Praise for the Author

"Hannah is especially good at portraying the emotional interactions and office politics of a fraught police force."
—*The Times* (London)

"This is top-notch British crime-writing from an author who writes with passion and draws you into the relentless pressure of a police murder hunt." —*Peterborough Telegraph*

"Brutal, shockingly realistic, and satisfyingly unpredictable, this is a thrilling, chilling tale with a formidable star player and charismatic location, ideally suited to the small screen. Move over, DCI Jane Tennison, there's a new kid on the block."
—*Lancashire Evening Post*

"DCI Kate Daniels: a Northerner to join the roster of top literary detectives." —*The Times* (London)

"Solid plotting . . . a satisfying and meaty read." —*The Guardian*

"Brutal and engaging. Mari Hannah writes with a sharp eye and a dark heart." —Peter James, internationally bestselling author of *Dead Man's Time*

Also by Mari Hannah

The Murder Wall
Settled Blood
Deadly Deceit
Fatal Games

Killing for Keeps

A Kate Daniels Mystery

MARI HANNAH

WITNESS
IMPULSE
An Imprint of HarperCollinsPublishers

First published in 2014 in the UK by Pan Books, an imprint of Pan Macmillan, a division of Macmillan Publishers Limited.

EPub Edition JUNE 2015 ISBN: 9780062387141

Print Edition ISBN: 9780062387158

10 9 8 7 6 5 4 3 2 1

For Oli
May you always feel that tingle

Prologue

THE THIRD BLOW sent Terry Allen crashing to the floor, striking his head on the toilet bowl on the way down. He blacked out. For how long, he couldn't be sure. When he came to, he didn't know where he was, much less how he came to be there. It took a moment before he could focus, a moment longer to register what he was looking at: his broken watch stopped at 01:34, spent tab ends, discarded condoms, gum, the odd dead insect, a flash of red – the sole of a high-heeled shoe.

Grant's club was heaving as usual, the seedier side of what Newcastle had to offer on a Friday night. Thumping music kicked its way through the walls into the gents. Just feet away, a punter was banging a local hooker up against the wall, too busy getting his end away to pay him any attention. There were some things worth turning a blind eye for. That tart for sure. She'd sell her soul for a line of coke. Terry had been there himself when his lass was in a strop and he was consigned to the spare room.

The music stopped suddenly and with it the vibration through the floor. The punter shagging the whore withdrew. Shoving her away, he told her to get lost in a voice Terry thought he recognized but couldn't place. When she held out her hand for payment, the man cuffed her hard with the back of his hand, splitting her lip wide open. Giving him a mouthful, she got the same again, then scooped up her bag and disappeared.

Zipping up his flies, the man turned, a smirk crossing his ugly face as his gaze fell on Terry.

Terry closed his eyes, felt his stomach lurch. Now he remembered how he'd ended up on the floor and why it was so important to get the hell out of there. But his left cheek was stuck fast against cold tiles ingrained with muck. He was, quite literally, frozen to the spot, unable to summon the energy to fight. Despite an attempt to push them away, images scrolled through his mind, striking terror into him: pliers, hammers, blowtorches and chainsaws . . .

Friday the thirteenth was about to live up to its reputation.

Startled by the sound of splashing water, he turned his head to see where it was coming from. Not quick enough. A size-ten boot pressed down on his neck – a warning to stay put. Terry complied, senses on high alert. Then it began, as he knew it would, a blow to the back, delivered with such ferocity that he heard bones crack, the air forced from his lungs. As warm liquid made its way down the inside of his new Versace shirt, Terry braced himself. But it wasn't blood trickling across his skin and pooling beneath him. He was being pissed on.

As the boot left his neck, a hand as big as a shovel grabbed him from behind. He was yanked to his feet and spun round, bringing him face-to-face with two pairs of the coldest eyes he'd ever seen: the O'Kane brothers – Glasgow's finest – a pair with a penchant for torture. He could see they meant business.

Craig O'Kane leaned in close. 'Give him up, Terry.'

Terry moistened his fat lip. 'Fuck off.'

Spitting in Craig's face was only inviting further punishment, but Terry had standards, a reputation to uphold. These heavies had just crossed an invisible line. There was no way he could let that go. He was scared. Undoubtedly. But he'd rather die than let them know he was in the least bit intimidated. Despite their obvious advantage over him, he feigned indifference.

Wiping Terry's blood and snot from his face, Craig nodded to his brother.

Finn didn't need telling twice. Raising a baseball bat high above his head, an evil glint in his eye, he brought it down hard on Terry's shoulder. Then he paused for a moment, a broad smile on his face as he savoured the sight of his victim clutching himself in agony, before hitting him again.

Terry cried out as a succession of blows rained down on him, each one harder than the last. On the deck now, he curled up into a ball, using his good arm to protect his head from the worst of it, taking full-on kicks to the body from both men. He knew he'd be wasting his breath begging them to stop. There would be no mercy from these two. Craig and Finn O'Kane were hell-bent on getting what they came for. Despite the pain, Terry was equally determined they would go home empty-handed.

Suddenly the blows stopped, but there was no respite from the terror. Terry knew all too well the consequences of going up against the O'Kanes. He'd seen the damage they could do when riled, the hideous injuries they had inflicted on those stupid enough to get on the wrong side of them: shattered bones, amputations, burns – even blindness for one poor sod. Resisting them was suicide.

Terry shivered, listening to them panting after their exertions, wondering what was coming next.

Whatever it was, he couldn't let his brother go the same way.

'Get the bolt cutters,' Finn said.

Six Weeks Later

Chapter One

DAVID PRENTICE HAD been a security guard for over twenty-five years, nearly half his life. He'd worked on the Silverlink Industrial Estate the last ten. In all that time there had never been a single incident on his watch. Nights were a pain, but he wasn't complaining. His line of work was, more or less, money for old rope. A piece of piss, in fact, allowing him time to study digital photography with the OU.

What was not to like?

Lifting his head from his prospectus, he took a long drag on his cigarette, rechecking his monitors. Perfect. Nothing to suggest he'd have to make the boring journey round the perimeter fence at five, no unusual sightings to report in the logbook. It was still. Quiet. He yawned. He'd be home and hosed by six-fifteen. Except . . .

Something wasn't quite right.

Prentice peered again at the monitors. The last one he looked at showed a van straddling the main gate. It wasn't there before. Pushing buttons on a keyboard, Prentice zoomed in on the vehicle, its driver's door wide open – no sign of its owner. The van was parked on the access road, so technically not his problem, but it soon would be if the idiot who'd left it there didn't get it shifted. Half an hour from now, delivery wagons were scheduled to arrive. Prentice imagined them backed up all the way to the coast road, waiting to get in.

Panicking, he rewound the footage.

A short while ago, he'd eaten his bait and taken a quick slash. He'd been out of his chair only a matter of minutes. In that time, two sets of headlights had approached the main gate at high speed: the mystery van and a light-coloured Range Rover following close behind. Prentice began to sweat as he viewed the screen. The two vehicles pulled up sharply. The van door flew open and a figure sprinted from one vehicle to the other. Before the door of the four-by-four was even closed, it was driven away at high speed, resulting in rear-wheel spin. It disappeared, leaving a plume of smoke in its wake.

What the hell was all that about?

Pulling on his uniform jacket, Prentice picked up his torch and went to investigate. As he walked to the exit, it occurred to him that what he'd seen might have been a diversionary tactic, a ruse to make him take his eye off the ball. The guy he'd seen running from the van and his accomplice could be parked around the back, ready to ram-raid the place. To be on the safe side, he returned to his office, rechecking his monitors, paying particular attention to the perimeter fence.

Satisfied that there was nothing untoward at the rear, he made his way outside. As he hurried towards the main gate, a distance of around a hundred metres, his eyes nervously scanned the delivery yard. It was a beautifully clear morning. Not yet light. Eerily quiet. No sign of anyone, suspicious or otherwise. His breathing slowed, returning to normal. Probably some daft kids messing around in a stolen vehicle. They had little discipline these days and fewer boundaries. What the parents were up to was anyone's guess.

Digging inside his pocket, Prentice took out his master key, then thought better of it and put it back, deciding to remain on site, call the police and set the monkey on their backs, as his late wife used to say.

They're paid a damn sight more than you.

Mrs P was right – they were.

Intent on getting away home on the dot of six, Prentice looked up, the flap-flap of the company flag above drawing his attention. The only other sound was the soft purr from the van's engine as he neared the main gate. Switching on his torch, he aimed it at the open driver's door. The vehicle was a newish Mercedes. Along the side panel, a sign spelled out a company name: HARDY'S ROOFERS. Beneath it, a website address and contact details were picked out in bold black lettering.

As he fumbled in his pocket for his mobile, Prentice decided it would be quicker and easier to contact the company direct rather than calling the law. The police would no doubt insist on a forensic examination and all sorts of other bollocks before the vehicle could be moved, leaving him stuck on site till lunchtime. Not to mention the shit he'd be in with his boss if he arrived to find the entrance blocked off.

The number rang out unanswered. He scanned the van again, moving the torch-beam to the rear wheels where something glistened, thick and shiny like oil, dripping on to the road below, pooling beneath the vehicle.

Oh Jesus!

Prentice ran.

Chapter Two

It HAD BEEN a hell of a night in the A & E department of the Royal Victoria Infirmary. Since midnight there had been a steady stream of walking wounded, as well as emergency admissions brought in by ambulance, some with blue lights flashing and sirens screaming, the whole works. At last count, a hundred-plus cases had been booked in: heart attacks, strokes, a small child rushed in with meningitis, casualties from multiple RTAs. Bursting at the seams, the department had coped – but only just. Then it all went quiet.

Totally spent, Senior House Officer Valerie Armstrong glanced around the waiting room, sipping cold tea she'd been given half an hour ago, relieved to have survived the general mayhem in the run-up to the August bank holiday weekend. Apart from one confused old man who'd just taken a seat, there wasn't another punter in sight. The place looked as if it had been burgled: wheelchairs abandoned at the door, chairs tipped over, food wrappers and polystyrene cups discarded everywhere, a baby's nappy dumped on the floor next to, of all things, an empty vodka bottle. She couldn't remember a night like it.

Behind a thick glass screen to her left, the department's twenty-year-old temporary receptionist looked done in. Louise was leaning on the counter, head propped up in the palm of her right hand, ID clipped to the pocket of a tight-fitting white shirt, a pretty silver chain around her neck.

Stifling a yawn, she took in the clock on the wall.

'What time you due to knock off?' she asked.

Valerie checked her watch. ''Bout an hour and a half,' she said. 'I'm ready to crash.'

Out of the corner of her eye, she noticed an unattended patient lying on a trolley in the corridor, just his head showing above the covers. To be fair to Louise, he was only partially visible from where she was sitting. But still . . .

The SHO pointed at the trolley. 'Whose patient?'

The girl shrugged. 'Maybe Dr Suri's . . . or Dr Templeton's.'

She was blatantly guessing.

Valerie didn't think much to either suggestion. Both doctors were long gone. She'd passed them in the corridor as she came back in after collecting her breakfast from her car. On call since midday, they'd had their coats on and were on the way out of the building.

'No,' she said. 'They've gone off duty.'

'Roger's then?' *Another guess.*

A staff nurse appeared, a manila folder under her arm, calling out to the old man. As the two shuffled off behind a brightly coloured curtain, Valerie glanced at a box on the wall where patient records were kept for those awaiting treatment. Curiously, it was empty. Her eyes shifted from the box to the man on the trolley, then back to Louise.

She tried not to sound cross. 'Any idea how long he's been waiting?'

'I'm sorry, no.' Louise looked worried.

Valerie attempted a smile of reassurance.

If in doubt, ask the patient.

She set off to do just that. But as she drew closer, her steps faltered, an inexplicable feeling of dread eating its way into her subconscious. Seized by panic, she stopped short of the trolley and glanced nervously over her shoulder at reception. Louise barely acknowledged her. Valerie's gaze shifted back to the patient. Steeling herself, she stepped forward, placed index and middle fingers on his neck. His skin was cold to the touch. No pulse. No need to call for the crash team. He was as dead as a stone.

Chapter Three

DAWN WAS BREAKING as Detective Chief Inspector Kate Daniels' Audi Q5 sped off the coast road en route to Silverlink Industrial Estate, Detective Sergeant Hank Gormley by her side. She was strangely apprehensive. Word from the control room had reached her only half an hour ago. The incident she was rushing towards was serious. As duty Senior Investigating Officer in Northumbria Police's Murder Investigation Team, that was a given. However, something in the controller's voice had raised her antennae, putting her on high alert for a case outside of the norm.

'Sounds nasty,' yawned Hank. He was barely awake.

'Maybe the eyewitness got it wrong.' Indicating left off the roundabout, Kate stopped at a red light, glancing at him as they waited to move off again. 'You know what they're like sometimes. In the dark they see things that aren't there. Panic sets in and we get half a story.'

'Maybe,' Hank said hopefully.

The lights changed to green. Kate floored the accelerator, keen to reach her destination. But as she rounded the corner, she was met with a sight that forced her to slam on the brakes, bringing the vehicle to an abrupt halt that nearly put them both through the windscreen.

'Or maybe not,' she said drily, her eyes glued to the road ahead.

The crime scene was bigger than either of them could have imagined. Blue lights flashed at either end of an access road empty of civilians but crawling with police personnel. Traffic officers had blocked off the grey strip of tarmac for as far as the eye could see. Arc lights were being erected and forensic officers in white suits were walking the line, placing tread plates every metre or so, a process that was ongoing.

Without another word passing between them, Kate and Hank got out of the car, ducking under crime-scene tape that warned others not to cross. As they neared a grey Mercedes van – the focus of everyone's attention – they saw Home Office pathologist Tim Stanton on his knees in full forensic kit, the hood of which was pulled tight around his head to ensure no contamination of evidence.

He looked up, a pained expression on his face.

From where Kate was standing, it was impossible to tell what he'd been looking at. But his eyes held a warning: *This is not something either of you want to see.* Receiving his unspoken message, Kate sent Hank to find the witness who had called the incident in. Only after he'd disappeared did she step forward, all the while hoping that her imagination was conjuring up worse images than she was about to view.

She was wrong.

Her heart rate increased as her tired eyes travelled down the side of the van to a place near the rear offside wheel. Despite the urge to look away, she knew she couldn't. No matter how gruesome a spectacle, she was paid to investigate murder. She couldn't afford to buckle. Still, she found it hard to make sense of what her eyes were transmitting to her brain, even harder to quell the silent scream inside her.

Suspended from the underside of the roofer's van was the naked torso of a white male – or what was left of it – a mangled mess of bloody flesh, missing limbs, a gaping jaw . . .

What is that? Bone? Teeth?

Don't look into his eyes.

Suddenly cold, Kate pulled up the collar of her coat. Doing up her top button was the only distraction available. She was calm on the outside, but traumatized on the in. Hank arrived at her side, his attention immediately focused on the victim. He tried his best to make out he wasn't moved by what he saw, but failed miserably. In fact, he seemed to shrink physically the longer he stared. When finally he glanced up, his eyes were dull with shock.

'The witness is pretty shaken up.' He swallowed hard. 'Can't say I blame him, now I've seen it for myself. He'll be having night-mares for weeks.'

'We all will,' Stanton said.

Kate mimed to Hank: *You OK?* Concern she wouldn't voice in the presence of the pathologist.

Hank nodded. The detectives would debrief later.

'Who found him?' she asked.

'David Prentice, security guard at this place.' Hank thumbed over his shoulder to the premises behind them, a two-storey warehouse in need of a paint job. 'Apparently the estate is like a racetrack some nights. He wondered if joyriders had hit a pedes-trian and carried on driving, not realizing there was someone underneath.'

'If he's under the impression that this is a tragic accident, he couldn't be more wrong.' Stanton didn't look up. 'The IP's body is secured to the chassis with a thick leather belt. See, here . . .' He beckoned the DCI with his index finger.

Kate crouched down as he pointed at a section of the torso that remained intact. Outrage and sadness competed for space in her head. What kind of despicable act of madness was this?

'Can you make it out?' Stanton's tone was impassive. 'The belt is looped in such a way as to make it impossible that this was anything other than deliberate. Judging by the trauma inflicted, the vehicle must've been travelling at terrific speed. The buckle is almost embedded in his stomach. There's no doubt whatsoever that we're dealing with a murder case. Forensics are trying to locate the rest of him – if they can scrape him off the tarmac.'

Kate had no words.

Stanton's tone softened as they both stood up. 'I'm so sorry you had to see this.'

Thanking him, she turned away, taking Hank with her. The road was lit up like a busy airport runway. They walked the route the van had travelled. Every few metres or so they saw pieces of the victim ground into the road surface: an ear, teeth, a section of scalp and bits of unidentified bone.

Halfway along, yellow chalk circles had been drawn on the road. Kate called out to one of the crime-scene investigators, asking what they were.

'Improvised plates,' he told her. 'We ran out. They'll guide you the rest of the way.'

Nodding, she walked on.

'You OK?' Hank asked.

'I've been better. You?'

Trying hard not to react to the revolting detritus on the road, even though it was affecting her deeply, Kate registered the absence of gallows humour from Hank this morning. No jokey routine to get him through the horror. There were times when it wasn't appropriate, and this was one of them. He was as disturbed as she was. No question. An hour ago, they had been in their respective homes, fast asleep, oblivious to the brutality taking place on this deserted stretch of road. Now they were viewing a scene so gruesome it would never leave them, illuminated by the volley of camera shutters and flashbulbs going off on all sides.

Kate took a deep breath. Their job was never pleasant. They had attended some nasty pile-ups and collisions in their time – including a particularly harrowing incident a couple of years ago on the A1 trunk road – but this was something else. It was deliberate.

It was sick.

A traffic officer approached wearing a fluorescent jacket, his eyes partially shaded by the peak of his cap. Introducing himself as the senior accident investigator, he asked Kate if she was the duty SIO. She nodded, giving her name and rank, presenting Hank as her second in command.

'You've done a great job,' she said. 'What's your take on this lot?'

'It stops, or should I say starts, adjacent to Halfords.' He pointed along the road. 'Looks like they stripped him, tied him on to the Mercedes, got in and floored the accelerator. The van did a reciprocal round the mini-roundabout – probably what killed him – then it travelled west at high speed along the main road here, round the roundabout at the top and back down again, turning sharp right, dumping the van where it is now. The victim never stood a chance.'

Kate's jaw bunched. 'According to the control room there was a second vehicle involved.'

'Yes, ma'am.'

'I want it found. Any sign of his clothes?'

'Not yet, but the CSI lads are on it.'

'That's good. Keep me posted.'

In the distance, Kate saw motorists abandoning their cars to stare in her direction. To the left of the roadblock a group of pedestrians stood behind flapping tape, craning their necks to see what was going on, probably crowing because they couldn't get to work. They would be demanding to know when the diversion would be lifted, resentful at being held back by officers as clueless about it as they were.

The DCI sighed. With forensic evidence spread over such a wide area, the site would remain closed for some time. Hundreds were employed on the industrial estate, and soon there would be delivery vehicles and shoppers adding to the congestion. 'I can almost hear the complaints pinging their way into my inbox already.' She grimaced. 'There'll be a million calls to handle: enquiries from the press, local MPs, headquarters – all wanting answers we don't have.'

'Yet,' Hank reminded her. 'But you're right, this'll end up feeling like we're working in a circus instead of a major incident room.'

Kate was exhausted just thinking about the day ahead. 'Well, they'll all have to wait. We have other priorities.'

A mobile rang.

They both went for their pockets.

It was Kate's. The screen showed *Pete Brooks*. She swiped to answer. 'Go ahead, Control.'

'Looks like we found your second vehicle, boss.' Brooks hesitated, checking details. 'CCTV picked up a Range Rover heading west along the coast road towards the city centre shortly after leaving Silverlink. It was found abandoned and on fire off Walker Road in the East End five minutes ago.'

'Damn!' Kate's shoulders dropped. 'The victim's clothing was probably inside. Are Forensics at the scene?'

'They just got there.' The controller paused as someone spoke to him at the other end. After a few seconds, he came back on the line. 'The fire is out, but don't hold your breath for a positive result. Forensics say it's going to take a while for the vehicle to cool down, then it'll be a question of seeing whether there's anything left to examine.'

'Problem?' Hank asked as Kate thanked Control and hung up.

'The Range Rover – it's been torched.'

He narrowed his eyes. 'What did you expect?'

Frustrated by the development, she looked away, her eyes finding the warehouse entrance. Something about her crime scene didn't quite add up. It was always difficult at such an early stage of an enquiry to second-guess what was going on. She expressed her reservations in a question to Hank. 'Why dump the Merc in full view of CCTV rather than on a piece of wasteland? God knows there are plenty of those scattered around the city.'

She didn't expect an answer. Didn't get one either. They both knew there was only one plausible explanation. Whoever was responsible didn't just want their victim to suffer. They wanted him dead. And they wanted him found.

Chapter Four

THE DEAD PATIENT was handsome, late twenties, early thirties. Only his head was visible. Dr Valerie Armstrong got a whiff of expensive aftershave as she said a silent prayer for him. The man had obviously looked after himself. His skin was perfect, his eyebrows waxed. He had long dark lashes, a straight nose and strong jawline. There was no pillow on the trolley, so his head was tilted back slightly, his mouth open as if inviting a kiss. What an absolute tragedy, that someone so young should die on a hospital trolley, unnoticed in the midst of all the frantic activity of A & E.

Wondering whether he was a family man, her eyes shifted from the face to the blue blanket that covered his body. It was then that she saw the blood, now a dark brown where it had dried out in the high temperature of the corridor, staining the open weave around the abdominal area. A sob left her throat as she pulled back the cover and saw that the dead man's elbows were bent, his hands resting on his stomach, a wedding band on his left ring finger – *his only finger*. Every other digit was missing, including both thumbs; not crushed or ripped off, as she would have expected had he lost them in an accident, but severed with a smooth blade. As the blanket fell from her hand she saw that more blood had pooled on the sheet either side of his torso, presumably from an injury to his back.

Valerie ran to reception and made an urgent call.

THIRTY MINUTES LATER, argumentative voices reached her as the medical director arrived in A & E, followed by the duty lead consultant. For the next few minutes, pointed questions were asked. The director was furious on two counts. One: because he'd been hauled out of bed. Two: because the consultant hadn't run her shift properly. As he threw his weight around, she bit back, citing understaffing and pressure in the department, shifting responsibility to him. Neither gave a thought to the identity of the dead man or how long he'd been there.

'Stop!' Valerie glared at them both.

The director bristled. 'Excuse me?'

The SHO flicked her eyes toward the entrance where a couple assisting a wheelchair patient were calling for help. Ignoring them, the director asked her to cover up the corpse.

'Or better still,' he suggested, 'move him out of sight to one of the side wards.'

Valerie refused point-blank. 'This is a police matter, we can't move him.'

'I insist!' the director whispered through gritted teeth. 'We can't possibly leave—'

'I agree with Valerie,' the consultant cut him off. Reminding him she was still in charge of the unit, she nodded to the receptionist. 'Make the call, Louise.'

As the girl hurried back to her desk, Valerie beckoned a porter. 'Get some screens over here. And see to it no one goes near the body.'

IT TOOK THE police less than five minutes to arrive. A male sergeant and female colleague, both in uniform, walked through the door with radios squawking. Ushering them to a side room where they could talk without interruption, Valerie explained the situation. Even in her head, it sounded incredible. It was painfully obvious that the officers were unimpressed. Whether that was because, like her, their shift was almost at an end and they could do without the hassle of staying on duty, she wasn't able to gauge. And, if it was, who could blame them?

The senior officer perched on the edge of the desk, asking her to repeat her account one more time. This time around, his colleague took notes in her pocket book. But it wasn't long before Valerie ran out of words. Much as she appreciated the importance of getting every detail straight, she could only tell them what she knew.

'I saw nothing,' she said. 'Right up until the moment I spotted him lying in the corridor.'

'Well, someone must have,' the sergeant said, an accusation almost. 'The way you described his injuries, Mystery Man didn't walk in unaided, did he?'

'No, I don't suppose he did.'

'So what's the sketch? Any idea how he managed to pull it off?'

Valerie's eyes found highly polished lino. She had no theories – at least, none that made any sense, none she cared to share. She'd just completed a marathon shift and was due for another in a matter of hours. All she wanted was to go home, crawl into her bed and sleep. She'd done nothing wrong and had no reason whatsoever to feel guilty. So why did she? The sergeant's hard eyes weren't helping.

A female voice pulled her back into the room.

'Doctor?' The PC stopped scribbling. 'The sergeant asked you a question.'

'I'm sorry.' Valerie shook her head, tried to focus. 'As I said, I have no idea how he got here, or how he came to be missed. We were extremely busy—'

'How about when he was found?' the sergeant asked. 'Do you have any ideas on that score?'

'That I can tell you. It was almost five-thirty. One of the admin staff asked me how long before I went off shift and I checked my watch. When I discovered he was dead, I put in a call and questioned the triage team myself while I was waiting for a response. It seems he wasn't assessed on arrival by any of the nurses on duty. I realize you'll also want to talk to them.'

'Except you didn't call us at five-thirty, did you?' he said.

'Well, no, not personally.'

'My information is that your receptionist called it in some time after six.'

'That's correct. But I'd reported the matter to the medical director. It's procedure.'

'Maybe a nurse went home,' the female officer suggested. 'Forgot to log the patient in?'

'I doubt that,' Valerie said.

'It happens, surely?' The sergeant eyed her sceptically. 'Someone goes sick . . . they rush off without finishing what they're doing. Not that the hospital trust would ever admit to such a thing, but you and I know different, don't we? Mistakes happen in all walks of life – no need for a cover-up.'

'Cover-up? If you're suggesting—'

'I'm not making allegations, Doctor – it's far too early for that. This unexplained sudden death isn't a matter my colleague and

I can handle on our own. We'll have to pass it upstairs, consult with the Murder Investigation Team. Until they arrive, I must ask everyone to remain in the building until further notice. And I'll need the names of everyone who was on duty at the time.'

Valerie offered no argument. The sergeant had a point, she supposed. As a health professional tasked with the job of saving lives, she wasn't happy about a patient in critical condition being left unattended in a corridor. And she was all too aware that the medical director would pass the buck in her direction if he thought he could get away with it. He'd do so in a flash if it would save his own skin.

The police sergeant stood up. 'Can you take us to the body now, please?'

Valerie led the way across A & E. The department was dark, the lights dimmed. At the request of the police, it had already been closed down and emergency admissions temporarily redirected to another entrance.

She rounded the screen that concealed the trolley from view and turned to face the two officers. From the glances they exchanged on catching sight of the victim, it was obvious he was no stranger to them.

Chapter Five

ON THE SILVERLINK Industrial Estate, DCI Kate Daniels had just finished overseeing a delicate and ghastly operation. Having called upon the Fire Service to jack up the Mercedes to enable crime-scene investigators to photograph her victim in situ, she'd looked on as the body was extricated from the underside of the vehicle and handed over to mortuary staff for transfer to Newcastle's city morgue.

The body-bag was zipped up, laid on a stretcher and loaded into a black van. Hank Gormley waved it forward, instructing a uniformed colleague to follow in a panda car. It was important to preserve continuity until the cadaver was in the care of Tim Stanton, who was standing by to carry out an urgent post-mortem. Police tape and cones were lifted, allowing the vehicles through inner and outer cordons, where they were joined by a Traffic car, its driver engaging blues and twos to ease the journey.

As the mini-convoy disappeared, Kate turned to face Hank.

'What was the name of our witness?' she asked.

'David Prentice. Forty-eight-year-old widower. No form. Lives on Benton Park Road. Father of two, grandfather of four.' He pointed to a sign behind them: *JMR Air Conditioning & Refrigeration Services*. 'He's in there, waiting for you.'

Kate found the man at his desk in the security office, hands cupped round a mug of sweet tea, a half-smoked cigarette dangling from his lips. He stubbed it out and stood up as she walked in. It was as if the room was shrouded in fog. Bizarrely, it had no air conditioning. Without asking permission, the DCI opened the window to let the smoke out. Then she sat down, taking the weight off her aching feet. The man looked grey. Was it any wonder? She wasn't feeling too hot herself.

'I'm DCI Kate Daniels. Are you up to answering questions, sir?'

'To be honest, I'd rather go home. I'm feeling a bit shaky.'

'That's entirely understandable. Finding a body must have been harrowing for you, especially in the dead of night.'

'I don't want to talk about it.'

He was a dead ringer for Kate's old guv'nor who was now the head of CID; a little younger perhaps, but the face was the same shape, with a generous mouth and greying hair at his temples. They could've been brothers, except Prentice was quaking in his uniformed boots and Detective Chief Superintendent Bright would never do that, no matter how unpleasant the circumstances. Then again, the security guard had probably never seen so much as an angry dog in his whole career, much less had to deal with one.

'I won't keep you long, I promise.' Kate gave a smile of encouragement. 'The sooner we get it over with, the sooner you can go home to your bed. It would help if you could tell me everything you know, a blow-by-blow account of your movements since you came on duty, including how and when you discovered the body. It's very important to establish what happened here so I can start looking for those responsible.'

Prentice took a deep breath. 'I started at ten o'clock. It was a normal, boring shift until I noticed the van a few minutes before five, after leaving the office for a moment or two.'

'Is that allowed?' Kate asked.

'It was that or piss in a bucket. Forgive the language, I—'

'Needs must, eh?' Another smile. Kate pointed at a hard-backed ledger on his desk. 'Is that your duty log?'

He nodded.

'May I see it please?'

Prentice pushed it towards her. He looked on as she opened it up and turned to the relevant page. The writing was neat but so small she was forced to use her reading specs. Scanning the entries, she noted that he'd made a tour of the perimeter fence every hour throughout the night until four a.m. The five o'clock patrol remained blank.

Picking up on her concern, Prentice was at pains to point out that he hadn't completed that circuit because he was too busy investigating the mystery van.

'That's when you called us?'

Sweating profusely, he nodded.

Kate shifted her attention from the man to a desk littered with paraphernalia: a half-completed crossword, an Open University pamphlet, a framed photograph of four grinning schoolboys she assumed were his grandchildren, a few jottings on a notepad and some literature on photography.

Oh God!

Along with a feeling of déjà vu, a young woman appeared in Kate's head: an amateur photographer she'd come across in a previous case who'd tried to cash in by selling images of a dead man to the press. That was the way things were these days; everyone carried a camera in their pocket, the means with which to capture a moment in time, no matter how miserable. People saw it as fair game. Images that sold newspapers were highly prized. Sadly, that particular photographer had paid the ultimate price, silenced for good by someone who didn't want their face made public.

'Keen photographer, are you sir?' Kate took in an enthusiastic nod. 'Take any snaps while you were outside? Because, if you did, I'd like the film and the camera.'

'I don't have one with me.'

'Mobile phone?'

'I didn't take any pictures.'

'That's fine.' Kate sent a warning shot across the desk. 'I just need to be sure. The incident I'm investigating is not one that should end up in the public domain. If that were to happen, you should understand that there would be consequences.'

'Check it if you don't believe me.' He pushed his mobile across the desk. 'There's nothing on it, I swear.'

'I'll take your word for it.'

Thanking her, Prentice shuddered as if something with more than two legs had walked across his skin. 'To be honest, I was so spooked when I realized what I'd found that I bolted back here. I dialled 999 in case he was, y'know, still alive. It never occurred to me to get my camera out. I'm no ghoul, Inspector.' He paused for thought. 'Not that I thought he could be – alive, I mean. But I'm no doctor, am I? You hear about people surviving terrible accidents.'

He hadn't been told.

Kate tried to find the right words with which to convey the unpalatable truth. 'Mr Prentice, I'm not here about a terrible accident. This is a clear-cut case of murder. As despicable as it sounds, what you witnessed tonight was a deliberate act.'

'What?' He looked horrified.

'I'm afraid so. I'm sure you'll appreciate how serious that is and why I need your full cooperation.' Unfortunately, Kate was destined not to get it.

Prentice immediately clammed up, floored by the realization that whoever she was after knew where he worked and when they could find him alone on the premises. Having seen what they were capable of, he had no doubt they would silence a witness without a second thought.

Chapter Six

No AMOUNT OF gentle persuasion made a difference. The witness was frightened. He had a right to be. Kate drove slowly through the traffic on the way back to the city centre. She was tired and under pressure but, if she were being perfectly honest, enjoying the adrenalin rush of a new enquiry, even though this one was more difficult to stomach than most. She could tell Hank felt it too. He was as high as a kite, on the phone to their guv'nor, Detective Superintendent Ron Naylor.

'The news isn't all grim,' he was saying. 'We already have a victim ID.'

Tuning him out, Kate turned her attention to the case generally. Identifying the victim was something she hadn't thought possible a couple of hours ago. But thanks to the timely intervention of crime-scene investigators, she was in possession of the most vital piece of evidence an SIO needs in the first few hours of a new case. Prints lifted at the scene matched some already on the database. That was good. The name of the person to whom they belonged was not. In fact, it was quite the opposite: enough to strike fear into the heart of most detectives, whether or not they knew the man personally. His reputation was legendary in the Northumbria force area.

Repercussions would surely follow.

Kate drove on, hoping she didn't have a turf war on her hands.

Having finished his call, Hank had gone quiet. A worrying development, unheard of almost. Not only was he not talking, he wasn't catching up on lost sleep either, something he did at every opportunity. Normally, he'd be hanging like a bat from his seat belt by now. The horrific nature of this case had got to him.

'Do yourself a favour,' she said. 'Don't think about it.'

'Since when did you take up mind-reading?' he asked.

She glanced sideways, a wry smile on her face. 'Try zoning out the images. It'll allow you to concentrate on the case rather than the pain of it, if that makes sense.'

'You do that?'

'Every time.'

'Does it help?'

'We're humans too, Hank.'

'Nice sidestep. I notice you didn't answer the question.'

'Complete detachment would mean we were robots.' Kate kept her eyes on the road. 'It may surprise you to learn that we are allowed to feel. In fact, it's obligatory. Number one on my list of coping strategies. It makes me try all the harder to catch the bad guys.'

There was another way she handled the nasty stuff and she'd already made up her mind to make the call as soon as the briefing was over, the murder enquiry underway. She'd talk it through with her friend and confidante, criminal profiler Jo Soulsby. Their discussion would take the form of a professional debrief almost. It wouldn't change a thing, but afterwards she'd feel a little less like she was dying inside.

Hank was still in a bad place. 'It's beyond me how Stanton manages. At least we don't have to look at it twenty-four seven.'

'Did I ever tell you Jo believes in meditation?' Kate said. 'You should try it sometime.'

'No offence, but that's bollocks.' It wasn't like him to be so dismissive. He liked Jo a lot, respected what she did for a living, valued the contribution she'd made since her secondment to the Murder Investigation Team.

'I was a sceptic too once,' Kate said.

Another wave of sorrow washed over her.

Who was she trying to kid?

BY THE TIME they reached the station, Naylor had set the wheels in motion. The incident suite was full of detectives and civilian personnel awaiting instructions from the DCI, all leave over the coming bank holiday weekend cancelled at short notice. No one minded. That was just the way it was. In fact, some welcomed the opportunity for overtime, an occurrence far less frequent than it used to be.

Taking her own advice, Kate forced herself to concentrate on procedure rather than dwelling on images she wished she'd never seen. Sharing the name of the deceased with DC Lisa Carmichael, advising her that crime-scene photographs were available for upload, she set her to work immediately, excusing her from the briefing, before turning to face the squad.

'Right, ladies and gents, can we have some quiet please?' She waited for the hum of voices to die down. 'We've got a distressing torture case on our hands. Nominal One is John Allen. That is *the* John Allen, for those of you in the know.'

There were a few raised eyebrows in the room.

Kate moved on. 'For the benefit of those new to the squad, he's a villain from a criminal family going back generations. He's also well known to the Serious Organized Crime Agency. Along with his brother and equally obnoxious mates, John Allen has dabbled in anything and everything, specializing in stealing high-end cars to order, selling them on, shipping them abroad. A very lucrative line of business it was too. Enough to buy them a pretty fancy lifestyle—'

'Not any more,' Hank said drily.

Kate glanced at the murder wall. On one side of a state-of-the-art digital screen, John Allen's name had appeared in large capital letters, alongside his age (twenty-nine), date of birth, address when last arrested, significant others and known associates. Underneath was a police mugshot Carmichael had lifted from the PNC. On the other side of the screen, horrific images were uploading; a macabre illustration of what Kate had seen at dawn on a deserted street a few miles east of the station.

The state of the body was such that several officers dropped their heads on one side, trying to work out which way was up: DS Paul Robson, DCs Neil Maxwell and Andy Brown among them. Andy, the quiet one of the three, grimaced as if he'd eaten a lemon whole. Silence spread throughout the room, except for the tap-tapping of Carmichael's fingers as they flew over her computer keys. The young DC had her head down as usual, so deep in concentration she was oblivious to the reaction her efforts were having on the rest of a team coming to terms with what was being shown.

'Let me be clear here,' the DCI said. 'No matter what criminal activities Allen instigated in his lifetime, he didn't deserve to end his days the way he did. My immediate concern is that his associates may take the law into their own hands, exact some form of retribution on those responsible for his death. Our first priority therefore is to find his brother Terry before all hell breaks loose.'

'We just did,' a voice behind her said.

All eyes were on the door.

Two uniformed police officers were standing on the threshold, the older a male sergeant most of them had known for years. 'Excuse the interruption, ma'am.' He held up an incident report. 'But this concerns you.'

'Did you bring Terry in?' Kate asked.

She had good reason to jump to this conclusion. As soon as victim ID was confirmed, she'd turned her attention to his relatives, in particular the delivery of a death message, a job easier said than done for two reasons: the Allens were antagonistic towards the police and their criminal lifestyle meant they moved around a lot. When they couldn't be found, she'd issued an action to trace next of kin.

'No,' the sergeant said. 'Terry Allen is also in the morgue.'

'What? Are you serious?'

'Deadly, no pun intended.'

For a moment, no one spoke. Then the silence was broken by rumblings of *Jesus Christ, good riddance* and other harsh words directed at the younger Allen brother. Kate asked for attention, giving the officer the opportunity to explain his attendance at the RVI, the fact that he'd personally identified Terry, an offender he'd arrested on several occasions, as the deceased patient who'd been found in a hospital corridor.

'You're absolutely sure it was him?' Kate asked.

The sergeant was nodding. 'His wallet and driving licence were in his pocket. We made some tentative enquiries, called out the duty pathologist. Apart from injuries we could see for ourselves – all bar one of his fingers were missing – the doc confirmed he'd been stabbed several times in the back. It's definitely a murder case, linked to the one you're already dealing with, unless you believe in coincidence. I suspect you don't.'

Two brothers . . .

Tortured to death on the same night . . .

Not for a moment did Kate believe this was a coincidence. Whoever killed the Allen brothers was switched wrong – a malicious sadist. She dreaded what would happen when word got out to family and associates. Like it or not, as SIO she had no right to withhold cause of death even in cases like this one, where the family had a history of dispensing their own brand of justice. She felt sure they would close ranks, put the shutters up and use any means at their disposal to track down those responsible. It wasn't hard to imagine what would happen next. She knew it wouldn't be pretty.

Chapter Seven

A NUMBER OF competing actions scrolled through Kate's head. At least two people were involved in John Allen's death: the drivers of the Mercedes van and the Range Rover. She needed to catch them both before his family did. Appointing DS Robson as statement reader, she asked DC Maxwell to take care of the CCTV they had appropriated from JMR Refrigeration. As usual, he had his head up his arse; he was so busy eyeing up MIT's newest female recruit, Kate suspected he hadn't heard a word she'd said.

'Neil, did you get that? Or do I have to repeat myself?'

Maxwell apologized, his face flushing.

'I said there's a DVD on my desk, footage from the main gate. Get it to Technical Support right away. Tell them I'm specifically interested in the section between four fifty-five and five past five. See what they can do with it and report back to me as soon as you can. I'm hoping they'll give us something we can work with, a vague idea of who we're looking for.' Having already seen the footage, she was doubtful.

Delegating other tasks, she turned lastly to DS Brown. 'Andy, see if you can pinpoint where the Range Rover went after it left Silverlink. Raise an action for any joyriders in the area: they may be potential witnesses or suspects. As soon as we get confirmation of the vehicle licence plates, I want you to hunt down the registered keepers. Hank, Lisa, come with me. I need you at the hospital.'

THEY REACHED THE Royal Victoria Infirmary a few minutes before ten and set about questioning staff. Kate concentrated on the SHO who'd found the body and consultants who'd been on duty at the relevant time. Hank took the receptionist, porters and ancillary staff, while Carmichael tackled the triage team. Two hours later, they met up in the relatives' room the hospital's medical director had set aside for them to use.

They had each drawn a blank.

Kate nodded as Lisa pointed to a Thermos flask that had been left on the coffee table, a handwritten note beside it: *Help yourselves.* Nothing, it seemed, was too much trouble for the staff of A & E.

Pity they hadn't paid the same level of attention to their patients.

The room was soulless, far too warm to be comfortable, and staged – an administrator's idea of showing respect to those in distress. Neutral walls vibrated with a million sobs, much like the waiting room at the city's crematorium where Kate had supported more families of homicide victims than she cared to remember in the years she'd been a murder detective.

Slumping down on the tan sofa, she dreaded the hours ahead. Delivering multiple death messages on the same day wasn't unusual. Conveying two separate non-accidental deaths to the same family was unprecedented. The words 'shoot the messenger' loomed large in her head.

Accepting a drink from Lisa, she waited for her to sit back down before speaking. 'So,' she said. 'Shall I go first?'

Lisa and Hank were nodding.

'OK, the SHO, Valerie Armstrong, pronounced Terry Allen dead at five thirty-five, half an hour before his brother suffered a similar fate at Silverlink. According to the attending pathologist, Terry had been dead approximately two hours.' Taking a gulp of coffee, Kate set the cup down on the floor beside her feet. 'The doctor claims she had no idea who the patient was until the police were called. I gather he wasn't seen on arrival by the triage team?'

'That's correct,' Lisa said.

'Hank? Is that your understanding?'

'Yup. He wasn't booked in at reception either.'

'How come he was missed?' Kate asked. 'He was in no condition to walk in unaided, lie down on a trolley and cover himself up. So how did he get here? More importantly, who brought him in?'

'Only one nurse admitted to seeing him lying on the trolley,' Carmichael said. 'Poor girl thought he was asleep. She's blaming herself. Thinks she may lose her job over it. She assumed he'd been assessed and was awaiting transfer to a ward. Apparently there was pandemonium last night, including a fatal RTA involving a bus with a number of elderly passengers on board. They were working flat out, boss.'

'That's also backed up by the receptionist's log,' Hank said. 'There were multiple casualties. Can't have been much fun.'

'Did any uniforms view the CCTV?' Kate asked.

Hank was shaking his head.

'Then we need to do that.' Picking up the internal phone, Kate dialled zero and asked for the security office. A few seconds later, a man answered, identifying himself with his first name only: Frank. Switching to speakerphone, Kate identified herself by name and rank and, to add weight to the call, as a member of the Murder Investigation Team. 'I'm in the building. I need to take a look at your CCTV right away.'

'I was expecting that,' the man said.

'Really?' Kate rolled her eyes at the others. 'You psychic or something?'

'Word spreads like wildfire in a hospital, Inspector. Much as it does in a police station, I imagine.' The guy had a deep gravelly voice, a pronounced Irish accent. 'Perhaps I should explain.'

'If you would please, Mr . . . ?'

'McGowan.'

'I'm listening.'

'Just a moment . . .' McGowan wasn't alone. Someone was talking in the background. He responded, asking a colleague to take over. Then Kate heard heavy boots on a solid floor, a squeaky door open and close, then the background noise disappeared and he returned to the phone. 'At around three this morning, the camera covering the front door of A & E flipped up suddenly and was pointing at the stars. It had never happened before so I called maintenance to check it out. The guy who examined it says that it had been deliberately angled away from the entrance. It couldn't have done that all by itself. There wasn't much wind and the camera had to be prised back in place, so it did. Then later, I heard about your man. I mean the poor guy who passed away without receiving treatment. When they mentioned that he wasn't booked in at reception, I put two and two together.'

'That's quite a deduction,' Kate said.

'Irish doesn't necessarily mean stupid, Inspector.'

'I'm sure it doesn't.' The DCI grinned at the others. She liked McGowan's candour. 'Thanks for the information, sir. I'll send someone up immediately to take a statement. I'd appreciate it if you'd stay put until they have.'

'I'm not going anywhere.'

'You've been a great help.'

As Kate hung up, her tiredness vanished. Tampering with equipment. Deliberately masking Terry Allen's arrival at A & E. She grinned at the others. They were in business.

Chapter Eight

HOSPITAL CCTV BACKED up everything McGowan had told them. Having commandeered the footage, the three detectives walked back to their car in glorious sunshine. Hank chuckled under his breath when he spotted a sticker for illegal parking on Kate's windscreen. Tearing it off, she slapped it against his chest, begging him to sort it when he got back to the incident room – one less problem for her to deal with.

'It'll cost you,' he said.

'And I'm sure you'll collect.' Kate turned away. 'Lisa, contact Forensics. We need the camera at the front door dusted right away.'

Pulling out her mobile, the DC dialled a number and lifted the phone to her ear. 'Can we visit the deli on the way back? I'm ravenous.'

Despite an early call-out, no breakfast, and the fact that she was also starving, Kate refused. There was no time for a detour today. Pleading with her to change her mind, Hank said something less than complimentary about the staff canteen that made both women laugh. Carmichael's sulk was gone by the time they reached the car.

Hank climbed in the front with Kate, Lisa in the back. 'Are we agreed: we've nailed the time Terry Allen arrived at the hospital?' he asked.

'Looks that way.' Belting up, Kate unhooked her sunglasses from the visor, put them on and fired up the engine. 'Not that it'll take us very far.'

'It'll aid the sequence of events—'

'True. But unless there are prints or DNA on that camera, we're screwed. I can't believe anyone with the savvy of a three-year-old wouldn't be gloved up while attempting to mask their identity, can you?'

'We're due some luck.' There was no conviction in his voice.

'Yeah, and pigs might fly.' Kate turned left towards Exhibition Park. Giving way at a roundabout, her eyes shifted to the rear-view mirror as Lisa ended her call, pocketing her phone.

'I'd love to know who took Terry to the hospital,' she said.

'Million-dollar questions are always tricky,' Kate said. 'Who-ever it was, they didn't want to be seen. Which strongly suggests we'd recognize them.'

Lisa gave a resigned nod. 'A family member, you reckon?'

Hank wasn't sure. 'Nah, they would wait around for a prognosis, surely?'

Kate listened as her colleagues continued throwing ideas around, each point stripped down, examined, ruled in or out. They were great, these two. Always gave their very best in pursuit of justice, even for victims as loathsome as the Allens. Handpicked by her old guv'nor, Hank and Lisa were the cream of the Murder Investigation Team. She counted herself lucky to have them on board.

Hank still wasn't buying the family angle. 'Wouldn't a relative want to find out how he was doing, whether he was going to make it or croak?'

'Well, if not family, then who?' asked Lisa. 'Unless he managed to call a mate—'

'With one finger and multiple knife wounds?' Hank made a *not likely* face.

'What then? Are you suggesting he was tortured, then a Good Samaritan comes along and takes him to A & E?'

'Part of that suggestion rings true,' Kate broke in. 'I mean, it *is* possible he was found by someone he recognized, someone who didn't dare walk by without helping. Terry begs to be taken to the RVI rather than dialling 999, thinking it'll save his life, but then loses consciousness. His shy saviour decides not to stick around for fear of being implicated in a serious assault. He may well have been a Good Samaritan but, make no mistake, he's also known to us. Law-abiding folks don't tamper with evidence—'

'Now you're talking sense,' Hank said.

'Either that or they were scared to death,' Kate added. 'And not necessarily of us. They wouldn't want to get on the wrong side of whoever did the torturing – or even Terry's extended family.'

As they continued theorizing, she took a right down Claremont Road, another right past the Civic Centre, arriving at the station a few minutes later. Keeping the engine running, she turned in her seat to face them. 'By all means grab a sandwich, both of you, but then it's heads down.' Hank leapt out of the car like a man half his age, eager to get to his bait before he died of hunger. 'Lisa, you know the score. I want you on close associates. Find out who was around, who was in prison. Try and get a handle on what's been going on in the Allen world in the past few weeks.' As Lisa got out of the car and shut the door, Kate dropped the window. 'Hank, hold the fort 'til I get back.'

He turned to face her. 'Where are you going?'

'Where do you think?'

Realizing she was planning to see the victims' family on her own, he protested vehemently. He wanted to go along in case there was trouble – the very reason she wanted to leave him behind. No amount of gentle persuasion could convince him that there was less chance of the family kicking off if he wasn't there when she delivered the terrible news. He tried to get back in the car but she'd locked the doors and was already moving off.

'At least tell me *where* you're going,' she heard him yell.

Chapter Nine

ACCORDING TO INTELLIGENCE, Mrs Allen senior had a penthouse apartment in a block near the Sage Music Centre on the Gateshead side of the Tyne. Kate parked on the north quay, deciding to walk across the Millennium Bridge to the south side of the river. She needed some air. Time to think. En route from the station, her mind kept coming back to the same thing over and over. Why amputate all bar one of Terry Allen's fingers? Why leave the ring in place? If it was a clue, she had no idea of its significance. *Yet*.

Taking out her phone, she rang Jo Soulsby's mobile.

The profiler answered with her first name only.

She was at home.

'Hi, it's me.' Kate tried to sound upbeat.

'Hey, stranger!' Jo sounded happy and relaxed. 'What you up to?'

'I need your help . . . again.' Kate looked around her, making sure no one was within hearing distance. 'I have a nasty torture case on my hands, a double murder this time – actually two murders that are most likely linked. Any chance I can swing by later and fill you in? Not sure what time it'll be, but I could do with your input. I'm about to tell the relatives of the deceased, and they are not going to take it well.'

'Why is that a problem for you?' Jo asked. 'You sound stressed. I know it's never a pleasant task, but it's not as if you haven't done it before.'

Stepping onto the bridge, Kate let out a big sigh. There was no point denying she was bricking it. The tone of her voice must have given her away. She didn't stand a hope in hell of keeping that from Ms Intuitive. There had been a time when they were so much more than work colleagues, but even though intimacy was no longer a realistic proposition – except maybe in her dreams – the friendship remained.

'Kate? You still there?'

'Yes, sorry . . . it's not a problem exactly, although I can't say I'm looking forward to it. My victims were killed in separate incidents, but they belong to the same family – and these people aren't big fans of the police.'

'Is Hank with you?' Jo sounded worried.

'Not this time.'

'Why?'

'I don't want to give them an obvious target to vent their anger on. They're going to be pretty pissed as it is.'

'Ring me the minute you're out.'

'That's won't be necess—'

'Ring me . . . please.'

It was easier not to argue. They had done enough of that to last them both a lifetime. They made arrangements to meet later at Jo's house and then Kate hung up.

Halfway across the bridge, her phone beeped twice. It was still in her hand. She stopped walking, leaned on the guard rail to check out the display, ducking as a gull swooped down from the roof of the Baltic into the murky waters below. Like most cities, Newcastle owed much of its wealth to the river on which it stood. Working shipyards further east were long gone, trading warehouses turned into upmarket riverside apartments.

The text was from Robson, asking her to get in touch.

He had news – none of it good – apparently.

She rang him back. 'Hi, it's me. What's up?'

'Examination of the Mercedes is still ongoing. They're reporting bolt cutters and severed fingers in the back. Unless John had more than the usual number, they're not his.'

'Terry's.' Kate wasn't asking, she was stating a fact.

'Looks that way. I think we found our second crime scene.'

Pocketing her phone, Kate walked on, chewing over this new intelligence. It seemed reasonable to assume that Terry Allen had been tortured in the same van that was used to kill his brother. But how, she wondered, had he managed to escape? Or had he? Perhaps he was tortured and dumped as a warning. If so, could it have been John who'd taken him to the RVI?

The questions were still whirring round in her head when Theresa Allen flung open the door to her penthouse apartment. It was clear from her appearance that she was expecting a visitor. Dressed smartly in a powder-blue linen suit, white T-shirt and strappy sandals, she had perfect hair and make-up. Either she was entertaining or she was on her way out to have fun. Had Kate not been about to give the woman the worst news of her life, she would have given anything to trade places with her.

'Can I help you?' A warm smile accompanied the question.

'Mrs Theresa Allen?'

'Yes.'

'I'm DCI Kate Daniels.' Kate offered up ID.

When Theresa saw the MIT label beneath Kate's rank and name, her face paled. Without saying a word, she moved inside, leaving the door wide open. Following her in, the DCI took a deep breath as she entered the living room. For a moment, Mrs Allen stood motionless with her back to the door, looking out through a picture window with a spectacular quayside view that Kate suspected she wasn't seeing. Theresa turned, removed her jacket and sat down on the nearest sofa.

Kate remained standing. 'I'm so sorry, I have some bad news.'

'I thought as much,' Theresa's Glaswegian accent was soft, nothing like the harsh version so often portrayed on the box. Although she'd guessed the situation was grim, she didn't cry. It was as if she'd already imagined a copper's knock a hundred times before. She sucked in a breath. 'I tried with my boys, we both did. Don't get me wrong, Inspector, I'm well aware my ex pulled some strokes in his time. Brian was no saint. But he never wanted our kids to go the same way. He died before they got into any serious trouble.'

Theresa paused, exhaling loudly before carrying on. She needed to talk and Kate let her. It was a tactic employed by many of the bereaved, a way of putting off the evil moment when they would be told a truth they didn't want to hear. It was the eyes that gave her away. On the brink of tears, she was barely holding on.

'They were too much like him.' Theresa's eyes drifted to a photograph of a handsome middle-aged man, large build, steely blue eyes you could dive into. 'Not violent,' she corrected herself. 'They were never like him in that way. They just thought they were above the law. I knew it would end badly.' She paused a moment, swallowed hard. 'Which one is it?'

Kate didn't know what to say. She wanted it to be one son, not both. She wanted to walk away and leave the woman be, not break her heart and pry into her personal life. She was sick and tired of being the purveyor of bad news.

Theresa looked away.

She'd already made the jump.

Placing a comforting hand on her shoulder, Kate sat down. This wasn't how she'd pictured the scene. Nothing like the reception she'd anticipated. She'd gone to the house expecting trouble and found cooperation. It would have been much easier had the woman been angry, if she'd told her to get the hell out of her house. But here they were, interacting, woman-to-woman, not a hint of animosity between them.

They spent an hour together. Kate made tea and listened patiently as Theresa talked some more. Many years ago, she'd begged her husband to put his past behind him and move away from his home city for the sake of their young family, to give their sons a better start in life than either of them had enjoyed.

'Except that didn't happen,' Kate said.

'No . . .' Theresa held her gaze. 'I did what I could.'

When Kate didn't comment, Theresa insisted she'd been a good mother.

Whether a person was genetically predisposed to be bad or made that way – the nature–nurture argument – was a familiar topic of debate between Kate and Jo. Theresa was adamant that she'd done her level best, insisting that her late husband had never abused her or the kids. So, she was asking, if their violent tendencies weren't learned or observed at home, where had such behaviour come from?

The doorbell rang, stopping her in her stride.

It was a rude interruption but a welcome one, allowing Kate to let the matter drop. 'You want me to get that for you?' she asked.

'No, it's OK,' Theresa said. 'I was going out. It'll be my lift.'

She left the room, leaving the door ajar.

Muffled conversation and sobs reached Kate through the wall. Curious to find out who was at the door, she stood up and moved into a position where she could see along the hallway without making it obvious she was snooping. Idly studying a bookcase, she was able to view what was going on out of the corner of her eye. Theresa was receiving a hug from a male visitor. Kate could feel his eyes on her. But the second she looked at him, he turned his face away. Half-expecting Theresa to return with her guest in tow, Kate went back to her seat. Seconds later, she heard the door close and he was gone.

'A neighbour,' Theresa said, as she walked back in.

'Oh?' Kate could see she was lying. 'Then I'm surprised he didn't stay.'

For a moment, the women locked eyes. Kate waited patiently. Experience had taught her that confrontation was not always the best policy in situations like these. And so it proved. Exposed as a liar, Theresa had nowhere else to go . . .

'You caught me out, Inspector. He's my new partner. I asked him to leave because he has no idea I have sons, let alone that my ex was a Glasgow thug. I told him there had been a family bereavement, that I'm OK and prefer to handle it by myself. I've not known him long and I don't want to lose him. Can we get on with this? I'm very tired.'

'Of course,' Kate said. 'It would help if we knew where John and Terry spent last night.'

'No idea, I've not seen them for a couple of weeks.'

'Did they talk about what they had been up to recently?'

Theresa was shaking her head. 'I assume it was probably illegal. I told you, Inspector: I wanted none of it. Mind you, I'm not surprised they had enemies. They were often in the papers, accused of this and that. John had been to prison on more than one occasion. I don't know which one.'

'You didn't visit him?'

'No.' Theresa lit a cigarette and threw the lighter on the coffee table. 'I thought that my disapproval would help him see sense, like it did his father. I was kidding myself. I'd already lost him and his brother. To be honest, they were good for nothing else. God forbid that they would get a regular job and settle down. Money was all they cared about. And before you ask, I never took a penny from either of them.'

Kate couldn't help but be impressed by the woman's ability to keep a rein on her emotions. Given the same circumstances, she knew she wouldn't have. This woman had seen some shit in her lifetime, the kind that hardens people. No wonder she had wanted to leave it all behind in Scotland and turn her life around. From the look of her penthouse, she'd certainly done that. Such a shame her sons hadn't followed suit.

The phone rang out a couple of times and was ignored.

'I don't expect you to believe this,' Theresa said, 'but when John and Terry were with me, they were just my boys, loving and generous, everything a mother could possibly want or wish for. John especially. After his father died, I don't know how I'd have got through it without him. They were in Spain together when it happened. A golfing holiday – boy's stuff, y'know.'

A tear formed in Theresa's left eye. A tiny liquid balloon sat on her bottom lid for what seemed like an age before gravity made it splash on to her bare shoulder. She brushed it away, composure returning. She took a long, deep drag on her cigarette. Smoke curled around her mouth as she moved it away.

Studying her closely, Kate was very much aware that she still had the hardest part to face. She couldn't shrink from it: certain facts had to be disclosed. Theresa's sons had both been tortured. How could she tell her that she only need identify the younger of the two, that formal identification by next of kin would be impossible in John's case? It would destroy her.

Theresa was still talking. 'I chose not to ask my sons questions I didn't want answers to, Inspector. I don't suppose that makes any sense to you, does it? But that was the only way I could cope.'

'I understand.' Kate had met many parents who followed the same policy.

It was time.

She told Theresa the truth, conveying the information as sensitively as she was able; only what she needed to know, nothing more. She was relieved that the mother didn't want specifics. In possession of an address for Terry's wife and John's girlfriend, Kate made arrangements for Theresa to view the body and for a Family Liaison Officer to call, then left the woman to grieve alone.

Chapter Ten

TERRY'S WIFE LIVED around the corner, so Kate went there first. When April Allen refused to let her in, she was forced to convey the sad news across the threshold before the door slammed in her face, followed by a mouthful of abuse from inside the house. Raising her hand to knock again, Kate thought better of it. She'd informed the next of kin. Job done. After the morning she'd put in, she wasn't waiting around for afters.

With a pressing appointment at the morgue and, if she were being honest, unable to face another death message, she called Hank and asked him to head over to John's place and break the news to his girlfriend, Vicky Masters. He was more than happy to take the weight off Kate and they agreed to rendezvous back at the office when he was done.

THEY MET IN the canteen an hour and a half later, both drained, in need of a break and a recap on the morning's events. There were no fresh developments from either crime-scene investigators or house-to-house. In the incident room, the Murder Investigation

Team were treading water. Bored and with little to keep them ticking over, Hank gave Kate grief for driving off without him, asking how she'd got on at the morgue.

'The usual,' she said flatly. 'You fare any better than me?'

He shook his head. 'Vicky Masters wouldn't talk to me. She was in a hell of a state when I got there—'

Kate flashed him a look. 'She already knew?'

'Oh, she knew all right.' He pointed at the machine. 'You want a coffee or something?'

'From that?' Kate grimaced. 'I'd rather stick pins in my eyes. I'm sorry, Hank. Theresa must have called Vicky right after I left.'

He pressed for hot chocolate. 'You never said anything about John to Terry's wife, did you?'

'Hardly. Anyway, she saw me off before I had a chance to pass on our condolences.' She gestured to a seat near the window. They moved towards it, took a moment to unwind, both feeling punchy.

Trying to work out where to go next, Kate looked out of the window. It was a beautiful day – sunny and not a cloud in the sky – but all she could see was a strip of tarmac smeared with congealed blood and bits of skin.

'So much for zoning it out,' she whispered under her breath.

Hank narrowed his eyes. 'Boss?'

'Nothing,' she said, an idea occurring. 'You know, it may not have been Theresa who told Vicky that John was dead.'

'Makes you say that?'

'Maybe whoever did the killing is bragging about it.'

'To scare the shit out of everyone?'

'You saw the state of the victims. You'd have to be barking to inform on them. Anyone brave or stupid enough would know they'd get the same treatment from the perpetrators. We need to find them or there's going to be a bloodbath.' Kate paused a moment, considering her options. 'If Theresa doesn't know where her sons were last night and their partners won't say, that only leaves us one option.'

Hank put down his plastic beaker. 'Which is?'

Kate hesitated – *time to go off-piste.*

Chapter Eleven

When on unofficial business, Kate liked to do things the old-fashioned way. No names, no pack drill. No mobile phones. No company. She'd known the man she was looking for since she was a DS on the drugs squad several years ago. Communication devices were not his thing – never had been. The only way to get hold of him was by visiting his haunts: the pubs, the betting shops or greyhound stadium.

Moving through the crowded pub towards the bar, she scanned the room casually. No sign. She checked her watch: three-thirty. Less than ten hours into a double murder case, she didn't have time to piss about. But, seeing as she was already there, she decided to give it a few minutes to see if her man surfaced.

Pulling up a bar stool, she sat down, ordering a gin and tonic with a twist of lime she had no intention of drinking. The barman smiled as he set her glass down and moved off to serve someone else. Acting as though she was in no particular hurry, Kate pulled a copy of the *Journal* newspaper towards her and stuck her head in it.

The words were a blur. She couldn't stop thinking about the mother of her two victims.

If Theresa Allen was to be believed, and Kate had no reason to suspect otherwise, she had done her utmost to bring up her sons in difficult circumstances. The fact that she'd failed miserably was immaterial. John and Terry were inherently dishonest. Despite her assertion that they were nonviolent, the DCI knew different. They were like their late father. Anyone who got in their way ended up being leaned on heavily – and they didn't make the same mistake again.

Kate pushed the paper away and pictured the scene back at the incident room. An information-gathering exercise would be well underway. She'd asked for a full history of the Allen family. Her team would be liaising with their Scottish counterparts to discover the circumstances surrounding their move south of the border. Would it have made a difference had they done it sooner? Jo would tell her it would. It was a child's formative years that were so important. By the time they reached adolescence, it was already too late.

What a bloody waste.

Pulling out her phone, Kate texted Carmichael, asking if she'd come up with anything that might throw light on what the two men had done to deserve such vicious treatment. Almost immediately, she received a text back: Negative.

Kate replied: Keep on it.

As she pocketed her phone, she glanced up at the mirrored tiles behind the bar and caught sight of the man she was looking for exiting the gents. A flash of recognition crossed his face as their eyes met. He gave a nod, almost imperceptible, a signal that he'd seen her. He didn't look happy. No wonder; he knew she was there to give him grief.

Wishing she could down the lot, Kate took a small sip of her gin and placed the glass back down on the counter. When she looked up, the man she'd made contact with had gone. That didn't concern her. They had an arrangement that if he saw her hanging around he would make his way to the Cumberland Arms. That would be where he'd gone . . .

She hoped.

She gave it a moment longer, then set off to find him. It was breezy outside, busy with pedestrians, all of whom seemed to be hurrying on a mission, as if their lives depended on them getting from A to B as quickly as possible. Hers too was urgent. As she made her way to the rendezvous point, she thought about her use of informants over the years, a practice widespread in every police force. In the fight against organized crime, snouts came in handy. Kate was a true believer; she knew from experience that trading favours solved crimes. The introduction of regulations had complicated matters. Informants now had to be registered, placed on 'Form A', money and the possibility of a reduced sentence the only carrots officers were allowed to dangle in exchange for information.

That was the official line.

Problem: Towner was unregistered.

The only form he'd appear on was a charge sheet – assuming he failed to deliver. But that was the least of Kate's worries. If she got caught not playing by the rules it would be a disciplinary offence.

C'est la vie – she had a double murder to solve.

THE CUMBERLAND ARMS was a popular, arty pub tucked away on James Place Street near Byker Bridge, a few minutes' drive from the city centre. Towner – not his real name – was sitting outside at a picnic bench, a fresh pint in front of him and something cool and non-alcoholic for her. Kate put on her sunglasses as she approached his table. She straddled the bench, held up her drink.

'Cheers,' she said.

'Don't mention it,' he grunted. 'You owe me seven quid.'

Same ol' Towner.

Setting her glass down, Kate slipped a twenty beneath his pint. Cast her eyes over him. She hadn't seen him for almost three years. They had met around the turn of the century. He'd come begging her to turn a blind eye to his sister's misdemeanours; in exchange he'd offered information on a major drugs deal that was about to go down. With a little gentle persuasion, he'd come good ever since.

He was thirty-eight years old going on fifty. Prolonged heavy drinking and smoking had aged him appreciably since last they met. His hair was grey and thinning, his skin an unhealthy yellow, his eyes bloodshot, his fingers stained brown with nicotine. But the only body parts she was interested in were his ears.

'I need your help, Towner.'

He glanced at the money. 'It'll cost you more than that.'

A group of girls were flirting with the young guys on the next table down, egging them on to get another round in and join them later at the Quayside. They looked joyful and healthy, the complete reverse of the forlorn individual facing Kate.

'How's Margie?' she asked.

'She's dead.'

Kate wasn't surprised. 'I'm sorry to hear that.'

'Yeah, right. Like you care.'

It was fair comment. Apart from being a druggie, his sister had been a prolific thief who'd steal her granny's eyes and come back for the sockets if she needed money. Kate had been well aware that

Margie was beyond help when she made a deal with her brother all those years ago. Towner liked his drink but was anti anything to do with drugs on account of what it had done to his sister. That worked to the DCI's advantage. His information had resulted in a drugs bust preventing hundreds of thousands of pounds' worth of cocaine hitting the streets. It also led to a commendation for a young DS before she was twenty-four years old.

'I want information on the Allen family,' she said.

Towner almost choked on his beer. 'I know nowt. And if I did, I wouldn't be telling you about it or I'd be joining our Margie downstairs.'

'I'm sorry you feel that way.' Her tone was softer when she spoke again. 'I would have thought you of all people would be celebrating today. The Allen boys were never on your Christmas card list.'

The comment was designed to provoke a reaction. It worked. She could tell from the expression on his face that he already knew about the two deaths that had brought her here. He wouldn't be sorry to hear of either man's demise. He despised the Allen brothers, John in particular; according to Towner, he'd been the one who got Margie into hard drugs in the first place.

'Am I a suspect?' he asked.

She almost laughed.

'Not your style, is it? You need a backbone for that kind of thing.' She eyeballed him across the table, her best don't-mess-with-me stare. 'I know what you're up to, Towner. I've been keeping my eye on you. If you want to stay out of custody, you need to start talking to me. Fast.'

'You know shit,' he said.

'I know you and your mates are thieving lead. I saw a movie of the three of you doing it a couple of months back. We detectives talk to each other y'know. I shopped the wasters you hang out with but kept my mouth shut about you. I don't have any lead on my roof so I'm not bloody interested. But if you don't come across for me now, my memory of who else was on that church roof is sure to come flooding back. Am I making myself clear?'

'Crystal,' he said.

'Glad we understand each other. Have another drink, then go home to that shit-pit of yours and have a good long think. When you've done that, use the phone.' She placed an unregistered mobile on the picnic table. 'Ring the incident room at Market Street. Ask for me and no one else. Got it? This is big. You've got twenty-four hours. I want to hear from you, Towner.'

'And if you don't . . . ?'

Kate smiled. 'You're getting locked up.'

He saw off his pint, scooped the note and the phone off the table, and walked.

Chapter Twelve

On the way back to the incident room, Hank rang. There was more news from the RVI. A wheelchair had been found abandoned in a linen cupboard with copious amounts of blood on the backrest that may or may not belong to Terry Allen. The chair had been collected by crime-scene investigators and sent for forensic examination.

Hank had more . . .

'What did we do before everyone and his dog installed CCTV?' Despite the fact that he'd been hauled from his bed too early, he sounded upbeat. He always got excited when the cards fell his way. 'John Allen was captured on camera leaving the hospital via the fire exit of a maintenance tunnel, a minute and a half after the main entrance video equipment was tampered with. It's him, no doubt about it. Where the hell have you been? I've been calling you for yonks.'

Kate sidestepped the question as another call came in.

Tim Stanton was calling from the morgue.

She put Hank on hold to answer. 'What's up, Tim?'

'I thought you should know: Terry Allen had substantial bruising – weeks, rather than hours old – as well as several broken ribs. Looks like someone gave him a right going-over and came back for more. The injuries would have required treatment by a physician.'

'Interesting. Thanks for letting me know. I'll drop by later on.' Kate hung up and went back to her call. 'Hank, you still there?'

'Where else would I be?'

'Still at the hospital I meant, Wally.'

'Yeah, I'm here.'

'Make your way to A & E.' Kate indicated to turn left. 'I'll meet you there in five.'

SHE WAS ACTUALLY there in three. Abandoning her car in a bay marked EMERGENCY VEHICLES ONLY she put a police notice on the dash and made her way inside. As luck would have it, Senior House Officer Valerie Armstrong was working a split shift and was back on duty. Even though she'd been up half the night, she looked amazing. Kate felt like she might contaminate her just by standing there, with images of death and torture scrolling through her head involuntarily, as they had done all day.

Pushing them away, she forced herself to focus on the doctor. Listing Terry Allen's injuries as Stanton had described them, she disclosed her victim's ID, asking the SHO to check the hospital records to see if he'd been treated in the recent past. The doctor's colour rose. For a moment, Kate thought she was about to refuse her request, but she was wrong. The man's identity had triggered a memory in the doctor's subconscious that took a while to surface and was only now clicking into place.

'I remember him,' she said.

'You've treated him before?'

Hank slipped into the room from the corridor.

'Yes,' Valerie said. 'If he's the man I think he is—'

'I don't believe this.' Kate didn't understand. 'Why didn't you say so earlier?'

'Did I miss something?' Hank asked.

Ignoring him, the house officer kept her focus on the DCI. 'Because I didn't know who he was.'

'How could you not?' Kate asked. 'If you were the one who found him—'

'Don't fight, ladies.' Hank was grinning. 'I can't stand the sight of blood.'

'Because he was unrecognizable from the man I saw this morning.' The doctor explained: 'He was badly beaten. I'm sure I don't need to tell you how much the face swells when traumatized. I thought there was something familiar about him. Now I know why. If it *was* the same man, it was weeks ago and he was very poorly.'

'I see.' Kate ran a hand through her hair. 'I'm sorry. It's been a very long shift, for both of us.'

'No apology necessary. Do you have a date of birth?'

Kate reeled off Allen's details. Picking up the internal phone, the SHO dialled a number, asking for hospital notes on Terence Allen, and then hung up. While they waited, Kate filled Gormley in. A moment later, there was a knock at the door. A receptionist entered carrying a thin manila file.

Valerie waited for her to clear the room before opening it. 'Ah,' she said. 'It is him. He was admitted in the early hours of Friday the thirteenth of July. As I said before, he was in an awful state. I suspected concussion. He was treated, but discharged himself a few hours later – against my advice.'

'Did he say how he came by his injuries?' Kate asked.

The doctor slid the medical record across the table, pointing at a handwritten note on the bottom, confirming it was hers, entered contemporaneously: *Patient evasive and uncooperative – refused offer of police assistance.*

Chapter Thirteen

THE PHONE ON Kate's desk rang before she'd even sat down. She stopped chewing, glanced at a half-eaten sandwich in one hand, coffee in the other, and placed them down in order to answer.

'DCI Daniels.' Kate listened but no one spoke. Background traffic noise suggested the call was coming from a public phone box.

Towner.

For a moment, she thought he'd bottled it. Finally, he came on the line, telling her that he had information and was willing to trade it in exchange for immunity from prosecution. Fair enough. Kate never went back on her word. He sounded nervous, understandably so. Whoever was dishing out the torture wouldn't think twice about seeing him off. He told her that Terry Allen had been given a right going-over last month. It was the first corroboration of what she already knew. Proof that he wasn't lying.

Her instincts had paid off.

'So, he got jumped,' she said. 'Thugs have a tendency to make enemies occasionally. You know I need more than that. Where exactly did this take place?'

'Grant's.'

'Nightclub?'

'Yeah.'

Kate picked up her pen. 'Who attacked him?'

'Dunno.'

'Stop wasting my time!'

'I don't, I swear.' Towner hesitated. 'Look, all I know is he's been lying low ever since. Word on the street is, he was lucky to survive. The heavies doing the kicking backed off when his mates arrived mob-handed, tipped off by a hooker who'd seen it happen. The guys who got hold of him weren't arsed about Terry. They were searching for John.'

Yes! 'Why?'

'Fuck knows.'

'Which hooker?'

'Dunno.'

'Try harder.'

No response.

'Fine, enjoy the rest of your day. It'll be your last in the sunshine—'

'Calls herself Sky,' Towner blurted out. 'I swear, that's all I have.'

'That was the right call,' Kate said. 'Next time you're on a church roof, say three Hail Marys for me.' She cut him off.

Making a note on a message pad for entry on to HOLMES, Kate timed and dated the form. In the bottom corner there was a box to fill in with the name of the person from whom the information had come. It appeared to get larger the more she stared at it. Lifting her pen from the paper, she paused, then scribbled four words: *Anon Female/Sunderland accent.*

SHE FINISHED HER tea before joining the rest of the team in the incident room for the early evening briefing. Carmichael kicked off the meeting. She'd been in touch with the Serious Organized Crime Agency. A list of known associates had gone out to Division for further investigation. It seemed that the Allen crew were not averse to crossing force boundaries to carry out their business. They operated in several cities: Manchester, Leeds and Glasgow among them.

Kate went next, disclosing her new intelligence on Terry Allen's hospitalization six weeks earlier. Then, as cool as you like, she shared her more recent tip-off, the fact that the assault may well have been witnessed by a hooker named Sky, information she believed might move the enquiry along a pace.

'Where did that come from?' DS Robson was often too bright for his own good. As statement reader, he was the linchpin of the murder enquiry. All statements passed over his desk and he was telling everyone that he didn't recall any mention of Sky. His focus was on the DCI. He was waiting for an answer she'd rather not give.

'It didn't come in a statement,' Kate explained. 'It was a phone call. I took it myself.'

That truth seemed to satisfy him. But on the opposite side of the room, it wasn't fooling Hank who, it had to be said, was a lot more switched on than Robbo would ever be. Feeling his eyes bearing down on her, Kate moved quickly on to Maxwell . . .

'Any news on the DVD from JMR Refrigeration, Neil?'

Maxwell shook his head. 'Technical support are working flat out. It's proving difficult to enhance. Light was poor. Both guys were wearing balaclavas. They're not holding out much hope.'

Kate wasn't impressed. 'What about the rest?'

'Rest?' Maxwell queried.

'Clothing, watches, jewellery, footwear. There must be something distinctive that we can identify. Or didn't it cross your mind to ask?'

'Have I done something wrong, boss?'

'No. Yes. Get back on to them. You need to up your game.' Kate scanned the room. 'That goes for the rest of you. I want enquiries made in the nightclubs in and around town. There's some real shite coming out of Grant's club lately. Start there.'

Gormley's eyes again.

Kate sucked in a breath. 'Andy, get in there tonight and see what you can pick up. Take Lisa with you. And for God's sake, be careful. We want results but we don't want to tip anyone off.'

The noise level rose as the team disbanded. Before Kate had a chance to slip away to the relative safety of Naylor's office – he'd asked for a personal briefing – Hank approached asking if he could have a word, flicking his eyes in the direction of her office.

Kate led the way, expecting earache.

She deserved it.

Hank closed the door behind him. 'What's going on?'

She threw herself down in her seat, trying to avoid looking at the message from Towner still lying on her desk. Hank remained standing, eyeing her with suspicion. Reading her. Making her feel uncomfortable. She wanted to laugh out loud. The best detective sergeant in Northumbria force, her favourite man in the whole wide world, was sulking – but only because he cared about her. On a previous enquiry they had fallen out when she'd not played by the rules. He'd told her then that if she dug a hole – however big – and jumped in, he'd be there to haul her out, no matter what the circumstances, but in exchange he expected honesty and openness.

He was staring at her. 'You wouldn't be using unregistered informants, by any chance?'

She used her best poker face. 'Makes you say that?'

'I know how your brain works. How devious you are.' He tried for a smile. 'I couldn't give a stuff either way, but we had an agreement to play nice, didn't we?'

It was true. She'd promised not to exclude him from her exploits ever again. But things were rarely that simple. She stared at him, weighing up the possibilities. Tell him, or protect him by keeping him well out of it? They were playing a game of blink first.

Hank was winning.

'So.' He sat down. 'Are you using a snout or not?'

'Might be.' Her eyes grew big. 'OK, I am. Happy now?'

He blew out his cheeks. He knew only too well that it could land her in hot water with Naylor, a disciplinary offence at best, a demotion at worst.

'My call,' she said. 'Nothing for you to worry about. And no Form A, understood? We want to catch these bastards, don't we? My source won't help me if it's official.' She made a smiley face. 'You in, or out?'

Hank grinned.

Chapter Fourteen

KINGS TERRACE WAS a tree-lined avenue in the leafy suburb of Jesmond, a couple of miles from Newcastle city centre. Kate was feeling decidedly jaded as she pushed open the gate to number 45, walked up the path and rang the bell of the smart Victorian house. Since being dragged out of bed she'd viewed two dead bodies, launched a double major incident investigation, delivered two death messages, worked all day, delegated, directed her team and briefed her guv'nor. She was ready to drop.

An arc of light flooded from the house as the door opened.

As Kate stepped inside, Jo Soulsby took her jacket and hung it on a peg in the hallway. Shutting out the dark, she gave Kate a gentle hug. Kate stood there, arms flopping by her side like a child at the arse-end of a school day, too grumpy and too tired to move. She didn't hold on for fear that it would be interpreted as another pathetic attempt at reconciliation.

Jo looked happy and relaxed. Kate could hardly remember what it felt like to take a day off and chill. It was warm and cosy in the house. There was a faint whiff of alcohol in the air, and she could hear music, a constant in both their lives when they hung out together. Just being there brought a rush of memories flooding back.

'Heavy day?' Jo asked.

Slipping off her shoes, Kate avoided eye contact. 'The first few hours are always the worst. It's bedlam in the office and this one's not straight by any stretch of the imagination. We've got victim IDs and bugger-all else. My guys are still in the haystack searching.'

'I wasn't sure you'd come this late.'

'I nearly didn't.'

Kate checked her watch – quarter to ten – almost nine hours since she'd promised to call Jo, sixteen since she'd started this particular shift. The role of SIO on the Murder Investigation Team was her dream job, one she'd worked hard to secure, but there were times when she questioned what she was doing with her life, when the position asked too much of her. Right now, she wished it would vanish, if only for a few days, until she recovered from the influx of cases that had wiped her out.

'Sure you don't mind?' she said. 'We can do this tomorrow.'

'We'll do it now. You look like you need a good talking to.'

Jo moved away, her tapered trousers and skinny T-shirt accentuating her figure as she walked towards the kitchen. Kate followed, trying to ignore her own reflection in a full-length mirror at the end of the hallway. She looked dreadful, longed for a soak in a hot bath and a change of clothes.

Inviting her to sit at the table, Jo handed her a bowl of soup and a chunk of brown bread, told her to eat while she poured them both a glass of wine. 'I take it you're finished for the night – unless that damn phone of yours summons you back.'

Mid-mouthful, Kate nodded.

The soup tasted good. It was homemade and warmed to the perfect temperature. A few feet away, Nelson, Jo's young Labrador, was curled up asleep in his basket next to the Aga, so peaceful she wished she could lie down beside him and drop off.

When she'd finished eating, Kate followed Jo through to the living room, her stomach churning as she walked through the door. The lighting was soft – very personal – and it wasn't for her. A couple of candles were burning away and there were signs of an intimate evening: two champagne flutes, wine glasses, empty bottles, corks and CDs littering the place.

Quite a party.

For a moment, Kate pictured Jo and A. N. Other. Shoes off. Snuggled up on the floor, listening to music, as they had once done. Sharing a joke. Possibly planning their next jolly jaunt. Making out.

Jo stifled a laugh. 'You should see your face!'

'Face?' Kate felt her cheeks burning even as she said it.

'No need to panic, Kate. The lads have been round: a celebration for James's graduation, remember? I asked you to join us.'

'Ohmygod.' Kate palmed her forehead. 'I totally forgot, I'm *so* sorry.'

'Don't worry about it. You missed them by minutes. They're off into town to meet some mates.'

With her jealousy out of the way, Kate could see more clearly. There were three, not two, wine glasses in the room. One had been left on a side table and there was a third champagne flute abandoned in the hearth of a fabulous marble fireplace, the pride of the room. She felt silly and a little emotional. Fatigue sometimes had that effect.

She cleared her throat. 'Am I allowed to ask how he did?'

'He got a 2:1.'

'Fantastic!'

'Bloody amazing for someone who put no work in whatsoever.' Even though Jo was smiling, her eyes were not. James had been tipped for a first but had been too busy shagging his tutor to do the graft. 'He could have done so much better.'

'Don't be disappointed,' Kate said.

'I'm not, I'm frustrated.'

'Why? Because studying an older woman floated his boat more than politics and economics ever could?' Kate smirked. 'No-brainer, wouldn't you say?'

'Yeah, I guess. Believe it or not, they're still together.'

'Wow! Must be serious.' Kate knew about the affair from way back. 'Have you met her?'

'Jill? Hell no!' Jo made a crazy face. 'Anyway, you didn't come to talk offspring. Sit. You look exhausted.'

'I'm fine.'

'Really? Take a look in the mirror.'

Kate ignored the dig. Any more tension and she'd surely snap.

Jo slumped down on the sofa, kicked off her pumps and tucked her legs beneath her bum. Kate sat down too, changing the subject to something less personal: work. Handing over crime-scene photographs, warning Jo that they were far from pretty, she looked on as the profiler viewed them. The temperature seemed to plummet the more information they shared, the main thrust of their conversation hinging on the level of violence used. It was way over the top in anyone's book.

'Torture cases are rarely impulsive,' Jo said.

'I agree. This one was definitely planned. Stolen vehicles, acquisition of tools – SOCO found bolt cutters.' Kate cringed as she said it. 'You'd expect that would guarantee Terry Allen's compliance. Except, he didn't talk – at least, we don't think he did, poor sod. Whoever cut his fingers off was organized enough to bring along the right implements to do the job. It's enough to make you puke—'

'Unless the tools just happened to be in the van they stole.'

'C'mon, you don't believe that any more than I do. Anyway, Robbo checked with the registered keeper as soon as the missing digits were discovered in the van. There were no tools in the Mercedes or the four-by-four. Whoever did this knew what they were doing and why they were doing it long before last night.'

'So what's your theory?'

'I'm not sure I have one, at least not fully formed. Either the offenders let Terry go and followed him, or else he escaped and managed to get a message to John. It wouldn't take a brain surgeon to work out that he'd require a major trauma centre. Which is the only plausible explanation why the brothers bypassed the nearest A & E. It didn't work though; I think the offenders were lying in wait to grab John as he left the RVI.'

'Why are you so certain that Terry was the bait, John the target?'

'I'm not. But that's the word on the street.'

'Then why bother torturing John? Why not just kill him outright?' Jo held up the photos. 'This is pretty elaborate, don't you think? Risky too. There must be more to it, surely.'

'There are certainly easier ways of committing murder,' Kate conceded. 'Killing him wasn't enough. They wanted him to suffer on the way out. According to SOCA, his offending has escalated in recent years. He and Terry were dabbling in all sorts. Extortion, mainly. Taxing local businessmen in exchange for protection they didn't want or need. Nasty stuff. Maybe this is someone fighting back.'

'If you lie down with dogs . . .'

'Exactly.'

'So what happens next?'

'I'll work on Terry's wife. She's not a fan of the police, but I'm hoping she'll want justice.'

'Is that a euphemism for revenge?'

'Either way, I'm probably the best person to hand it to her, whether she likes it or not. I intend to play up that angle, make her understand that killing those responsible would be swift but a lot less satisfying than watching them go down for life. I'm not sure it'll wash though.'

'What about John's girlfriend?'

'Same difference.'

'Maybe not. If she's young and has a kid, she might be more amenable—'

'Hank tried. She was equally uncooperative.'

'With all due respect, Hank isn't you. You have a way with women.'

Kate managed a half-smile. 'I'll see what I can do.'

Hoping Jo was right about April Allen, and that she might also be able to talk some sense into Vicky now she'd had the chance to calm down, Kate let out a big sigh. 'I'm not sure I have the where-withal to pull it off this time.'

'Of course you do.'

'Do I?' Kate met her gaze with a look of defeat. 'I've hit rock bottom, Jo. I'm under so much pressure to perform, I can hardly breathe. Everyone at the office is relying on me to put these cases to bed, even Hank. To do that, I need to break down an impenetrable wall of silence and hostility. Allen territory is rough terrain. Any witnesses are going to be too terrified to speak out. Where the hell do I start?'

'If anyone can get through it, you can.'

Kate was shaking her head, the mask she wore at work peeling away, leaving her exposed and vulnerable. 'You don't understand. I just don't have it in me to take another big enquiry, not after the caseload I've been carrying the last few months. But try telling that to Naylor – the man's a bloody machine.' Kate went quiet – toying with the Celtic necklace Jo had bought her the previous Christmas – meeting her compassionate eyes across the room. 'I'm not being defeatist – I'm being brutally honest – I'm struggling here.'

'I didn't say it would be easy.' Jo gave a sympathetic smile. 'You'll have to draw heavily on your reserves. You're bound to feel depleted occasionally, but you have the patience and experience to unlock this. I'm not just saying that because we're mates. You know it's true.'

'Thanks for the vote of confidence.'

'That said, you need to be very careful. These are sadistic, organized psychopaths. They enjoy inflicting pain. They're not your average thugs.'

'I'm not interested in labels. I just want them off the streets.'

'You need to warn the team they won't come quietly.'

'*I* need to find motive – and *you* are preaching to the converted.' Seeing the hurt on Jo's face, Kate apologized immediately. Jo was an easy target for her rage, the only one she could yell at without fear of retaliation, but it wasn't fair to use her that way. She sighed. 'Know what I need most?'

'A kick up the arse?'

'A hug.'

Kate looked on as Jo uncurled herself from her chair, picked up the wine bottle and joined her on the sofa. Taking Jo's right hand in her left, Kate laid her head on the profiler's shoulder – a perfect fit – a minute of peace and quiet after a wretched day.

'Forgive me being grumpy?'

'Don't be daft. I rather like being your punch-bag. Makes me feel I'm contributing.'

'You are . . . you always do. Why do you think I'm here?' Kate lapsed into silence for a moment, her mind back on the case. 'Know what my first thoughts were when I viewed John Allen's body? I was thinking that the torture was more important than the killing. Does that make any sense to you?'

'It wouldn't surprise me. It was certainly very personal.'

'What the hell goes through the minds of these people?'

Jo combed a hand through Kate's hair, soothing her. 'You'll work it out. How many times have I heard you tell the squad that, if they look hard enough, they'll find a way to build a case? Any case.'

'You're right. But the extent of our knowledge is thin, to say the least. We've got two vehicles and sod-all else. Both nicked on the outskirts of Hexham, within minutes of one another, far enough from the city so as not to be clocked. That's classic behaviour for car thieves: fail-safe device in case anyone remembers a number plate. They're savvy. Professional. I'm not sure that takes us any further.'

Easing herself out from under Kate's head, Jo reached for the wine bottle.

'Not for me,' Kate said. 'I'm already feeling drowsy and I've got the car.'

'Live a little. It's Friday night. You can't keep up this relentless pace—'

'Ahem, didn't you just finish telling me I can?'

'Good point.'

'Who am I kidding? I can hardly bail a day into a double murder enquiry, can I? Much as I might like to.'

'No, but how many times have we had this conversation?' Putting down the wine, Jo turned to face her. 'You drive yourself too hard. Remember when Stella Bright was dying and things got on top of your old boss? Who advised him to delegate? You should take your own advice, Kate. By all means give your team direction, but then let them get on with it. There's loads of them and only one of you. They'll share the workload. You're good for nothing otherwise.'

Kate was welling up. There were no actual tears. Even if there had been, Jo would've made nothing of it. Her support was unconditional. There would be no bullshit offers from the force psychologist at *her* recommendation. No reminding her of it later. What was said in her living room would stay there. Kate could rely on her integrity.

Fighting sleep, she sat up straight. It was true that she'd been feeling the strain for a while and had failed to do anything about it. She was doing the work of two. Her annual leave had gone untouched. She'd been working flat out for months and it had to stop.

Jo had read her mind. 'Is there no chance you can take time off?'

'You coming with me if I do?'

'Try stopping me.'

Kate looked at her. 'Promise?'

'Cross my heart and hope to die.'

'Please don't say that unless you mean it.'

'I do mean it. I'm a lot of things, but a tease isn't one of them. Of course I'll come with you. I hate to see you like this. You can barely stay awake. Besides, I'm a doctor. I've made a diagnosis and come to the conclusion that you need my special kind of therapy to make you well.'

'I am well!'

Nothing wrong with a little pretence.

'Are you, really?'

Kate dropped her gaze.

'I'm worried about you. Let me take care of you.' Jo stroked Kate's cheek with the back of her hand, eyes on fire. 'Would it help to know that I have an ulterior motive? I want you, desperately. Maybe we could start where we left off on Valentine's night.'

Leaning her head back, Kate shut her eyes as the memory took hold: a rudely interrupted and sexually charged moment that had taken them both by surprise, an encounter that had seen them scrambling into their clothes – just as things were getting inti-mate – in order to drive to a police station to rescue a friend whose daughter had gone missing.

Kate heard the glug of wine as it left the bottle. Even though her weekend was in ruins, she was spent, far too tired to object.

'Maybe we could start tonight,' Jo chuckled. 'I don't know about you, but I'm well out of practice.'

Her voice sounded far away.

Jo picked up her glass and sunk back into the soft cushions of the sofa. Sliding her free arm round Kate's shoulders, she sighed, expecting a kiss at least. There was no response. Her former part-ner had surrendered to tiredness and fallen asleep.

Chapter Fifteen

TURNING OVER, KATE pulled her knees up to her chest and the covers over her head as dawn crept into the room. Even in her semi-conscious state, something wasn't quite right. Feeling the heat of breath on her hand, she tried to wave it away without success. Forcing her eyelids open didn't work. She was drifting down and down into the comfort of sleep again. When something wet touched her face, she tried to rub it off.

She was freezing, cold and frightened.

A shadow, dark and indistinct, moved closer. She saw blood, sticky and congealed, a gaping jaw, an empty eye socket, a silver belt buckle embedded in raw flesh. Waking with a start, sweaty and confused by her surroundings, she shook her head, trying to dislodge the nightmare but the crime-scene images refused to budge. It would be a long time before she could rest easy, in bed or out of it.

Reality kicked in as Nelson stuck his cute head on one side, a curious look on his face, his eyes never leaving her. She stuck out an arm to stroke him, receiving another lick in return. At some point during the night, her shoes had been removed, a blanket lain across her. Jo's living room was tidy now. No dirty glasses or empty bottles. No trace of the candles she'd seen last night. *God!* She must've been out for the count if Jo had managed to clear that lot up while she was sleeping.

Drawing the cover back, she sat upright, rubbing her eyes. She'd slept but could feel no benefit from having done so. Combing her tangled hair with one hand, she tried straightening her clothing with the other. It was a feeble effort. The creases were there to stay. It was gone six according to the carriage-clock on the mantelpiece.

Time to get a move on.

Hauling her aching bones off the sofa, Kate crept towards the living room door, intending to sneak away without waking Jo, but as she reached the hallway, the smell of fresh coffee hit her senses. Little did she know that her host had been up for hours.

Kate found Jo in the kitchen, radio playing gently in the background. Dressed casually with hair scuffed back in a bun at the nape of her neck, muddy wellingtons on her feet; she'd already walked the dog.

'Morning . . .' Kate gave her a peck on the cheek. Her voice was thick with sleep. 'I'm sorry.'

Jo's brow creased. 'What on earth for?'

'Everything . . .' Repressing a full-on yawn, Kate pointed at her dishevelled state. 'Bet you wish you had a shirt like this.'

'Very attractive. I didn't have the heart to wake you.' There was a flash of mischief on Jo's face.

'Did I miss something?' Kate asked.

'You could say that. It's not often women fall asleep in my arms.'

'Damn! Couldn't you have pinched me or something?'

They laughed and let the matter drop.

Kate glanced out of the window. It was tanking down, the plants in Jo's tidy back yard receiving a thorough soaking. Pulling out a chair, Kate sat down at the kitchen table set for breakfast: fruit, cereal, yoghurt, boiled eggs and homemade marmalade. Placing two thick slices of bread in a toaster, Jo lifted the left-hand hood off the Aga and slid it into place, laying out new house rules as she waited for it to brown: no guests allowed to leave without first having something to eat. It was a fait accompli. No point arguing.

'I took liberties with your car keys,' she said, looking over her shoulder. 'Your overnight bag is upstairs and there are fresh towels in the bathroom.' She pointed at the toast. 'I'll keep this warm, if you like.'

ON HER DRIVE into work, Kate tuned to Radio 4 and caught the news headlines at seven-thirty. Another gunman had been on the rampage in New York. People had been shot. One dead, several injured. The person responsible had been taken out. Fifteen minutes later, Hank greeted her with a glance at his watch and a wry smile as she entered the incident room. It was unusual for her not to beat the team in and he'd known where she was headed the night before. He'd played Cupid in the past, would like nothing better than to see his two favourite women settle their differences and get back together.

Bending down as she passed his chair, she whispered: 'For such a tough guy, you're as soft as clarts.'

A wide grin spread across his face. 'I rang you at home and got no answer.'

She pointed at his messy desk. 'Haven't you got work to do?'

As he picked up the phone, chuckling to himself, Kate looked around her. She'd given DCs Brown and Carmichael permission to come in late after a surveillance operation at Grant's, but they were both at their desks. Like her, they looked washed out, the result of too little sleep. She'd make it up to them – *eventually*. Carmichael was busy with her computer, a look of total concentration on her face.

Leaving her to it, Kate approached Brown instead.

'Anything new to report, Andy?'

'Maybe.' He swivelled his chair to face her, his hopeful expression raising her expectations. 'There was a bit of an atmosphere in Grant's last night. Lots of speculation about who'd collared Terry to get at John, who had the guts to rock them both off. Your anonymous caller was right about one thing: Terry hadn't been seen for quite a while. It seems he stuck his head above the parapet at just the wrong time.'

Ignoring another smirk from Hank, Kate asked, 'What's the SP on John?'

'Also keeping his head down, though for different reasons. Rumour has it he's been playing away from home with someone else's missus. I heard the name Amanda mentioned. Didn't catch the rest. I was hiding in the bog at the time. Bastards walked away mid-conversation. Some people have no consideration. It might mean something. Or not.'

He'd done well.

Kate glanced at Carmichael, then back at Brown. 'What's Lisa doing?'

'She's going through the information we received from SOCA yesterday to see if the name Amanda is mentioned anywhere.'

Carmichael looked up. 'Nothing so far, boss.'

'Keep at it, Lisa. Andy, give Grant's management a bell. Find out what archaic recording device they happen to have on the premises. Any update on Sky?'

Brown shook his head. 'Lucked out there, sorry.'

That was disappointing, but Kate was delighted that the youngest members of her team were taking the initiative to trace John Allen's mistress without waiting for her to action it. Maybe she should come in late more often. Her mood changed as a horrible thought struck her. Towner's monotone voice popped into her head, reminding her of the earlier assault upon Terry Allen: *Word on the street is he was lucky to survive. The heavies doing the kicking backed off when his mates arrived mob-handed – tipped off by the hooker who'd seen it happen.*

According to officers on the outside team, Terry's mates weren't talking and there was little chance of them changing their minds. But was the same true of Sky? If she'd witnessed the beating and was blabbing about it she was in grave danger. Kate needed to find her – *fast!*

Chapter Sixteen

KATE CLOSED HER office door, hoping for some quiet time. Reflection was difficult in the midst of a hectic incident room. She sat down at her desk. Avoiding her in-tray, she pulled a pad towards her and picked up her fountain pen, her mind swimming with competing actions – none making any strong connections in her head. She began jotting down notes:

- *Sky – trace – question – protect?*
- *CCTV from Grant's – if any exists.*
- *Talk to the WAGS – establish where John and Terry were meeting up.*
- *T – he must know Sky!*
- ~~*DNA results!!*~~

Scrubbing out the last entry – it would be days before DNA results were available – she sat back, her frustration rising. The severed fingers found in the back of the Mercedes van might well be *her* priority, not necessarily that of a national forensic science laboratory;

she spent half her life waiting for others to do their jobs. But it was the remaining finger on Terry's hand that intrigued her the most. Why leave one finger intact? It had to be noteworthy and she added it to her list. She hadn't seen the ring he'd been wearing. It too was being forensically examined. More waiting. According to the property list, it was no ordinary wedding band either, but a seal ring with a family crest.

Flash bastard.

Kate had always wanted one of those.

She wondered if it had been bought or handed down the genera- tions. Theresa Allen claimed that her husband's death had had the opposite effect on his offspring to that which she desired. Rather than forget him and his criminal ways, Terry and John had been hell-bent on emulating him. They had placed him on a pedestal, and done their best to live up to his formidable reputation as a hard-nosed gangster.

Someone tapped on the door and it swung open.

Hank stuck his head in. 'You OK?'

Kate nodded. 'Sit down, take the weight off.'

'Where next?' he asked, the chair creaking under him.

'I wish I knew. I could lean on Towner again but I want to gauge the temperature of the relatives first.'

'John's girlfriend might talk, now her meal ticket is gone.'

'Jo thought so too. Vicky is younger than Terry's wife, she could be more amenable.'

Hank agreed, but made the point that her age had nothing to do with it. As John hadn't married her, Criminal Injuries Com- pensation wouldn't recognize her, he explained. Besides, Vicky had a criminal record of her own. Nothing sinister – petty theft and one count of possession of Class-C drugs – but enough to make her ineligible for a government-funded payout.

'And there's her kid,' Hank said. 'Apparently, John never acknowledged the bairn. If that's true, there's every chance his family might cut her adrift to fend for herself.'

'The opposite could also be true,' Kate ventured.

That threw him.

'That baby is the only grandchild Theresa Allen will ever have,' she told him. 'Think about it: she's a mother who's lost her only children. Despite their wayward lifestyle, she doted on them. It stands to reason she'd want to maintain a link with the next generation. I would, given the same set of circumstances.'

'Good point.'

'C'mon.' Kate stood up. 'We need to get going.'

As they passed through the incident room, Brown confirmed that CCTV footage was available from Grant's. Kate asked Maxwell to retrieve it.

'Lisa, go with him. Ask around. You see any prostitutes hanging around outside, bone them about Sky. If they give you anything, follow it up. Make damn sure you're not followed though. I suspect we're not the only ones keen to make her acquaintance.' Taking a twenty-pound note from her pocket, Kate handed it over. 'Don't part with that unless you get any intel . . .' She flicked her eyes towards Maxwell. 'And keep him on a tight leash.'

Laughing, Maxwell promised to behave himself.

Instructing detectives on the phones to feed anything important through the Receiver, Kate asked DS Robson to deputize for her and left the building with Hank. They took her car, neither of them relishing another row with bereaved partners. But what other choice did they have? They were desperate to pinpoint the movements of their victims in the hours leading up to their deaths. The conversation was as pivotal as it was crucial. In any murder enquiry, building a sequence of events came second only to discovering the identity of a victim. If they could establish where the brothers were before they died, they would find witnesses for sure.

'What's Theresa Allen like?' Hank asked casually, a few minutes into their journey.

'Personable,' Kate said. 'Considering she's two kids short of a family.'

Accelerating as she crossed the Swing Bridge, Kate glanced to her left, taking in his concern. She could see he wasn't happy. 'Something bothering you? Because if there is, I'd like to hear it.'

'It might be nothing.'

'Hank! Don't do that!' Shooting through a set of lights, Kate pushed her way into the left-hand lane and then slowed down as another set of lights turned red. 'I'm too tired to play guessing games. If you have something to say, I want to hear it.'

'You won't like it.'

'I already don't. Give!'

Hank wiped his face with his hand. 'I just find it hard to imagine that a woman who's lived with one of Glasgow's biggest villains is now enjoying the good life in a penthouse paid for through honest hard work. What does she do for a living, anyway?'

'I have no idea. I never asked.'

'Maybe you should have.'

'Yeah,' Kate scoffed. 'Good idea! Mrs Allen, your sons are dead; mind telling me how you finance such a fancy lifestyle? You can't blame the woman for the sins of her kids, Hank. Anyway, you wouldn't have said that if you'd seen her. She was wearing a blue linen suit and a string of bloody pearls. She looked like the president of the local WI.'

There was no retort, amusing or otherwise.

For a moment, silence filled the car. Somewhere inside Kate's head, alarm bells rang. Although very obliging, Theresa had lied about her boyfriend and been caught out. An unnecessary and provable lie, though in truth she'd covered it up with a credible excuse.

Hank was talking again, suggesting that Theresa was more likely to have taken over the family business than turned the other cheek and gone against her boys, a clear dig at Kate's judgement. Unlike her, he didn't have much faith in the powers of rehabilitation.

Kate's mind went into overdrive. Yesterday, Theresa had come across as genuine, but that little lie and Hank's warning shot had sown a seed of doubt she was now struggling with. What if he was right and she was wrong? 'It pays not to judge without even meeting the woman,' she protested.

'Then why are you looking so worried?' Hank glanced her way. 'You know your trouble?'

'No, but I'm sure I'm about to find out.'

Biting her tongue, telling him to drop it, Kate pictured the male caller Theresa had sent away yesterday, a sinking feeling in the pit of her stomach. When she told Hank about him, he damn near exploded.

Chapter Seventeen

'YOU ARE JOKING!' he said.

'No, I'm deadly serious. I offered to answer the door, but she declined. When I clocked him in the hallway, he looked away. I thought he was upset, shaken by the news, the old macho no-tears thing. To be honest, I half-expected her to invite him in. When she didn't, I could hardly go running after him, could I? Why would I? You're not suggesting *she* had anything to do with her sons' torture, surely?'

'No, but—'

'There you go then. She seemed perfectly genuine to me.'

'Yeah, well she would, wouldn't she?' Hank turned in his seat to face her, a serious expression on his face. 'No offence, boss, but you were a bit shaken up yesterday. You've not been yourself for weeks. You should've taken me with you. Two heads 'n' all that.'

'You been talking to Jo?'

'No!'

'Then what's with the interrogation?'

'You're right.' He sighed. 'Forget it.'

IT WAS CHUCKING down as Kate brought her car to a halt on Newton Road, High Heaton – typical bank holiday weather. Vicky Masters' house was close to St George's United Reform Church, a place of worship for many who lived in the area. As she got out of the car, Kate wondered if the congregation had prayed for John, whether he was considered worthy now he was dead. He sure as hell wasn't when he was alive.

She rang the doorbell.

Vicky didn't answer immediately – not until she realized they weren't going away. When she did finally open up, a baby was pinned to her hip, his big blue eyes fixed on the detectives.

'What do you want?' She glared at Hank. 'I could've sworn I told you to get lost.'

Kate held up ID. 'I'm—'

'I know who you are,' Vicky interrupted. 'And why you're here.'

'May we come in?' Kate asked. 'I'd like to help.'

'Oh yeah, how you gonna do that?'

The two women locked eyes. Kate urged her to do the right thing for all their sakes, including the little one who would one day begin to ask questions. Vicky was a pretty girl, twenty-two years old with corkscrew auburn curls. Dark eyeliner made the whites of her eyes stand out. And she was nowhere near as hard as she was making out. After a few moments of uncertainty, she walked away, leaving the door wide open, an invitation for them to follow her in – a hint that all was not lost.

Relieved that they weren't wasting their time, Kate entered the house, Hank bringing up the rear. The flat was contemporary and nipping clean inside. Not flash, but these two wanted for nothing, except maybe the guy who paid the bills. A photograph of Terry and John holding champagne flutes at a wedding celebration caught her eye as she scanned the walls – both good-looking lads.

'We're very sorry for your loss,' she said, hoping the young woman didn't ask too many questions about the circumstances surrounding her boyfriend's death. There was no point dancing round the subject. The DCI wanted information. They all knew that. The sooner she got it, the sooner she'd be on her way. 'You've met DS Gormley. My name is Kate Daniels, Murder Investigation Team. We need to talk.'

Stroking the child's head gently, Vicky eased him into a high-chair, made him comfortable and applied a plastic pelican bib he didn't want to wear. 'Talk if you want. I need to feed the bairn.'

'What's his name?' Kate asked.

'Nathan.'

'Hello, Nathan.' Kate turned from the child to his mother. 'How old is he?'

'Nine months.'

'He's cute.'

As if he knew he was being talked about, the child began bouncing in his seat, stopping only when his mother lifted a nursery-rhyme bowl from the kitchen bench and sat down beside him. Kate looked on as his chubby little hands grabbed for the spoon each time it came within striking distance – a picture of domestic bliss. But very soon, his expression changed from eager anticipation of more food to concern for his mother. As young as he was, he'd picked up on a change in atmosphere and was distressed by the silent tears rolling down Vicky's face. He glared at Kate as if it was all her fault.

'HOW THE HELL does a girl like her get mixed up with the likes of John Allen?' Kate whispered, letting herself out, making a beeline for her Audi. 'I mean, she's bright, intelligent, caring – a good mum too. You only need to look at her little boy to see that he's thriving. What an absolute waste.'

Hank shrugged, meeting her eyes across the roof as they climbed in. 'There's no accounting for taste. Anyway, she coughed. I call that a result, don't you?'

Kate agreed.

Securing the name of the club where the victims were planning to meet the night they died was a tangible lead she felt sure would uncover witnesses to what happened, why it happened and who was responsible. Sticking her key in the ignition, she glanced back at Vicky's front door. The whole time she'd been in the house, something had niggled away at the edge of her consciousness, her eyes drawn back, time and again, to the photograph of two young men smiling into the camera, triggering a chain of thought she couldn't share with Hank until they had left the house.

'He must've been an amazing brother,' she said.

'Which one?' Hank strapped himself in.

As an only child, Kate had no references from which to draw. She was trying to imagine the power of love between siblings, the bond between blood brothers whose lives had been linked from birth and strengthened through the death of a father they both idolized.

'John,' she said finally.

'What about him?'

'You love your brother, Hank?'

He gave her an odd look. 'What kind of a question is that?'

'You do though, right? You'd do anything for him?'

'Of course.'

She held his gaze. In her head she was back at the morgue, viewing Terry Allen's body, Stanton giving her a running commentary of what actually killed him. The fact that there were traces of chloroform round his mouth and nose. How he'd suffered before drawing his last breath. The thought of what he'd endured sent shivers down her spine all over again.

'How many fingers would you be prepared to lose before you gave him up?' she asked. 'One? Two? A handful? Terry Allen wasn't Superman. He didn't squeal because he couldn't – he didn't have the answer to whatever question they were asking him. He didn't know, Hank. He didn't bloody know.'

Chapter Eighteen

AT PRECISELY FOUR o'clock, Kate stood up to address the squad in an incident room packed to the rafters with police and civilian personnel. Frantic activity and the hum of conversations died down as she called for order. In seconds, the room was still, all faces turned in her direction, every member of staff paying attention, waiting for what they had already been told was a breakthrough in the case.

Glancing at a hastily scribbled aide-memoire, she was about to begin speaking when Jo Soulsby slipped quietly into the room at the back, miming a sorry. She'd agreed to assist the enquiry from this point on, an unusual occurrence in a gangland feud, but the level of violence was such that Kate had made a good case to her superiors on the grounds that they couldn't afford to have a couple of sadists running amok on the streets of Newcastle. Besides, there were no guarantees that the Allen brothers were the only targets. On a personal level, Kate was pleased to see Jo back where she belonged after a year out on secondment to a local prison, a disastrous move on so many levels.

'Right,' she said. 'I have a lot of ground to cover, so get your notepads ready. We now know from his hospital admission sheet that Terry Allen suffered a serious assault on Friday, thirteenth July. He was treated for his injuries and discharged himself the same night against medical advice.' She scanned the room, finding Maxwell. 'Neil? What's the state of play with CCTV from Grant's?'

'There's very little historical footage,' he said. 'The digital revolution passed the management by, I'm afraid. They still record to disk, which they wipe and reuse to save money. The earliest dates they have are only a fortnight old. I haven't spotted Terry or any of the scum he hangs out with, but I think I may have identified Sky.' He paused as the DCI congratulated him on a job well done. 'She's there most nights, hanging round the door, picking up punters.'

At his request, Carmichael uploaded an image of a leggy brunette to the murder wall. Wearing a strapless sparkly top, short skirt and thigh-length boots, she was standing near the doorway smoking a black cigarette, obviously plying her trade as customers entered and left through the main entrance.

Kate asked Carmichael to zoom in on her face so the team could examine her features in greater detail, but no squad member was able to ID her.

'Get a copy to Vice.' Kate was looking at Maxwell.

'I have done. They're clueless.'

Kate's enthusiasm plummeted. 'Must be new to the patch.'

Maxwell nodded. 'You want me to try and find her? She's hot.'

The DCI scowled at him. 'She's a kid!'

No one except Maxwell was laughing. The office fanny rat, he thought he was a player where women were concerned. He leapt at the chance of making their acquaintance at every opportunity.

Detectives bowed their heads, expecting him to get a more serious ticking off for not taking the briefing seriously. There was no piss-taking, no letting off steam. The SIO was right to be angry. Despite an attempt to hide it, Sky could only be a teenager – a young one at that.

Maxwell's smile melted away under the intensity of the boss's glare.

'It must be your lucky day, because finding Sky is exactly what I want you to do,' Kate said. 'Consider yourself on nights, kerb-crawler and official sleaze-ball for the next few days.' The squad were now laughing. 'Wear your best cravat and make damn sure you don't get locked up. You're excused as soon as this meeting is adjourned. Who's next?'

One by one detectives took their turn updating the team on the state of play with their particular enquiries. A dozen or so statements had come in but, because the offences had been committed in the dead of night, there was nothing in them that Kate could identify as worthy of further investigation. No one had seen anything of interest and, if they had, they were keeping it to themselves. The wall of silence surrounding the Allen family was proving difficult to scale. The DCI worried that the enquiry would stall.

'Where are we with joyriders?' she asked.

Carmichael raised a finger. 'I pulled a few names from the PNC – offenders who've been locked up in the past in and around North Tyneside, one or two living in close proximity to Silverlink. Division were issued with details of the vehicles we're interested in. One young lad seemed rather nervous when questioned. Turns out he nearly came to grief when a Range Rover shot over the round-about the wrong way at high speed.'

'Could be our vehicle,' Kate said. 'By nervous, I take it you mean disqualified?'

'He's already on probation. Banned from driving for two years.'

'No wonder he's jumpy. Get him in here, Lisa. Maybe he knows more than he's prepared to admit. If he doesn't cooperate, put him in a cell and give his probation officer a call. That might jog his memory a little quicker. In the meantime, I want to talk about the ring found on Terry Allen's finger, the only one he had left. Finger, I mean, not ring.'

DC Brown jumped up, handing out a stack of photocopies with a blown-up image of the ring in question. It was an engraved antique, not worth that much, but it was vital to have its provenance checked out. Raising an action to facilitate that, Kate glanced again at her notes. She was flagging but couldn't let it show. The team were restless too. Everyone keen to bugger off and get on with the job, except Robbo, whose kid had kept him awake half the night.

Raising a hand, he spoke through a gaping yawn, for which he apologized profusely. 'We still don't know where John was between three a.m. when he dumped Terry at the hospital and five a.m. when he was next seen wrapped round the rear wheels of the van that killed him. Those missing hours are vital. Assuming he was grabbed at the hospital, whoever dumped him at Silverlink didn't go there straight away or Prentice would've seen them on his security monitors much earlier.'

'Division are monitoring CCTV, all routes between the two,' Maxwell volunteered. 'But don't hold your breath. They found nothing so far. It looks like they drove John round for a while in order to extract information. Probably showed him his brother's severed fingers while they were at it. Sick bastards. That would be enough to make most men talk.'

'Especially you,' Carmichael muttered under her breath.

Hank grinned at Lisa. She tolerated Maxwell, but there was no love lost between them. She thought he was a lazy git with no redeeming qualities. He thought she was a smart arse, a young sprog with far too much to say for herself, the bosses' favourite. In a personality contest, she'd win hands down.

'What about mobile phones?' Hank said. 'Terry managed to communicate with John somehow.'

'Not necessarily,' Carmichael said.

Hank asked her to explain.

'It could've been the offenders, couldn't it? If they told John what they had done to Terry, they'd expect an instant reaction. Even if John suspected a trap, he'd set off to find his brother no matter the risk to himself, wouldn't he? He was a thug. They all think they're bulletproof.'

For once, Andy Brown disagreed with Lisa Carmichael. 'If that was the case, they would've chosen somewhere isolated, a spot where they could grab him without any difficulty—'

'Not the way I see it.' Carmichael stood her ground. 'The boss said that leaving John's body in full view of CCTV at Silverlink was like giving someone the proverbial finger. A public spectacle, she said. An execution wasn't enough. The offenders not only wanted him found, they wanted to advertise what they had done to him.'

Kate could see both sides of the argument. 'I don't know why, but I can't help thinking that Terry escaped all by himself. I don't know, maybe he played dead, did a runner while their backs were turned. But Hank is right, we need to chase up the comms.' She singled out Brown. 'Andy, I'd ask Lisa but she has a lot to do. Can you talk to the service providers for me? See if either brother has a mobile registered. I think they're too clever for that, but it's worth a shot.'

'Check out John's landlines too, while you're at it,' Hank said.

'No, don't,' Kate said. 'I'd like to tackle Vicky myself on that score.'

Brown looked at her. 'It's no trouble.'

'Thanks, Andy, but Hank and I went to see her earlier. She won't take kindly to another detective knocking on her door. Besides, we're practically best friends.' The DCI was being facetious. 'She gave us a pretty good insight into her relationship with John. She was highly suspicious of him. He often went off with his mates, leaving her alone for days on end. She was guarded in what she said, but I got the feeling she didn't always believe he was where he said he was. She reckoned he was screwing around.'

'Amanda,' Andy suggested.

'Probably.' Kate *so* wanted to get a handle on her.

'Possible motive? People have killed for a lot less.'

'I agree, but usually in a fit of temper, not in the organized way our offenders have gone about it. In my humble opinion there's more to this case than a pissed-off husband with his nose out of joint. Anyway, now it's my turn. I saved the best 'til last, so listen carefully. Vicky Masters claims John and Terry were due to meet each other at the QC Club on Thursday night. That's since been corroborated by April Allen, who saw no point in denying it once we had the information, so we have our first real lead.'

The news received a mixed reaction. Kate could see it in the eyes of her team. A nightclub was never a good hunting ground for information. On a Thursday night, any place of entertainment would be heaving, the clubs especially. Identification would be a 'mare. Detectives would have to trace and eliminate hundreds of witnesses – some pissed, others stoned – it didn't get any worse than that. She wondered if her victims had been lured to the club or if a chance meeting had contributed to their deaths. Brown was asking for an address. The QC was relatively new. He couldn't immediately place it.

'Broad Chair, next to the Wig and Pen,' Hank told him. 'Directly opposite the Crown Court, side entrance. That, my friends, means more CCTV.'

There was an audible groan in the room. So far this case consisted of nothing else. It was a pain in the arse, but an obvious place to start. Kate began delegating jobs, directing squad members to keep at it. The QC Club was their absolute priority now. Every millisecond of the footage required forensic examination.

A telephone rang, stopping her in mid-flow.

Hank swiped it off the desk, identified himself, leaving the caller in no doubt that the interruption was unwelcome, that the team were in the throes of an important briefing and weren't to be disturbed.

After listening to the response, he covered the handset and eyed Kate. 'It's Sam at the morgue.'

'Something wrong?' she asked.

'No idea.' He made a face. 'She wants the organ grinder. Seems to think it's urgent, though.' He held out the phone, avoiding the eyes of amused colleagues.

Allowing him his little joke, Kate took it from him, lifting it to her ear. 'What is it, Sam?'

'Apologies for interrupting, Inspector. I thought you'd like to know that Mrs Allen didn't turn up to view her son's body as arranged. I waited an hour and called her home, several times, but she's not picking up. In my experience, that's never happened before.'

'Did you send a car round?'

'I did – but the attending officer got no response. You don't think something might have happened to her, do you? I have a really bad feeling about this.'

Kate's stomach turned over. *You're not the only one.*

Chapter Nineteen

KATE HUNG UP, told the team she was heading out to Theresa Allen's penthouse, and made straight for the door with Hank on her heels. On the way downstairs, he pointed out that there was a plausible explanation for the missed appointment: Theresa couldn't face the grim task of seeing her son on a mortuary slab. But Kate could tell he wasn't really buying that. And, it had to be said, neither was she.

'Unless she's topped herself,' he added, getting in the car. 'Or worse, she's the next target. Or her new squeeze is.'

'I hope none of the above is true.' Kate really didn't want to go there. The idea was alarming but credible. Taking off like a bullet from the station car park, she engaged a blue light as fears she didn't even want to acknowledge grew louder in her head. Hank was still theorizing . . .

'It's possible that the man you saw in her apartment had gone there to kill her rather than to buy her afternoon tea. He might have changed his mind when he realized she already had company.'

'Oh great.' Kate shot him a look. 'Is that supposed to make me feel better?'

'Just doing my job.' Hank stopped talking.

The rest of the journey was a blur of pedestrians, traffic lights, slow-moving vehicles and nightmarish thoughts. Kate couldn't stop her brain working overtime. Conjuring up images of raw flesh and blood, the aftermath of cruelty she'd tried and failed to forget, she imagined Theresa Allen's tortured body on the floor of her penthouse, a thought that repulsed her all over again.

Lacking the stomach for another corpse, she screeched to a halt at the base of the tower block, drawing the attention of pass-ers-by, as well as lower-floor residents who'd seen and heard them arriving.

The detectives jumped out of the car, their normally relaxed walking pace turning to a sprint as they neared the entrance, nei-ther of them sure what they expected to find.

They took the lift to the top floor.

When the doors slid open, Kate led the way, praying she'd find Theresa alive and well, right where she'd left her yesterday. When there was no answer at the door, she flashed an anxious look at Hank. The penthouse lacked a letter box – mail was delivered to the ground floor only – so she put her ear up against the door and listened for movement from within.

Eyes on Hank, she shook her head.

'You waiting for a warrant or shall I kick it in?' he asked. 'If we're really lucky, she might still have some fingers left.'

Kate's whole body shuddered.

'Do it!' she said.

Standing well back, heart hammering in her chest, she looked on as he shoulder-charged the door. With two family members dead already, they had reasonable cause to suspect the occupant might be in mortal danger. Their first duty was to preserve life. Kate was prepared to argue the case for unwarranted entry to her superiors or a court of law should any surviving member of the Allen family complain about her actions later.

The door held, so they joined forces and hit it again.

This time it flew off its hinges. They rushed inside, calling out to Theresa. The living room was empty. Kitchen too. Nothing out of place and no signs of a struggle. By anyone's standards, the apartment was immaculate. That meant very little. Theresa was a slight woman. Faced with someone prepared to do her harm, she wouldn't necessarily have put up a fight. She may not even have had a chance to defend herself.

Leaving Hank in the living room, Kate wandered down the passageway, checking bedrooms on either side. All clear. The bathroom was pristine, the towels bone-dry, no evidence of recent use. She was about to leave when something odd registered but then disappeared. Whatever it was, it was gone. Lingering in the doorway a moment, she scanned the room, her eyes eventually coming to rest on an empty glass shelf devoid of the personal items she might expect to see: toothpaste, deodorant, body lotion. To the right of it, the electric toothbrush charger was empty.

Opening the mirrored bathroom cabinet, she looked inside.

'Shit!' She shut it again, taking in her own miserable reflection.

'What's up?' Hank wandered in. 'I've seen better-looking dead folks.'

'She's gone,' Kate said. 'Not taken by force. Just gone.'

'YOU'RE TOO LATE, love,' a female voice said as they let themselves out of the penthouse. The woman to whom the voice belonged was leaving the only other apartment on the top floor, a key still in her hand. Dressed in a blue camisole, cheap jeans and flip-flops, she was old before her time, stick thin and anaemic-looking, with hollow eyes.

'What do you mean?' Hank asked.

She flicked her eyes to the door beyond them. 'The tenant scarpered first thing. I clean for the neighbour here. When I came in this morning, they were leaving in a hurry with a couple of travel bags.'

'They?'

'You're the cops, yeah?' She didn't wait for a reply. 'Doesn't surprise me, to be honest, I knew there was something dodgy 'bout those two the first time I clapped eyes on 'em, him in particular – cold as ice.'

Kate and Hank exchanged a look.

'Do you know who this man is?' Hank asked.

'Kiddin', aren't ya?'

'I take it you were never introduced.'

'Suits me fine. Terrifies me, he does.'

'You're absolutely sure the lady who lives here went willingly?' Kate asked.

'*Lady?*' the cleaner scoffed. 'That's stretching it a bit, pet.'

'I'm not asking for a personal reference. Did she go willingly or not?'

'Too right.'

'I don't suppose you know the man's name?' Hank said.

'I heard her use it once. He didn't like it either. Shoulda seen the look he gave her.' The woman gave a slight shake of the head. 'Nah, it's gone, sorry. I can't remember.'

'Can you describe him?'

When she did so, Kate knew she was talking about the same man she'd seen yesterday. She handed the woman her business card in case the name should come back to her later. As Hank took down her details, Kate pressed for the lift. She couldn't get out of there quick enough. Theresa Allen *had* lied to her. And now she'd done a runner with an unsavoury character whose ID the DCI didn't know. She could only surmise that one or both of them had reason to be in fear for their own safety. What the hell was going on? If they were together, who were they running from?'

'What they been up to anyway?' the cleaner asked, pulling Kate back to the present.

'We just need to speak with them,' she said.

'Won't be anything good, I reckon.'

Kate wasn't drawn by the comment. She had too much on her mind. Despite Hank's assertion that she should've taken him with her when she went to see Theresa Allen the first time round, there was nothing she would have done differently. She'd gone there in a welfare capacity, delivering a double death message to an unfortunate mother. She had no cause to suspect the woman or to interrogate her visitors.

So why did she feel so bad about it?

If Hank was right about Theresa, she deserved a BAFTA. That very small lie began to grow bigger in Kate's head: *A neighbour . . . you caught me out, Inspector. He's my new partner . . . I've not known him long.*

As a bell signalled the arrival of the lift, Kate turned to face the cleaner. 'This man Mrs Allen was with? Long-standing boyfriend is he?'

'Seems to be. They've been together a canny while.'

'Can you be specific?'

The woman shrugged. 'Eighteen months, give or take.'

So, more than one lie.

'And who would you say wears the pants?' Hank asked.

'Eh? I'm a cleaner not a fucking shrink—'

Kate waited. It was an intelligent question from Hank. The answer could provide insight into Theresa Allen's relationship. 'You look like an intuitive woman,' she said. 'Go on, give us your best guess.'

'*He* does.' There was no hesitation.

All three got in the lift and travelled down in silence. Hank raised a sympathetic eyebrow as they made their descent to the ground floor. Kate didn't need to tell him how bad she felt. Theresa Allen and her fancy man had played a blinder.

Chapter Twenty

BACK IN THE incident room, Kate was on her feet 'fessing up to colleagues. 'There are only two possible explanations for Theresa's disappearance: either she fears for her own safety or someone else's. While I was with her yesterday, she had a male caller. Sadly, we were never introduced. I have no ID but I got a good look at him. Today we struck lucky. We have a witness who saw him back at the flat this morning. I want this man traced as a matter of urgency.'

Hank was nodding, a show of solidarity; at least that's how it would appear to the team. Kate knew different. On the way back from Theresa's apartment they'd had words when she almost crashed into a vehicle with a clear right of way. The near miss had given them both a fright, likewise the other driver who was heavily pregnant and in tears when Hank got out of the car to make sure she wasn't hurt.

Kate's attempt at passing the incident off as a momentary lapse in concentration didn't work. When he got back in, Hank had gone mental, telling her to take her head out of her arse or let him drive. She had to admit that her performance had fallen below the standards of an advanced police driver, or any driver, particularly one whose car was her most prized possession. Still . . . How dare he accuse her of underperforming? Didn't he know she was doing her level best?

And what business was it of his anyway?

Hank was on his feet now, trying so hard to make amends it left her feeling more guilty, not less. The team were all ears, every one of them giving their undivided attention, barring her. She hadn't heard a word he'd said. Seconds later, he paused for breath, looked at her.

'Shall I continue?' he asked.

'Be my guest. Never let it be said that I'd stop a colleague in full flow.'

Hank carried on. 'The boss and I strongly suspect that Theresa Allen, her boyfriend, or both, may be the next target. Either way, they've put themselves in a position where they don't have to talk to us. Terry and John's partners claim they don't know where Theresa is, which we are prepared to accept – if she's running scared, she's hardly going to advertise where she's hiding. But they also deny any knowledge of the boyfriend – which, if I may say so, is bollocks. I've met enough liars in my time to know one when I see one.' Again, he looked at Kate.

'I agree,' she said, fighting her agitation. She should be leading from the front, not Hank. Trying to slow her breathing wasn't working. She almost gagged on her words. What the fuck? 'I mean, I agree that . . . well, it was obvious that they were covering for him. Hank thinks the boyfriend may be up to his neck in the family business, and I'm fast coming round to that view. I'm pissed that I let him slip through my fingers, I'm really sorry.'

Jo sprung to her defence. 'How were you supposed to know?'

'At the time, I wasn't . . .' Kate pinched the bridge of her nose. She stuttered awkwardly. 'Hindsight . . . is a wonderful thing. Maybe Terry and John were just foot soldiers, not as far up the organization as we . . . as we initially thought. Maybe Theresa's boyfriend is in charge these days.' Her eyes found Hank. 'Sometimes it's hard to tell who's the boss.'

Hank got the message.

'So, who's to say he's not your killer?' Jo pointed at the murder wall with its array of gory crime-scene photographs. 'It's possible, isn't it, if those two stepped out of line?'

'Absolutely right.' Hank chanced his arm. 'Which is why we need to find him.'

The discussion lasted a while. Either their mystery man was a raving loony who'd killed John and Terry, or the poor sods died trying to protect him, or else they didn't know of his existence when someone thought they did and now he was next on the hit list. As her team threw ideas around, voices faded in and out. Kate gave up trying to follow what they were saying; she could feel the blood draining from her face, and her head felt like it was about to explode. Massaging her temples, she struggled to organize her thoughts but they were all over the place. She hated falling out with Hank. He didn't deserve the treatment she was shoving his way.

Even in the midst of her confusion, Kate was clear about one thing: she alone was to blame for the dilemma facing the team. She could have kicked herself for being sucked in by Theresa-I've-had-it-with-crime-Allen. The speed with which the woman had upped sticks and fled the penthouse should have come as no surprise; even a complete rookie ought to know that organized prigs always had an escape route mapped out. Presumably Theresa had a bolthole, another toothbrush charger. Kate wondered whether her intention was merely to make herself scarce in the short-term, lying low till the police caught whoever was responsible, or if she and her boyfriend had scarpered for good. They hadn't taken much from a penthouse packed with objets d'art, some of which looked valuable. She wondered too how the search team were doing.

What else have I missed? Think!

'Kate?'

The DCI turned towards the voice. Jo had an odd look on her face, Hank too. In fact, the whole team were frozen like statues, all staring in her direction.

'Sorry . . . Andy . . . have you . . . you got anything for me?'

'Boss, it can wait. You don't look well.'

'No. I'm fine. Really, I'm fine. Let's hear it.'

'You want some water?' Jo asked.

'What? No!' Suddenly hot, Kate pulled at the neck of her shirt. 'Don't fuss.'

Jo backed down. Kate asked Andy to carry on. He'd been waiting patiently to take the floor. A skilled officer, he rarely missed a trick and this occasion was no exception. He'd been checking CCTV footage from the QC Club and made a positive ID of Terry Allen arriving at ten past eight the night he was killed. It was fast work, a Eureka moment, one that would normally be met with congratulations and a flurry of activity, but Kate hardly reacted.

'Any sign of John?' she asked.

'Not so far but, unlike Neil, I have no heavy date so I'm here for the duration if you need me.'

'Thanks. Have your . . . report on my desk, first thing.'

The stutter was back, along with the stares, the loss of concentration and confidence. Kate couldn't continue. What in God's name was wrong with her? She told herself to breathe. Jo was on her feet, holding out a plastic beaker of water.

'Lisa, can you open a window?' she said. 'It's very hot in here.'

Kate took a long drink as Jo tried to cover for her, floating the idea that she too was dehydrated. Inwardly, Kate was panicking, struggling to convince herself that her incapacity was temporary, brought on by this particular case. The scale of the violence disturbed her; of all the stabbings, beatings and shootings she'd dealt with in her career, this one was the worst. It was evil, gratuitous, way over the top – even for the most hardened of professionals. From the moment she'd viewed what was left of John Allen's body, she'd been going downhill at a rate of knots. It wasn't just cumulative stress, the result of long hours, little rest and clawing her way up the rank structure, trying to be the very best detective she could. She knew she ought to take her own advice and try zoning out the images, but when the job dominated her every waking hour that was easier said than done. Living alone, she had no one to distract her, no one to unwind with, no one to hold her hand. That was nothing new – it had always been that way. There was no point dwelling on it. Wallowing in self-pity wouldn't solve a thing. She dismissed the squad.

THANK GOD NAYLOR *hadn't made the case review.* An appointment with Chief Superintendent Bright, Kate's former guv'nor, had kept him away. It was getting on for eight o'clock when he resurfaced and they finally sat down for a progress report. He seemed a little preoccupied and she hoped it wasn't anything to do with her wobble in the incident room.

After the briefing, she'd gone for a walk with Hank to get her shit together. She'd apologized for yelling at him, for not giving him the lickings of a dog in the briefing, and then sent him home to see his wife and son. His marriage had been hanging on a thread for years, but recently there had been a turnaround, a change of heart from his wife, Julie. Having told him she couldn't live with him, she'd since decided she couldn't live without him either. Right now, Kate understood how she felt. At times of stress, she couldn't cope with Hank's sympathy. His sarcasm had always been much easier to take.

Naylor looked tanned and relaxed after a recent holiday on the Greek island of Mykonos, spent in a luxury apartment owned by one of his many friends. He was discussing her forced entry into Theresa Allen's penthouse, an action he supported unreservedly.

'There was nothing in the flat of any interest, guv.'

'No hint of where she might've gone?'

'According to the search team, no.'

'And she's a woman of considerable means?'

'The kit in her apartment would suggest so, yes.'

'Passport?'

Kate shook her head. 'That was the first thing we looked for when we discovered she'd packed her toothbrush. I have to accept that she could be out of the country by now.'

Naylor shrugged. 'There's not much you can do about that, except keep your eyes and ears open.'

'I'll try Vicky Masters again.' Kate felt calmer now, her panic attack a thing of the past. 'She's proving to be the weak link in the Allen family chain.'

A tap on the door made her stop talking.

Hank walked in, a sheepish look on his face.

Kate asked him what he was doing back, even though she knew the answer. She couldn't say so in front of Naylor but – however well-intentioned – Hank's interference was beginning to piss her off. She didn't need, much less want, a babysitter.

'Julie's out on the town, so I'm off the hook.' He smiled at Naylor. No point smiling at Kate; she wasn't buying his bullshit. 'I didn't want to leave in the first place, guv. Kate insisted. I know she's trying to give my relationship a half-chance of survival, but I've always been a bugger for punishment. The wife and I are doing OK anyhow. So far so good.'

Their guv'nor wasn't fooled any more than Kate was. 'You didn't want to miss anything, more like.'

'So where's Julie gone?' Kate asked.

'No idea.' Hank shrugged. 'I dropped her off in the Bigg Market. She wants picking up at eleven. Can't go home and sink a few, can I? May as well put in a couple more hours here.'

Kate looked at him. He could lie, but not to her. He was worried about her. Unable to bear the heat of her gaze, he quickly changed the subject, telling Naylor that Chelsea had beaten Newcastle two nil so he'd lost all interest in watching *Match of the Day*. Not a footy fan himself, Naylor had nothing to contribute. Then, having exhausted the topic, Hank slung his hook, grumbling about the woes of being a Toon supporter as he left the room.

Intending to follow suit, Kate got up.

Naylor shook his head, waved her back into her seat. Cupping his hands behind his head, he leaned against the backrest, running his eyes over her, making her feel self-conscious. She wanted to get back to work, but he ordered her to go home. 'Have a long, hot soak in the tub and a few hours' kip and come to the case fresh in the morning. You're useless to me burnt out. And you need to be in early tomorrow. Bright's coming in.'

'To see me?' She was suddenly on the back foot. 'On a Sunday?'

Naylor nodded. 'That's what he said.'

'He thinks I'm losing my touch, is that it?'

'Hey, why so defensive? He told me it was something he could only convey face-to-face. And, before you ask, I told him nothing. I know nothing, do I? Unless there's something you haven't told me . . . ?'

'No, guv.'

So he knew. Although it wasn't Naylor's style to mention it to Bright, it didn't mean that the head of CID hadn't heard about her little drama in the incident room from elsewhere. A loose tongue in the canteen could expedite a rumour to HQ quicker than a Boeing. It would reach his ears eventually, as most things did. And, if it did, she'd have some explaining to do.

Chapter Twenty-one

KATE LET HERSELF in to the incident room at five to six. Even by her standards, that was early for a Sunday morning. She'd woken at four and started chewing over why Bright wanted to see her so urgently and hadn't been able to get back to sleep. It was drizzling. No point going for a run, so she decided to skip breakfast and go in early. With no cleaner at the office to disturb her, and no squad due in 'til seven, she had plenty of time to skim the newspapers and organize a plan for the day ahead.

She didn't linger in the MIR but went straight to her desk, made herself a pot of coffee and put her feet up. According to her paper, it was National Marriage Sunday. Roman Catholic priests were spouting their hatred again. Cardinal Keith O'Brien, the leader of the Church of Scotland – the man who'd previously described gay marriage as a 'grotesque subversion of a universally accepted human right' – had apparently stopped talking to First Minister, Alex Salmond.

Marriage . . . Kate whispered. *Not gay marriage, you bigoted arseholes.*

The article did nothing but convince her to stay in the closet. Pushing her anger and her newspaper away, she checked her in-tray. A hard copy of Brown's report was right on top where she expected to find it, marked for her attention. Clipped to the front, a précis of what he'd gleaned from the CCTV she'd asked him to look at. At ten past eight, Terry Allen had entered the QC Club. Half an hour later, at twenty to nine, John joined him. Both broth-ers arrived alone, Brown noted. They left together at nine forty-two. At the bottom of the page was a handwritten note . . .

This is where it gets interesting.

Intrigued, Kate left her desk and walked into the MIR, switch-ing on the lights on her way in. Dead computer screens, like giant eyes, watched her as she moved across the room to Andy Brown's workstation. Opening his top drawer, she found what she was looking for: a USB pen drive, an exact copy of the DVD he'd retrieved from the QC Club.

Wondering how long it had taken him to complete the task, she counted herself lucky that she had such a dedicated team member prepared to stay late for the sake of the job and not because he was making shedloads of overtime. There was an embargo on at present. Headquarters were holding a tight rein on budgets. She'd have to go cap in hand to beg for an increase if the enquiry ran on.

And this one surely would.

Back in her office, she slipped the USB pen into her computer. She poured more coffee and then sat down to see what had fired Brown's imagination. Before she had a chance to access the file and fast-forward to the relevant time, her office door opened and Hank walked in, a huge grin on his face.

She glanced at her watch.

Six-fifteen.

'You sure Julie's back?' Her eyes shifted to the screen in front of her. 'Mustn't have been a very good night out.'

'Ha! Very funny.' He pointed at her monitor. 'You got an adult movie on there?'

'Touché! Pull up a seat for the Andy Brown show.'

Dragging a chair round behind her desk, Hank took off his jacket and sat down beside her. He smelled divine: his favourite shower gel. She sensed he'd turned the corner and was finally getting his life back on track. He'd lost more weight, was drinking less and looking all the better for it. She loved it when they were the only ones in. It was times like this when they did their best thinking.

Winding the timer to eight o'clock, Kate let the footage run on in real time. 'Keep your eyes peeled while I read this.' She tapped a few keys. The screen split in half – the footage on the left, Brown's report on the right – side by side so she could check them off against one another, noting that a copy had been sent to the Receiver, Detective Sergeant Harry Graham.

'Looks like Andy did a good job,' she said.

'Lisa too.' Gormley's eyes never left the screen. 'I told her to get herself away home. She insisted on staying to help him.'

'You do surprise me. I'll have to have a word with those two. They're spending far too much time together. You think they'll ever—'

'Nah, they've got more sense.'

'You getting at me and Jo?' She nudged him with her elbow.

'Get off me!' He grinned. 'I'm trying to watch this.'

She smiled. 'I wish you would.'

Kate relaxed. They never stayed mad at each other for long. That was the strength of their relationship.

Continuing to scan the report, she began typing actions into the remarks column in bold font. When she'd finished, she suggested that they run through the footage a couple of times, checking the accuracy of the report along the way. Not that she doubted Andy or Lisa, just because it was pertinent to do so.

'What's remarkable is the fact that Terry and John were in the club for less than an hour,' Kate said. 'And not by design either, judging by the expressions on their faces as they left. Not the cocky bastards of old, are they? They seem bloody nervous to me. Terry in particular, don't you think?' She didn't wait for an answer. 'Wait a minute!' She paused the footage, replayed part of it, freezing the final frame and zooming in on the brothers as they went outside. 'Who the hell is Terry looking at?'

'Whoever it is, they're out of shot.'

They both glanced at Brown's report . . .

To: DCI DANIELS
From: DC Brown
cc: DS Harry Graham

Report re: Action 36

DVDs RECOVERED FROM QC Club – Evening of Thursday, 23 August 2012 – Exhibit references AB3 (Front door) AB4 (Dance floor) and AB5 (SE Corridor)
I have to report as follows: I've examined all the CCTV as outlined above and have come across Nominal 1 (John Allen) and Nominal 2 (Terence Allen) on only four occasions. FYI, there is a discrepancy between the CCTV clock and real time. Clock running seven minutes slow, hence time on DVD and actual time recorded below:

Ref: AB3 – Front Door

CCTV Time	Actual Time	Description	SIO Remarks
20:03	20:10	N2 enters wearing dark shirt and trousers. In this frame, in front of him is one blonde female: mid 20s, red dress. Also two white males behind: both dark-haired wearing dark pants, light dress shirts and no jackets. No words shared. No reason to believe they are together.	**Raise action Blonde F/2 males**
20:33	20:40	N1 enters dressed in a grey casual jacket/white T-shirt. No one in close proximity.	
20:34	20:41	Sequence ends.	

Ref: AB5 – SE Corridor

CCTV Time	Actual Time	Description	SIO Remarks
20:45	20:52	N1 and N2 talking. They don't appear happy. They seem keen not to be overheard. Stop talking when approached by female – short dark skirt/revealing strapless pink top, brunette, lots of bling.	**Raise action One Female**
20:47	20:54	Both N1 and N2 talking on Black-Berry phones. At this time they're approached by a bouncer – thickset, shaved head. Obviously known to N1, as they exchange a high five.	**Ditto Bouncer**
20:50	20:57	Sequence ends.	

Ref: AB4 – Dance Floor

CCTV Time	Actual Time	Description	SIO Remarks
20:52	20:59	N2 on dance floor talking into iPhone. One female nearby – overweight, thin legs. Very drunk. Purple silky sleeveless dress. N2 shouts at her and she leaves.	Raise action One Female
20:54	21:01	Sequence ends.	

Ref: AB3 – Front Door

CCTV Time	Actual Time	Description	SIO Remarks
21:35	21:42	N1 and N2 leave together, N1 shouting into his phone, N2 looking over his shoulder at someone out of shot.	Who? Raise action
21:45	21:52	Sequence ends.	

They needn't have bothered checking it. Andy's account was spot on, no inconsistency with what they themselves had seen. The case had indeed just got 'interesting'.

Chapter Twenty-two

NEWTON ROAD, HIGH Heaton. Kate rapped on the door so hard it hurt her knuckles. For some reason, Bright had delayed his visit to the incident room until eleven o'clock. Still, she was pushed for time. Following information received, she needed to speak to Vicky Masters urgently. A British Telecom contact of Carmichael's had been swift to assist the police. He'd told her that John Allen paid for the privilege of a line rental but never used the phone. His landline was a broadband connection only. No calls, local or international, had ever been made or received, despite the allocation of a dedicated number. Even worse news from Lisa: there was no record of a mobile contract for either John or Vicky with any major service provider. It was as the DCI had expected – unregistered mobiles were a criminal's best friend.

'What now?' Vicky's shoulders dropped as she opened the door and saw her standing there. The young mum was still in her pyjamas, her son Nathan nowhere to be seen.

'I need to talk to you,' Kate said. 'Can I come in?'

'Do I have a choice?'

The DCI gave her a pointed look.

Without a word, Vicky spun on her heels and walked away. In the living room, she went back to a pile of ironing. There were fresh bouquets in vases and condolence cards scattered about. The TV was tuned to some kind of talent show, the contestant proving only that he couldn't sing. Seeing the look of disapproval on Kate's face, the girl picked up the remote and killed the set. Folding baby clothes was the method she employed to avoid eye contact.

Kate didn't hang around. 'I'd like to examine your phone,' she said.

Vicky looked up, rattled. 'I don't have a phone.'

'You expect me to believe that, in this day and age?'

'Believe what you like.' She was lying and not very well.

'What about John? I bet he had plenty.'

Vicky's colour rose ever so slightly. 'Didn't you find it on him?' she asked.

'Stop wasting my time, Vicky. I'm trying to get the people who murdered him and I need your help. Don't you want them caught?' Kate waited. The girl remained silent. 'OK, I happen to know he had a phone with him because I saw him using it at the QC Club. It looked like a BlackBerry. And no, it wasn't on him. If his phone is in the wrong hands, I hope you weren't daft enough to use your real names in the address book, or this bloodshed won't be over.'

There was more clothes-folding – frantic now.

Vicky glanced at a photograph of John. 'I want to see him,' she said.

'I'm afraid that's not possible—'

'Why?'

'Technically, you're not his next of kin.' Kate acknowledged how difficult that must be to accept and hurried to change the subject.

'The phone, Vicky . . . he was shouting at someone on the phone. Was it you?'

Vicky looked up. 'No! What are you on about?'

Kate backed off, allowed some time to pass, putting the pressure on her to answer. Somewhere in another room, the baby stirred and then went off again. After a while, the girl couldn't stand the lull in the conversation and began to fill the silence. Thank God she'd finally seen sense.

'I binned all the phones,' she said.

'You did what?' The DCI was furious and it showed.

'It's not against the law. John told me to.'

'He rang and asked you to?'

Vicky shook her head, guilt creeping across her face. 'Ages ago, he told me that if he didn't come home your lot would probably have locked him up and I was to get rid fast. When I got up to see to Nathan at five on Friday morning, he wasn't there. I just did what he asked with all the phones in the house, mine included.'

'How? Where?'

'I burned them on the BBQ. The bits that were left, I chucked in a disposal bin at the hospital. John said all their waste is incinerated every day.'

Kate raised her eyes to the ceiling.

This wasn't what she wanted to hear.

Chapter Twenty-three

CHIEF SUPERINTENDENT PHILLIP Bright looked immaculate, as always. He entered Kate's office bang on eleven o'clock, shutting the door behind him. His appointment as head of CID had been the best thing to happen to the department in years. He was a no-nonsense copper, a detective of the old school, feared by the shirkers and loved by everyone else. He was quite simply the very best detective the Northumbria force had ever seen, the man who'd chosen Kate to follow in his wake, the policeman who'd taught her all she knew – and then some. He'd told her that one day his job would be hers, if she played her cards right.

Kate sighed.

At this moment in time, she didn't fancy her hand.

Opening the button of his jacket, Bright hoicked up his beautifully pressed trousers and sat down, crossing one leg over the other. His shoes were bulled to perfection, so much so that he could've been a guardsman on parade. Draping his left arm over the back of the chair, he looked at Kate, no doubt noting how tired she was, but telling her it was great to see her.

'You too, guv.'

A smile began at the corner of his mouth and spread quickly – *always a good sign.*

Mindful of her recent drama, Kate wondered if she should mention that this week hadn't been her finest. She decided against. He'd had plenty of disappointing weeks himself over the years, not to mention twice as much aggravation on account of the way he approached his job, as well as a fair amount of associated stress.

'Ron said you wanted a face-to-face,' she said.

'Don't look so worried. It's not about Theresa Allen, if that's what you're thinking. By the way, I know her of old. Came across her back in the days of the regional crime squad when I was a rookie. She's one piece of work, is Theresa.' He chuckled. 'I hear she did quite a job on you.'

Kate wasn't finding it funny. 'I can't believe I swallowed her garbage.'

'Hook, line and sinker, is the word on the grapevine. It happens, Kate. Move on.'

'So that's not why you're here?'

'Would I lie to you?'

They both laughed.

Of course he would.

'Why then, guv?'

A flicker of something behind his eyes was hard to identify. 'Later,' he said. 'Given that I am here, that I'm also an authority on Allen family history, it might be as well if I chip in. I want to help if I can – unless you feel it would undermine your authority. I got on the wrong side of you once before, remember?'

He was teasing her.

She stared at him – almost a glare. 'How could I forget?'

The words were out of her mouth before she had a chance to stop them. The case to which he was referring was her first as SIO. On that occasion, he'd been the one making errors of judgement – with catastrophic results for Jo Soulsby, who ended up in custody, wrongly accused of her ex-husband's murder. Although the memory was painful for all concerned, it was water under the bridge now.

Still, it was a lesson to all that the great man was himself fallible.

Kate stretched, easing the tension in her shoulders. 'I don't mind you holding my hand, guv. To be perfectly frank, I could do with your advice. If I don't get this right I have a feeling that Stanton will be screaming for space down at the morgue.'

He pointed to her cafetière. 'Better get the coffee on then.'

HIS VISIT PROVED timely and invaluable to the investigation. There were few detectives with his ability to recall details of old cases with such clarity. Of particular interest to the SIO was his knowledge of the older generation of the Allen family, especially their flight from Glasgow to Newcastle when their children were small.

Kate convened a 'special' meeting and, with the whole squad gathered round him, Bright was soon on a roll. It was like old times. Like he'd never been away. With his usual panache and good humour, he shared what he knew about Brian and Theresa Allen – a formidable couple who had made a fortune from other people's misery.

'Back then, Brian Allen was fearless,' Bright said. 'Although Strathclyde force never proved it, it was strongly suspected that he and his partner in crime killed a rival gang leader in Glasgow, sending a wreath to the family with the message "We done it" pinned to the front, taunting them.'

'Rival gang leader?' Kate was taking notes.

'Dougie O'Kane. Nasty piece of work.'

'The note was anonymous, I take it?'

'Yes, but no one was in any doubt who'd sent it.'

'How long after this did Brian bring his family south?'

Bright ran a hand through silvery grey hair. 'Five, maybe six years.'

Kate was in the zone. 'Do you know why, guv?'

'Word on the street was, he wanted to get away from the next generation of gangsters. Dougie O'Kane's sons were maybe twelve and thirteen when he died, into all sorts. As they got older, threats were made – threats Brian knew they were capable of carrying out. Dougie was a hate figure. No one shed a tear when he croaked.'

'Good riddance to bad rubbish, eh?'

'You could say that. On the other hand – and this is going to sound strange – I liked Brian Allen. He was a hard-ass, but charismatic, renowned for his barefaced cheek when it came to criminal activity. Even as a cop, you had to admire the guy. His kind doesn't exist any more. It was them versus us – Brian understood that – respected it even. It was a two-way street. Today's prig is probably sitting behind one of those –' He pointed at the computer on Lisa's desk. 'They don't need to shift off the sofa nowadays, let alone get their hands dirty.'

Kate scanned the faces of the Murder Investigation Team. They were like nursery children, mesmerized by Bright's story-telling, hanging on his every word. And, boy, did he have stories to tell – some that would make their hair curl. He'd been a hard-ass himself when he was younger, the Gene Hunt of Northumbria force in his heyday. What he was saying resonated in Kate's head. When she joined the police almost twenty years ago, you didn't sit around waiting for DNA results to come in. You had to go out and find the clues. It was as upfront and personal for the police as it was for the offenders.

Sometimes people got hurt.

'So Brian effectively ran away to save his skin and died of a heart attack while playing golf?' Maxwell said. 'Doesn't sound very fearless to me, guv.'

'Not for his own sake.' Bright focused on him. 'He'd never do that. It was to protect Theresa and the kids. Like you, people thought he'd gone soft. His best mate took a lot of flak for it at the time. But I know different. Let's just say Theresa was the love of his life. He'd do anything for her, even drag himself out of the gutter.'

Kate's pen was poised over her notepad. 'Who was this mate?'

'A heavy called Arthur Ross McKenzie.'

She wrote the name down. 'Is he still alive?'

Bright shrugged. 'Far as I know.'

Kate was way ahead of him. 'Lisa? Start typing – a middle name will cut down the possibility of multiple hits on the PNC.' She turned back to Bright. 'How old, approximately?'

'Mid-fifties. Last I heard, he was banged up.'

Lisa's fingers flew over the keys. She waited, but not long, before a list popped up on screen. Scrolling through it, she paused, pushed a few more keys.

Kate continued to question Bright. 'Did McKenzie know Theresa, guv?'

'Intimately, but only in his dreams.' Bright was almost blushing, something he rarely did. 'McKenzie had a thing for her. To be honest, we all did. Wouldn't surprise me if he didn't hook up with her the minute she was available. He was a thug, not stupid. He wouldn't have dared cross Brian when he was alive. He'd have lost his gonads if he had.'

Detectives were grinning, enjoying the banter.

'Found him.' Carmichael could hardly contain herself. 'Remanded in custody for attempted murder in 1998, sent down in '99 by the Glasgow High Court. Spent a couple of months in Barlinnie in isolation, several years at Shotts Prison.' Her eyes were fixed to the computer screen. 'It appears he was moved from maximum security in 2008. Jesus!' She paused, looked up. 'Guv, he was released in 2009 from Acklington. Since then, he hasn't put a foot wrong.'

'I very much doubt that.' Bright pulled his reading specs from his pocket as Carmichael turned her screen around to face the team. 'What you mean is, he hasn't been caught.'

'Why Acklington?' Kate asked, getting to her feet.

Bright frowned. 'It's not unprecedented to transfer prisoners across the border.'

'No, but it is unusual,' Kate reminded him. 'Lisa, get on to the Scottish Prison Service and find out. In fact, call Jo and ask her to do it on our behalf.'

'Boss?' Lisa was almost sulking.

'Do it, Lisa. Asking Jo is no reflection on you. She has contacts we don't have. I want the unofficial reason for McKenzie's transfer, not the official one, and Jo is the best person to get it for me. We don't have time to piss about. Ask her to get back to me as soon as possible.'

Bright moved closer to take a look at Carmichael's screen. 'Yeah, that's him.'

The squad gathered round, peering over his shoulder to view a photograph of McKenzie, before parting to let Kate through. All eyes turned in her direction as she viewed the image for herself. When the phone rang in her pocket, she ignored it; there was no disputing that she'd found her man.

'Gotcha!' she said. 'Guv, that's the man I saw at Theresa Allen's apartment. He's aged a bit since this photograph was taken, but I'd recognize him anywhere. He must be the target.' Her phone rang again. She pulled it from her pocket, her eyes never leaving the screen.

Maxwell's voice hit her ear.

'Slow down, Neil, what is it?'

'Boss, I found Sky.'

Kate punched the air. This was turning out to be her lucky day.

Chapter Twenty-four

THEY STILL DIDN'T know her real name. Maybe they never would. The leggy brunette lay sprawled in the mud, wet hair draped to one side, a large gash to the back of the head, dead eyes staring at nothing, lips slightly apart. She was dressed in the same sparkly top, short skirt and thigh-length boots she'd worn on the CCTV. For a moment, Kate's mind played tricks on her. She could see her alive, smoking a black cigarette outside Grant's nightclub, flirting with punters as they traipsed in and out the door – a tragedy waiting to happen.

It paid to be clinical in situations like these. Kate was finding it hard. She was a person first, an SIO second, and death by homicide was never easy to deal with. Glancing back at the girl, all she could see was congealed blood and brain matter, mascara-stained cheeks the colour of plaster. She didn't need a forensic pathologist to tell her that Sky been struck with a heavy object from behind. Or that wiping away her make-up would reveal a child of no more than sixteen, not long out of school.

In the pouring rain, Kate closed her eyes and tried to breathe, desperate to cover the kid up – afford her some dignity while she remained on this earth, but that wasn't possible because it would contaminate the body. Even after death, the unfortunate girl would be prodded, poked and forensically examined for trace evidence of who might've killed her.

Suddenly aware of Hank's presence, Kate met his gaze, an unspoken message passing between them: there were times when the job was too much to stomach. He said something she didn't quite catch as another panda car arrived on the scene – blues and twos engaged. There was no need to hurry. Not now anyway. Maybe if help had arrived a couple of hours earlier, Sky might have lived. *She might.* Kate glared at the officer who got out of the car. He hurried off in the opposite direction. Hank was asking if she was OK. She nodded, grateful for his concern.

'Along with a bit of loose change, this was found in her pocket.' His expression was sombre as he extended his arm, handing her the scanned image of an unborn child. 'It's dated last Friday. Should be able to get an ID.'

'Whatever.' She turned away, her comment drifting away in the wind. 'Will anyone care?' She turned back, letting out an audible sigh. 'I'm sick of all this, aren't you?'

'You don't mean that. Sky needs us. She needs *you.*'

'I know she does . . . I need someone too, Hank.'

It was a rare moment of vulnerability from the DCI. Hank had no answer. Under the parapet of the Byker Bridge they stood facing one another, police tape flapping in the wind, the rain hammering down on the pavement beneath their feet in an area flooded with police cars and forensic vans, while officers rushed to erect a tent to preserve the scene and screen the body from prying eyes. Others stood around, awaiting instructions on how to proceed – expecting Kate to take the lead, unaware that she wanted to walk away, get as far away from police work as she possibly could. She wanted to give it all up and make a life with Jo. She'd need her later. She needed her now.

Chapter Twenty-five

ONLY HALFWAY THROUGH the third day of a major enquiry and Kate already felt jaded. Back at the MIR, the mood was sombre. Sky's death – the fact that she was pregnant had raised the tempo of an investigation that was escalating in seriousness by the hour. Fielding calls from all quarters, the DCI was being asked by the media to comment on yet another murder in the city. Three in as many days made people nervous.

'They're screaming for a press conference,' she said to no one in particular. 'If they knew my schedule, they wouldn't ask.'

'Don't worry about that.' Naylor arrived by her side from his office. 'I'll sort it later.'

'Thanks, guv, I appreciate that.'

'On one condition.' He dropped his voice. 'I'm worried about you.'

'Why?' She met Hank's eyes across the room. 'Listen, if Gormley said anything—'

'He didn't. Grab your jacket and come with me.' It was an order, not a request.

Leaving the incident room, they went outside to stretch their legs and get some air. As they would be pushing through into the night, Naylor insisted they nip across the road for something decent to eat. The inevitable consequence of working long hours meant that detectives had to eat on the hoof: takeaways, sandwiches, crisps and chocolate. A few days into an enquiry they all began to look and feel unhealthy.

'Except Carmichael.' Naylor had already begun to cross the road. 'I notice she never eats anything green.'

'What, guv?' Kate practically had to run to catch up with him, dodging stationary traffic waiting for the lights to change. 'Look, it's nice of you to shout me lunch, but I haven't got time. Besides, it's hardly fair. My team's working flat out—'

'And one by one they'll be following us.' He used the old cliché about armies marching on stomachs. 'Whine all you like, but I'm not taking no for an answer.'

They turned down Pilgrim Street, then right on to Mosley Street heading along the Diamond Strip, an area promoted by local businesses as Newcastle's answer to London's W1. It was essentially two streets that ran from the Swan House roundabout to the city's Central station. Streets that had chic-sounding, contemporary cocktail bars like Bijoux, Floritas, Baby Lynch and Madame Koo representing the upmarket end of what the city had to offer.

The Living Room was on Grey Street, not far away. Naylor was well known there and got a table right away. Explaining that they were short of time – that he'd be putting more diners their way in the course of the afternoon – he ordered Sunday lunch for two.

'Any drinks?' the waiter asked.

'Water . . . Beer,' Kate and Naylor said together.

The waiter hurried off.

Minutes later, he was back with their drinks, and not long after that steaming plates of roast beef and Yorkshire pudding arrived. Content that this was a working lunch, Kate picked up her cutlery and got stuck in, bending Naylor's ear about the case before he'd even raised his fork to his mouth.

'So what do you reckon, guv, linked enquiry or not? Any number of punters could've slapped Sky on the head just because they could. She was a vulnerable kid. You know as well as I do child prostitutes get beaten every day.'

'Or maybe there was a motive,' Naylor suggested. 'Albeit a weak one. She might have been killed because she was carrying a baby belonging to one of her punters.'

'I don't think so,' she said. 'It's more likely that Sky saw too much in the gents at Grant's, don't you think?' She broke off as the waiter returned, asking if their meal was satisfactory. They both nodded, thanking him. The food was delicious.

As she waited for him to move away, Kate felt reenergized, more able to concentrate on the case away from the distractions in the office. She should've eaten breakfast. Naylor had been right to take time out. As Hank had so eloquently pointed out, Sky needed her, all the victims did. Through her they would get justice. She was the voice they no longer had. No way she would let them down.

'It's your call,' Naylor said. 'What do you want to do?'

'I want to run the incidents together. If it becomes clear that it's a father-to-be who wasn't ready to acknowledge a child, then it's very easily hived off into a separate incident.' Kate put down her cutlery, propped her cheek up with her left hand, her elbow resting on the table. 'I want to link it for two reasons. One: I don't want my guys taking their eye off the ball while we're looking into this. Our priority has to be finding the evil bastards who are riding roughshod over our patch.'

'And two?'

'Sky worked the area surrounding Grant's. A lot of the witnesses will be the same people in both incidents. I don't want anything missed while we're investigating her death that might impact on the enquiry we're already running.' Kate paused a moment, unsure whether to be absolutely honest with him. 'Guv, between you and me, there is a third reason.'

Naylor put down his beer. 'Which is?'

'We might get a little more finance out of headquarters if they think the incidents are linked and the body count is rising and likely to rise further. That might make me sound like a devious cow, but I've a feeling we're going to need it.'

'You are a very clever woman, Kate Daniels.' Naylor smiled. 'Go for it! I can't imagine you'll get any grief from Bright. By the way, what did he want to see you about?'

'He didn't say. We got so caught up in the Allen family history, it must've slipped his mind. He's coming back for the briefing later. I'll let you know.'

Naylor looked away, not soon enough to hide his thoughts: *Must've slipped his mind, my arse.* Kate didn't challenge him, just took the hint that it was something important if Bright wanted to see her on a day he'd much rather be playing golf. For reasons she didn't quite understand, that thought made her very nervous.

Chapter Twenty-six

WITH KATE'S BLESSING, Naylor split the team in two to ensure continuity and sent them off in pairs to eat. For operational reasons, it wouldn't do to have both detective sergeants missing at the same time. So he sent a DS with a DC, Hank and Carmichael first, a list drawn up for the remaining squad members to follow suit in a kind of tag-team arrangement.

While Hank was away, Kate called Jo and Bright asking if they could get into the office for a briefing at five o'clock sharp. They both agreed. Another call to Vicky Masters' landline went unanswered and, for the next three-quarters of an hour, a mountain of paperwork kept the DCI occupied.

Tackling only high-priority stuff, she dumped the rest in a pile to be dealt with later and tried Vicky again, but still she didn't pick up. Putting the phone down, Kate slipped on her jacket and left her office, arriving in the MIR at the exact same time as Hank returned from the restaurant.

'Don't bother sitting down,' she said.

He looked at her, a guilty expression on his face. 'Am I in trouble?'

'Why, have you done something wrong?'

'I was just—'

'Sticking your nose in where it didn't belong? That about sums it up, I think. We're going out, that's all you need to know, seeing as you can't be trusted to keep it shut.'

Hank received and understood the message. Slapping his left hand with his right, he tried to make light of the situation. Kate wasn't laughing. Fearing a row, detectives working nearby kept their heads down. Not that there had been many spats between the SIO and her trusted DS over the years, but it paid not to get involved when there was a falling out.

On the way out of the incident room, Hank dropped his voice. 'Am I forgiven, or are you going to sulk all day? I hate it when you get arsy.'

THEY ARRIVED AT Vicky Masters' house bang on three-fifteen. There was no answer at the door so Hank bent down, lifted the flap on the letter box and peered in. He listened. No noise from the flat whatsoever. No radio. No chat between mother and son. He stood up, shaking his head as a young woman arrived at the house next door pushing a double buggy with identical twin babies inside.

She fixed them with a wary look. 'Can I help you?'

So young, Kate thought. No more than eighteen, by her calculation, but already tied down for the next eighteen and looking like she knew it. Her eyes were dull with black circles underneath. Something about her appearance struck a chord. It was the same downtrodden expression the DCI had seen a thousand times before. Pound to a penny she was in an abusive relationship. There

were no bruises visible. There never were. Those who inflict violence against women were often clever enough to strike where it
wouldn't show.

'I'm trying to find Vicky Masters.' Kate held up ID. 'Any idea
where she might be?'

'She's at the park with Nathan.'

'Paddy Freeman's?'

'Yeah, I just came from there.'

The park they were talking about was popular, a spot much
loved by locals, a place where they could play safely with their
kids, walk their dogs, play tennis or kick a football around. Abut-
ting Castle Farm playing fields and Jesmond Dene – a nearby
wooded valley – it was possible to get lost along its twisted paths
and hidden walkways. With a child in a buggy, Vicky could be
away several hours.

Kate didn't have time to wait. 'Where did you see them exactly?'
she asked.

'In the kids' play area, near the pond. She can't bear to be in the
flat since, y'know—'

'Yeah,' Hank cut her off. 'I can imagine it must be hard for her.
Thanks for giving us the heads-up. We'll make sure she hears of
your concern. We'd love to stop and chat but we must get on.'

The girl scowled at them as they got back in the car.

Angry that he'd dismissed her so abruptly, Kate told him off,
pointing out that she might need the police one day and he'd done
nothing to foster an opinion that they were in any way approach-
able. Hank winced and apologized for not picking up on the abuse
angle she was still banging on about, grateful that the park was
only a few minutes away and hoping their arrival would bring an
end to his reprimand.

Kate managed to squeeze her car into the only available space in the small car park. Most times, it wasn't possible to get in there. People visiting sick relatives at the hospital opposite were charged inordinate amounts to park in the hospital's own parking bays, so they often used the free one belonging to Paddy Freeman's instead.

Getting out of the car, the detectives followed the path to the water's edge, turning right towards the play area. There were scores of folks milling around, many with kids. Vicky and Nathan were not among them.

'Damn!' Kate said. 'We missed them.'

'Unless they're in the cafe.' Hank pointed to the single-storey building behind them, a favourite stop-off point for hungry detectives passing to and fro. Good coffee and snacks never went amiss when they were working flat out. Officers grabbed what they could whenever they could. 'You want me to check it out?'

Kate nodded. 'I'll skirt the Dene. See if I can spot them. Bring me an ice cream.'

Hank didn't move. His attention was drawn to something over her shoulder. Kate turned to see what it was. Vicky was sitting alone at a picnic table in the shade of an overhanging tree, handing Nathan bread with which to feed the ducks. To the untrained eye, it was a happy scene replicated right across the park, except the girl was weeping.

'You still want an ice cream?' Hank asked.

'What?'

'An ice cream. Still want one?'

'It was for Nathan, you daft sod, not for me.'

As he loped off in the direction of the cafe, Kate made her way over to mother and son. She sat down on the bench beside them and spoke without looking at the girl.

'Vicky? How are you coping?'

The girl sniffed. 'He won't settle. He misses his dad.'

'I can imagine,' Kate said. 'If it's any consolation, he'll stop fretting eventually. I'm not suggesting he'll forget – you wouldn't want that – but it's true what they say: time is a great healer. I can see you're heartbroken. In the coming months you'll see beyond John's death and remember the good times you had together.'

'Thank you.' It was almost a whisper.

'You were helpful to me before,' Kate said. 'Now I need something more from you.'

'I don't have any more.' The girl pulled a chunk of bread off a loaf and gave it to her son, who threw it at the ducks, hitting one of them on the head, making the rest squabble over it and the child squeal with delight.

Kate stared straight ahead. On the field opposite, a few bare-chested young 'uns were kicking a ball around using their T-shirts as goal posts. One scored a goal and did a dance, emulating the professionals he'd probably seen at a match or on television. She swivelled round to face the young mother. 'I want to reassure you we're making headway with the enquiry. We already know who Theresa's boyfriend is.'

The girl gave herself away, her hand freezing in mid-air as she offered more bread to Nathan.

'I'm not blind, Vicky. I can see you're terrified of him,' Kate said. 'But I need to find him fast. He has no idea that you're talking to us. How could he? I need answers because, believe me when I say that there are things about this case that make McKenzie seem like a really nice guy. I want to make sure you and Nathan are safe. Do you understand?'

'I can't help you.'

'Vicky, look at me, please.'

The girl turned her head away.

'There's always a nice way and a nasty way to deal with potential witnesses,' Kate said, urging her to see sense. 'Please don't make this difficult for me, for yourself. For what it's worth, I believe you are an innocent in all this. I think you had very little idea of what John was up to, am I right? Vicky, please look at me.' When she didn't respond, Kate tried again. 'I happen to think you're better than John and his kind. Isn't it time to stop buggering about and tell me everything you know? I'm trying to keep you safe, can't you see that?'

She waited but still Vicky didn't bite.

Kate was losing patience. 'Look, if you don't help, I'm sorry to have to say it, but you're on your own.'

Silence.

Hank was back.

He handed Nathan a cornet.

'Take him for a stroll,' Kate said.

'Boss?' He raised an incredulous eyebrow. 'Is this about before?'

'Do it.' Kate glanced at the boy's mother, letting him know that they were halfway through a delicate subject. 'Is that OK with you, Vicky?'

Vicky nodded.

'What if he cries?' Hank was beginning to panic.

'That's what the ice cream was for,' Kate said.

Hank pushed the buggy away, muttering expletives under his breath.

Kate smiled inwardly. Served him right for talking behind her back to Naylor. He'd think twice before doing it again. They were partners, and partners didn't grass, no matter how well intentioned.

It was time to stop teasing him and get down to serious business. She turned to face Vicky, taking something from her pocket. 'I didn't want to have to do this, but you forced my hand. I'm going to show you a photograph that you'll never, ever forget. It's John. Your John – or should I say, what's left of him.'

The girl looked horrified. Her imagination was obviously working overtime.

Her comeback was emphatic: 'I don't want to see it.'

'Makes two of us,' Kate said. 'I didn't want to either. Now it's the only image I see every time I close my eyes. You probably think I'm a cruel bitch. Well, here's the thing, in my line of work you have to be cruel to be kind sometimes. My job isn't only chasing villains, Vicky. A big part of it is protecting the public. I have good reason to believe that what happened to John may well happen to the man we're searching for. As sad and awful as it sounds, John was collateral damage. I believe Arthur McKenzie is the real target.'

At the mention of the name McKenzie, a flash of recognition crossed Vicky's face, enough to convince Kate – not that there'd been much doubt in her mind – that he was indeed Theresa's boyfriend. All the DCI needed now was a little cooperation from this frightened young woman and she'd be on her way.

But things were rarely that simple.

'Listen, McKenzie's right to hide,' Kate said. 'I don't give a shit what he has or hasn't done. I just want to ask him some questions, find out what he knows – and, believe me, that's plenty. For starters, he knows who did this. And that the reason they killed John and Terry was to get at him. I need a statement from him. Vicky? Are you listening? These are scary people I'm talking about. They won't stop until they find McKenzie, and God help him when they do.'

Kate wasn't getting through.

'You ever wonder why I didn't ask you to ID John's body?'

Vicky's eyes shifted from her lap to the DCI. 'You said I wasn't his next of kin.'

'I lied. I was sparing you the heartache of finding out how bad it really was. I guarantee that when you see this photograph you'll wish you'd cooperated before it came to this.'

'I won't look at it. You can't make me.'

She was weakening.

Kate was running out of ideas. She gazed into the middle distance. Hank had been once round the lake and was now walking back towards her, chatting away to Nathan like a proud father. Vicky followed her gaze as the DCI kept her focus on the child, commenting on how much he resembled his dad.

'So cute,' she said. 'I hope he gets the chance to break some hearts one day.'

'Stop!' Vicky stood up.

'No, you need to hear this.' Kate stuck the knife in and twisted it. 'John and Terry were tortured to death. How long do you think you'll last when they come for you? You're in grave danger and so is Nathan.' Hank pulled up right in front of them. Kate bent down, stroked the child's hand and then glanced up at his mother. 'How do you think these thugs are going to get you to talk? Ever thought about that?'

Reality was sinking in. A sob left Vicky's throat. Grabbing Nathan up in her arms, she held him close, terror in her eyes.

'I can offer you both protection if you tell me where I can find McKenzie and Theresa. It's entirely a matter for you. Look at Nathan. Look at him! You can't afford to say nothing.' Kate slid a card from her pocket and threw it on the picnic table. 'Give me a call when you see sense.'

Chapter Twenty-seven

HER WORDS HAD been necessarily harsh. Bereaved or not, the DCI was sick of dancing around Vicky Masters. The threat of showing her a photograph of her tortured boyfriend had been merely a ploy to get information, a tactic designed to scare her. Kate had no intention of carrying out the threat. In fact, the snap she'd taken from her pocket was of Jo. In the end, she'd wasted her time. The girl refused to cooperate.

With the Murder Investigation Team assembled, Kate took the floor in the crowded incident room. There was much to discuss. Maxwell kicked things off; he had no further information about Terry's antique ring, but on the plus side he had made a positive ID on Sky, a development Kate invited him to share with the others.

'Sky's real name is Bethany Miller.' Maxwell could hardly look his colleagues in the eye. 'She's fifteen years old, from Barrow-in-Furness; an only child, according to the Cumbrian officer who visited her parents to break the news. They threw her out in January following an argument over money she'd spent on a bloody mobile phone. The parents are en route to the morgue to make a formal identification. It's a given, unfortunately. She gave her real name and former address to the hospital that scanned her. Sounds like she had plans to go home and patch things up with her folks.'

'If only she'd gone sooner,' DS Robson said.

The temperature seemed to drop a few degrees.

Kate cast her eyes around the room. The death of any child had a sobering effect on the team. She couldn't afford to let their heads go down for a second. To avoid them dwelling on Bethany, she moved on, singling out Lisa Carmichael, who had news the DCI felt sure would lift morale. The nervous joyrider who'd been interviewed by Division had been invited into the station for further questioning. On Daniels' say so, Lisa had informed him that they'd overlook the Driving Whilst Disqualified offence he'd committed in exchange for information that might assist with a more serious enquiry she was dealing with.

'He responded to that,' Lisa said. 'He told me that the Range Rover he'd seen in the early hours of Friday morning had "shot out of Silverlink like a bullet", crossing the roundabout on the wrong side of the road, heading straight for him.'

'Go on,' Kate said.

'The driver and passenger apparently laughed as the kid swerved to avoid them, narrowly missing the offside of his car, nearly wrapping him round a lamppost in the process.' Lisa Carmichael's exuberant tone was an indication that there was more to tell – a potential leap forward that enthused everybody present. 'That roundabout is well lit,' she continued. 'The lad got a good look at the idiots in the Range Rover, good enough to see that one of them was ginger.'

The squad began to mutter among themselves. It was the first clue to the identity of one of the offenders they were seeking.

Across the room, Bright raised an impressed eyebrow, congratulating Lisa on her contribution. She sat down, chuffed that the head of CID had been in attendance when she broke the news – knowing it wouldn't be forgotten.

Maxwell was pulling a face.

For her part, Kate had enjoyed the exchange. Their former guv'nor had tipped Lisa for the top, as he had *her* years ago. No wonder: Lisa was both intelligent and conscientious, two attributes that went hand in hand. Without one, the other was useless. His endorsement was totally justified. The opinion of such a senior officer carried a lot of weight in Northumbria force. Right now though, Kate's own wisdom was kicking in. Like the ball on a roulette wheel, something inside her head whizzed round and round and fell neatly into place on a winning number.

Shutting her eyes, she dragged a memory up from the depths of her subconscious, a snippet of information she'd filed there long ago. She had no idea where it came from. Only that it was important. Scotland had the highest proportion of redheads in the UK. Around four out of every ten Scots carried the redhead gene.

'Kate?' Bright's voice cut through her thoughts. 'You want to carry on?'

She dropped her head to one side. 'Guv, what colour hair did Dougie O'Kane have?'

'What?'

'Was he a redhead?'

His answer came in a smile.

This new snippet of information galvanized the Murder Investigation Team. They couldn't yet prove it, but the consensus among them was that one or both of Dougie O'Kane's sons was reaping revenge for their father's death. Unless they were a mile wrong,

Craig and Finn O'Kane were gunning for Arthur Ross McKenzie, taking out anyone and everyone who was stupid enough to get in their way.

'Have you all got a copy of Andy's report on the QC Club?' Kate asked.

Some detectives did, some didn't.

Instructing them to share, she stepped forward. 'The last action I raised on there was to establish who it was that Terry was looking at as he left the premises. We think we know who it might be. I want the footage re-examined from that point on in order to ID as many clubbers as humanly possible, especially any that have red hair. For argument's sake, let's call this new action "Sequence of Events – QC". Everyone clear on that?'

There were nods of confirmation.

'I want frame-by-frame photographs of every movement to run all the way round the incident room where you can all see them. I want times, names, the whole nine yards. Bearing in mind the fact that John and Terry left early, I appreciate that it's a massive undertaking. It's necessary though, and I'm confident you're up for it. Whoever killed them – and possibly Bethany too – I honestly believe is in this club.' She pointed at the murder wall, a frozen image of Terry Allen looking over his shoulder. 'He's bloody scared. In my humble opinion, he's looking at the man or men who assaulted him six weeks earlier on the thirteenth of July.'

The team agreed with her assessment.

'If we're on the right track, Craig and Finn O'Kane will be on that footage somewhere. Only a halfwit would risk chasing someone out of a club in full view of CCTV. A sophisticated prig would mingle, bide their time, walk out with a crowd. These people are professional criminals, organized and savvy.'

'In that case, they would make straight for the nearest fire escape, wouldn't they?' The suggestion had come from Jo Soulsby.

'We have it covered, Jo. Andy recovered CCTV from all exits.' Kate could feel the excitement building in the room as she focused on Brown. 'Same goes then,' she said. 'I want frame-by-frame shots running right up until the last man or woman out of the QC turns the key in the damned lock. Let's get moving.'

Chapter Twenty-eight

TWO HOURS LATER, Kate raised her head to a tap on her office door.

'Got a minute?' Jo walked in and sat down without waiting for an invitation. 'You keeping out the way?' She thumbed over her shoulder. 'There's a mass wallpapering project going on out there.'

'How are they getting on?'

'Wonderfully, by the looks.'

Kate glanced at her watch: 20:10. 'Thought you'd have been long gone. Can I help you with something?'

'Other way round. I think I can help you.' Stretching her legs out in front of her, Jo placed her hands loosely in her lap. 'I just got off the phone with the Scottish prison service. Arthur Ross McKenzie was apparently a model inmate at Shotts. He was moved for his own safety in 2007. I asked why not to another prison north of the border and met a brick wall, so I rang Acklington, the receiving prison, or HMP Northumberland as it's now known. They told me that special permission was sought to move him south from the Scottish system. And guess what else? In the last few months of his sentence, he had a visitor.'

'Theresa?' It was an educated guess.

Jo grinned. 'And that's not all—'

'What did I tell you?' Bright breezed in through the open door. 'Theresa was always a piece of work. She's been a pathological liar since the day she was born.' He nodded a hello to Jo and then focused on his DCI, resenting the fact that the profiler had got to her before him. 'What does she look like these days anyway? Still good enough to eat?'

Kate made a face. 'Depends how hungry you are, guv.'

They all laughed.

The good humour was welcome relief from the seriousness of the offences they were dealing with. It helped to displace the elephant in the room that seemed to appear each time these three were together. Before his wife died, Kate had supported her boss through some difficult times. The two had become very close. In a brief moment of weakness – Kate would say madness – he'd let it be known that he wanted more than a working relationship with her, altering the dynamic between them for ever. It was ridiculous on two counts. First, Kate had only ever seen him as a mentor and father figure. Second, she was still in love with Jo – a state of affairs that he was unaware of.

When Bright had made a play for her, he'd been ignorant of her feelings for women – for Jo in particular. He'd taken the news on the chin, but there was a residual resentment over the relationship that hung like a dark cloud over them all. Kate regretted how the news had come out: an anonymous letter sent by an offender stirring up trouble. It wasn't as if she'd plotted to make a fool out of her former guv'nor – although sometimes it felt like that. She'd merely been keeping her sexual preferences to herself, as she was fully entitled to do.

So why did she feel so bloody guilty?

It got up her nose that two of the three people she loved most in the world – Hank being the other – would never get on. Or would they? Bright was making an effort tonight. If he noticed her studying him, he didn't let on. Realizing that Jo hadn't been party to his earlier insights on the case, he recapped on the chronology of Arthur McKenzie's fall from grace for her benefit, underlining the most important details, that he was a hard-nosed thug and Brian Allen's right-hand man when the two allegedly murdered Dougie O'Kane in 1993.

'And after Brian disappeared to Newcastle with the family . . . ?' Jo asked.

'McKenzie assumed the mantle. He hung around, took over where Brian left off. For a while there were no challengers to get in his way, so he was top dog in town. But when the O'Kane boys grew into men, things started to go tits-up. Actually, that's why I'm here. According to SOCA, McKenzie was on a hiding to nothing from the start – not as high up the pecking order of the Glasgow gangs as he thought he was. He had a lot of enemies.'

'You said "that's not all" before,' Kate reminded Jo. 'What did you mean?'

'Sorry, I nearly forgot. The first time I rang Shotts Prison, the officer I wanted to speak to wasn't on duty, so I called back. He told me that McKenzie survived a nasty assault by another inmate, a man named Wallace Whittaker—'

'Let me guess,' Bright said. 'A buddy of Craig and Finn O'Kane?'

'Correct. There's no hiding place in prison, not unless you opt for solitary confine—'

'Not Arthur's style,' Bright interrupted. 'He likes to rule the roost.'

'So I understand.' Jo had more. 'Prison officials couldn't force him into solitary, so they had to protect him in some other way. If an inmate is targeted inside, it causes massive problems for staff because they dare not take their eyes off them, even for a second. In order to keep the lid on the problem, they moved him out of harm's way, no doubt frustrating the O'Kane boys in the process. If they were, as you suspect, planning to avenge their father's death, they would put feelers out for information.'

'Prison grapevines extend across borders,' Kate said.

'Exactly.' Jo paused, collecting her thoughts. 'Inmates come and go. Believe me, they don't miss a trick. It's not beyond the bounds of possibility that Craig and Finn found out where McKenzie had been moved to, when he was being released, who his visitors were – all via word of mouth.'

'I'm surprised they weren't waiting for him at the gate,' Bright said.

'Maybe they were. But guess what?'

The detectives turned their eyes on Jo.

'So was Theresa.'

There was still a long way to go, but the case was shaping up nicely.

Chapter Twenty-nine

DESPITE THE FACT that it was Sunday evening, Kate rang her counterpart in Strathclyde force, DCI Matthew Trewitt. She had no qualms about disturbing his day of rest: Senior Investigating Officers were on call 24/7, every day of the year, including Christmas Day.

He answered his mobile on the second ring.

Having identified herself, Kate explained that she'd got his number from the control room and was calling in connection with a current investigation on her patch: two separate linked murders by torture involving members of the same family. Very nasty offences. She didn't go into too much detail on the phone, preferring to keep it brief.

'We have reason to believe that Craig and Finn O'Kane may be responsible.'

'Sounds right up their street.' Trewitt's response was immediate, his tone matter-of-fact, as if torture were an everyday occurrence in Scotland. 'I hope you've got plenty of evidence, because they're a couple of slippery customers.'

'I can see that from their rap sheet,' Kate said. 'Tell me about them.'

'Not to put too fine a point on it, they're scum. They've been on the wrong side of the law since birth, just like their father before them. Minor thefts and assaults, graduating to drugs, prostitution and money-lending as they got older – for which they charge a massive amount of interest – and then some. Those who don't pay end up in a very bad way.'

'Anything recent?'

'Aye, you could say that.' Trewitt exhaled. She could tell he was smoking a cigarette, could swear she could actually smell it.

'And . . . ?'

'Thrown out, no case to answer,' Trewitt said. 'Happens all the time. They get as far as the court steps. Everyone bottles. Witnesses disappear. I'm sure I don't need to draw you a picture. If memory serves, a couple of assaults remain on file for the Procurator Fiscal to consider. In fact, some sad bastard is still lying in hospital, too scared to give evidence. The O'Kanes like torture. Section 18 woundings are their speciality. Intent is their middle name.'

'What kind of torture?' Kate asked.

'You name it, they're into it: fingers, toes, kneecaps – and they especially like jaws.'

The word 'jaws' made her shudder.

Trewitt was still talking. 'By the time they're done, their victims either hobble everywhere or end up sucking their dinner through a straw. Sometimes both.'

Asking him to report any sightings of her two suspects immediately, Kate hung up. Too wired to go home, and with a lingering image of that gaping jaw, she remained in the incident room long after the others had gone home to spend a couple of well-deserved hours with their wives and families. Only DC Lisa Carmichael insisted on staying on.

With a magnifying glass each – looking like a caricature of Sherlock Holmes and Dr Watson – the two walked around the room, viewing the results of the team's efforts that evening. As Kate had requested, frame-by-frame photographs had been posted round the walls with meticulous attention to detail. Each one had been labelled with the time and a list of anyone already identified.

Kate rubbed at her tired eyes. After a while, faces on the stills became indistinct blobs, each one merging into the next as she studied them, paying particular attention to anyone with red hair, a task made more difficult by lighting both inside the club and in the street directly outside. She took a break, suggesting Lisa do likewise. They made a cup of tea and then started again, prepared to work late into the night if necessary.

'Where are you?' Kate whispered under her breath.

Convinced that her targets were Craig and Finn O'Kane, and that their motive was revenge, she had the distinct feeling she was missing something that was staring her in the face, an impression she shared with her young DC.

'Like what?' Carmichael asked.

Kate shrugged. 'If I knew the answer to that, I'd be home in bed and so would you.'

Walking across the room, she picked up a hard copy of Brown's report that someone had discarded on a desk. She scanned the notes she'd made in the right-hand column. The bouncer was easy. Contacting the QC key-holder led to an immediate name and address. Brown had gone to see him and, together with other detectives drafted in to assist, he'd spent much of the evening piecing together evidence of who was who.

Information was sketchy. Some regular members the bouncer knew, others he recognized only by face. The team were lucky in one respect: professional doormen were paid to be observant. They were able to make associations between clubbers it would've taken the Murder Investigation Team months to establish. Who was friendly with whom in the queue to get in, who was passing drugs, who was trouble, who was canny. The bouncer had even given them information as to where some of the punters lived. In short, he knew the clientele inside out. Except – *surprise, surprise* – for John Allen, who, he claimed, just happened to be a member of the same gymnasium.

'Our only contact outside of the gym was at the QC,' he'd told Brown.

'Yeah right,' Kate muttered as she scanned the image in front of her, the two men's hands frozen in a celebratory high five. 'What was that all about then?'

'You're talking to yourself again,' Lisa said.

Kate didn't answer. She'd moved to another section of footage, her mind racing as she realized what she was looking at.

Stop, stop, STOP!

She'd prioritized the examination of CCTV from ten o'clock onwards around the hospital and Silverlink, based on the time Terry and John had left the club, and yet . . . Kate blinked, thinking that her eyes were deceiving her. Was she seeing things? She stared at the images again. 'Jesus!' she said under her breath.

Her exclamation brought Carmichael rushing from the other side of the room.

'Find something?' she asked, following her boss's gaze.

'I don't know, Lisa. Tell me what you see.'

Carmichael raised her magnifying glass, studying the images. She pointed at some figures: John Allen, Terry Allen and a young girl already identified by her distinctive red dress – the blonde seen entering the club in front of Terry at ten past eight on Thursday night. Her name was Rose, although the team didn't yet have a surname.

'Anyone else?' Kate asked.

Carmichael rechecked. 'No.'

'Look at the timeline.'

Lisa stared at the wall for a long time, then glanced at her boss as she realized what was so wrong about the picture. The frame they had been examining was timed at 1:06 a.m. It was clear to both detectives that at some point during the night they died, Terry and John had doubled back to the nightclub, which meant that the squad had been wasting precious resources on the wrong time frame.

'We need to start again, Lisa. Find out when exactly they returned and, more importantly, when they left again. You up for it?'

It was a daft question.

Chapter Thirty

THIS WAS NO ordinary grey and rainy Monday morning. No amount of depression in the weather could dampen Kate Daniels' spirits. She was on a roll, finally making headway, in possession of unequivocal proof that she was on the right track. Her discovery that Terry and John made not one but two visits to the QC club on Thursday, 23 August wasn't the full story. With Carmichael's help, she'd established that the brothers had re-entered the premises shortly before midnight; they then came running out again at eight minutes after two. John was screaming into his phone as they separated, legging it in different directions. A few minutes later, two men were seen climbing down the fire escape, coats over their heads in order to mask their identity – *or their red hair.*

Kate had slept for less than four hours. She didn't feel tired – just depressed by the prospect of meeting Bethany's grief-stricken parents, a task so grim the worry of it had deprived her of the little time she had to rest. Try as she might to imagine how they were feeling right now, in her heart she knew she wouldn't come close. Pushing away that gloomy thought, she allowed the adrenalin rush she'd felt the night before to bubble to the surface, knowing from experience that it would carry her through until the Millers arrived.

CCTV sightings of the Allen brothers at the QC nightclub had cut the time frame down considerably, allowing her to target her enquiries more appropriately, leaving far less time unaccounted for than she had originally calculated between their exit from the premises and the discovery of their bodies at the RVI and Silverlink Industrial Estate.

Kate had issued a TIE action to trace, implicate or eliminate her suspects, Craig and Finn O'Kane. Her gut instinct was that they were responsible. The onus was on the Murder Investigation Team to find enough evidence to prove it in a court of law and she'd instructed the squad to do a job on them. An information gathering exercise to uncover recent photographs, current and past addresses, what vehicles they drove, who their associates were, what offences they were suspected of, details of significant others and current financial position.

'Every scrap of intelligence is being checked.' Kate was heading along the corridor with Jo towards the staff canteen, a chance to escape the mayhem of the incident room for a few minutes and talk without interruption. 'Finding them is the hard part. They're thugs, not down-and-outs living on the street. These men are clever criminals hiding behind reputable businesses in Glasgow, Edinburgh and other cities too.'

'Can't you put out a general alert?' Jo asked.

'You mean flash it all over the papers?'

They turned the corner, pushing open the door. Perfect: the room was empty. They got water from the machine and took a seat beneath the window, Kate telling Jo that it would be unwise to involve the media at this early stage. On the one hand they could be very useful – it would give her many more pairs of eyes if local people knew what the O'Kane brothers looked like – but the last thing she wanted was some have-a-go hero getting hurt tackling a pair of dangerous psychopaths.

'I have to be so careful not to spook the public or drive the offenders underground,' she explained. 'Maintaining a silence means the O'Kanes won't know what we know. I want to keep it that way.'

Jo fell silent, lifted her drink to her lips and sipped gently, leaving no lipstick on the white beaker. How the hell did she do that? How, despite the demands of her job, did she manage to turf up at work as if she'd stepped out of a photo shoot? Kate's eyes travelled unashamedly over Jo's pleated navy shirt, the alluring split at the neck, a tiny button the only thing keeping it from slipping from her shoulders.

'I've contacted Strathclyde police,' she said. 'I've been very guarded, putting feelers out to find out what the tale is, but only with my operational equivalent. People talk. It pays not to trust anyone. The fewer people who know we're sniffing around, the better. The O'Kane brothers have no idea our disqualified driver spotted red hair, or that Vicky told us where John was headed the night he died. They'll be hoping that none of that information is available to us. Fortunately, they're wrong.'

'You think they're still on the patch?'

Kate shrugged. 'They could still be here, waiting for McKenzie to stick his head above the parapet. On the other hand, they may have gone off home until the heat dies down. Our lot are well briefed to keep a lookout. On the off chance they're already across the border, the SIO up there has been primed to give me a shout.'

'Did you find John and Terry's phones?'

'No, I didn't. That reminds me, mind if I make a call?'

Taking her phone from her pocket, Kate dialled a number.

A woman answered. 'CSI Northumbria.'

Kate grimaced. *They were SOCO! What was with the fancy name?* 'This is Detective Chief Inspector Kate Daniels, Murder Investigation Team. I'd like to talk to the officer who inspected the burnt-out Range Rover in the East End . . . yes, part of the Allen enquiry. Quick as you can, please.'

The line clicked and a male officer picked up, identifying himself, telling her he'd completed his report and was about to call her.

'Good. You have something for me?'

'Negative. I'm afraid there's no sign of any components of mobile telephones in the vehicle.' Kate thanked him and hung up. It was not the result she was after.

Chapter Thirty-one

'HA!' GORMLEY CHUCKLED. 'Turns out the Essex Lion is no more than a large domestic cat called Teddy Bear.' He was referring to reports of a wild animal roaming the tiny village of St Osyth. The news had taken the media by storm, triggering the involvement of experts from Colchester Zoo as well as police firearms teams. 'Witnesses reported having seen and even heard the ruddy thing roar. Divvis!'

Kate grinned. It was much-needed light relief from the serious offences they were dealing with. She'd come from a fraught meeting with Bethany Miller's parents, who, having formally identified their daughter's body, had stayed in Newcastle overnight, insisting on speaking to the Senior Investigating Officer before returning home to Cumbria – as was their right. Kate had taken the opportunity to find out more about the girl, whether she'd been in touch, whether she had any friends she might have stayed in touch with. But the parents were vague – no, more than that, they were downright evasive and uncaring – leaving her in no doubt as to why Bethany preferred prostitution on the streets of

Newcastle to life with them. Maxwell was mistaken. There was little love in that family; no chance of Bethany patching things up and moving back in, with or without a baby. And now the Millers had the effrontery to demand justice for the poor girl.

Shame they hadn't been so concerned when she was alive.

The rest of Kate's morning was spent with her team, a recap of where they were at. The consensus of opinion was that the O'Kanes were unaware they were being hunted – or they didn't care. The brothers' arrival at the club did not feature in the frame-by-frame pictures on the incident-room wall, and all they had of their departure were shots of two figures leaving via the fire escape, faces obscured by their coats. Brown suggested the O'Kanes had sent someone ahead to open a toilet window on the ground floor so they could slip in unobserved. Security wasn't foolproof by any means.

Kate looked out through the grubby window on to the street below, preoccupied with thoughts of Terry and John, particularly their missing phones. She needed to find them. Outside, the rain had cleared. The wind was getting up as people hurried along Market Street in their lunch break, passing a row of police vehicles parked all along the road. Getting out of an unmarked vehicle was a DS she'd had a brief fling with at training school.

Two-timing bastard.

The relationship was history, however, the recollection prompted a thought about cheating other halves. It made her wonder about Amanda – John Allen's latest squeeze, according to the gossip Brown had overheard at Grant's. She'd still not been located. SOCA didn't have her down as one of his known criminal associates, so the connection had to be pleasure rather than business. CCTV footage showed that he'd called someone twice from the QC Club. If he was two-timing Vicky and it wasn't her he was calling, maybe it was Amanda.

And what of Terry's phone? His wife was point-blank refusing to speak to the police. Assuming he hadn't lost it in his rush to escape his torturers, it was safe to assume that John had taken possession of it before leaving him at A & E.

Kate sighed. If John had been overpowered before he had time to dump the phones, it stood to reason that these vital devices had fallen into the hands of his killers. Even now they could be going through the address books, trying to find someone who could lead them to McKenzie. They'd be particularly interested in recently dialled numbers, so Amanda could well be their next port of call.

Somehow, Kate had to get to her first.

IN DESPERATION, KATE called Towner. He didn't pick up. She tried again. Same result. So she texted: phone me! Frustrated, she tried to get on with her work. At a little after one p.m., her mobile rang. Towner refused to talk. He was petrified. People were nervous and he was leaving town, he told her.

'Listen to me, you piece of shit!'

The phone went dead before she'd finished yelling into the receiver.

Hank arrived in her doorway as she slammed it down. 'Problem?' he asked.

'My snout hung up on me!'

'Your politeness probably put him off.'

Kate laughed, the tension gone. She called Towner back, listening as the number rang out, rolling her eyes at Hank. 'John called somebody from that club, Hank. You saw the footage. He was agitated, screaming for help. He's got to be calling someone close by, someone able to render assistance in the form of a hiding place or reinforcements to see off the O'Kanes. We need to talk to Amanda, if only to rule her out. Personally, I reckon he was calling McKenzie.'

'I agree. McKenzie isn't stupid though. Wherever he is, he's well hidden.'

'Yeah, but . . .' She held up her phone. 'This scumbag knows more than he's letting on.'

KATE FLOORED THE accelerator. If Towner wouldn't come to her, she'd go to him. Turning left out of the station, she drove down Pilgrim Street and took the exit off the Swan House roundabout heading for the East End, Hank by her side. They were pleased to be out and about. Since Bethany Miller's death, a new wave of information was coming into the incident room: statements, documents, telephone messages, intelligence from the house-to-house. All of this intel was being acted upon, but so far they had no concrete proof that the incidents were linked.

'I don't know how Harry does it,' Hank said.

He was referring to the Receiver, a key member of the team. It was Harry's job to work out which pieces of evidence were crucial, which bits less so. His was a desk job. He was continually reading. What came his way could change the whole emphasis of an enquiry as stuff dropped out and something new came in. He spent endless hours updating information for officers on the ground which, in turn, generated more actions going forward. There was a constant reappraisal of priorities going on.

'I couldn't agree more,' Kate said.

An hour ago, she'd been offered the services of a part-time detective for her incident room. She'd fought against it. What use were they to an SIO if they didn't know what had happened in the three days they were off duty? Threads were dropped. They weren't up to speed. It was impossible to keep up with a fast-running enquiry.

Turning left, Kate stopped at the lights to let an old lady cross the road. As she waited to move off again, her thoughts turned to the murder wall and the special box flagging up new events. It was the first thing she looked at each time she entered the major incident room. In her job, you could go out in the morning and come back at lunchtime to discover that everything had been turned upside down by some new development. That was why briefings were so important, why she insisted on everyone being there.

Her phone rang.

She answered, putting it on speaker through the hands-free.

Robson sounded excited. 'I just took a call from the cleaner you met at Theresa Allen's flat. She wanted to speak to you urgently—'

'She remembered McKenzie's name?'

'Even better – she said to let you know that there were two Scottish thugs hanging about earlier. They were asking after Theresa. And get this: one of them had red hair. It looks like the O'Kane brothers are still around.'

Kate and Hank high-fived. It was great news. Now more than ever, they had to find Towner and get a handle on Amanda, McKenzie – or both.

WHERE IS HE? Kate barged through the pub door and out into the sunshine, heading for her car. Pushing the button on her key-fob for the umpteenth time, she yanked open the door and climbed in.

'Where now?' Hank asked.

She looked blankly at him. 'I have no bloody idea.'

They had visited just about every pub in the East End, a string of betting shops and various cafes without success. Having exhausted all of Towner's haunts, they had no choice but to return to Kate's office and hope that he made contact.

They didn't have long to wait.

As they entered the incident room, Kate's pocket vibrated: a text from the man himself. She caught Hank's eye, held up her hand with fingers spread to indicate five minutes, and hurried straight into her office to call Towner back. He didn't answer. Swearing under her breath she tried again. The ringing tone stopped and the connection was made.

Towner was shitting himself. She could hear it in his voice, his nervousness proof that he knew more than he'd let on.

Deciding the restrained approach might work, Kate put in a few minutes of gentle persuasion. It paid off: Towner admitted he had information that might help, but told the DCI that he was too terrified to get involved. If John and Terry's associates didn't silence him, the men who killed them soon would. He wasn't prepared to test that theory by grassing anyone up.

'I won't let that happen,' Kate said. Her assurances were met with a long silence. 'C'mon Towner, you know me. Have I ever let you down?'

Still he didn't bite.

Raising her eyes to the ceiling, Kate held on to her temper, even though she was ready to rip his head off. Finding him was bad enough. Talking to him was something else altogether. With careful handling he usually came over, but, for once, she wished he'd do so without making her sweat.

'I can offer you safeguards,' she said.

'Oh yeah?' Towner gave a nervous laugh. 'That even sounded like a lie. What d'you take me for? What you going to do? Give me close protection for the rest of my days? I'm going to need it, if I talk to you.'

'Where are you?' she asked. 'I'll—'

'Up the creek without a paddle, that's where.'

'Fuck's sake! Stop messing me about, Towner.' Time to change tack. What this needed was the personal touch. 'I'll meet you. Usual place in ten.'

'No way!' he yelled. 'Anyway, I'm not around.'

'So where are you?'

'Whitby.'

'You're kidding. Why?'

'Why d'you think? I'll meet you at Botham's teashop at half four.'

'Are you taking the piss?' Kate glanced at her watch. It was three-fifteen. 'You know I'll never make it.'

'Half four. Come alone or forget it.'

'Wait! Listen—'

'They close at five,' he said. 'If you're not there by then, you'll never see me again.'

The dialling tone hit her ear.

She hit redial: *unobtainable*. The bastard had either thrown the mobile in the drink or taken the SIM out. She grabbed her coat and ran . . .

Chapter Thirty-two

WITHIN MINUTES, SHE was tearing across the Tyne Bridge heading south. Despite Towner's warning to come alone, Hank was in the passenger seat in case they needed to bring him back. Kate had only once made the mistake of driving an offender somewhere on her own and nearly came to grief when the mad woman grabbed the steering wheel on the coast road at seventy miles an hour. She'd vowed never to do it again.

Turning left out of Gateshead town centre she took the Felling bypass. Frustration getting the better of her, she glanced at her watch but then forced herself to ease off the accelerator rather than risk being flashed by speed cameras on a road notorious for catching drivers out. Hank yawned, settling back in his seat for the journey as she pressed on, passing a sign for South Shields, then turning right on to the A19 towards Sunderland and Teesside.

On a good day it would take an hour and a half to get to her destination, never mind find the premises her snout had chosen as a rendezvous. The miles flashed by in silence. They barely exchanged a word, and at one point Hank fell asleep. That was fine by her. It gave her time to think, an opportunity to calm down. She'd need her wits about her if Towner came across with vital information that might tip the enquiry on its head. As Jo had rightly pointed out, McKenzie and the O'Kanes were hard to handle. They weren't about to put their hands in the air and come quietly.

Three-quarters of an hour later, Hank stirred in his seat, his eyes blinking open. Taking in their current position, he yawned, apologized for sending the zeds up for the best part of their journey. 'You OK?' he asked. 'Want me to drive?'

Kate shook her head. 'Looks like we'll make it,' she said.

'Where's the meeting place?' He peered out of the window in search of a road sign.

'Whitby.'

'Where?'

She gave him an odd look. 'North Yorkshire.'

'Yeah, I've got a Geography O Level. I meant where in Whitby?'

'I don't know.' She'd been to Botham's many times with her mother. It was an institution in the seaside town, reputed to be the oldest surviving teashop of its kind in Britain. 'Look up the postcode and plug it into the satnav on my phone, will you?'

Hank did as she asked and then called the office. Progress was mixed: Brown was still working with staff from the QC club. With the doorman-cum-bouncer's help, he'd identified and traced more clubbers. That was good, but there was bad news too. Most were uncommunicative, claiming they'd been so pissed by midnight, they couldn't remember their own names, let alone ID anyone making trouble. No one would admit to knowing the Allen brothers – hardly surprising, under the circumstances.

PUSHING OPEN THE door, Kate and Hank stepped inside. Despite the fact that the tearoom was due to close in a little over twenty minutes, a line of customers were queuing at the counter to be served. Mounting the stairs to the restaurant was like entering another era. The place had the genteel atmosphere of a bygone age. A courteous young woman behind the till greeted them on the floor above. Kate told her they were meeting someone. The girl led them to a table near the window, taking their order for a pot of tea, much needed after their frantic search for Towner in Newcastle and the long drive south.

Problem was, the man himself was nowhere to be seen.

'I hope he's not playing silly buggers,' Kate said under her breath.

Hank grimaced. 'Why here and not in a pub?'

Kate shrugged. 'Well, we're not going to meet any riff-raff or angry gangsters here, are we?'

'This him?' Hank flicked his eyes to a customer arriving.

'No, relax.'

'What's he look like?'

Before she had time to answer, Towner appeared at the top of the stairs, more nervous and bedraggled than usual. As soon as he clocked Hank, he ran. Kate gave chase, belting down the stairs after him, out through the open door and along the road. He'd run the wrong way; Towner was in no condition for an uphill marathon. Dodging in and out of pedestrians, the DCI closed the distance and seized him by the collar. She swung him round, uncomfortably aware that the pursuit had attracted attention. Not wanting anyone to call the law, she hissed in his ear:

'Walk!'

Towner shrugged her off. 'We had an arrangement,' he reminded her. 'Come alone or no deal. You've always insisted on that. You can't change the fucking rules just because it suits you.'

'Your fault!' she said. 'How the hell was I going to get here on time without someone to park up if I had to abandon my car? Now get walking.'

Towner set off. 'Who was he anyway? Your minder?'

'A colleague, you daft sod – who the hell d'you think? And he's trustworthy, so if you ever need me and I'm not around, ask for DS Gormley and he'll sort you out. He's a good bloke. You two share the same dry sense of humour. You might have found that out if you'd stuck around.'

At the top of the street they turned right, heading for the sea. A few moments later, they sat down on a bench facing a vast expanse of shimmering water with nothing whatsoever on the horizon. It was a view that would normally lift the spirits, but neither Kate nor Towner were in the mood to sightsee. She wanted information. He wanted money. It didn't take long for him to ask for it.

'I'd like to help you out,' he said, 'But it'll take a shedload of cash to make it worth my while. By the way, you can have this back.' He handed her the mobile she'd given him. It was smashed to pieces. 'I want out. This is too heavy for me.'

'So tell me something I don't already know. Three people are dead, Towner. I need you to help me before anyone else gets hurt.'

'Like me, you mean?' Glowering at her, he lit a cigarette.

Kate could see how spooked he was. He dropped his head into shaky hands, smoke drifting through his fingers, his nails bitten to the quick. Right this minute she could do with a fag herself, a large drink to go with it, a nice hot bath, scented candles and good music.

Like that was on the cards anytime soon!

'I want you off my back, once'n for all,' he mumbled.

'Up to you,' Kate said. 'You come across for me this time, I might forget our alliance permanently.'

'You mean it?' He wiped a thin film of sweat from his upper lip.

'Depends. You need to start talking to me. Christ's sake, you have the chance to do some good for once. Please, Towner, I need your help to get this shit off the streets.' Her plea went unanswered. Time to up the ante and stop buggering about. 'OK, you had your chance. When I catch those bastards, I'll make it my business to let them know the information came from you. How's that sound?'

He glared at her. 'I gave you nowt!'

Kate got to her feet. 'They won't know that.'

'You can't do that,' he protested.

'I'm a copper. We can't afford ethics. Who's Amanda?'

Towner's expression was inscrutable.

'I will make it worth your while.' Taking fifty pounds from her wallet, Kate sat down, placing it on the bench between them, keeping her hand on top so it didn't blow away. It was her own money, nothing she could claim back from the force on account of his unofficial status, but she didn't care. It would be worth it to see the O'Kane brothers banged up.

'I need an address,' she said. 'Tell me where Amanda lives or where I might find her. Then you can start talking about the O'Kanes.'

Towner said nothing.

Sliding the cash out from under her hand, he looked out to sea, letting out a big sigh. For a moment, she thought he'd come across. Then he bolted from the seat, taking her completely by surprise.

The sound of screeching brakes and the thump as the car hit him made her shudder.

A small crowd had gathered by the time she made it off the pavement. Barging her way through to the front, she knelt down beside him, her heart kicking a hole in her chest from the inside. He stared at her through fading eyes as bubbles of blood spilled out of the left side of his mouth, ran down his cheek, settling on the tarmac beneath him.

An elderly woman arrived on the scene. Punching numbers into a mobile phone, she lifted it to her ear, her eyes on Kate. The woman was sheet-white, having witnessed the accident from the other side of the main road.

'He just ran,' she said. 'Do you know him?'

Kate shook her head.

She was vaguely aware of a female voice asking for police and ambulance. The elderly witness was explaining their location, telling the operator what she'd seen. Traumatized and bloodied, Kate looked down at Towner, feeling guilty for having denied him. Then Hank's voice came from left field: *Poor sod! Anyone know him? Anyone see what happened?* People were shaking their heads. The consensus of opinion was that Towner ran off the pavement into the path of an oncoming vehicle.

'What an idiot!' someone said. 'The poor driver had no chance of avoiding him.'

'Yeah, tragic.' A young woman's voice trailed off.

The sound of emergency vehicles could be heard in the distance. Towner stirred, tried to speak, something Kate couldn't make out. She leaned forward, her ear to his mouth. She could almost feel his dying breath on her cheek as he repeated it.

'What did he say?' the elderly witness asked.

Kate lied: 'He said his name was Alan Townsend.'

The woman pointed at the approaching ambulance. 'I'll let them know.'

Kate looked down at Towner, gave his hand a squeeze, reassuring him that help was imminent. What he'd actually said was 'Amanda'. As she removed her hand, he grabbed at it, keeping a tight hold. 'Across the street from Grant's . . .' He coughed, a spray of red spotting his chin. 'Blue door.'

Chapter Thirty-three

THE LARGE, STEADY hand on her shoulder was familiar. Hank pulled her back as the ambulance crew emerged with the stretcher, one medic shouting at the crowd to give them room to do their jobs. Kate glanced over her shoulder, feeling the weight of guilt eat away at her insides. She met the eyes of her DS. There were no accusations there, just an expression of total incredulity. He was talking to her but Towner's words were louder . . .

I want you off my back once'n for all.

Kate was struggling to put one foot in front of the other as they left the scene. In her head, she pictured the medics checking for signs of life. They were wasting their time; the minute he'd uttered the words 'blue door' Towner was gone. She had her information, but at what cost?

Have I ever let you down?

'I pushed him too far,' she cried. Her words were almost inaudible, her explanation incoherent and jumbled as she tried to justify her actions. Hank still had his hand on her shoulder, steering her clear of onlookers flooding the scene to gawp at Towner's crumpled shape lying in the middle of the road.

'He ran of his own free will,' Hank said. 'I saw that much. You're not a psychic. You couldn't have predicted that, Kate. No one could.'

'Yeah, well maybe I should have.' Palming her forehead, she stopped walking and drew in a long breath. She studied her professional partner, desperation in her eyes. 'I was seen, Hank! I was seen chasing him from the teashop, grabbing the silly bastard in the street. Jesus! I could lose my job over this. I've got to come clean. We have to go back.'

'Are you serious?' He swung her round as she tried to walk away, held on to her. 'That's bordering on professional suicide, and you know it. There's nothing you can do for him. Let's go.' His eyes held a warning she couldn't take in.

Incapable of straight thinking, she could only blurt, 'I can't!'

'Yes, you can. Calm down and think about this for a minute.' He pulled her away from other pedestrians, dropping his voice to a whisper. 'You go back and you'll be suspended for months. You'll never see SIO again. There'll be an enquiry. You know how it works when you're a copper – guilty or innocent, you're shafted. Are you prepared to lose your rank and possibly your job over a piece of shit like Towner?'

'It's not as simple as—'

'Yes, it is. You didn't chase him. He ran away. You didn't push him under the car. He. Ran. Away. You weren't putting him under any pressure whatsoever.'

Kate couldn't concentrate with him glaring at her like she'd gone completely mad.

'Walk away,' he said. 'You went off-piste. No point losing your bottle now. For Christ's sakes, get a grip!'

Hank was right about one thing – she hadn't been in pursuit of Towner when he legged it. He'd jumped up and bolted before she knew what was happening, there was no way she could be held responsible.

So why did she feel that she was?

Towner was a weak individual. Vulnerable. Always had been. Someone she could push around at will in order to get results – a fact she'd frequently taken advantage of, over the years. Informants were how detectives got lucky, how they cracked cases, earned recognition, achieved promotion. Nevertheless, she feared what she was turning into for the good of the job.

Hank told her she was talking rubbish. Towner was a loser, destined for a sticky end. He had no one. No family to mourn his passing. No one who cared enough to make a complaint or demand an enquiry from the Independent Police Complaints Commission. He wouldn't have told a soul that he knew her, for fear of losing street cred.

'And now he can't tell,' he added. 'So think yourself lucky. Jesus! He even gave you the phone back!'

'If that's supposed to make me feel good, it doesn't.'

'Well, it should.' Hank strapped himself in. 'We need to head back.'

Kate didn't move.

'We were never here,' Hank said. 'No one is going to come looking. Towner is an RTA statistic. All the witnesses said it was his fault—'

'He held my hand, Hank!'

'Exactly – you were there for him at the end when no one else was. You think he'd have told you about Amanda if he blamed you in any way?'

She hadn't thought of that.

'Drive,' he said.

As she drove away, he held up his phone. 'Do I make that call?'

Nodding, she put her foot down, putting as much distance between herself and Whitby as she could without attracting a speeding ticket. Hank phoned the office, asking Carmichael to check out the information on Amanda as discreetly as possible. Three-quarters of an hour later, Lisa rang back. Amanda was indeed living behind the blue door opposite Grant's.

'Shoot, Lisa.' Kate put the phone on speaker. 'Who is she and what did she have to say for herself?'

'Last name Hitchins,' Carmichael said. 'Claims she broke up with John a few days before he died. Wanted him to leave Vicky. He refused, on account of the kid. John adored him, apparently, even though he wasn't sure he was the father. And no, he didn't call Amanda Thursday night. I checked her phone. She's playing it straight, boss. Looks like you were right. It must've been McKenzie he was phoning. We might have some news on that, by the way. Neil has the gen. OK if I put him on?'

Unable to hide the disappointment in her voice, Kate told her to go ahead. Finding Amanda had seemed vitally important earlier in the day. The fact that she had no information that would take the enquiry any further was a bitter blow. Towner had died for nothing, and Kate couldn't live with that.

Maxwell came on the line, forcing her to concentrate.

'What you got for me, Neil?'

'Call came in earlier from an off-duty copper, Dixie Price.'

'The name means nothing to me.'

'It won't. He's from Durham force. Claims he has good intel on McKenzie's whereabouts. As you and Hank are out and about already, Robbo figured you might like to meet with him personally. He's waiting to hear from you.'

Maxwell reeled off a number.

'Did you check him out?' Kate asked.

'Yup. According to those in the know, he's a good bloke. His supervision said if he has information you can be sure it'll be kosher.'

Chapter Thirty-four

DIXIE PRICE LIVED deep in Catherine Cookson country in the exquisitely tranquil village of Blanchland. Situated on the Northumberland–Durham border, the conservation village was at the upper end of the Derwent Valley, not far from the reservoir of the same name. Built from the stone of a twelfth-century abbey, the village hadn't changed in centuries. Daniels knew it well. Surrounded by woods and open countryside, it was a favourite stop-off for tourists. There was nothing there bar a post office, a shop, a public house, a church and tearoom – nothing like the one she'd fled from a matter of hours ago, leaving her tea untouched.

Poor Towner.

Hank was staring at her expectantly.

Kate couldn't shake the image of the accident. 'Sorry, I missed that.'

'That's because you weren't listening.' He made no attempt to hide his frustration, telling her to pull herself together and stop dwelling on Towner. He knew her so well. 'I said we should meet Price over a meal at the Lord Crewe Arms. You look completely shagged out and I could do with some grub if we're pushing on through.'

'Fine. Whatever.' Kate had no stomach for food.

'Don't look so sour-faced. I'm not like you,' Hank grumbled. 'I can't survive on a lettuce leaf or a boiled egg.' He pointed at the glove box. 'You got anything decent to eat in there? Kit-Kat, bag of crisps, chicken tikka masala . . . ? I'm famished.'

Smiling, then crying, Kate could only shake her head. He was like a child over food and journey times. *Are we nearly there yet?* Wiping away a tear with her sleeve, she was so grateful to have him with her. He was still looking at her with pleading eyes when she remembered that the Lord Crewe had closed down for renovation. When she relayed that fact, he grumbled some more. She glanced at her watch. It was getting on for seven-thirty. In the sticks, nothing else would be open at this time of night. They would have to meet Price at his home address.

THE RENTED COTTAGE was set back off the main street, picture-postcard pretty with roses round the door, a little garden at the rear. Thick walls and stone floors made it feel cool inside. The décor was cosy: rugs on the floors, subdued lighting, sketches on the walls. Price was quite an artist in his spare time. With just a dog for company, there was little else to do in Blanchland.

Kate received a firm handshake.

The Durham officer had grey eyes, bushy eyebrows to match and an unusual streak the same colour running through short-cropped hair the colour of sand. Introductions over, he offered them tea and something to eat, lightening Hank's mood a little. Disappearing to the kitchen, he returned with a tray bearing tea

and enough sandwiches to feed the whole of the Murder Investigation Team – and then some.

As he set it down, Hank didn't stand on ceremony. He showed
his appreciation by filling his plate, telling their host he hadn't
eaten since breakfast. As Hank got stuck in, Price explained why
he was so keen to talk to them. He'd recognized Arthur McKenzie
from the photo Naylor put out on an internal bulletin that very
afternoon.

'This is bloody great!' Hank held up a half-eaten sandwich,
wiping butter from his chin with his free hand. 'You don't need a
lodger, do you, mate?'

Price grinned. 'Dig in, I've eaten.' He turned towards Kate.
'Ma'am, please help yourself.'

Declining food, she accepted a mug of steaming hot tea. She
wished Hank would shut up. He was asking Price how long he'd
been in the Dog Section. The officer told him six years. He was due
a transfer in a few weeks, finally making detective after years of
trying, and couldn't wait to bin the uniform. His dog had put his
paws up last year after an injury acquired while on duty had put
him out of action. It was then that Price had decided to reapply to
join the CID – this time successfully.

Hank eyed the springer spaniel, who in turn eyed him – or
rather the food in his hand. 'What's his name?'

'Molly's a bitch, aren't you, girl?'

A tail wagged. Ignoring her handler, the dog inched closer to
Hank.

'Aren't most police dogs male?' Hank was clueless on such
matters.

'Hank!' Losing patience, Kate glared at him. 'Eat, will you, and
let me get some answers, or we'll be here all night.' She turned

to Price. 'A member of my team said you saw McKenzie, is that correct?'

'Yes, I did.'

'When was this?'

''Bout four o'clock. I was sitting in the White Monk and the bugger walked in, large as life. I finished my shift at two and called in for a bowl of soup on my way home. I know the owners, Tony and Viv, quite well. They feed me, and in return I keep an unofficial eye on the place when it's closed, check that it's secure, that type of thing. I'm a key-holder actually.' Price got up, threw another log on the fire. He remained standing, his back to the fireplace, feet slightly apart, hands by his sides, almost to attention. 'McKenzie ordered stuff to take out – rather a lot for one person, I would've said. That's what drew my interest. When he turned around, I clocked him straight away. I didn't follow him out in case he saw me. By the time I made it outside, he'd disappeared.'

'And that's going to help me how?' Kate was beginning to lose the will to live.

'He's still in the village—'

'Makes you say that?' Hank stopped chewing, finally interested in doing some police work. 'I thought you said he disappeared.'

'Did he drive away or not?' Kate queried.

'No, he didn't.' Price told them that the population of Blanchland was less than a hundred and fifty. Strangers couldn't hide for long. He'd initially thought McKenzie was passing through, except he hadn't driven by. Price was clear about that. He'd kept his eyes on the road beyond the cafe window the whole time, he explained. 'If you know the White Monk, you'll know it's strategically placed to see what's coming and going. I guarantee no cars drove through the village either way. If they had, I'd have seen them.'

'So how come we're hearing about it now?' Kate asked.

Price flushed slightly. 'Your team said you weren't answering your mobile. You or DS Gormley.'

'We were tied up.' Hank moved quickly on: 'Couldn't McKenzie have been eating his scran in his car?'

Price shook his head. 'No, I made it my business to check parked cars in the vicinity before I called the incident room. To have vanished that quickly, he'd have to have gone into one of the houses in the village.'

'Problem is, which one?' Kate's eyes scanned the quiet street outside, wondering if she'd already been seen arriving. 'I don't want to tip him off. Not that he's done anything wrong; it's what might be done to him that worries me.' She refocused on Price. 'The guys after him are serious shit from Glasgow.'

Price grinned.

He knew something she didn't.

'Only one house has been advertised "to let" in the past few weeks,' he said. 'And spookily it was rented by a couple who aren't too friendly, by all accounts. I asked around, people I trust. You're in business, ma'am.'

Chapter Thirty-five

THE VILLAGE WAS silent. The street deserted. Price led the way along the road, pointing out a house at the end of a short terrace. Kate felt as if she was being watched from the houses round the square. There were no curtains twitching, but in villages like these, as Price had already pointed out, people were wary of strangers. Not surprising, given that the police presence would consist only of a drive-through every now and then to show the flag. Rural crime had rocketed since the recession hit. Prigs were having a field day, burgling at will, knowing they'd be long gone by the time the law showed up. Folks round here looked out for each other.

They had to: no bugger else would.

Kate glanced at Price, deciding what action to take. 'Hank and I will take the front door. You take the back. If they do a runner, there's not a lot we can do. If you can try and persuade them not to, I'd appreciate it. If we get in, we'll text you, so you can stand down.' She tapped Hank on the arm. 'Ready?'

He gave a little nod.

Price set off around the side of the property. Kate gave him a few moments to get into position and then knocked at the front door. She couldn't see anything through the window – or hear a sound – but she sensed someone inside. Whether they would answer or not was anyone's guess.

More eyes on her back . . .

Seconds later, the door opened, the chain still on.

'Remember me, Theresa?' Kate peered in through the narrow opening. 'Can we come in, only we don't want to be standing on the doorstep in full view of the whole village, do we? You never know who else might be watching.'

The veiled threat worked.

Satisfied that there was no one else in the street, Theresa undid the chain and the door swung open. She stood back to let them in, glaring at them as they walked past her into the hallway. Dressed in jeans and an old T-shirt, she had no make-up on and seemed to have aged since Kate had last seen her, baggy eyes testament to a sleepless night. Kate shifted her gaze. McKenzie hadn't moved from a fireside chair. He was fit, younger than his years. On the floor next to him was a full-sized and well-used baseball bat.

Hank pointed at it. 'Been having a knock around in the garden, have we?'

McKenzie gave him a hard stare. He sent Theresa to fetch him a drink, the pink tinge to the whites of his eyes suggesting that it wasn't the first that day – maybe a good thing that the bar across the road was closed. Theresa returned with a tumbler of neat whisky, the smell of food drifting in with her as she re-entered the room. There was no music on. No TV. No books or magazines scattered about.

These two weren't relaxing, that was for sure.

'Let's not bugger about, eh?' Kate identified herself and came straight to the point. 'You appreciate that if I found you, other people could.'

McKenzie took a slug of his drink. 'How did you find us?'

She gave him a pointed look. 'I'm asking the questions.'

'You make it sound like we're in danger, Detective Chief Inspector.'

'Tell me about the O'Kanes.'

'Who?' McKenzie asked.

'Cut the crap,' Kate said. 'You know who's after you and so do we. I can see from your face that they mean business. Otherwise you wouldn't be hiding away in the back of beyond now, would you?'

McKenzie dropped the attitude and made a plea for legitimacy. 'I'm clean since I got out of the pokey. If you bastards were doing your jobs properly, you'd know that. I've had my head down, setting up an antiques business. And before you ask, it's genuine. Not that I expect a polis to believe that.'

'He's right,' Theresa added. 'What he did in the past stayed in the past.'

'We're glad to hear it,' the DCI countered, her focus shifting from Theresa back to her boyfriend. 'Whether that is truth or fantasy doesn't concern us – that's not why we're here. You know *exactly* why we're here. You also know who else is interested in your whereabouts and the reason for that. The O'Kanes think you killed their father.' Kate pointed at Theresa. 'Along with her ex.'

'That had nothing to do with me!' McKenzie protested.

'Oh yeah?' Kate said. 'All Brian's fault, was it? Easy to say, when he's not around to defend himself. You should show more respect for the dead, sir.'

Theresa sat down on the arm of McKenzie's chair, slipped her hand into his. 'Arthur paid his dues for the things he did, and that wasn't one of them.'

He pulled away. 'Stop defending me, Theresa. These arseholes aren't listening.'

The room fell quiet.

Swirling his whisky round his glass, McKenzie swigged it off. This was a man under pressure, no matter the impression he was trying to portray. Kate couldn't imagine what Theresa Allen saw in him. Or why she still wanted to be with him after the horrendous events of the past few days. Her sons' remains were lying in a freezer in the city morgue and Kate felt compelled to nail the bastards that put them there. She directed her next comment to McKenzie: 'Whether you killed a rival or not, the O'Kanes are convinced you did. Either way, you're on a loser.'

'Making a run for it isn't going to convince them of your innocence,' Hank added. He looked at the DCI. 'Strange how criminals never think they'll get old, eh, boss? Not such a hard man these days, is he?'

'I was concerned for Theresa,' McKenzie bit back. 'That's why we did off.'

The detectives exchanged a look.

Kate didn't appreciate Hank locking horns with McKenzie when she wanted his cooperation – the most important thing to consider was the man's welfare and that of Theresa Allen. Getting into a punch-up wasn't going to help.

'What did John say when he called you Thursday night?' she asked.

'What are you on about?' McKenzie showed no emotion. 'He didn't call me.'

'Theresa?'

'He didn't call me!'

'One or both of you is lying.' Kate eyeballed Theresa. The hard-nosed cow didn't flinch. The DCI smiled at her, let some time pass. 'Do you remember a DS called Bright?' It was clear from her reaction that she did. 'He's my ex guv'nor, a cracking detective, best I've ever worked with – apart from this guy.' Keeping her eyes on Theresa, Kate thumbed in Hank's direction. 'Bright's a Chief Super now and he's been talking about you—'

'Fondly, I hope.'

'He tells me you were quite something when you were younger. What was it he said . . . ?' She paused, feigning memory loss. 'Ah, now I remember. He said, quote: extremely attractive and not short of admirers from both sides of the law. End quote. It must've come in quite useful for a girl like you, being able to twist men round your little finger. Bet you shagged one or two, to get your own way. Did Brian know what you were up to?'

Theresa smirked, showing her conceit.

McKenzie turned his head towards her.

She didn't return his gaze.

'Bright also said you were a pathological liar,' Kate added.

'I'm not lying.' She'd lost the grin. 'John didn't call me. Check my phone if you want. My sons are dead. Why would I lie?'

'Have it your own way,' Kate said. 'I want you both in a safe house.'

'Do me a favour!' McKenzie scoffed. 'You can keep your poxy safe house – every prig in the area knows where they are! No thanks. If it's all the same to you, Theresa and I will take our chances here – as long as you and the comedian keep your gobs shut, of course. Think you can do that?'

Kate stood her ground, considering his words. She couldn't force him to move or accept her protection. Silly man. 'If you're making your own arrangements, that's fair enough,' she said. 'Don't forget, the O'Kanes are patient souls. They're not on a short fuse like normal scum. You know as well as I do that's not how they operate. They're happy to bide their time. From what I've seen so far, they prefer inflicting pain to shooting folks and getting it over quickly, but we happen to know they own firearms so you'd best be ready for every eventuality.'

'Don't you think he knows that?' Theresa glanced at McKenzie. 'Show them, Arthur. Show them what their bastard mates did to you.'

'That won't be necessary,' Kate said. 'We have friends in high places. Shotts Prison sent me the photos.' She made a show of wincing, then shifted her attention from Theresa to McKenzie. 'That must've been quite scary at the time. Being locked up in there with nowhere to hide. I heard you were lucky to survive. John and Terry weren't so fortunate. Which is why I'm concerned for your safety.'

'My arse!' McKenzie put his drink down on the carpet, his eyes never leaving her. 'We're staying put, so take your partner and piss off.' He put his arm around Theresa. The pressure was clearly getting to her.

Kate eased off as Towner popped into her head. 'I urge you to reconsider,' she said.

The hard man gave an emphatic, 'No.'

'That's the wrong choice.' Kate's eyes settled on Theresa. 'Want to lose the last man standing, do you?'

Silence.

'Well, if you're hell-bent on staying put, I insist you have an officer with you in the house at all times, preferably one who's firearms-trained.' Kate was thinking of Andy Brown. He'd be perfect for the job. Surveillance was his thing, but he was also cleared to carry a gun. She intended to ask Durham force if she could borrow Price until she could organize round-the-clock backup. She liked Price. His instincts were spot on. Besides, the dog could be useful.

'That's all you have, one fucking firearm?' McKenzie let out a hollow laugh. 'You're really selling it to me, hen.'

Ignoring the put-down, Kate told them they were lucky to be getting any protection at all. 'The off-duty officer who spotted you isn't a million miles away. I'm going to ask him to step inside so you know him when he comes to the door with your protection. OK with you?' She pointed at the baseball bat. 'I don't want that thing wrapped around the wrong person's skull.'

Unable to sustain a show of bravado, Theresa buckled as the gravity of the situation closed in on her. She pleaded with McKenzie to accept help. At first, he refused. Then he nodded, reluctantly.

Kate turned to Hank. 'Get Price in here.'

It wasn't ideal but it was better than nothing.

Chapter Thirty-six

EARLY NEXT MORNING, Kate left the house to meet Jo. Officially, she wanted to update her on developments. Unofficially, she wanted to talk to someone other than her immediate colleagues. They met at the eastern end of Jesmond Dene so they could get some fresh air before driving into town together. Jo's car was in for a service. It was a lovely morning: sunny, windy, warm enough not to wear a coat. They walked the length of the wooded valley and sat down on rocks by the waterfall.

Jo handed Kate a croissant and a small bottle of fresh orange juice.

Kate smiled as she took it. Al fresco breakfasts were Jo's speciality. *Al fresco anything, in fact.* Kate's phone rang, piercing the silence of the dene, an unwelcome interruption so early in the day. It was Andy Brown. She spoke to him for a few moments and then hung up, her mind off her pastry and back on the job.

'All quiet in Blanchland?' Jo asked.

Kate nodded. 'Andy's relief arrived.'

'You got lucky yesterday.'

'With Price? Yes. Nice to know someone had their eyes and ears open for a change. Serendipitous isn't a word I can often use in relation to any incident of mine. If Theresa and McKenzie had chosen a different village, it could have been months before we found them. I now have two priorities: their security and finding the O'Kanes.'

'How was Theresa?'

'Not good.' Kate pulled a piece off her croissant and popped it into her mouth.

'And you?'

Kate stopped chewing. 'I've been better.'

'I can see that. Did you sleep?' When she didn't answer, Jo turned to face her, concerned that she was getting the brush-off. Despite their break-up, she'd always been there for Kate, in good times and bad, always willing to listen or offer advice. 'You going to tell me what's bothering you?'

Looking into the pool beneath the waterfall, Kate sighed. 'You don't want to know.'

'But I do.'

'Better you don't. I've done something I'm not very proud of.'

'Kate?' Jo put a comforting hand on her forearm. 'You're hurting. What's wrong?'

Laying her hand on top of Jo's, Kate stroked it gently. She didn't pull away. Kate was desperate to pour her heart out and confess all, but she couldn't. Not just for her sake, for Hank's too. He'd never forgive her if she blabbed to anyone about their ill-fated trip to Whitby. The truth was, she hadn't slept. She'd spent the whole night tossing and turning. Every time she closed her eyes, she saw Towner, heard the death rattle.

'What is it?' Jo asked.

If only she could answer. But how *could* she bang on about her precious career – the one she'd placed above all else, including Jo? The career she might lose if her gung-ho escapade was discovered. Kate dropped her gaze. She needed disapproval. All she got from Hank was support she felt she didn't deserve. Jo was studying her, trying to work out what was wrong, probably wondering why on earth she was looking so glum when the case was going so well. The team had identified the perpetrators of two, possibly three murders. Now all they had to do was find them. Not even that thought lifted her spirits with Towner's death dragging her down.

'Don't freeze me out, Kate. Talk to me . . . maybe I can help.'

'Not this time,' Kate said softly.

'Why not?'

'You just can't.'

'Oh, for God's sake! You're acting like you killed someone!'

The lump in Kate's throat grew bigger. She threw the rest of her pastry into the water, watched a couple of ducks fight over it, an explanation for her depressed mood on the tip of her tongue. Then Hank's voice barged its way into her head: *You went off-piste. No point losing your bottle now . . . get a grip!*

'Let's go.' Kate got up and walked away.

BACK AT HER office, the guilt over Towner's death continued to gnaw at her. Giving instructions to the team not to disturb her for the next quarter of an hour, under any circumstances, Kate logged on to her computer, typing two words into the search field. The homepage of the *Whitby Gazette* loaded, and there it was, dead centre of the Local section, just as she suspected it would be: news of a recent RTA. Under the headline – Fatal Road Traffic Accident – was the report of Towner's death.

Emergency service personnel were called to the scene of a traffic accident yesterday after a man was knocked down by a car on North Terrace. We understand that the casualty was not from the area. He was pronounced dead on arrival at Scarborough Hospital. His identity is not being released, pending further enquiries. Police are appealing for witnesses with any information to contact Whitby police on 101 quoting incident number NCL40965270812.

Oh God!

In her head, Kate broke the number down. The last part was easy: 270812 was merely the date of the incident. The middle part would be the force-wide incident number, the FWIN, but it was the prefix letters that worried her. She'd given Towner's name only and yet the police had already established that he was from Newcastle, unless the lettering was randomly generated, and she didn't believe that.

Palming her brow, Kate feared repercussions, both personal and professional. If she was mentioned by any one of the many witnesses, would the police come looking? Not unless she'd been seen arguing with Towner minutes before he died. Then they might. And not just for her, for Hank too – and he'd done nothing wrong. Would she be able to persuade the powers that be that he wasn't involved off grid with an unregistered snout? Debatable. He stood to lose his job. Would he ever forgive her? Would his family? Scooping up the internal phone, she rang him, asking him to join her in her office right away.

ALTHOUGH HANK HAD been busy with something else, he reacted immediately to the urgency in her voice, arriving at her door seconds later, anticipating trouble. Despite the open window, he noticed a whiff of nicotine in the air. She must be worried. It was years since he'd seen her smoke. He didn't mention it. He just took a seat and listened patiently as she explained about the press coverage, the fact that police were talking to witnesses, appealing for information. It was all basic procedure. If she'd been in her right mind, she'd know that. Instead, it seemed to have added to her woes, increasing her agitation and sense of foreboding.

'Is that all?' He relaxed. 'Jesus! I thought from the way you were talking that you'd received blue forms. Right now, white coats are more in order, wouldn't you say? You keep going like this, you'll end up on the funny farm.'

'I'm so sorry.' She'd completely missed his attempt to cheer her up and calm her down. 'I thought at the beginning of the enquiry that things couldn't get much worse.'

'They can,' he said. 'And they will, unless you hold your bottle.'

'What if they suspect—'

'Suspect what?' He leaned forward, dropped his voice. Looking deep into her tired eyes, he spoke slowly, assuredly. 'Kate, listen to me: aside from the two of us, nobody knows fuck-all. There's nothing to worry about. You've got to stop fretting. No one is going to suggest you were running after Towner when he was hit. You weren't. I know that, and so does everyone on that street. I told you before, it was an unfortunate RTA. End of story. Keep it in perspective. You could do with some downtime. Why don't you go off home—'

'What, and talk to the walls?'

'Just for a couple of hours.'

'I don't want to go home. I want to stay here, with you.'

'OK, OK. So stay.' Hank sighed. His amazing boss sounded like a child. He wanted to reach out and give her a big hug but he knew that in her present frame of mind she'd only push him away. In the absence of anything better to do, he got up and put the kettle on, asking if she wanted tea or coffee.

'Whatever, I don't care. What if my name comes up?' She continued to agonize over every detail. It was so unlike her. With his back to her, Hank shut his eyes and then opened them again, trying to decide what to do. 'Hank? Did you hear me?'

'How can your name come up?' he said. 'No one knows who you are. You were here on duty with me, weren't you?'

Hank knew she was in a very bad place, but he had no idea how to help her snap out of it. Maybe Jo could talk some sense into her. No, he couldn't tell Jo. Kate would never speak to him again. He had to think of something else. For now he got on with making the tea.

As KATE MADE her way to her car, Hank caught up with her. She'd noticed him keeping an eye on her all afternoon, but they had been in with the team and nothing more had been said in relation to Towner or their flight from Whitby after his death. The issue, though, continued to gnaw at her. Like subtext, it lay just beneath the surface, waiting to rear its ugly head, fooling no one. She just couldn't let it go.

'You really think I'm making too much of it?' Kate took in his nod as he stopped walking and turned to face her. She could tell that he was bluffing. She hated all that macho crap. He wasn't fooling her. He looked as anxious as she felt. 'I'm not, you know. Quarrelling with Towner in a busy street in full view of the public was stupid. It might cost me my career, Hank. I couldn't live with myself if it also cost you yours.'

'Kate, stop! That was ages before the accident.'

'What the fuck am I going to do?'

'You'll be fine. People row in the street every day. No one gives a shit.'

Dropping her head, Kate tried to suppress her agitation, tried desperately to justify her actions and save herself from spiralling into a deep depression. She'd seen it happen to a lot of officers in her time. Hank was right: she had to get her act in gear.

She looked up. 'Thanks for looking out for me, Hank.'

'Hey, we're a team. Who else would I look out for?'

They walked on.

Kate tried for a smile but didn't make it. In some ways it was worse because he was there, because he knew. If she'd been on her own, maybe she'd have come to her senses, kept her gob tightly shut and walked away. *Maybe.* Any copper worth their salt would. They'd say nothing to nobody. They would never have given it houseroom. If they had seen it, done it, they'd have left it alone. There were nice people in the world to worry about and Towner wasn't one of them. He was a good-for-nothing lowlife . . .

No, Kate thought, as they reached her car. He was more than that. Underneath his alcoholism and bad life choices, he'd been a pathetically sad man who'd needed help. She'd let him down.

Chapter Thirty-seven

THE WEEK DRAGGED on with no further developments – at least, not in relation to the enquiry, and not in Whitby, where Towner's death had been written off as a tragic accident. Hurricane Isaac had thrown all it had at New Orleans, Newcastle United managed a one nil win over Atromitos FC in their first European home game for more than five years, forest fires had ravaged large parts of Marbella, but, despite a force-wide search, the Glasgow thugs Kate was hunting had evaded capture. The investigation had ground to a halt.

The last day of August was dull and grey, much like the mood in a meeting room at Fantasy Island – the nickname for force HQ. It was day eight of the enquiry and Bright wanted answers. He'd summoned the A Team – Kate, Hank and Naylor – to provide them. The table around which they were seated was littered with papers, used coffee cups and all manner of other stuff, including the Detective Chief Super's favourite Garibaldi biscuits, laid on by Kate in an effort to soften him up.

It wasn't working.

Bright's tone was harsh. 'You must have something!'

'The bastards are lying low,' Kate said. 'I wish I had better news, guv. But there's none to give.'

'You've done everything in your power to find them?'

'Everything. I think it's time to talk to the press.'

'Hold on,' he said. 'Let's not get too hasty. What's the position with McKenzie and Theresa Allen?'

'Sitting pretty, I'd imagine.' Kate sighed. 'I appreciate that babysitting those two was my idea, but it's tying up physical and financial resources, placing a hell of a burden on the team, not to mention the budget. Taxpayers shouldn't have to bear the brunt of keeping them in their love nest for much longer. Besides, I'm bored, and so are the rest of the squad. I want to be more proactive.'

'What are you proposing?'

'As I said to you on the phone, there's no longer any reason to keep the O'Kanes' identities from the media. It's time we took the initiative.'

Bright shifted his gaze to Naylor. 'You happy with that, Ron?'

'If that's the consensus round the table, I'm not going to argue. Hank? Any thoughts?'

'I'm with Kate on this, guv. We need to flush them out. We've got nowt from Strathclyde or Lothian and Borders forces. We considered going north, but there's really no point. There have been no sightings of the brothers in Glasgow or Edinburgh. The police up there think they're hiding out on our patch. We've been hoping they would come out to play, but it just hasn't happened—'

'They have to come out sometime,' Kate said. 'They've got to eat. I suggest we go public as soon as possible. We need help. Let's face it, we've got bugger all else. By the way, Theresa is offering a reward of twenty K.'

'I didn't know that,' Hank said. 'How very motherly of her.'

'Never underestimate the power of cash,' Bright said. 'Or the power of Theresa Allen. She knows the score, that one. She also knows that a high reward will bring a weasel out of his hovel to talk to us. We need information and we're not going to find it sitting on our arses twiddling our thumbs. Have you no snouts you can lean on?' He was talking to Kate.

Blankly, she returned his stare.

'No, boss,' Hank answered for her. 'None that are talking, anyway. Prigs are understandably nervous. They're saying nowt, and I can't say I blame them. Kate's right: maybe we'll fare better with the general public.'

Kate felt hot and hoped it didn't show. 'While we're on the subject of press conferences, Bethany Miller's parents presented themselves at the station the day before yesterday demanding the opportunity to make a televised appeal.'

'Maybe they should,' Bright said.

Kate gave him a hard stare. 'Not while I'm SIO.'

'Why not? They've lost a daughter.'

'Because I have nothing but contempt for them. Their sole interest seems to be getting themselves on the telly to show the world how much they're grieving when they're doing nothing of the sort. They threw that poor kid out in the dead of winter without a second thought. Despite their . . .' She used her fingers as inverted commas. '"Deep concern" over her welfare, they didn't even file a missing-persons report. I'm not letting them wail to the cameras for sympathy. Their misfortune is their own doing.'

'OK, if you feel that strongly.'

'I do.' Kate paused. 'Guv, I think you should know that they've gone home to Barrow-in-Furness threatening to make a formal complaint.'

Bright shrugged. 'It's not your first. Don't suppose it'll be your last.'

Thanking him, Kate got to her feet and gathered up her papers, exchanging a brief glance with Hank. *How true that was.*

ARRANGING THE PRESS conference for two o'clock, Kate called Andy Brown from headquarters. There was nothing happening in Blanchland, but McKenzie and Theresa Allen had made him very welcome. Understandably nervous of having an armed officer in the house, they had eventually relaxed enough to manage a few laughs. They played cards to pass the time, even caught the odd movie.

'OK,' Kate said. 'Stay alert.'

'Will do, boss.'

'Put Theresa on, will you?'

The phone went down on a hard surface. Kate could hear Brown calling out Theresa's name. A few seconds later, she came on the line sounding out of breath, as if she'd run to the phone. 'Has something happened?' she asked. 'Andy said you want to talk to me.'

Kate was quick to reassure her. 'There's nothing new to report. I just wanted to make you aware that there'll be an appeal on local television channels tonight for witnesses and information in connection with the case. I didn't want you turning on without warning and thinking there's something afoot.'

'You haven't found those bastards then?'

'No, that's why we're going live.'

'Are you even trying?' She sounded stressed.

'We're doing our very best. The idea is to flush them out of their hiding place, assuming they're still in the area.'

'I'm not going in front of the cameras—'

'I wouldn't ask you to. Don't worry about that. It'll be me, DS Gormley and possibly our guv'nor.'

'Bright?' Theresa asked, a little too quickly. Her reaction made Kate wonder if anything had ever happened between them. Despite his devotion to his late wife, he'd always had a reputation as a ladies' man. Whether or not that was justified depended on who was doing the talking. The DCI had never witnessed him playing away.

'No,' she corrected her. 'I meant my new guv'nor, Detective Superintendent Naylor. We, or rather I, will appeal for witnesses to come forward. Then we'll warn the general public not to approach the O'Kanes if they see them. It's as simple as that. There may be questions from the press – I might answer them, I might not. I wanted to make you aware of it so you don't read anything into it that isn't there. I've told you everything there is to know. It's a press conference, nothing more.'

'Thanks for keeping me informed.'

'You still happy to put up the reward we discussed?'

'More than happy.'

Thanking her, Kate hung up and then made a similar call to Bethany Miller's parents. They weren't best pleased to hear that the planned press conference did not include the two of them. Mr Miller spent the next half-hour haranguing her, telling her that a letter was already winging its way to the Chief Constable, that she'd better enjoy her time on the TV because it would probably be her last appearance in front of a camera, in or out of uniform.

By the time she'd put the phone down, Kate was punchy. Picking up her pen, she began jotting down the salient points to be covered at the conference. She'd no sooner started than the phone rang. She scooped it up, frustrated with yet another interruption.

'Yes?' She didn't even try to hide her irritation.

'Hi, it's me,' Jo said quietly. 'Can you talk?'

'Not really, I have a press release to write.'

'Kate, let me help. I'm worried about you.'

'Don't be. It's nothing I can't handle. Anyway, it's sorted. There's no longer a problem.'

'Are you sure? I got the impression that you were—'

'Look, I shouldn't have said anything, OK? To be honest, I wish I hadn't. Leave it be, will you?'

'Fine!' The line went dead.

It was times like this Kate hated her job.

Chapter Thirty-eight

CAMERAS FLASHED. THE large conference room was filled with the sound of shutters going off in quick succession as the DCI was shown to her seat in the centre of a long table, the force logo at her back, Gormley on one side, Naylor on the other, a microphone in front of her. The room was busting at the seams, not a spare seat to be found. Everyone facing Kate was sporting a VISITOR PASS lanyard.

Directly in front of Kate was a man she recognized: Ian Payne from ITV's local news channel. Next to him was a BBC news presenter whose name she couldn't recall, and behind them were journalists from several national newspapers. Further back, she could see representatives from the local rags: *Northern Echo*, *Newcastle Chronicle*, *Evening Gazette* and *Hexham Courant*. It was standing-room only at the rear.

Kate waited for the hum in the room to die down, keen to get the conference over with. Tapping his microphone, an admin officer called for order. Instructing everyone to turn off mobile phones or switch to silent mode, he checked that they were all in receipt of press packs containing details of both victims and suspects.

Satisfied that he'd covered everything, he sat down, giving Kate the nod.

Thanking everyone for attending at such short notice, Kate introduced herself as the SIO in charge of the case they were assembled to discuss. 'Ladies and gentlemen, I asked you here this afternoon as a result of serious matters that have occurred in our force area in the last few days. You're aware that the body of John Allen was found on the Silverlink Industrial Estate in the early hours of Friday, twenty-fourth August. Shortly afterwards, the body of his brother Terence Allen was discovered at the Royal Victoria Infirmary. A murder enquiry was launched into both deaths.' The DCI paused, giving the reporters time to make notes. Glancing to her right, she noticed Detective Chief Superintendent Bright sneak into the room quietly. Their eyes met briefly, then she carried on. 'There is a third victim, Bethany Miller, a fifteen-year-old girl from Barrow-in-Furness. I must stress that at present I am unable to say for sure whether this third death is linked to the other two. What I can tell you is that she knew John and Terry Allen. Before I say anything more, on behalf of Northumbria Police I'd like to extend our condolences to the families and friends of all three victims.'

The press officer stood up. She wore a figure-hugging tailored suit, hair tied back and too much slap, the badge on her large left breast spelling out her name: Constance Blackett. Looking straight to the television camera crews positioned at the rear of the room, she made sure she got her sound bites in . . .

'I must point out that this incident is one of the most harrowing in the history of Northumbria Police and one of the worst Detective Chief Inspector Daniels and the Murder Investigation Team has ever had to deal with. I'd like to commend the detectives involved for their dedication and commitment in trying to apprehend those responsible.'

Inviting Kate to carry on, she received a thousand-yard stare in return. Blackett dropped her head, unable to face the message being transmitted across the room: *Sit down and keep it shut.* Kate hated the way these conferences were handled, especially the showboating by civilian press officials and senior officers trying to make a name for themselves. She'd make it her business to have a word with Ms Look-How-Important-I-Am-Blackett later.

The media were getting twitchy.

'My enquiries have revealed the names of two Scottish men who may be responsible for the offences outlined,' Kate continued. 'They are Craig and Finn O'Kane – thirty and thirty-one years old respectively.' She pointed at images pinned to the wall, then turned to face the bank of cameras in front of her, pausing a moment to get everyone's attention. 'Take a good look at these photographs. Have you seen these men in your local pub, nightclub, newsagents or grocery store? It's imperative that we trace and interview them.'

Glancing at the bullet points of her press release, she added, 'I'd like to make it absolutely clear that no one should approach these men. If anyone has any information on their current or past whereabouts – particularly where they might have been since late on the evening of Thursday the twenty-third of August when they were last seen at the QC Club – I'd urge them to contact their nearest police station or the incident room – or any police officer. The telephone number will be given out at the end.'

The press officer again: 'We have a large team of detectives waiting to take your calls.'

Kate wanted to punch her lights out. She had six detectives and four civilians waiting to take calls. Bearing in mind several hundred might come in within the hour, that was hardly adequate. On her right, Bright rolled his eyes, displeased with the unnecessary interruption at a pivotal moment in the process.

A hand went up. 'Chief Inspector?'

'I'll take questions in a moment,' Kate said as more flashes went off. 'It's vital that readers and/or viewers understand that these men are capable of extreme violence and *must not* be approached.' She waited for the scribbling to stop. 'I'll take your questions now.'

Pre-empting a question from the woman who'd interrupted her, the DCI looked the other way, gesturing towards another journalist she knew quite well: Gillian Garvey, crime reporter for the *Journal* – ex Reporter of the Year – a woman with her finger very much on the pulse of the city. She was bloody good at her job. As Hank had pointed out on more than one occasion, she had more sources that the Mississippi.

In the crowded room, a phone went off at exactly the same time as the one in Kate's pocket began to vibrate. Apologizing, Garvey drew an iPhone 5 out of her bag, quickly checked the display and then turned it off. When the reporter raised her head, her expression sent a warning to the DCI. It was one she'd seen many times before: *triumph*. A statement rather than a question was already forming on her lips . . .

'I've been informed that one of the men you're after is having a laugh with his mates in a Glasgow pub, Detective Chief Inspector.' Garvey spoke matter-of-factly, as if it was of no consequence, knowing the reaction it was likely to receive. Like the aftermath of an explosion, silence descended on the room. Then she twisted the knife further, eyes like lasers on the DCI. 'Instead of standing here talking to us, shouldn't you be locking him up?'

Trying not to show her emotions, Kate checked her own mobile phone. *Snap.* A text: Finn O'Kane spotted entering rough pub in

Glasgow. Officers dispatched to check it out. As she focused back on Garvey, it was plain to everyone assembled that she was far from happy. Momentarily wrong-footed, she covered the microphone and bent down. Using her hand to shield her mouth, she whispered to Hank: 'How is it that Gillian has a hotline to Strathclyde Police and no one's telling me about it?'

'She has more money than we do,' he whispered back.

'Sort it,' she hissed.

He got up and left the room.

All eyes were on Garvey. The smug journalist was milking her moment, enjoying herself at the DCI's expense. She knew fine well Kate wouldn't/couldn't tell her where to get off with an audience and cameras rolling. They were like Alpha females battling for supremacy in full view of the assembled press, not to mention Naylor and Bright.

Kate was losing.

'Before I entered this room,' she said, 'there was no information on either suspect's whereabouts. I checked.' Her eyes never leaving her opponent, she continued: 'Can you tell me how you came by that information, Ms Garvey?'

'An anonymous source.' She was almost grinning. 'A very reliable source.'

'Detective Chief Inspector, is it true that one of the victims was chained to the underside of a vehicle?' another reporter asked. 'I think the public have a right to know if there's a couple of madmen on the loose—'

'That kind of wild speculation isn't helpful, sir.' Kate moved on. 'Next question?'

Another hand went up, this one belonging to Andrew Jackman, a Scottish hack who had been around as long as Kate could remember. Balding, big smoker, sallow complexion – the man looked positively ill.

'Yes, Mr Jackman?'

'Is it right that Bethany Miller was working as a prostitute?' he asked.

'I have no information of that nature.' Kate had to restrain herself. This was a child he was talking about. Why didn't he show some respect? There was no way she would admit or deny the fact that Bethany was on the game. Her mother and father weren't in the room, but they would be watching at home. Whatever her opinion of them as parents, Kate felt for them. How hard must it be to hear your daughter referred to as a prostitute on or off national TV? 'As far as I'm aware, this unfortunate child was caught up in what I can only describe as a violent feud between rival gangs. Next question.'

But Jackman wouldn't let it go. 'It was my understanding that she was a working girl.' He used the old cliché: no smoke without fire. 'Is there no truth in it then?'

'Whatever information you think you have did not come from my office,' Kate spat the words out, eyes boring into Jackman. 'I think you should go and check your facts. Or better still, if you have any information about Bethany Miller, feel free to contact the incident room and make a statement to that effect. I will personally see that you are accommodated.'

He smirked – they both knew what she meant by that.

They both knew she was lying.

A male voice, unidentified: 'It sounds as though you have no leads, Chief Inspector.'

This was not going well.

Kate took a sip of water. More cameras went off and she was suddenly on the back foot, her awful week getting worse by the minute. Before she had time to respond, someone asked another question.

'Can you reassure the public that they're safe in their beds?'

'All I am prepared to say at this stage is that the motive for these offences appears to be personal. I have no reason to believe that the general public has anything to fear from these men, unless they are challenged. We believe the motive was revenge, the details of which I cannot disclose at this time.'

Kate tucked her hair behind her ear as other questions were fired in quick succession, the first from ITV News presenter, Ian Payne. 'What advice would you give members of the public who might have knowledge of the O'Kane brothers?'

'They should call 101 and officers will be dispatched immediately to take a statement.'

'And if they actually have them under observation?'

'They should dial 999 and they'll get an emergency response.'

Garvey dropped another bombshell. 'I heard that torture was used.'

Looking straight at her, Kate came clean: 'We strongly suspect that the men we want to talk to were after information and were prepared to torture their victims to death in order to get it.' She looked away, addressing the whole room. 'As I said, these were violent crimes, which is why we've asked for your help in tracing those responsible. We have full cooperation with Strathclyde, Lothian and Borders and other neighbouring forces. This matter is our priority. These men will be found.'

Chapter Thirty-nine

HANK WAS WAITING outside the conference room. Kate rolled her eyes as she barged through the door and went straight to the ladies. She turned on the tap and splashed cold water on her face. As she grabbed a paper towel, Press Officer Constance Blackett entered. Kate swung round, let her have it with both barrels, telling the silly cow never to interrupt her again in full-flight.

The woman rushed off.

Hank had heard every word.

'That was a bit harsh,' he said, as Kate joined him in the corridor. 'You can add her to your list of complainants!'

'Oh, you think so? Like I give a damn. You'd better ring Julie and warn her we're off to Glasgow.'

'What, now?'

'Yes, now.' As he fumbled in his pocket for his phone, out of the corner of her eye, Kate saw Gillian Garvey a few metres further down the corridor. She was leaning against the wall, talking on her mobile. Leaving Hank's side, Kate approached the journalist. Round two. Different opponent. 'A word, if I may.'

Garvey hung up, telling the person on the other end she'd call them back.

'What the hell is wrong with you?' Kate glared at her.

'Just doing my job, Kate. No need to take it personally.'

'Oh yeah?'

'Boss?' Ending his call, Hank tried to attract Kate's attention. 'We need to get going.'

'Wait!' She glowered at him before turning back to Garvey. 'You're experienced enough to know the rules, Gillian. It's basic procedure to turn off your phone. You obviously don't know what silent mode is. Next time you want my help, you'll find out. That special relationship we have? Forget it. You've pulled one too many strokes and I don't appreciate being made to look stupid in front of the national press, my boss and the head of fucking CID! I'm sick of your stupid games—'

'Boss?' Hank thumbed towards the door. 'We've got to go.'

'When I'm ready,' she barked. 'Wait in the car.'

He held his ground, sending her a silent message that another public row wasn't a good idea. She glared at him, prepared to order him out if necessary. She was exhausted, the stress of working flat out for the past week without any time off finally getting to her. Towner's accident and her spat with Jo hadn't helped. Gillian Garvey's antics were the tipping point.

A sharp tap on her shoulder made her turn around.

She came face-to-face with Bright.

Looking beyond her, he smiled at Garvey. 'Well done, Gillian. You pipped us to the post again, I see. Give us a minute, will you?'

He glanced over his shoulder. 'You too, Hank.' Then, to Kate: 'A word in your shell-like, if I may? My office.'

'We need to go, guv,' Hank said. 'The lads from Strathclyde have been on the blower—' He stopped talking mid-sentence, a warning look from Bright telling him to back off.

Garvey saw it too, made her excuses and left.

Kate's brow creased. If Bright couldn't say what was on his mind in front of Hank, it must be serious. If he was angry with her, or disappointed with her performance, so what? That made two of them. Surely he could see that she was in a hurry. With the sighting of Finn O'Kane in Glasgow, she was desperate to get a shift on.

Garvey could wait. For now.

Acutely aware of Hank's eyes drilling a hole in the side of her head, she glanced in his direction. 'I'll meet you at the car.'

Concern spread over his face.

Kate realized then that he'd tried warning her, that Bright must've been standing there the whole time she was yelling at Garvey. Not the way he'd want his star pupil to behave to a member of the press. A bollocking was private. As the Senior Investigating Officer of a high-profile case, she should've had more sense.

The Detective Chief Superintendent remained tightlipped as he led her down the corridor, a walk that seemed longer than usual. She felt much like a schoolchild being taken to the headmaster for a telling off. Instructing Ellen Crawford, his PA, that they weren't to be disturbed, he entered his office first and sat down, inviting Kate to do the same, meeting her eyes across his desk.

After what seemed like ages, she felt obligated to fill the silence with an apology. 'Guv, I'm sorry about the press conference. I let Gillian get the better of me. And that silly cow from the press office is as bad.' Kate shook her head. 'The woman is a complete liability. Someone should have a word with her.' She could feel herself blushing. 'Other than me, I mean. I'm sorry. I shouldn't have barked at her like that. I don't know what got into me.'

'That's not why I wanted to see you.'

'Oh?' Kate relaxed.

Thank God!

For a moment, she thought she'd misread the situation. He'd been meaning to tell her something for days. She was dying to know what it was and hoped that it was better news than his intense expression suggested.

She'd seen happier undertakers.

'What the hell were you doing in Whitby?' he asked.

The question winded her like a body blow. The room suddenly got smaller, the mere mention of the town sending shock waves to her brain. The man she revered so highly had caught her out. She felt hot, unable to think straight, and hoped it didn't show. Her response was pathetic. 'When, guv?'

'Oh, so you weren't there?'

'Sorry,' she said. 'You've lost me.'

His jaw bunched, demonstrating his irritation with her. Kate studied his face. There was no humour in his eyes, no sarky smile on his lips. His favourite DCI wasn't feeling the love. Wasn't feeling anything. She was staggered by this development – totally numbed by what might come next. He wouldn't tolerate any more nonsense.

She eyeballed him. 'How did you know?'

'Hank told me.'

'No he didn't. How did you find out?'

'You think chief superintendents have nothing better to do than sit at their desks with their feet up, drinking tea and bending paperclips?' He picked up his *Journal* and chucked it at her. 'I read the newspapers, Kate. Suspiciously, an old informant of yours was run over while crossing the road in North Yorkshire on the very day you and Hank were tied up doing extensive enquiries out of area and couldn't be contacted. I put two and two together and made four . . . because I'm a *detective*. I am still a detective, you know, even though I haven't got a proper job. Was Alan Townsend registered?'

'He's not an informant now.'

'He's not anything now!' Bright had fire in his eyes. 'I asked you a question that demands an answer. Was. He. Registered?'

'No, guv.'

'Did you tell Naylor where you were going?'

Kate shook her head.

'Why not?'

'I needed information!' She stood up, began pacing up and down. 'Guv, I did what I thought was right. When people ring up with information, I don't question it, I act on it. You taught me that, in case you'd forgotten.'

'Sit down! And don't get arsy with me.'

'I'm not!' Retaking her seat, she sucked in a big breath, realizing that she was in deep trouble. 'Towner wanted to meet in that location. I thought he sounded serious enough to pursue it. So much so that I was prepared to get in my car, drive all the way down there and fly by the seat of my pants. When I saw him, he was frightened. Terrified. I knew he had information to give and when I mentioned the O'Kanes, he got up and ran away. Bang! The car hit him a split-second later.'

'Jesus!' Bright's eyes found the window. His expression was grave when he turned to face her. 'What have I told you about breaking the rules? I've warned you so many times to run things by me first. You were out of the force area, pursuing someone who is now dead. Tell me he didn't run from you.'

Kate studied her shoes.

'Did you run after him?'

'Yes.' Kate's answer was spontaneous and emphatic. 'Quarter of an hour before, not when he died.'

'Come on!' He was shaking his head. 'You don't expect me to buy that!'

'It's the truth, guv, I swear.'

'Any witnesses?'

'Plenty.'

'Is that code for Hank?' Bright snorted. 'He'd say anything to save your ass.'

'He wasn't even there.'

'Do not lie to me!'

'He wasn't! He came along afterwards. I promise you, he knows nothing about it. This is my neck on the line, not his!'

He shook his head. 'You and your damned loyalty—'

'You've had your fair share of that from me too, guv. I've saved your ass once or twice.'

There was an awkward silence between them, a moment of high tension as they stared each other out. In the days he was her guv'nor, he'd always been in her face – but equally he'd always supported her. They were as close as it was possible to be. Yet Kate knew she'd overstepped the line once too often. He could go either way. He could help her or feed her to the IPCC. What she said next would determine which one of those options it was going to be.

Chapter Forty

'I WASN'T CHASING him, guv. I swear. I wasn't intending to arrest him. He ran away because he was stupid. He called me that afternoon. I had reason to believe that he had vital information in relation to a triple murder. He blurted out his location and hung up. What else could I have done? He's given me stuff before. Remember the Jackson case? *His* intel . . . the botched jewellery heist in 2008 when the owner was shot? *His* intel.'

Her former guv'nor's expression hadn't softened any.

Kate couldn't maintain eye contact. A lump as big as Texas formed in her throat. Her precious career was as good as over. Resigned to take the consequences of her actions, she waited. She thought about apologizing and decided she'd be wasting her breath. Tears stung the back of her eyes. She was only just holding on. Then suddenly she lost her composure. She hadn't been herself since Towner died. She'd been horrible to Hank, to Jo. Bright was the only thing standing between her position and a first-class ticket to the office of Professional Standards – or the dole queue.

'I realize there'll be an enquiry,' she said.

'Who said anything about an enquiry?' Bright looked almost as upset as she felt. 'It never happened. Neither did this conversation.'

She tried to thank him but couldn't speak. She wanted to yell at him and hug him at the same time. He was offering forgiveness that in her heart she didn't feel she deserved. She had great people round her and yet she pushed them away, time and again, when they reached out to give her a hand.

She was an emotional wreck.

The week's events kept flashing through her head: John Allen wrapped round the wheels of a Mercedes van, his brother's severed fingers, Bethany's head caved in. The thumping sound as the car hit Towner, his hand in hers as he slipped away, Jo's angry face, Gillian Garvey's smirk, the look of disapproval on Bright's face right now. His mouth was moving but she hadn't heard a word.

'Are you even listening to me?' He sat forward, placed his elbows on his desk and linked his hands together to support his chin. For a moment he said nothing, showed no emotion whatsoever, then his eyes took in a photograph of his late wife before coming to rest on Kate. 'Remember the night I made an arse of myself?'

He was referring to *that* night. It was before Stella died. She was horribly disabled but he was suffering too, struggling to cope with the demands of his job while caring for her at home. Late one night, the consequences of his refusal to allow her to end her days in hospital hit him like a brick when she asked him to put a stop to her pain permanently. At his request, Kate had gone round to help him over that traumatic event. In a moment of weakness, he'd asked her to spend the night with him.

Of course she remembered – how could she forget?

'Is there a point to this, guv?'

They had agreed never to mention it again, another thing that never happened. Relieved that she'd keep her rank for a while longer, Kate's detective mind was already focusing on the O'Kane sighting in Glasgow.

She checked her watch. 'Hank's waiting, may I go?'

Bright's jaw clenched. 'You're a piece of work sometimes, you know that? I bet Townsend was terrified of you.' He paused. In all the years they had worked together they had always had a love/hate relationship. Right at this moment, it was oscillating between the two. Leaning back in his chair, he crossed his arms over his chest and let out a long sigh. 'My *point* is one you'll take on board, if you have any sense. I was in a bad place then, Kate. You helped me out and I'd like to return the favour. With the benefit of hindsight, I can see that it was the lowest point in my life. I think this is yours—'

'With all due respect, that's bollocks, guv. I'm busy, that's all.'

'Sit down!'

She did as she was told – for once.

He cleared his throat. 'You don't make it easy for people. You're the very best detective I know, but I could do without the aggro. I'm warning you. This is the very last chance you get. Do I make myself clear?'

'Yes, guv.'

'When this case is over, take some leave. Whether you're willing to accept it or not, you've hit rock bottom. To be perfectly honest, I think you're unfit for duty. That opinion will stay in this office while I decide what to do with you. Anyone else would be off the case and handing in their warrant card. Now, get the hell out of my sight.'

Of all the things he could've said to her, 'unfit for duty' was the most hurtful. From the look on his face, he knew it too. Without another word, Kate walked out, closing the door quietly behind her. As she passed his office window, she was weeping.

Chapter Forty-one

HANK BINNED HIS cigarette when he saw her leave the building. Even at fifty metres away he could tell by her gait and the way her head was down that her meeting with Bright had been a difficult one. She was ashen when she arrived at the car. Not knowing how to handle the situation, he didn't say much, just held out his hand.

'Gimme your keys,' he said. 'I'm driving.'

'Thanks.' It was almost a whisper. 'Get me out of here.'

Without argument, she handed her keys over and climbed into the passenger seat. Unheard of. Driving was one of the pleasures of her life. She was never happier than behind the wheel, except maybe on her motorcycle. Placing her mobile on the dash, she strapped herself in. Hank reversed out of their parking place, glancing at her as he used his wing mirror.

She'd filled up, was fighting to maintain self-control. This was worrying. He'd seen her upset before – frequently angry – but never like this. Their eyes met briefly and she looked away, telling him she'd explain on the way. Enlightenment wasn't forthcoming. For miles and miles she sat motionless, staring through the windscreen at the road ahead, deep in her own thoughts, until he felt compelled to break the ice.

'What's the tale with Garvey?' he asked.

Preoccupied with what had occurred in Bright's office she seemed confused by the question.

'Gillian,' he pushed. 'What was all that garbage in the press conference?'

'Nothing important,' Kate said. 'She got a message on her bloody phone, same time as I did. She's got her hooks into someone in Strathclyde force. Wonder what it cost her to receive that timely tip-off?'

'She was right though.' Hank used his indicator, accelerated to overtake a tractor and then pulled in.

'About what?'

'She was only doing her job.'

'Yeah, well there are ways and ways. Shafting other people isn't one of them, even if she is a fucking journo.'

'Kate, calm down.'

She went quiet for a while and then swivelled in her seat to face him. When he looked at her she was visibly upset. 'I dropped myself right in the shit, Hank. The guv'nor knows about Whitby.'

'What? Tell me you're joking!' He took in the shake of her head. 'You never admitted it?'

'I lost it, Hank. I'm sorry.'

Oh fantastic. That was both their jobs down the pan. She should've kept her mouth shut.

What was she thinking?

Seeing the anxiety on his face, Kate told him not to worry. Bright wasn't going to shop them or do anything about it. He'd said as much. Her reassurance wasn't working, so she decided to elaborate. 'The conversation didn't happen,' she said. 'I'm on a final.'

Hank was incredulous. 'So why the tears?'

She rubbed at her brow, unable to answer.

'Kate, don't do this. You're worrying me.'

'He said I was unfit for duty.'

Taking his left hand off the steering wheel, Hank patted her arm. He didn't entirely disagree. She was like a ticking bomb. It wouldn't take much to tip her over the edge. As her number two, he saw it as part of his job description to protect her from herself. He'd known exactly how she'd react from the moment the car bumper smashed into Towner's legs and threw him up in the air on his final journey, even though she'd not actually seen the gruesome spectacle. By the time she had turned round, it was all over. The aftermath wasn't pretty. The reason she was blaming herself was because she cared deeply about people. All people. She was a good person. More compassionate than anyone he knew – hard on the outside, soft as shite on the in. Right now, she needed rest. He could do with some himself.

'Ever want to keep driving and never look back?' she asked.

'Sometimes,' he admitted.

She sighed loudly, the weight of the world on her shoulders.

'Why don't you call Jo?' he suggested.

'Yeah right, like she'll want to speak to me.'

'She's the one person who would,' Hank said. 'Apart from me, I mean.'

'Later maybe.'

Her phone rang. Hank half-expected Jo's number to show up on the car's display. Wincing as he saw that it was Bright, he glanced at Kate, a question in his eyes: *You wanna answer that?* There was a split-second's hesitation, a deep breath in, then a nod.

Hank pushed a button on the steering wheel to take the call.

Kate made a huge effort to sound upbeat.

'What's up, guv?'

'Are you two OK?' Bright asked.

'We're fine. Making good progress. There's nowt on the roads, to be honest.'

'Good, I want you here with some positive information, soon as you can. Let's put this one to bed, Kate. Then you can take that time off we discussed.'

Hank stiffened. She hadn't mentioned that. Their former guv'nor wasn't a man to mince his words. He'd obviously kicked her in the solar plexus and it would take a while to recover from that. Hank had been there himself, more times than he cared to remember, mostly, though not exclusively, with the same man on the other end of the dressing-down – Bright could be a twat sometimes. Satisfied that Kate was fine, the Detective Chief Superintendent levelled his parting shot at him.

'You owe me one, Hank,' he said. 'And I intend to collect.'

The dialling tone filled the car.

Hank said nothing. Although Bright was a demanding boss – not to mention a bully on occasions – he was fiercely protective of those he cared about. Hank thanked his lucky stars that it was him and not someone else who'd discovered their fateful trip south. The silence in the car was deafening. He imagined the monologue running through Kate's head: the what-ifs, the snippets of conversation between the two of them as they fled Whitby, her row with the head of CID. The guilt Hank knew she was still feeling. That self-examination nonsense he could never understand. It was over – end of. What was to analyse?

A few more silent miles went by before she uttered another word.

'Have you spoken to Andy?' she asked. 'I forgot.'

Hank nodded. 'There's nothing to do and nothing for you to worry about. He's got it covered in Blanchland. He'll let Theresa and McKenzie know about the sighting up north. That'll take the pressure off them and he'll remain in situ until stood down.'

'He could be there a while.'

'Get your head down, Kate. We've got a long drive ahead of us. Have a moment's peace for once. I'll give you a nudge in a bit.'

KATE WOKE TO the sound of a ringing phone. She'd been in a deep sleep and it took a few moments to drag herself awake, to figure out where she was, to remember what had gone on before she collapsed from sheer exhaustion. She glanced at her watch: five forty-five. They had made good time, were already passing a sign for Hamilton.

Not far to go.

Hank answered the phone.

A DC from Strathclyde came on the line, introduced himself by the name of Anderson. 'Bad news, I'm afraid. There's no sign of Finn O'Kane. We've tried interviewing possible witnesses, but if you knew the pub he was seen entering, you'd know there was never any fear of the punters saying a word to a polis.'

'You are still keeping obs on his house?' Hank asked.

'Houses,' Anderson corrected him. 'Finn O'Kane has more homes than Persimmon, spread over a wide area, as well as several other premises in which he and his brother can hide, all posing as legit businesses, some they admit to, some not. No joy there either, I'm afraid. We've put feelers out. My guv'nor thinks they fled your patch because they were about to be plastered all over the box on the six o'clock news.'

Hank couldn't help himself. Kate wasn't the only one angered by clever-arsed journalists and bent coppers. 'And how could they possibly know that?' he said. 'Unless someone your end told them – maybe the same person who likes talking to the press? One of your lot is on the take, pal.'

'That's quite an allegation to be making when you're asking for our help.'

'And I'll be pleased to repeat it to Complaints if it happens again,' Hank said. 'Do we understand each other?'

The detective sidestepped the question. 'Chances are, if Finn O'Kane is here, Craig won't be far behind. They're as thick as thieves, those two – no pun intended. Tell your boss we'll do our best to locate them for you.'

Kate studied the scenery, hoping Anderson would live up to that promise.

Chapter Forty-two

RUSH HOUR WAS well underway when they left the motorway and pulled into the car park of the Marriott Hotel, Argyle Street. Taking the overnight bag she always kept packed in the boot of her car, Kate led the way into reception. After booking in, they went upstairs, peeling off in different directions to find their rooms, with an agreement to meet downstairs five minutes later.

The view from the sixth floor was grim: a grey and miserable cityscape that matched Kate's mood, a spaghetti junction of main roads chock-a-block with commuters, the Hilton Hotel directly opposite, half-empty car parks as people left their jobs for the weekend.

Lucky them.

Dumping her bag on the bed, she glanced around.

The room was fine, nipping clean with crisp white linen and bright flowery prints on the walls, an attempt to add some cheer to the time she'd be spending there. Hopefully it wouldn't be long. In the bathroom, she washed her face and changed her shirt, repaired her make-up to give herself some colour and went in search of

Hank. She found him at the desk, asking the duty receptionist if she could tell him how to get to the city centre police station.

'Of course, sir.' The girl pulled a map towards her. 'It's on Pitt Street, left out of the hotel here.' She was drawing the route in red pen. 'Left at the first set of lights into Douglas Street, left again and turn right here.' She marked the destination with a cross.

'Is it far?' he asked.

She was shaking her head. 'Five minutes, tops.'

They decided to walk. They needed the air.

DETECTIVES FROM STRATHCLYDE CID were scratching their heads when they got there. DCI Matthew Trewitt had laid on tea, coffee and a mini-briefing in the station conference room for 7 p.m. His officers had scoured Finn O'Kane's known haunts and come up with zilch. Not a sighting. Not a whisper of any kind. Of him or his brother. It was clear from the subsequent chat that they were no further forward than Kate and Hank had been before they drove north.

It didn't take the Northumbria detectives long to realize that Finn and Craig O'Kane were a cut above John and Terry Allen in terms of criminality. Over the years, the pair had made a great deal of money out of their illegal enterprises, and acquired a reputation for ruthlessness in protecting their interests.

'Especially when it comes to taking out the competition,' Trewitt said.

'This isn't a turf war, Matthew.' As far as she was able, Kate explained the background to the double, possibly triple, murder case she was investigating, the motive being revenge for Dougie O'Kane's demise years earlier. 'We suspect their target is Arthur Ross McKenzie. An associate of theirs, Wallace Whittaker, made an attempt on McKenzie's life in 2008, while he was an inmate in Shotts Prison.'

'That sounds like Wally. He's a total scumbag.'

'Whittaker was charged with attempted murder, subsequently reduced to GBH,' Kate said. 'He got six years consecutive to the eight he was already serving. Should keep him out of our hair for a while.'

'D'you know where McKenzie is now?' Trewitt asked.

'Haven't a clue.' She wasn't falling for that one. Trewitt seemed nice enough, and he was a policeman. Didn't mean she could trust him. No point in offering McKenzie close protection and then telling the world where he was.

'It wouldn't take a genius to work out his release date and track him down,' Trewitt said. 'The O'Kanes have the means and the muscle to secure information they shouldn't be party to, if you get my drift. They're fond of flashing the cash.'

'Bit like journalists,' Hank said.

His sarcasm went down like a lead balloon. He'd never make a diplomat. Daniels shot him a look, half-expecting her Scottish counterpart to chew his head off for making allegations he couldn't prove. She needed Strathclyde detectives onside. This was no time to argue the toss over what had or hadn't gone down earlier in the day with Gillian Garvey.

Fortunately, Trewitt let it go.

'What's their mental state?' Kate asked.

Trewitt gave a non-committal shrug. He wasn't a shrink, he told them, and then proceeded to offer a diagnosis: 'Psychopaths, both of them, the type you don't want to meet on a dark night, or any other time, frankly.' He leaned back in his chair and clasped his hands behind his head. 'Think I'm in the wrong job, Kate. They drive great cars, pull stunning birds and live in wealthy areas; Finn outside the city, his brother in a smart villa in Barnton.'

Kate was impressed. Barnton was an affluent area, north-west of Edinburgh. She'd been there once or twice with a friend whose parents owned a house there. Properties were pricey. She certainly couldn't afford one.

'What's security like at Finn's place?' she asked.

'The best money can buy. Doors and windows like a Bank of Scotland safe.'

'Guns?'

'Oh yes! By the way, if you're thinking of storming the place, you've got a job on your hands. Even if you get beyond the perimeter fence – and you'll need a tank to do so – there'll be a couple of hungry Rottweilers waiting on the other side to rip your throat out.'

Kate shivered. 'First thing in the morning, can one of your guys show us where it is?'

'I'll do it myself. It'll get me out from behind my desk.'

'Thanks. Can you fill Hank in on how you go about applying for a double-U round here? Sounds like we're going to need one.'

'No problem. Anything else?'

'I'm going to need some bodies – live ones, I mean. Who can you spare?'

'One of my old DCs has made a career out of chasing the villains you're after. You're welcome to him.'

'He hasn't caught them yet,' Kate said drily. 'Doesn't sound like my type, to be honest.'

Tickled by the dig, Hank grinned.

'He's a good bloke,' Trewitt insisted, humourless eyes on Hank. 'And really clued up on the O'Kane family. He's had more complaints than Scottish Gas because of his efforts to get those two sods convicted. He's a little obsessive, I grant you. I think you'll be impressed when you see the dossier he has on them.'

'We'll take your word for it,' Hank said.

'What's his name?' Kate asked, trying to deflect the other two from an all-out fight.

'Randy,' Trewitt said. 'DC Randolph, if you're feeling overly formal. How about I throw a couple of uniforms in too. That do you?'

'We're taking major players out, Matthew.' Kate's expression said it wasn't enough.

'Better ring your guv'nor then.' Trewitt picked up the landline, proffered the receiver. 'You wouldn't want to meet mine after the discussion we had when I told him you were coming. If you need extra manpower, your force will have to pay for the privilege.'

HAVING ARRANGED A 5.30 a.m. start they called it a day with the agreement that Strathclyde officers would keep up the search through the night. Kate and Hank got to the hotel at five to nine. As she wandered into the lounge bar, he went off to buy a new toothbrush and a disposable razor in the hotel shop. He hadn't brought one along – hadn't brought anything along. A new pair of shreddies was on his priority list he informed her as he walked away.

Kate chuckled, then grimaced. *Too much information.*

Hank caught the shop before it closed and joined her a few minutes later, a pink toothbrush sticking out of his breast pocket. Taking off his jacket, he loosened his tie and sat down, stifling a yawn. It had been a bloody long day and he was done in. They both were.

'You want a drink?' he asked.

'Already on order,' she said. 'I got you a beer.'

'Great. Menus too? I'm bloody starving.'

Nodding, she held up her phone. 'I spoke to Bright.'

'Oh yeah, how is the grumpy bastard?'

'Still simmering.'

It was strange to hear Hank disrespect the man who'd hand-picked them both and paired them to work together all those years ago. Notwithstanding her promotion to Detective Chief Inspector, it had been the very best day of her professional life. She had a lot of respect for Bright, and Hank was like the brother she never had. He and Kate had grown closer and closer in the past few years and she simply couldn't do without him.

'I've given him an update,' she said. 'Told him to get his cheque-book out.'

'Bet he didn't like that.'

'He was fine with it.'

'He's trying to get back in your good books.'

When the drinks came, they ordered food. It didn't take long to arrive. They discussed strategy while eating. The plan was to meet with Trewitt and DC Randolph at the station early and then stake out Finn O'Kane's main residence. Only then could they decide what further action to take, what extra manpower and resources they required to mount an operation. There was much to do.

Kate drew her eyes away from her meal. 'Depending how it goes tomorrow morning, I'm going to leave you here to organize the warrant while I jump on the train to Edinburgh.'

'To do what?' Hank yawned again, blinking his eyes to keep them from closing.

'I called the duty DCI and told her I'd be over. She'll get the same spiel I gave Trewitt. It merits the personal touch. A request for assistance from Lothian and Borders will be better coming from me.' No offence was meant and none was taken.

'Fair enough,' Hank said. 'Sure you're not swanning off to Harvey Nicks to get a peace offering for Jo?'

Kate managed a smile. 'Another time, maybe.'

'You don't trust me, is that it?'

'Not as far as I can throw you.' She winked at him. She could feel herself relaxing now she'd spoken to Bright in private. He hadn't mentioned their row on the phone. And when she'd asked for financial resources to be made available, he acquiesced without a fight. Kate outlined her plan. 'I know some of the Murder Investigation Team in Edinburgh. I thought maybe they would pull a few strings. In the meantime, you can liaise with Trewitt and gather the necessary resources for an assault on Finn's place while I'm gone. He likes you, I can tell.' She made a crazy face. 'Soon as I return, we're going in, so be ready. I'm going to collar those evil toerags if it's the last thing I do.'

Hank raised his glass. 'Welcome back, boss.'

They clinked glasses.

Chapter Forty-three

Dawn . . . somewhere on the outskirts of Glasgow. A mist hung over the valley. All was still. Surrounded by woodland and farms on three sides, Finn O'Kane's main residence was a mansion by English standards. Kate was standing on high ground, viewing it through binoculars, trying to work out a strategy. The only sound was birdsong and there was no sign of anything untoward.

The approach wasn't good: a six-foot high fence, *Keep Out* gates, a long drive leading to the front door and CCTV. All the shutters were closed, so no chance of seeing anyone walking around inside. Trewitt was right: mounting an operation without anyone getting hurt was a logistical nightmare.

This could go horribly wrong.

On the way to their location, Hank and Trewitt had travelled in one car, Kate and Randolph in her Q5. He was nearing retirement, a man with the physical characteristics of a front-row forward. That might come in handy, bearing in mind the fear that their suspect wouldn't come quietly. Throughout the journey, he talked constantly about their target. It was clear he'd taken a special interest in Finn O'Kane and his older brother Craig, tracking their every move in the past ten years.

Shame they'd managed to evade his scrutiny last week, Kate was thinking, but didn't say.

Randolph's voice brought her focus back to the house. 'Can't believe he'll be there when he knows we're after him. He's got more off than that. He's a cunning bastard, make no mistake.'

'That's precisely why I want it searched,' Kate said, without taking her eyes off the property.

'Ma'am?'

The DCI lowered her binoculars. Before she could answer, a truck loaded with logs coasted by on the dirt-track road, the female driver giving her the once-over. Kate shifted her gaze to Randolph. 'Best place to hide is right under our noses. Happened to me once: a guy I was hunting bought the police house right next door to the station. Paid cash too – probably from his ill-gotten gains. Took us months to find him.'

'Class!' Randolph pointed at the house. 'What d'you reckon then?'

'Can't see any dogs,' Hank said, to no one in particular.

'Doesn't mean they're not there,' Trewitt offered.

'I agree.' Kate glanced at her Scottish colleagues. 'If they're as ferocious as you say, we're going to have to incapacitate them. Doesn't sound like a noose will do it. I want two dog men, a vet, a couple of DCs, someone from SOCO and a TSG Group – one sergeant and seven. Can you fix that up?'

'Is that all?' Trewitt was being sarcastic.

'We're paying for it, Matthew. Why should you care?'

'Fair comment,' he said. 'Consider it done.'

'Any other escape routes?' Hank asked.

Randolph was shaking his head. 'On foot, maybe, but they're hardly going to make a run for it, are they?'

Kate scanned the house again, then told Trewitt she'd seen and heard all she needed. He got in his car and drove off alone, promising to rally the troops she required.

'Ready to go?' Hank asked.

She stood her ground.

'You really think he's in there?' Randolph asked.

Kate didn't offer an answer. She could tell from his expression that he reckoned she was off her trolley even considering it as a possibility. Maybe he was right. She'd had better weeks. But even so, she had the distinct feeling that her luck was about to change.

She was close. She could feel it. And that was good enough for her.

LEAVING DC RANDOLPH in position until arrangements could be made for someone to relieve him, Kate drove Hank to the hotel, promising him the meal he'd missed when they left at five-thirty. They had a long day ahead of them. It might be hours before they had another chance to fill up. The dining room was full and they had to wait for a table. Kate wondered if it was always this busy or if there was some kind of convention on, or maybe a major gig in the city. Her idle musing triggered a thought: if O'Kane was into music, it might draw him out from wherever he was hiding.

Making a mental note to check it out, she glanced at her watch, desperate to get going.

Hank grimaced, thoughts of a disappearing breakfast too hard to bear. The waitress arrived in the nick of time, showing them to a table and taking their order straight away. After they had eaten, Kate signed for the food. Scooping her bag off the floor, she stood up, telling Hank she wanted the operation on O'Kane's house ready to go in four hours maximum.

'The warrant included.' She gave him her car keys. 'You can drop me at the train station first.'

'You sure you don't want to take the car?' he said, as they walked to the Q5 and got in. 'I could put the bite on Trewitt for one of theirs.'

'No, you keep it.' Drawing her seat belt across her, she reminded him that on a Saturday morning it would be as quick by train. 'Besides, I want you mobile in case O'Kane makes an appearance.' She narrowed her eyes. 'But it's my car, so no parking it anywhere dodgy. And remember, you're not Starsky or Hutch.'

'Aww,' Hank grinned. 'You're no fun.'

'I mean it,' she said. 'Any damage comes out of your pay.'

They drove to Glasgow Central station in silence, rain hammering on the windscreen. People sheltered under umbrellas as they headed into work, passing the old and the new of what the city had to offer: dilapidated red sandstone buildings in the foreground, contemporary pieces of architecture in the distance, a poster for the Glasgow Royal Concert Hall, an advertisement for the Bank of Scotland *Great Scottish Run.*

Kate checked the date on her mobile phone. Race day was tomorrow, Sunday, 2 September.

'Pull up here,' she said, as they neared the station.

Hank brought the car to a halt on double-yellows. She asked him to fetch a newspaper and a return ticket for her journey while she made a call to let Edinburgh officers know she was on her way. The paper was to check out what was on in the city, she explained. She could do that on the train. 'According to Randolph, Finn O'Kane likes the high life. If he's such a flash bastard, maybe he'll crawl out from under his rock if there's something good on tonight.'

'Safety in numbers?' Hank offered, getting out.

'Something like that.' Kate checked the street. 'I'll wait here. We don't want to get done for parking illegally.'

As he walked away, she pulled out her phone and called Lothian and Borders HQ, asking for directions and letting the duty DCI know she'd be there in a little over an hour. As she rang off, Hank yanked open the door and got in the car empty-handed.

'You can cash a cheque in there and put a bet on,' he said. 'You can't buy a newspaper.'

'It's a train station!'

'You can't get a train there either, I checked.'

She looked at him oddly.

'There's only one an hour. You missed it. You'll have to go to Queen Street where they run every fifteen minutes.'

KATE RAN UP the steps, passing a bilingual English/Gaelic sign: *Welcome to Queen Street – Fàilte gu Sràid na Banrighinn.* Securing a return ticket to Edinburgh Waverley, she grabbed a coffee to go and called Jo as she waited for the 08:45 train due into the capital at 09:37. Jo didn't pick up, so Kate climbed on board.

Her first journey by rail between the two cities took her through places she'd never heard of, Croy being one. It reminded her of the Tyne Valley line, the train she used to get from Newcastle to her father's home in Corbridge – in the days when she used to visit, before they fell out. The landscape was very similar and it even had a golf course alongside the track. Although it was double the distance, the journey time was much the same with fewer stops along the way.

Edinburgh was as grey as Glasgow had been – only prettier. If she hadn't been such a fan of her home city, this was the one place Kate would choose to live. It wasn't looking its best on account of the construction of the city's new tramway. There were steel barriers everywhere, blocking off roads, preventing shoppers from crossing Princes Street. Fortunately, it didn't affect her as she was hailing a cab.

Chapter Forty-four

GORMLEY TOOK THE warrant from the court clerk and made his way to Pitt Street police station, arriving a little after eleven forty-five. Despite their spat the day before, Trewitt had been busy. He'd made an operations room available for the Northumbria detectives: a desk, two chairs and a phone they could use either internally or to get an outside line. It wasn't a palace, but it was a lot better than some places they had been asked to work in.

DC Randolph had also done his bit, supplying aerial photographs of Finn O'Kane's home from his extensive dossier. He'd stuck them on the wall, telling Hank they had been taken by the land agent responsible for the property before it changed hands. There were detailed maps of the interior to go with it.

'My boss will be impressed,' Hank said.

'Don't get too excited. There's no news on Finn's whereabouts.'

'What about Craig?'

Randolph shook his head.

It was depressing news and, because they had turned over O'Kane's so-called business premises, they had lost the element of surprise. Hank had nothing to do but wait and hope that Kate was on the right track.

Come late morning, Randolph led him to the canteen. In the course of a coppers' chat over a bacon sandwich, it turned out they knew some of the same detectives, including Detective Chief Superintendent Bright. Randolph and Bright had joined the police around the same time and worked a few national crime squad jobs together.

'Small world,' Hank said.

'He was a flash git when he was young.'

Hank laughed. 'Hasn't changed much.'

'His wife Sheila was nice.'

'Stella. She died: car crash.'

'Oh, I'm sorry to hear that.'

Hank changed the subject: some friendly banter about Bright's meteoric rise to the top. Eventually the topic of conversation worked its way round to the current case, Randolph confessing that Scottish crime rates would drop considerably if Kate could take out O'Kane.

'What's she like?' he asked. 'Seems a bit uptight to me.'

Hank ignored the swipe. 'She's a one-off, a great boss, even better detective.' He wanted to add, *And very upset right now and as mad as a box of frogs half the time*, but kept his thoughts to himself.

'She'll be *my* favourite detective, if she pulls this off,' Randolph said. 'Then I can die a happy man.' He stood up, suggesting they return to work, and they continued their conversation as they walked out of the canteen and along the corridor. 'I've tried putting Finn away for years. We've all tried. Problem is, he, his brother and the lowlife scum they hang around with know our faces. Every time we get wind of their wrongdoing, they see us coming a mile off and pull out.'

'You've not heard of undercover surveillance then?' Hank said.

Randolph grinned, appreciating the humour. He opened the door to Hank's little office. 'Your boss is an unknown quantity to them. Maybe she'll have more luck. Only, she's not going to be in a position to walk up and introduce herself, is she?'

''Fraid not,' Hank was forced to agree.

'Maybe this time we'll get lucky. Question is, can she out-think them?'

Hank sat down. 'If anyone can, *she* can.'

'You really rate her, don't you?' Randolph pulled up a chair.

'Bright does too. He's supported her throughout her career.'

'She must be good. From my recollection, he doesn't impress easily.'

'His faith in her is well deserved. If there's any justice in the world, she'll follow him to the very top, fill his shoes when the time comes. But that assumes a meritocracy, or at least a level playing field. You and I both know that's bollocks. I'm biased, but she does more work in her bait time than the brass do in a week, and gets very little thanks for it. It'll be the same here, no doubt.'

'If your face fits . . .' Randolph allowed his comment to trail off to nothing. He pointed at the photographs of O'Kane's imposing property. 'Your boss obviously thinks there's someone in there.'

'And you don't?' Hank asked.

'Nope, and I know them a damn sight better than she does.'

'Fiver says she's right.' Hank stuck out his hand, a confident look on his face. 'I don't want any of your funny money, mind. Back in Geordistan my newsagent is loath to accept Scottish dosh.'

Chuckling under his breath, Randolph shook on it, a camaraderie developing between the two detectives. 'Think I'll step outside for a smoke. You coming?'

The landline rang.

Hank picked up, answering with his name, waving away the offer to join Randolph outside. As the Scotsman left the room, an excitable voice hit Hank's ear. The officer keeping covert observations on the target property spoke so quickly it was all he could do to make out a word he said. 'Hang on mate,' Hank said. 'You're going to have to slow down and give me that again.'

'Dogs!' the officer said. 'Going crackers.'

'Inside?'

'It's hard to tell, with the house sitting in a valley the way it does. Could've been an animal on one of the adjoining farms. Look, I know this area like the back of my hand. It's a hunting, shooting, fishing community. Could be someone rabbiting in the woods. I just thought your DCI would want to know.'

Thanking him, Hank put down the phone. Presumably Finn O'Kane had chosen the property for that very reason; what better place to possess firearms than in a farming community? Hank knew farms in 'the shire' – Hexhamshire in Northumberland – where you could take a gun into a pub after a day's shooting but couldn't smoke a tab because of health and safety.

Crazy world.

That worrying thought lingered in his head as he left the building. O'Kane could do target practice and no one would bat an eyelid. For all Hank knew, there might be an arsenal inside that house that no one was aware of. As soon as he was en route, he called Kate to update her, suggesting she might consider a firearms team.

She was already on the train, minutes away from Queen Street station. She'd spent an hour with Lothian and Borders, who were now on board. She'd mustered forces, she said. Edinburgh officers were waiting at the nearest nick for her signal. They hadn't been told where they were going or what was going down. They were on standby, with a trusted team leader on hand to give the go-ahead when the time was right.

'The idea is to hit both homes at the same time,' she said.

Hank concurred. 'Sounds like a plan.'

'As soon as we're on the move, I'll brief them,' she added. 'Look, I've gotta go, train's pulling in. I want everyone in position and standing by. Sit tight and wait for me. I'll be there as soon as I can. Let me know if there are any further developments.'

KATE RAN FOR the nearest taxi. She got in, telling the driver she'd pay double if he put his foot down – no easy task on a Saturday lunchtime in the centre of Glasgow. As he pulled away, she called the Lothian and Borders team leader, asking him to mobilize his squad and wait for her signal. Coordinating a double hit was vital for a successful outcome. She was relying on him to play his part.

She hung up, checked her watch. It was quarter to one.

The driver was watching her through his rear-view mirror, no doubt wondering who she was and what on earth was going on. He'd probably never had a senior police officer in his cab, directing operations on something so serious. Kate was grateful he had the good sense not to ask questions, but she wished he'd get a shift on.

As they left the city behind, the sun came out and the sky turned blue, but it wasn't the improvement in the weather lifting her spirits. It was the adrenalin rush she always felt when she was closing in on a target. The hideous image of John Allen's body chained to the underside of a van had remained with her all week, acting as her motivation to keep pushing on. She ached to apprehend those responsible and put them away.

Short of her destination, her phone rang. Robson asked how things were going. She talked in code, letting him know she was setting up 'a two-pronged approach to her problem', knowing he was astute enough to work the rest out for himself.

'Any more sightings?' he asked.

The driver's eyes again.

'Sadly, no. Listen, I can't speak now. Hoping to have news later.'

'There's been a development this end,' Robson said.

Kate glanced out of the window. Although she'd visited Finn's home that very morning, the landscape wasn't familiar. Putting Robbo on hold, she leaned forward, tapped the driver on his shoulder, asking him how much further. He told her two minutes and she went back to her call. 'Can you be quick, Robbo? I need to pay my driver and keep this line free in case Hank calls. There's a lot of stuff going on.'

'Think I have a handle on Terry Allen's ring. A silversmith called the incident room. He'd seen the press release and thinks he may be able to help. I've sent someone out to take a statement. If it checks out, I should have more for you by close of play.'

'Great. Everyone else OK?'

'They're fine.'

'And the rural babysitter?' She couldn't mention Blanchland or DC Andy Brown by name with the cab driver listening to her every word.

'Far as I know.' Robson paused. 'It's been a while since he checked in. McKenzie was getting agitated, slinging his weight around, giving Andy earache. Nothing he can't handle.'

'Try and raise him. Let me know what gives.'

She had another call waiting and rang off.

Gormley also had important news. 'On scene,' he said. 'Minutes before I arrived, the obs guys heard what they thought was a car starting up. A moment ago, a vehicle went along the ridge. I saw it myself—'

'Description?'

'Dark, possibly a four-by-four, only the roof was visible beyond the hedgerow. At first, I wasn't too concerned because it's not actually on O'Kane's land—'

'And now you are?'

'TSG got a call from Control: reported trespass on the farm next door in which a vehicle was used – a dark green Range Rover. One male driver, no passengers.'

'Hold on, Hank.' She spoke to the driver. 'Pull up here.'

He narrowed his eyes. 'You sure you have the right place? There's nothing here!'

'What were you expecting? A brass band?' Then, to Hank: 'Have we got a call out for the Range Rover?'

'Yep, no sign yet.'

The cab swerved to one side and came to an abrupt halt.

Shoving money into the driver's hand, Kate told him to disappear. Then she was out the door and running along a dirt-track road, arms going like pistons. There was no way she could allow the cab to jeopardize her operation.

As she neared the brow of the hill, she could see two dog men getting out of their van wearing protective clothing. The TSG were in full riot gear, their team leader giving last-minute instructions to his men – if they were all men; it was difficult to tell under their combat suits and helmets. A firearms marksman was also standing by.

Everyone was ready.

Attaching a radio to her jacket, Kate took binoculars from Hank and surveyed the scene. Not a sound from the house. Not a chink in the shutters. No sign of anything untoward. She didn't want a hair on her head or anyone else's harmed. It was now or never.

At one o'clock she called Edinburgh.

'It's a GO, GO, GO – best of luck.'

Chapter Forty-five

WITH THE POLICE marksman covering her back, the TSG flanking her on either side, each with a specific area to cover, Kate walked up the driveway towards the front door, senses on high alert. Scanning each shuttered window in turn, she wondered whether anyone was watching her through some unseen spyhole. She had no idea what reception she'd get or how many people might be inside. Could be one or both brothers – with or without a dozen other thugs as backup – hands in the air, or spoiling for a pitched battle with the police.

The O'Kanes were facing a life sentence – they had absolutely nothing to lose.

As she neared the front entrance, Kate half-expected the door to open, unleashing two savage beasts – the four-legged type, not humans. Fortunately for her, it stayed shut. Glancing to her right, sharing an anxious moment with the TSG leader, she gave the nod for him to proceed. He in turn gestured to a member of his team.

An officer stepped forward.

A battering ram wasn't strong enough to attack such a solid door – he'd be forced to hit it time and again – particularly if it had been reinforced on the inside, as Kate suspected it might be. He'd brought along a spreader, a hydraulic piece of kit that would do the job with no effort whatsoever.

In seconds, the door was off and the TSG were storming forward into the building. It was dark inside. Kate hung back, shone a torch at the alarm board.

Wires dangled loose. The power had been cut.

It didn't bode well.

As she entered the house, two scenarios played out in her head. Either the lowlife who lived there had knocked out the electricity so as to hide more effectively and get the jump on the police, or he'd left the house empty and the place had been burgled. Given Finn O'Kane's reputation, she was inclined to dismiss the second option, unless it was a burglar with a death wish. There was a third option: maybe her radar had let her down this time. She hoped that wasn't the case.

Beyond the outer hall, it was pitch-black. Officers moved like shadows through the cavernous hallway, flashlight beams shifting left and right as they spread out, each one taking responsibility for their own section of the house. Keen to play his part, Hank followed one group up the stairs. Remaining on the ground floor, Kate listened as boots scurried across the ceiling above her head. For a split-second, the house was silent as officers upstairs and down listened for movement.

Then she heard it: the most terrifying, primitive sound. And it was coming from only a few feet away.

Her whole body tensed. Time stood still. She wanted to raise her torch, wanted to see what was in front of her. Or did she? She froze, hardly daring to breathe, her professional training deserting her. Instinctively, she stepped away, the hair on the back of her neck standing to attention.

She was not alone . . .

A growl didn't quite cover it.

With nothing but a police-issue torch with which to defend herself, Kate imagined the dog already at her throat, tearing flesh, shaking her like a toy. It was so close she could smell it. Any minute now . . .

It took all her nerve to resist the temptation to scream for someone with a firearm to shoot the animal dead. She didn't dare yell out for fear she might trigger an immediate attack. Another step backward, then another, quicker this time. A trip sent her crashing to the floor, landing with a solid thump as she hit the deck, injuring her left wrist as she reached out to break her fall. Putting her right hand out to help herself up, she let out a yelp as it sank into warm hair and flesh.

A low voice on her radio: 'Unit One: all clear outside. Nothing to report.'

Kate felt sick. 'Unit One, I need assistance. Get someone in here, now!'

'Unit One: Affirmative.'

Responding to her distress, Hank came on the radio: 'Boss? You OK?'

Another growl. She couldn't speak.

'Kate, where are you?' Hank sounded stressed to death. For a moment, the house was silent. Kate could hear her own heartbeat. In her head, she imagined officers all around the house stopping dead in their tracks, waiting for her response, each and every one of them alert to the potential danger within. 'Drawing room,' she managed, her voice sounding higher than its normal pitch. 'Beware of the dog.'

Training her torch on her right hand she could see it was covered in blood. Beyond that, the beam of light caught the open eyes of a dead dog lying beside her, a bayonet sticking out of its neck.

Hank thundered down the stairs with two TSG officers hard on his heels.

'It's still warm,' Kate said, as he helped her to her feet.

The all-clear was given. Even in the roof void and cellar there were no signs of life. Light flooded into the hallway as the shutters were opened. The noise that had petrified Kate had come from a second dog, its chilling growl reduced to a whimper. The animal, barely alive, was lying on its side with a stab wound to its chest, a bloody lump of steak hanging from its mouth, a stunt to distract it from attack. There was more fresh meat scattered around the room.

Clever, Kate thought.

Calling for assistance, she asked if the animal could be saved. The vet shook his head, said he'd take care of it. Saddened, but relieved that it would soon be out of its misery, Kate turned to the TSG officers.

'Have you checked the garage?' she asked.

'Not yet.'

'OK, come with me.'

Chapter Forty-six

KATE STEPPED OUT of the way to allow three of the tactical support group to enter the quadruple garage before her. With no power available, there was very little light in the windowless space as she followed them in. Despite the fact that it was only September, it was freezing in there. Fear hung in the air. She could tell by their cautious approach that her Strathclyde colleagues were nervous. There was no gung-ho entry, no shouting – no exchanges going on – merely officers going quietly and methodically about their business.

The tension was almost palpable.

For a moment, they stood in silence, their torches illuminating the back wall. A bank of metal shelving with tools of every kind, some that could do real damage: spanners and screwdrivers of every size, pliers, hacksaws, torque wrenches and claw hammers. Bolt cutters, a torturer's best friend.

Some tools were missing – a worrying thought.

Parked nose-in, there were four vehicles in the vast space. Kate wondered why. If Finn O'Kane wasn't home, how had he left? He was hardly the public transport type. She supposed he'd been picked up by an associate or taken a cab, or maybe the flash bastard had other toys to play with and these highly polished and pristine beauties were the ones he cherished the most. As a car enthusiast, she could understand that.

Unless he hadn't left.

There was plenty of space to hide, in or out of vehicles. Officers worked quickly, taking the room in sections. One got down on the floor, shining his torch along the ground, checking the underside of the first vehicle he came to, a silver Porsche 911, and beyond to the far end of the building.

A shake of his head as he stood up told her there was nothing there.

Another team member had already checked the interior of the car, given the all-clear. He was examining the second vehicle, a red double cab Toyota Hilux. As he moved around to the rear end of the vehicle, he stopped dead in his tracks. Staring at the rubberized floor, he lifted his foot as if he'd stepped in something sticky.

Kate followed his gaze. There was a dark patch beside his right boot, directly behind the rear bumper. Trying to work out if there was anything sinister there, he put a finger to his mouth and pointed at the tonneau cover. Kate selected a Stanley knife from the shelving unit and handed it to him.

He slashed open the cover – the cargo area was empty.

Shining his torch on to the floor, the officer crouched down. Kate looked on as he dipped a forefinger in the dark pool. Rubbing it together with his thumb, he brought his hand to his nose and gave it a sniff.

'Oil,' he said softly.

Relieved, they moved on to the third vehicle, a black BMW 7 Series. Again, they found nothing untoward. That left only a black Range Rover, polished to perfection. Kate was beginning to hate Finn O'Kane, but her jealousy was fleeting. She was about to take a step forward when the officer in front of her tensed and glanced over his shoulder, an expression of revulsion on his face. Kate peered over his shoulder at the vehicle and saw that the front passenger window was open. An orange rattan strap fixed to something inside the vehicle was stretched to breaking point. On the other end of the strap was a hand attached to its owner, Finn O'Kane.

Kate had found her target.

WITH THE SEARCH over and the place secure, Kate stood the TSG down so she could preserve the scene until the Glasgow Murder Investigation Team arrived. Only her own trusted DS was allowed in. As Kate waited for him to arrive, she stood for a moment, surveying the scene.

Finn O'Kane's arms were splayed out over the bonnet of the vehicle. His head had lolled to one side, blood seeping out beneath the gag in his mouth, eyes staring straight at her. The straps that secured him to the car were the ratchet-type, like the ones she used to tie down her motorcycle on ferries when she went abroad. Once tightened, the Glasgow gangster never stood a chance.

Moving closer, she saw that there was liquid on the floor where Finn had pissed himself, the smell of shit where his bowels had emptied, vomit on the bonnet of his precious car. She didn't need Forensics to tell her that the Range Rover hadn't been driven at speed. It was obvious in her mind that it had been edged towards the wall, inch by inch, with the intention of delivering the maximum pain and distress to the victim. Two thousand eight hundred kilos of metal, an engine of four and a half litres, crushing Finn until his internal organs ruptured and his bones shattered. No wonder his final expression was one of pure terror.

'Those who live by the sword,' Hank said cruelly as he arrived by her side. 'Lothian and Borders have been on the radio. They drew a blank. Craig O'Kane wasn't at his Barnton flat.' He looked at the body. 'Someone enjoyed doing this.'

Kate couldn't agree more.

What was wrong with these people?

Something over her shoulder caught Hank's eye.

'Christ Almighty!' He pointed at the car. 'What the hell is that?'

Kate had been so engrossed with the methodology of the crime, she hadn't examined the vehicle or noticed the bloody handprint on the driver's side of the front windscreen, its fingers spread wide, as big as a shovel. The print was dead centre, not scuffed or smeared. It had been deliberately placed there – and not by Finn O'Kane.

She looked at Hank, trying to process the find.

Whoever had left the print there wanted his identity known, probably to scare the living daylights out of Finn's brother, Craig. A message. No, a statement: *This isn't over . . . not by a long chalk. I'm coming after you.*

This was someone who wanted Finn O'Kane to suffer as John and Terry Allen had done. But who?

McKenzie?

Kate felt a wave of nausea as she remembered Robbo telling her there had been no contact from her close protection officer in Blanchland: *It's been a while since he checked in. McKenzie was agitated, slinging his weight around, giving Andy earache. Nothing he can't handle . . .*

Andy!

'Oh my God!' Her voice caught in the back of her throat as she imagined something too awful to contemplate. Already she feared the worst. 'Hank, get hold of Andy. Now!'

Chapter Forty-seven

McKenzie had a good motive for killing Finn O'Kane. The question on Kate's lips was this: was he still in Northumberland under close protection, or in Scotland gunning for Craig? It had been over four hours since Andy last reported in; ample time for McKenzie to drive to Scotland, murder Finn and make good his escape. It was in everyone's interest to know where he was. Both forces needed to find him, fast.

Right this minute, Andy was her priority.

Please God, let him be OK.

Following her withdrawal from the crime scene, Kate had travelled to Pitt Street police station with Hank and taken up residence in the office they had been allocated – a drab room no bigger than a broom cupboard. Hank was seated, Kate pacing up and down, the phone to her ear. Andy's number had been ringing out for ages but still he hadn't picked up. The DCI felt sick. She didn't even want to consider the what-ifs. The Murder Investigation Team was her family. She'd be devastated to lose an officer – any officer – on or off duty.

'Where the fuck is he?' she muttered under her breath, imagination in overdrive.

Already she was blaming herself for putting Andy at risk, asking herself if she should or could have done things differently, bearing in mind McKenzie's reputation as a hard man. Although she was trying not to panic, she couldn't shake off the image of a coffin draped with the Northumbria force flag, a police helmet on top, a guard of honour in full dress uniform lining the route to Newcastle crematorium. She'd attended too many funerals. They were acutely distressing, occasions that no officer would ever wish to repeat.

Like Kate, Hank had also been trying to raise Andy, desperate to find out if he was in one piece or lying in a ditch somewhere with his head caved in or shot by his own firearm. He made another call. She didn't need to ask to whom. This time he was trying Andy's home again, in case he'd suddenly been taken ill. If so, he could well have made alternative arrangements for the protection of McKenzie and Theresa. Perhaps he'd left a message to that effect, but for some reason it hadn't yet filtered through to Robson in the incident room.

Kate wasn't buying that. Andy was as strong as an ox. He'd never taken a day's sick leave in all the time he'd been in the Murder Investigation Team. Besides, he was a stickler for keeping in touch with base.

Hank shook his head, left another message and hung up.

For a while they sat in silence. The murder investigation launched by DCI Trewitt into Finn O'Kane's death was not their problem. O'Kane had been killed in the Strathclyde force area and it was nothing to do with them. All the Northumbria detectives needed was samples from his body for use as evidence in their own murder enquiry. Short of giving statements to the SIO, Kate and Hank were free to leave.

'Try the office again,' Kate said.

Hank dialled the number and got the same response. Andy was still unaccounted for.

Kate glanced at her watch. *Two-fifteen.* Robson hadn't heard from Andy since ten this morning. Assuming for one minute that he'd been overpowered by the man he was supposed to be protecting, he might be tied up, making it impossible for him to call in. If McKenzie was in a state of high anxiety earlier in the day, had he been planning something all along? It would certainly explain his agitation.

Kate stopped pacing and sat down, trying to separate fact from speculation.

As if reading her mind, Gormley told her, 'He'll be fine.' But there was no conviction in his voice. He sounded as if he was trying to convince himself. 'You know what prigs are like under safe house conditions. They're happy enough at the start, getting their food delivered, DVDs on demand, but it doesn't take long for them to go off on one. Remember that guy a few years back, went totally apeshit, screaming to be let out?' His laughter was forced.

'Yes, Hank, I remember him. Stop trying to cheer me up. I don't give a toss about McKenzie. I just want Andy back.'

'Pound to a penny, he's in a pub somewhere supping a pint with his charges—'

'So why's he not picking up? Answer me that.' Decision made, she stood up. 'Come on, we're going home.'

'You're joking. We can't!'

'Why? Why can't we?'

'Trewitt wants your input at his briefing. I thought you said—'

'I changed my mind.' Pulling on her jacket, Kate opened her briefcase and scooped all her paperwork into it. As she charged out of the office, Hank tagged along, trying to convince her to stay: Trewitt wouldn't be happy. They would find Andy safe and well. There was bound to be a perfectly reasonable explanation for his absence. She rounded on him. 'Such as?'

'I'm just saying—'

'Andy knows the rules, Hank. Give me one good reason why he's failed to obey them, why he's not made contact with me, you, or the team.'

Her mobile rang, stopping the row as they got in the car. Robson had been dispatched to McKenzie's rental property and Lisa Carmichael had insisted on accompanying him. The news wasn't good. The place was empty. No sign of Brown, McKenzie or Theresa Allen. The only saving grace was that Andy and Lisa had found no sign of anything untoward either. The village of Blanch-land was as peaceful as ever.

Kate fired off question after question in quick succession, most of which Robson had already answered. She needed to be sure he'd covered all the bases. 'Is the place secure?'

'Yes, all locked up.'

'Any signs of a disturbance?'

'No, thankfully.'

'Did you speak to the neighbours?'

'Yes—'

'No one heard any fighting or shouting?'

'No. That's good, isn't it?' He was trying to make her feel better. 'No one has seen hide nor hair of them. Or Price, for that matter. I can't get hold of him either.'

'Jesus! Break the door down and get your arse inside.' She waited for what seemed like an age. Heard a loud clash as either a bat-tering ram or Robson's shoulder hit the door. She imagined him checking the interior of the tiny cottage, the chair where McKenzie had taken the piss last time she'd seen him. Robson was talking her through his search. He sent Lisa to search the rest of the ground floor, and then Kate heard his feet thundering on the stairs . . . and then everything went quiet. 'Robbo?' Nothing. *'Robbo?'*

Still nothing.

The line was dead.

Kate called him back.

He picked up immediately. 'Sorry, I lost the signal. Everything appears normal here, boss.'

Her relief came out in a loud sigh. 'Put Lisa on.'

Carmichael came on the line. Although Lisa was strong, gutsy and a fabulous asset to the Murder Investigation Team, Kate didn't want to ask her outright how she was coping. She knew only too well that any sympathy from her would result in floods of tears from the young officer. She and Andy were inseparable. He was her friend as well as her colleague. She knew better than anyone that it was completely out of character for him to go AWOL.

Kate had to work hard to sound upbeat and calm. 'Lisa, is Andy's car there?' she asked.

'Yes, it's round the side. First thing I checked.' Her answer came out like a croak. She cleared her throat but couldn't keep the tremor out of her voice: 'Something's happened, I know it has.'

'Lisa, listen to me. We will find him.' Kate took a deep breath, trying to keep her own heartache at bay. Her place was with her team, not here, a hundred and fifty miles away. She knew she should say more, but how could she tell Lisa to keep faith when she was fast losing all hope?

She ended the call, feeling that she'd let Lisa down. She'd let them all down, especially Andy.

KATE DROVE TO the hotel like a woman possessed. Passing through the crowded reception area, she headed straight for the lift. When it reached her floor, she practically ran to her room. Hurriedly, she packed her gear, left a brief message for Trewitt and then joined Hank in the foyer downstairs.

By ten past three, they had checked out and were on their way to Newcastle.

Weather-wise, it was a perfect afternoon for motoring. Not wet. Not sunny. Just cool and dull. Not that Kate felt much like driving. Right now, she wasn't moving. One of the dual carriageways close to the hotel was blocked off in readiness for the Great Scottish Run. It was causing a bottleneck of mammoth proportions, frustrating everyone, her especially.

It took the best part of ten minutes to clear the car park, another ten before she managed to exit the main roundabout. Checking her directions, she waited for a gap in the traffic and followed the signpost for Glasgow airport (M8), Kilmarnock (M77), Carlisle and Cambuslang (M74). Once clear of the logjam, she floored the accelerator, her speed climbing . . . sixty . . . seventy . . . eight-five miles an hour.

Aware that Hank was watching the speedometer, she kept her eyes on the road, closing on an Audi TT, its driver hogging the outside lane, one of those I'm-doing-the-national-speed-limit types that got right up her nose on a regular basis. The stupid sod wouldn't move over and let her by.

She flashed her headlights but still he didn't move.

Hank urged her to back off, but she took no notice. Instead, she turned on her blue light. Technically, the situation didn't warrant it, but Andy's plight was a true emergency in her eyes – and still the git in the TT didn't move over. She undertook the car, glaring at him as she came alongside. The driver was oblivious, hadn't even known she was there.

Kate drove on.

If McKenzie harmed one red hair on Andy's head she'd make it her business to hunt him down. In the meantime, all she could do was be patient and wait for news. Even if there was a shout for assistance, she was too far away to be a first responder. Despite her faith in her team, it didn't come easy, trusting others to do their jobs and deal with the situation until she returned.

A few miles on, Hank got his head down and fell asleep. With no one to talk to, Kate began dwelling on her altercation with Bright, her take on the matter going back and forth like a ping-pong ball. He'd practically ordered her to take a leave of absence. The words 'unfit for duty' had been a real slap in the face, questioning her credibility and professionalism, everything she stood for. She'd been replaying the same thing over and over like a mantra in her head ever since the words left his mouth.

If it had been anyone other than Bright, she'd have shrugged it off. Laughed even. But therein lay the problem. Bright wasn't anybody – he was her mentor, the man she admired more than any other, except Hank – the detective who'd taught her everything she knew.

That didn't mean she could forgive him for what he'd said.

Hadn't he fallen short in his career too? Hadn't she covered for him?

Now they were even.

So what if he'd questioned her judgement. He'd done it before. Several times. What made him think he had the right to look at her as if she'd crawled out from under a stone?

The reason she couldn't let it go was because it mattered – because it came from someone she respected and looked up to.

There was no getting away from it. She needed to see him. Apologize properly. She'd think twice in future. Rein in her maverick tendencies. Stop making rash decisions.

Yeah, right.

Living on the edge was part of her personality. He knew that. Wasn't that why he'd taken her under his wing, nominated her over and again for promotion? She didn't have to make him believe she was up to the job. She *was* up to the job. If he wanted a conformist, he'd picked the wrong horse.

Exhausted with the argument raging inside her head, Kate eased her foot off the pedal. There was little traffic on the road. No need to rush. Time to calm down. The scenery was stunning beneath a leaden sky, the windscreen dotted with a few raindrops, one or two at first, then a torrential downpour, causing her to slow down even further. Hank stirred in his seat, opened one eye, then closed it again.

The phone rang, startling them both.

Robson had located Andy.

Chapter Forty-eight

DC BROWN WAS standing to attention, hands behind his back, feet slightly apart, facing his boss's desk. Half an hour ago, he'd been relieved of duty in Blanchland and summoned to the MIR by Naylor. Five minutes ago, Kate Daniels had burst into the incident room, nearly taking the door off its hinges. Without checking the murder wall, something she always did, she marched across the room and ordered him to her office, humiliating him in front of the squad.

'Lunch?!' Her face was almost crimson. 'You went for *lunch*?'

'And then a walk in the woods,' Brown said. 'I weighed up the odds and made a decision.'

'The wrong one!' she yelled.

Swallowing hard, Brown didn't know what to say. His boss looked jaded. Drawn. He knew she'd had a hell of a day; a hell of a week. He'd seen her angry before – but never like this – and still she wasn't done.

'Let me rewind here.' She crossed her arms, her eyes boring into him. 'Hank and I are up at a murder scene in Glasgow thinking that the guy you're babysitting has rocked you off, and you're sitting in a pub somewhere filling your face? Tell me that's not true, Andy! Make me understand how you thought that was a good idea.'

'With respect, boss, it was! McKenzie and Theresa were stir crazy. Price was on a rest day. He did a forward recce before we set off. I took all the necessary precautions. Asked him to check the route first, make sure there was no one dodgy hanging around. There were the usual suspects walking their dogs, couple of people fishing on the reservoir. He knew who they were. He even came along with his dog to cover my back.'

'Oh, that's OK then. Are you *mad*? Do you have *any* idea the trouble you are in?'

'Why am I in trouble?' Brown knew that sounded lame even before the words had passed his lips. From the minute he'd been summoned from Blanchland he knew he was for the high jump, if not from Naylor, then from her. Fortunately, Naylor had been called away to HQ and wasn't in the office when he arrived. 'Boss, McKenzie wasn't locked up or under arrest.'

'Don't backchat me, Andy. I'm perfectly well aware—'

'Will you hear me out?' He paused, apologized for raising his voice and interrupting her. Aware of the eyes of the team through her office door, he felt ridiculous standing there, trying to vindicate himself. Since he'd joined the Murder Investigation Team, the DCI had only good things to say about him. Until today, they'd never exchanged a cross word. He'd dealt with the situation as he saw fit. He didn't feel he deserved such a public reprimand. Again, he tried justification. 'My role was saving their lives, not detaining them.'

'It wasn't their lives that concerned us. It was yours!' Kate took a breath, dropped her voice a touch. 'Jesus, Andy! Did you not think for one millisecond how going AWOL might look to the rest of the squad if they tried getting hold of you? How it would look to me – to Hank? To anyone else with a brain bigger than a walnut?'

'They were hell-bent on going. If I hadn't gone along, they'd have walked out anyway.' Brown resented the implication that he had no sense, even though he could see how worrying it might have appeared to her. 'There was nothing I could do! Theresa was even worse than McKenzie. She wanted out of the house and I couldn't convince her otherwise. She can moan for Scotland, that one. She had to get out of there and, to be perfectly honest, so did I.'

'Ah, I understand.'

'No, with all due respect, I don't think you do, boss.' Brown shifted his weight from one foot to the other. 'I did everything I could in order to make it as safe as possible for all concerned. I'm sorry, OK? I'm a townie. How did I know you can't get a mobile signal up there if you move more than two metres from the house?'

Kate huffed. 'You should've called first!'

'I never thought—'

'Why the hell not?' Kate's voice was getting louder by the second. 'Hank and I have been going crackers, thinking something awful had happened to you. Lisa is in chunks. You owe her *big-style*. You bloody idiot! You never *ever* do that again! Do you understand?'

And suddenly he did. He felt like a kid being scolded by a parent for running off, or a dog whose owner slaps it for not coming to heel when called – *which is precisely why they never do*. This was her way of showing him how much she cared. How worried she'd been. He'd rather have had a Bonio.

HAVING VENTED HER anger on her young DC, Kate called the squad together for a full briefing. When it was over, she sent Hank off home to see his family – it was the least she could do after the day he'd put in. Grabbing a sandwich to go, she left the station, bound for Blanchland, taking Andy Brown with her.

There was no way he was going home yet.

He had no bloody idea how relieved she was to hear that he was safe. At first he seemed almost oblivious to the anxiety he'd caused his colleagues in the few hours he'd been off the grid. She'd enlightened him good and proper, terrifying him in the process. Although he didn't know it yet – she intended to let him stew a while – she had absolutely no intention of taking the matter further. Technically, he'd broken the rules. But hey, who was she to point the finger? No, it was over: Junior was back with his mummy.

IT WAS DARK by the time they reached McKenzie's cottage: eight thirty-three, to be precise. Andy Brown rapped hard on the door. Creeping around outside wasn't to be recommended with an armed officer in the house on high alert because some raging lunatic was out to get McKenzie. When Craig O'Kane found out about his brother, all hell would break loose.

The latch came off and the door opened.

Kate showed ID, asking the armed officer to remain in the hallway while she and Andy had a word with the occupants. Andy led the way into the living room. Acknowledging Theresa with a nod, he stepped aside, letting his boss take centre stage. McKenzie was sitting in his usual fireside chair, legs raised on a footstool, newspaper on his knee, not one but two crisp packets on the floor beside an empty plate – the remains of his supper.

The DCI got straight to the point. 'Right, Arthur, I want to know who it is.'

McKenzie's eyes slid over her from head to toe, a method employed by his kind when they were trying to put professional women down. Kate was used to it, immune to it even. It made her all the more determined to make his life difficult until she was ready to leave. And that would depend very much on his reaction to her line of questioning. Not that she expected straight answers. She was only there to gauge his response – to see the whites of his eyes, so to speak.

'What the fuck are you on about?' he said.

Kate so wanted to wipe the grin off his face. Her eyes took in both McKenzie and Theresa. 'You two think you've played me, don't you? Well, I've got news for you. Detective Brown here may have babysat your alibi, but I know you sent someone up to Glasgow to kill O'Kane, and I'm going to prove it if it's the last thing I do.'

'O'Kane's dead?' McKenzie grinned. 'Ace! Which one? We'll throw a party.'

'You know fine well which one. And believe me when I tell you, the other one's not going to be a happy bunny. If I were you, I'd dig in for a while. Because Craig is coming after you and I might not have the funds to provide any more protection – unless you cough up a suspect.'

'Is she always this dim?' McKenzie was smirking at Brown. Another put-down. Address the male officer and ignore the female, irrespective of rank. 'Even if I knew what she was harping on about, does she really believe that I'd implicate myself in something as serious as a murder? The stupid cow is talking shite.'

Brown told him to show some respect.

Slowly, McKenzie shifted his gaze to the DCI and slipped his hand into Theresa's. 'I told you once before, I'm going straight. Theresa and I both are. We're not the same people we were years ago. Ask anyone. We run a reputable business. We have a solicitor and everything. In fact, if you continue to make such wild accusations, Detective Chief Inspector, I might have to give him a call.'

Chapter Forty-nine

THE INCIDENT ROOM was in semi-darkness when Kate arrived, shortly before ten o'clock. Everyone had knocked off and gone home. Lights were dimmed, computer screens blank, as she made her weary way towards the glow of her office at the far end of the room. The blinds were half-closed but she could see a figure waiting there, way before she reached the door.

Bright.

Kate slowed. *Not now.*

After going ten rounds with Andy, and ten more with McKenzie, she couldn't stomach another row – especially with the head of CID. Tired and agitated, she'd left McKenzie in a strop, accusing her of harassment. It was useless talking to him. The tosser deserved all he got from whoever was currently dishing out the violence. Shame she couldn't butt out of his dispute with O'Kane and let the stupid sods kill each other.

For a moment, she considered tiptoeing away, making out that she'd gone straight home. But unless Bright had changed his after-shave, she knew it wasn't him before she reached her office door. A whiff of Jo Malone – Dark Amber & Ginger Lily – identified her visitor as Jo Soulsby. Kate had bought her the cologne for her birthday.

Jo's presence, even at this late hour, was a nice surprise, if not a little baffling. Given that they hadn't seen each other for days, or spoken since their brief squabble on Friday morning, Kate wondered why she was there so late in the evening when she could be tucked up in bed or lounging in front of a good movie.

Trying not to appear as downhearted as she felt, she turned the handle and opened the door. Jo was sitting in the easy chair Kate had bought from an antiques shop and installed for the comfort of visitors, feet tucked up beneath her. She was casually dressed in a pair of old jeans and a rugby shirt, hair tied up loosely, a few strands hanging loose around her face. A pair of tatty sneakers lay untidily on the floor, kicked off to make her even more at ease in her surroundings.

She looked right at home, engrossed in a novel: Louise Welsh's *The Girl on the Stairs*.

'Good choice!' Kate was pointing at the book. She bent down and planted a kiss, first on one cheek, then the other. 'To what do I owe this pleasure?'

'Sit down, I'll get you a coffee.'

Closing the paperback, Jo stood up and gave her a hug, hanging on for a bit too long. Kate told her not to bother with the coffee. It was too late in the day for that and she had a much better idea. She needed something stronger after the day she'd put in. She was technically off duty, on her own time. Opening her bottom drawer, she took out two shot glasses and a bottle of Jim Beam Devil's Cut bourbon.

Pouring them both a dram, she held up her glass. 'I so need this,' she said.

'I don't think you do,' Jo said awkwardly. 'Not for me.'

'Not a social call then?'

Kate was right about that. Jo told her that she knew all about O'Kane's death, Andy's disappearance and McKenzie's alibi. As part of the team, most of that was understandable, but she'd left the best 'til last and didn't hold back.

'I also know about Whitby, Towner, and your bloody awful row with Bright.'

'How the hell?'

Meltdown . . .

Hank had grassed her up.

Kate downed her drink in one, felt the bourbon do its job, warming her insides as the amber liquid entered her system. Even without the alcohol, she was punchy. Having told her to forget all about Whitby, in the time it had taken her to drive to Blanchland and back, Hank had blabbed to the one person in the world whose approval mattered.

Kate wouldn't forgive him this time.

OK, so he was concerned about her. That didn't give him the right to involve Jo in her screw-ups. When was he ever going to learn to keep his nose the hell out of her business?

Lifting Jo's untouched glass to her lips, Kate slugged off the bourbon, picked up the bottle and poured another, slopping some on her desk in the process, not bothering to wipe the excess away. She didn't know what to say, what to think.

'You could have told me, you know,' Jo said gently.

'What, and risk the condemnation I can see in your eyes? Or is that for the drink? It's hard to tell these days.' Kate stared Jo down. They were no longer together. There was no reason to explain her actions. Why should she? She had nothing to feel ashamed of or guilty about. She wasn't about to apologize for doing her job. If she felt like a bloody drink, she'd have one. Resentment bubbled to the surface and she blurted out exactly what was on her mind: 'If I'd wanted you to know, I'd have told you myself. He had no right!'

'He had every right. Don't be angry with him, Kate. He meant well.'

'Oh yeah? Wonder who else he's told.'

'What? Come on! You know he'd never do that! He thinks I can help.'

'Well, you can't. No one can. I'm a big girl. I have to work this out all by myself.'

'You're not though, are you? Working it out, I mean. He said you weren't. He told me how upset you were. How you weren't—'

'Coping? Is that what he said?'

'I was going to say feeling your best. That's true, isn't it?'

Kate didn't believe her. She glanced out of the window at the building across the street. It was dark. Empty. Just like her. So, now she wasn't merely 'unfit for duty', she wasn't coping. *Jesus Christ, was this a conspiracy?* Did everyone think she was heading for a mental breakdown? She turned back to Jo, her face set in a scowl. 'Roll up, roll up for the freak show. The great Detective Chief Inspector Daniels does it again. Is Hank selling tickets yet?'

'What's Hank got to do with it?' Jo looked genuinely bewildered.

Kate stared at her as the penny dropped. If it wasn't Hank who'd grassed, it had to be Bright – but why? He and Jo had never seen eye to eye. For him to confide in her went beyond unusual, it was unprecedented. The sharing of such confidential and potentially harmful information came as a body blow to Kate. And with it came an epiphany.

She desperately needed help.

Chapter Fifty

SUNDAY MORNING WAS glorious, warm and sunny. Kate had slept soundly, if only for four hours, despite a heartbreaking face-to-face lasting until after midnight. By that time she was incapable of driving, so Jo had dropped her off at home. Persuaded to stay for a nightcap, she eventually left around half past twelve. In between arriving home and Jo leaving, Kate had gone through a range of emotions: anger, aggression, guilt, and most of all sadness for having pressurized Towner and disappointed Bright.

Jo, as always, had listened patiently while she spewed out all the reasons she was feeling so ghastly. She had wept and drunk more alcohol than was good for her, purging herself to the point of exhaustion. At some time during the conversation, she'd acknowledged she'd been pushing herself too hard and promised to slow down. Whether she'd keep that promise rather depended on her case.

Before Jo left, she'd helped her upstairs to bed and held her until she fell asleep. Unless Kate had imagined it, they had reiterated their intention to take a holiday together when the investigation was over – which it wasn't, not anywhere near. Kate had a vague recollection that they had talked about themselves too, specifically about *that* topic, the one she wasn't to mention ever again – why their relationship had gone horribly wrong.

In the course of a one-way conversation, Jo had told her some home truths. She'd accused Kate of limiting her choices, seeing only two alternatives – being out and proud, or staying in the closet – when most of their gay friends were busy just getting on with their lives. They didn't need to bang on about their sexuality or beat the drum. Why should they? Jo argued. The phrase 'private life' meant just that. Like they gave a shit what anyone else thought. Jo was insistent: there was only one person stopping them moving in together and starting over, letting others make up their own minds what was going on, and it wasn't *her*.

You're the only one placing barriers in our way.

Kate knew she was right.

The thought that their relationship might still have some life in it lifted her spirits as she showered and brushed her teeth. Within twenty minutes, she was on her way to work with renewed determination to solve her case and plan some time off afterwards. It wouldn't be for long though. Ambitious police officers didn't ask for special dispensation for an extended period of leave, not if they knew what was good for them. It didn't show the right level of commitment – at least, that was how it would be viewed upstairs. A sabbatical was out of the question. If she took one of those, she'd be guaranteed a job at the end of it, but not necessarily the one she already had. HR might put her back in uniform and she wouldn't risk that.

SHE ARRIVED AT the incident room at six forty-five. It was exactly as she'd left it the night before. No one in yet, no laughter or chatter, no hum of the well-oiled machine that was the Murder Investigation Team. Her office smelled faintly of alcohol. The shot glasses were gone, tidied away by the cleaner, not the best impression for a DCI to give. What the hell? It had never happened before in all her years in the force. She had enough to fret about without adding to the list.

Drinking copious amounts of water to rehydrate her body and downing a couple of painkillers for her aching head, Kate even managed a bacon sandwich from the staff canteen to soak up the alcohol. By seven-thirty, she'd completed her admin. She'd made a few phone calls, including one to Trewitt. He was tied up in a meeting. She hoped it meant good news. Leaving a message for him to get in touch, she put down her mobile as Hank arrived in the doorway. Gone was the bedraggled look, the five o'clock shadow he'd been sporting when last seen. He was freshly shaven and raring to go.

She felt guilty for having doubted him.

The tenth morning briefing was due to get underway at nine o'clock. Bright surprised everyone by arriving at the MIR unannounced. He gave no valid reason for wanting to sit in, made out that he had nothing better to do on this fine Sunday morning, mitigating his presence by reminding everyone that he knew the Allen family well. He'd taken a personal interest in the case and was curious to know how things were progressing.

Kate wasn't fooled. It was all bollocks.

Bright was shadowing her – protecting her – something he'd done for nearly fifteen years. After her first case as SIO, he'd stopped doing it. Until now. He wasn't exactly treating her like a rookie, but not far off. Although she didn't like it, she had to accept that he was genuinely worried about her. So she bit the bullet, pushing away any residual ill-feeling, hoping to convince him she was perfectly well and capable of carrying out her duties without interference or anyone holding her hand.

The noise in the room increased as the squad took their seats.

The murder wall had been updated. Under Finn O'Kane's image, his name was underlined. Beneath it someone had written the words: *Deceased – TIE action ongoing.* Kate stood up, signalling that she was ready to start. She began by confirming that there was no new intelligence on the whereabouts of Craig O'Kane, and no evidence that any of McKenzie's cronies had been involved in the murder of Finn O'Kane.

Kate was inclined to believe McKenzie. 'If I've read him right,' she said, 'although he joked about throwing a party when he found out Finn was dead, he was shocked by the news. I'm certain of it. He tried very hard to mask his surprise.'

Andy Brown was nodding. 'I agree with the boss. He couldn't hide it.'

'So,' Kate said. 'If he wasn't behind Finn's death, then who was? Unless—'

Her phone rang.

'Unless?' Bright said. 'You going to enlighten us?'

Kate ran a hand through her hair as she took in the display on her mobile phone. She looked up. 'It's Trewitt, guv. I've been waiting on news from Scotland. I'm hoping this is it.'

The Chief Super nodded his consent for her to take the call.

To avoid wasting precious time relaying everything that was said to the team, she put the phone on speaker. There was a short delay before Trewitt came on the line.

'Guess whose print was on the windscreen of Finn's car?' he asked.

The squad were all ears. He'd asked the question in a way that implied Kate must know the answer. And it turned out she did. Overpowering O'Kane and strapping him to his vehicle took strength, suggesting that the person responsible was a well-built male. The handprint was *definitely* male. There were few possibilities from which to choose. If it wasn't McKenzie or one of his associates, it had to be Finn's brother, Craig, or . . . *who else, who else?* It was the question Kate had been asking herself all morning. The answer had come to her in a flash. It had been on the tip of her tongue when the phone rang.

'Brian,' she said. 'Brian Allen.'

'No one likes a clever shit,' Trewitt replied. 'How did you work it out?'

'Process of elimination.' Kate ignored a round of quiet applause.

Chapter Fifty-one

As she put the phone down, Bright stood up, still clapping his hands in a show of appreciation. A little choked by the gesture, Kate managed to hide it well. There was no doubt that it was a pivotal moment in the case. It explained so much, most importantly the issue that had bugged her since day one: the identity of the person John Allen was calling on the night he died. She had her answer. He was screaming for his father's help when he made that call.

'Jesus! The guy's got some neck,' someone said, pulling her back into the room.

The nerve it must've taken to pull off Finn's death under the noses of three police forces and get away scot-free – especially when you were dead – required a certain level of *je ne sais quoi*. It didn't surprise Bright. According to him, Brian was the most audacious criminal he'd ever come across. Fearless too. But even Bright had to admit, he hadn't seen that one coming.

'A legend in his time,' he said. 'Not one to use violence for the sake of it, but if someone crossed him he'd get his revenge – and then some. If Finn'd had a hand in killing his sons, he'd have no qualms using a vehicle to squash him like a fly against the wall until his eyes bled. He would have walked away without giving the matter a second thought.'

'Nowt wrong with an eye for an eye,' Robson said emphatically. 'Can't say I wouldn't do the same in his shoes. I'd be prepared to swing if anyone touched my laddie.'

'Too right,' Hank added, the only other father among them.

Bright was nodding. 'Now can you see why I liked him?'

'I'm beginning to like him too,' Hank said.

Kate rolled her eyes. 'Will you lot listen to yourselves? Revenge was the motive that triggered the violence in the first place. It solves nothing. Anyway, Brian is Strathclyde's problem, not ours. All *they* have to do is find a dead man. Dead or alive, *we* still have to prove a case against Finn and the evidence, so far, is circumstantial. We might be convinced of his guilt, but that's not enough.'

'The DCI is right,' Bright said. 'You need to find Craig before Brian does and get a confession out of him.'

Hank looked at him. 'Guv, with all due respect that's as likely as my being appointed Chief by the end of the day.'

A chuckle went round the room.

Kate didn't need reminding that if Brian got to Craig first it would change things dramatically. It would mean she'd have to prove the case to Bright, rather than a court of law. If both brothers were dead, before the case could be classed as detected and written off in the system, it had to satisfy the head of CID. The report she'd have to write would be lengthy. She'd have to prove beyond the bounds of possibility that the O'Kanes were responsible for John and Terry Allen's deaths. It would be a massive undertaking, one she'd do anything to avoid.

'I need proof, guys,' she said. 'No ifs or buts.'

'You have *no* real evidence?' Bright asked.

Kate was shaking her head.

Carmichael was the first to offer an answer. 'I hate to state the obvious, but Bethany Miller was the only witness we're aware of and she's dead. The van was burned out and SOCO say there's nothing in it of use to us. The only other thing we have is the young lad who saw a flash of ginger hair in the Range Rover in close proximity to Silverlink at silly o'clock the morning the Allen brothers croaked.'

'Bring him in,' Bright said. 'Put an album of redheads in front of him.'

Carmichael advised that she was on it. 'I don't hold out much hope, though. The Range Rover was being driven at speed. Can't see him making a positive ID, can you?'

'Anything else?' Bright asked.

Most team members were scratching their heads.

'Brian seems to think he was guilty,' Hank said. 'The man's been officially dead and buried for years. Why would he come back to life to right a wrong if he wasn't one hundred per cent sure Finn had something to do with his sons' deaths? John Allen was terrified. I think he told his old man exactly who was responsible.'

'For what it's worth, I do too,' Robson said.

'The history also fits,' Kate reminded them. 'The bad blood, I mean.'

'We do have one other witness,' Carmichael said. 'The cleaner .at Theresa Allen's apartment block got a good look at the blokes who paid her a visit.'

'Good thinking,' said Kate. 'Get her in here, Lisa. Have her take a look at an album of redheads too. We may never have physical evidence linking Finn and Craig to the scene, but if we have a witness who can ID them driving away and another witness who'll testify they were trying to get to Theresa, we'll be cooking on gas. Let's face it, they had no reason to be in either place unless they were involved.'

Bright sent her a silent message: the protégé he'd nurtured for years was back.

It brought a lump to her throat. Things were looking up.

Chapter Fifty-two

BLANCHLAND ON SUNDAY lunchtime, particularly when the weather was warm, took on a persona of its own. People swarmed there to soak up the atmosphere, to stroll in the fresh air, picnic at nearby Derwent Reservoir or stop off at the White Monk for lunch. It was a much-loved haven of tranquillity in people's busy lives. Just as well the tourists and villagers had no inkling of the goings on in one tiny cottage in the village.

Kate was visiting McKenzie and Theresa yet again, this time with Hank. On their way into the house they had been warned by the couple's close protection officer that the pair were already half-cut and argumentative. In the few hours they had been awake, they had fallen out with him and had a go at each other. Despite the smell of a Sunday roast permeating the room, the atmosphere could only be described as hostile.

Domestic bliss this was not.

Apart from being unbearably hot, the house reeked of booze and fags. McKenzie was sitting at a small dining table, yesterday's *Journal* spread out in front of him, an open pack of cigarettes, a lighter, an empty beer glass by his side, waiting to be refilled. Not bothering to raise his head, not interested in a word they had to say, he'd called Theresa through from the kitchen to see to their guests. She arrived, decidedly flustered, hands covered in flour, a dab of white powder on the left side of her cheek. She was wearing a black apron Kate's father would call a pinny, a check tea towel draped over her left shoulder. Her eyes were red, whether from too much alcohol or upset was anyone's guess.

Apologizing for calling unannounced at such an inconvenient time, Kate invited Theresa to sit.

'I prefer to stand, if it's all the same to you.' Theresa raised her hands. 'As you can see, I'm busy.'

'As you wish.' Kate cleared her throat, wondering how to word the information she was there to impart. It was important to establish whether the woman was aware her husband had faked his own death. The subtle approach wouldn't work with someone like Theresa, so Kate dived right in. 'I have something to tell you. It might be news to you. Then again it might not. Chief Superintendent Bright told us you were a pathological liar, but I'm prepared to give you the benefit of the doubt.'

'Fuck does that mean?' McKenzie stood up suddenly, knocking his chair over. He loomed over Kate, furiously demanding, 'What is your problem, lady?'

The DCI stood her ground, unfazed.

When McKenzie pointed his finger in her face, Hank stepped between them, eyeballing him. They were like a pair of prizefighters flexing their muscles before a bout, psyching each other out. The state McKenzie was in, Kate was confident he'd be on the deck with the snips on if he decided to take a pop at her DS.

'I think it's you who has the problem,' Hank said. 'Back off and listen.'

'Or what?' McKenzie leaned forward until their foreheads were almost touching.

'You don't want to find out,' Kate said. 'So shut it or we'll be having this conversation in a cell. You'll be right at home.'

Placing his fingers on McKenzie's chest, Hank pushed him away roughly. Then bent his forefinger, beckoned him forward, willing him to kick off. McKenzie was about to rise to the bait when Theresa took hold of his arm. Shrugging her off, he withdrew, sat down in his favourite armchair, demanding that she bring him another drink.

Kate asked her to stay put. 'I'm not finished with you yet.'

McKenzie glared at her. 'Spit it out then, Detective. Then fuck off to where you came from and leave us be. Have you no manners? Can you not see we're about to eat?'

Keeping her focus on his other half, Kate ignored him. 'We have categorical evidence that Brian didn't die in Spain, Theresa. He's alive and well. And less than twenty-four hours ago, he was up to his old tricks in Glasgow.'

Theresa took a step backwards, put a hand out to steady herself. Her knuckles were white as she gripped the tabletop. She was almost hyperventilating. If she was bluffing, she deserved a BAFTA.

Allowing the woman a moment to compose herself, Kate asked her outright if she had known that Brian was alive and studied her reaction carefully.

Theresa swore she didn't.

'John did,' Kate said.

The noise that left Theresa's mouth was a strangulated wail. She sat down at the table, drew McKenzie's fags towards her and lit one, taking the nicotine deep into her lungs. Her floury hands were shaking so much she could hardly hold the cigarette between her fingers. As she took another long drag, the tip glowed red and then died off. She glanced up at Kate. 'There must be a mistake.'

Kate shook her head. 'I'm sorry.'

'The bastard. I had no idea, I swear to you.'

Kate looked at McKenzie. 'How about you, Arthur?'

'Are you fucking serious? Why would he confide in me?' He was chuckling, apparently finding the whole thing hilarious. 'Anyway, you think I'd be with Theresa if he had?'

'I was wondering about that,' Kate said. 'What impact will his resurrection have on you?'

'Well, if he's going after the other cunt, he has my vote. I'd be the first to shake his hand, because guys like O'Kane never stop.'

'That's not what I meant.' Kate left that one floating.

'Oh, I see.' McKenzie shrugged. 'We're not in danger from Brian, if that's what you're suggesting. He and I were practically family. Ask Theresa.' He looked to her for confirmation, but there was no response; Theresa's face was almost as white as her hands. Unconcerned, McKenzie trained his eyes on the detectives. 'If Brian *is* alive, it was his choice to disappear. He's got no dispute with me, or her. We both thought he was dead – and she had every right to get on with her life.' *Another grin.* 'It suits me fine. I always did prefer screwing married women. Forbidden fruits are so much sweeter.' He scowled at Hank. 'Don't you agree, pal?'

Hank couldn't help himself. 'I hope Brian appreciates your attitude to married life.'

Kate told them to cut it out. She hadn't come for a fight, much less a discussion on morals. Despite McKenzie's confidence, she couldn't afford to assume that he was correct in his assessment of the danger Brian posed to him and Theresa. So far as she was concerned, Brian Allen was an unknown quantity. He'd proven himself capable of extreme violence, and she had no idea of his current whereabouts. Bearing that in mind, she wanted McKenzie and Theresa moved to a bona fide safe house. She couldn't force them to go. And if they insisted on staying, as they had once before, she'd need to make arrangements to extend their protection for the foreseeable future.

IN THE END, McKenzie and Theresa agreed to move, if for no other reason than a change of scenery. Tasked with making the necessary arrangements, Andy Brown was put back in charge of their ongoing protection and excused from all other duties.

Back àt the incident room, there was no consensus of opinion. The team was split right down the middle, one half prepared to accept Bright's contention that Brian wouldn't harm Theresa. Quite the contrary: he'd do anything for her, even drag himself out of the gutter, even fake his own death. The other half of the squad remained to be convinced. Like Kate, they thought it was stretching it to believe that he'd been motivated solely by the desire to protect his wife and sons from the wrath of the O'Kanes.

Superintendent Ron Naylor put forward another suggestion. 'Maybe we're all missing the point. Couldn't it be much more simple than that? Maybe he found someone new and pissed off to a place in the sun.'

'A new start?' Kate queried.

'Just so,' Naylor said. 'It's not as if it hasn't happened before, is it?'

'That's true,' Carmichael chipped in. 'The guv'nor said he was quite the ladies' man. A real charmer.'

'I'm with the Super on this,' Robson said. 'If Brian moved his family south to protect them, chances are he faked his own death for the very same reason, so the Glasgow mob would hear of it and stop hunting him down, if indeed that's what they were doing.'

'C'mon!' Hank was shaking his head. 'Giving up the love of your life is too high a sacrifice, surely? I agree with Ron. He probably got sick of Theresa and the kids weighing him down and cleared off while he was young enough to enjoy life and start again.'

'Then why go to the trouble of faking his death?'

They were going round in circles, getting nowhere fast.

'Robbo's got a point, Hank,' Kate said. 'Anyway, it doesn't matter why he left her. As I keep telling you, he's not our problem. Strathclyde can argue that one. The important thing here is that one or both of the O'Kane brothers found out he was still alive and committed murder and mayhem on our patch, a mess that you and I have to clean up.'

'You think Brian was unlucky?' Carmichael asked. 'That he got spotted by some other lowlife in Spain or wherever, after all these years?'

'Who knows?' Kate paused for thought. 'Lisa, see what you can find out about Brian's "death". John shipped the body home, so he was obviously complicit in his father's vanishing act. Maybe he confided in someone and was double-crossed. Knowledge like that is worth a shedload of money.'

'If so, his loose tongue cost him,' Maxwell said. 'You reckon Vicky knew?'

'No,' Kate said. 'I think it highly unlikely. I'm pretty sure Terry didn't either. If he had, he'd have blabbed before losing his fingers. It begs other questions though, very worrying ones.' She had the whole squad's attention. 'What exactly did John give up while he was being tortured? What I mean is, does the surviving O'Kane brother know where to find Brian?' Kate studied the faces of her team. 'Maybe the sole reason for killing John and Terry was to draw Brian out into the open, bring him back to the UK.'

'Well, it backfired,' Carmichael said. 'He's out for revenge now, and if he found Finn . . .'

'Yup, he'll find Craig,' Hank said. 'One down, one to go.'

'Not if we find him first,' Kate said. 'Lisa, get Trewitt on the phone. Let's do some graft.'

Chapter Fifty-three

ALMOST TWO WEEKS into the enquiry and they were still no further forward in the search for Craig O'Kane. There had been no sightings whatsoever, in England or north of the border. For all they knew, Brian might already have found Craig O'Kane and delivered his retribution. If, on the other hand, Craig was still alive, he might be the predator rather than the prey, looking to avenge his younger brother's death.

The words *blood bath* didn't quite cover it.

The only new information available to the Murder Investigation Team had come from DS Robson. The silversmith who'd come forward in response to the appeal for information had since identified Terry's ring as his own handiwork. Although he couldn't recall the man who'd commissioned it, he'd written it up in his order book as a twenty-first birthday gift. The date corresponded to Terry's coming of age and was not long before Brian Allen disappeared off the face of the earth.

Kate had always thought that the ring was a clue, some kind of sick message for John that the O'Kanes were coming for him. That theory only held up if Terry had told them where it came from and what it meant to him. Whatever the story, she'd uncovered its significance too late. If she'd known Brian was alive before driving north to Glasgow, she could have put the Strathclyde, Lothian and Borders forces on alert.

No one had been looking for a dead man.

There was a mountain of paperwork on Kate's desk, most of it relating to Brian's falsified death in 2005. John Allen had been with his father when he allegedly collapsed from a heart attack and took his last breath. It was John who'd called the medic and obtained a death certificate. He'd even spoken to the British Consul, who in turn contacted the UK police to inform Theresa. Then, bold as brass, John had repatriated the body for cremation at Newcastle's West Road Crematorium.

Easy.

Particularly as there was nothing that would flag up the death as unusual. It wasn't as if the 'deceased' was a fugitive on the run from the police, either in Spain, the UK or anywhere else in Europe. Assuming anyone even bothered to check. For all intents and purposes, it was just another sudden death of a tourist on a golfing holiday. It wouldn't surprise Kate to learn that John had reclaimed the entire cost from his insurance, such was the audacity of the man.

She wondered how he'd pulled it off.

It was anyone's guess whose body was actually in the coffin. She knew only that it was a middle-aged male. She felt sad for the dead man's family; they might go on searching, possibly for the rest of their lives, for a missing man who would never be found, dead or alive – his body reduced to dust nearly two thousand kilometres away from home in a city he'd probably never even heard of.

Picking up some of the documentation pertaining to Brian Allen, she sifted it in her hands. For every Spanish form, there was a corresponding English translation.

It all appeared lawful . . .

It was anything but.

In the course of her enquiries, she'd spoken to a local registrar and also an undertaker about the procedures involved in repatriating a body from abroad. The corpse would be embalmed in the country where death occurred, arriving in the UK in a zinc-lined casket for transfer to a burial coffin. Official forms had to be completed in the language of the dispatching nation and then translated into English before a body could be released for shipment. To Kate's surprise, no formal identification was required on this side of the water.

'You take it at face value?' she'd asked, incredulous.

'Pretty much.'

'No fingerprints taken, dental records . . . ?'

'No,' the expert witness said. 'The casket arrives. The family takes the translated death certificate to the Registry Office. So long as the papers appear to be in order and the district coroner sees no reason for further investigation, away we go.'

Kate couldn't believe it was that simple.

Although Theresa Allen was a piece of work, the DCI felt sorry for her. The poor woman still had photographs of bouquets displayed in the crematorium garden after the service. Dozens and dozens of them, all lined up along the pathway to be viewed by mourners after the ceremony.

What a sham.

KATE PUT DOWN the phone. The question of Brian's death certificate had bothered her for days. Convinced that either the form itself was dodgy, or the doctor who'd certified death was, she'd put out an action to Spanish police and had a long conversation with the enquiring officer. He concluded that the female GP was in the clear. She'd reported a death certificate stolen a few months after Brian's death, alleging it was removed from the back of a tear-off pad. She hadn't noticed it was missing until she reached the end of the book. Her signature had been falsified and she would not be facing charges.

Kate jumped as a shout went up in the incident room beyond her office door. Through the blinds she could see detectives on their feet, all smiles and pats on the back, Carmichael and Maxwell among them – almost a group hug taking place. Hank emerged from the centre of the scrum, an expression of delight on his face as he high-fived Robson.

Seconds later the two arrived at her door.

'We're on,' Hank said. 'Trewitt's team spotted Craig O'Kane on CCTV at Edinburgh airport at the easyJet check-in desk. He was travelling light, hand luggage only – a light-tan Hidesign leather holdall. Flash bastard.'

Kate's interest waned as Robson gave her the corresponding bad news . . .

'The downside is, this was five past five yesterday morning, not today.' He grimaced. 'I'm sorry, boss. It seems O'Kane got the jump on us. He took the six o'clock flight to Alicante.'

Kate was a little confused. Her suspect leaving the country was hardly a cause for celebration. Before she could ask why the victory-dance, two modest pieces of information fell into place. Glancing at the papers spread out on her desk, she shuffled through them, eventually found what she was searching for . . . an A4 sheet.

She held it up. 'This is the transit documentation for a zinc-lined casket. Alicante is the departure airport. Robbo, get on to Trewitt. Tell him I want CCTV checked for *all* Alicante flights from Scottish airports from Saturday lunchtime onwards.'

Gormley and Robson exchanged a look.

There was more.

Kate's eyes darted between the two. 'What?' she asked.

'Trewitt and his team aren't as daft as I thought,' Hank admitted sheepishly. 'As soon as they clocked O'Kane, they repeated the action for Brian. He jumped on a Jet2 flight bound for Alicante out of Edinburgh the day Finn died. Clever, eh? He kills Finn, then goes straight for his two-thirty flight after leaving his calling card on the car, knowing full well that our heads were all turned the other way.'

Kate sat for a moment, considering.

'If Craig's looking for Brian, you and I need to follow the trail to Spain.'

Chapter Fifty-four

THEY WERE IN seats 19a and 19b, too far from the front of the plane for Kate's liking. From her aisle seat she had a good view of passengers entering through the forward door that, sadly, was still gaping open.

She exhaled loudly.

No matter where she was off to, it seemed that there was always one tosser who managed to hold up her flight, postponing take-off and inconveniencing other passengers. She wondered how long the captain would wait *this* time. The alternative didn't bear thinking about. She knew from experience it would involve unloading the luggage to identify the one bag checked in by the absentee, a missed flight slot – an unnecessary delay.

She was bored already.

The complaint was on the tip of her tongue.

Before she had a chance to voice it, a round of applause filled the cabin as a group of well-served middle-aged men and women welcomed the late passenger on board. The arrogant shit was smirking as he walked down the aisle sporting the same stupid black D & G T-shirt others in his party were wearing. According to lettering on the back as he turned round, the group were bound for a piss-up in Benidorm – a fortieth birthday party for one of their number.

No Dolce & Gabbana here.

Written beneath the iconic D & G image, were two words: *Drunken Geordies.*

Kate ignored a growing desire to say something as he threw himself down in his seat, joking loudly to his sniggering mates. Tipping her head back, she tried to relax and found she couldn't get comfy. Hank's bulk in the next seat gave her little room for manoeuvre. The seatback facing her was a foot away, an advertisement for cheap lager – Buy 2 cans of Stella and save £1 or €1:50 – in her face. She had a feeling those bound for Benidorm would be taking full advantage.

Grateful that she wasn't squashed into a window seat, the slope of the aircraft shell making her feel even more claustrophobic than she already did, Kate paid attention as cabin crew went through their emergency routine, wondering what her chances were of ever getting a life jacket over her head in such a confined space, let alone being able to pass the straps around her waist and clip them together as she was being instructed to do.

Once airborne, she considered the task facing her. As the SIO trying to solve three connected homicides in the Northumbria force area, she'd been given a free hand to conduct the investigation in whichever way she chose by Naylor and Bright. That meant a lot, bearing in mind her recent failure to impress the latter.

Annoyed that Scottish ports had been checked too late to prevent Craig O'Kane from leaving the country, she was faced with the mammoth task of finding him. According to Spanish police, he'd passed through airport security before a message filtered through to be on the lookout for him. Her best chance of finding him was to locate Brian Allen, and the only link to him had come from hurried conversations last night with John Allen's mother and girlfriend. Both had been surprisingly helpful.

Theresa had given her a photo of Brian taken weeks before she 'buried' him. Comparing it with images sent by Immigration directly to her phone, it was clear that his appearance hadn't changed much since faking his death in 2005. There was no sign of plastic surgery and not much evidence of the natural process of ageing. Seven years on, his hair was fairer. It didn't appear dyed. A little greyer round the temples perhaps, probably lightened by the sunny climate on the Continent. He'd also grown a beard.

An Oliver Reid lookalike, Kate thought, but tanned and toned, *a Glasgow hard man who could handle himself.* She'd know him anywhere.

Theresa had also supplied a photograph of Brian and John together. They were standing side by side, arms round each other's shoulders, smiling for the camera. A happy father-and-son snap Theresa wanted returned when Kate had finished with it. It was the only one she had of the two men together.

Hank's voice broke her chain of thought. 'You OK, boss?'

She glanced sideways. 'I'm thirty thousand-odd feet above the ground, jammed into a tin tube and can't hear myself think. Why wouldn't I be OK?'

He chuckled. 'You think we've got a hope in hell of finding him?'

'O'Kane or Allen?'

'Either,' he said.

She shrugged. 'We'll give it our best shot.'

'They'll be looking over their shoulder now, for sure.'

'You reckon? I don't think either of them will give a shit, Hank. If you can tie someone to a van and run him over, or crush him against the wall and leave irrefutable evidence that it was you who did it, you must be some mad bastard. O'Kane and Allen deserve each other. They must be pretty certain they have the means to get away with cold-blooded murder.'

Hank made a face. 'You make them sound so nice.'

'Yeah, I'm dying to make their acquaintance.'

'They're not going to be best pleased to see us.'

'If we ever find them.'

'Why do you think Brian showed his hand?'

Kate gave him a pointed look. 'You being funny?'

'Not intentionally.' He wasn't. 'He didn't need to tip us off, so why do it?'

'For the right price, people talk. He'll be under the impression that Craig is as well connected as he used to be, perhaps with a journo or bent copper in his pocket, someone who'd keep him up to date with any interesting developments. It was a terror tactic. Brian wanted him to know that he took out his brother and was coming after him.'

The man in the window seat had taken off his headphones.

Hank lowered his voice. 'Then why piss off back to Spain with the job half done?'

'I don't know the answer to that. Maybe he was hoping to disappear into the ether again, lie low until the heat died down, then come for Craig when the case was lower on our priority list.' She pointed at the phone lying on the drop-down table in front of him. 'Any news from Lisa?'

Hank picked it up, checked the display.

Carmichael was liaising with Spanish police. She'd promised to text any developments as and when they occurred and also interview Vicky again to see if there was any evidence available as to John's movements in Spain. If they had that, they might be able to track down his father. She'd already given them two till receipts she'd found in the pocket of a linen jacket still hanging in John's wardrobe. Both receipts were for a restaurant where he'd eaten while in the country six months ago.

As Hank accessed his messages, his expression gave him away.

Had they got lucky?

'Tell me,' Kate said.

'Vicky remembers a photograph John sent of his holiday villa one time.'

Kate's head went down. 'How does that help us? She destroyed her phone.'

'She forwarded it on to piss off her sister who she can't stand the sight of. Depends if the sister saved it or not. Lisa's checking it out and will be in touch if anything comes of it.'

With her fingers tightly crossed, Kate glanced across the aisle as the plane tipped slightly, altering direction. Fluffy clouds below resembled whipped meringue. She wished she could lay her tired body down on top of them, curl up and fall asleep until this unsavoury affair was over and done with.

She turned back to Hank. 'Get some kip,' she told him. 'It's going to be a long day.'

He didn't need telling twice. Within seconds he was gone but, less than three minutes later, he was awake again, a transmission over the flight intercom dragging him from sleep: a chance to win ten grand on a scratch card, a reminder that fragrances and gadgets were available should passengers wish to purchase them.

Kate wished the steward would shut up. She wanted rest, out of the tin tube, her feet back on terra firma.

Hank drifted off again.

Unable to rest, Kate opened the novel she'd brought along to pass the time – *Headhunters* by Norwegian author, Jo Nesbo – a tale in which the hunter becomes the hunted, according to the blurb on the back. She wondered if that was what was going on in Spain. Was O'Kane hoping to get to Brian before he had a chance to get to him?

If so, he was playing a very dangerous game.

She glanced at her sleeping DS. Between them they had spent many years hunting down wrongdoers, a job that rarely took them out of the UK. *Thank God*. Kate preferred home turf. She hated being constrained by the protocols of another police force. Not being a warranted officer was like operating in a straitjacket. It didn't feel right. Hank, on the other hand, couldn't give a monkey's. Working in someone else's jurisdiction was fine with him, so long as it involved a stretch of sandy beach and a few pints of local beer at the end of the day. Not so for her. Wherever they were headed was too far from the Tyne Bridge for her liking.

Chapter Fifty-five

KATE STOPPED DEAD at Passport Control, unable to believe her eyes. In recent years, her job had been made more difficult by the lifting of border controls. This state of affairs was a bloody joke. Every immigration booth – and there were several – was abandoned. Not a police officer in sight, let alone anyone from Customs or Immigration.

Her tone was sarcastic. 'No one stopped them coming in then?'

Hank had no words.

Taking the escalator to the ground floor, they followed the signs to the exit, bypassing baggage claim areas on their right, having opted for hand luggage only to ensure a quick getaway. The drunken Geordies were pissed already, one female practically incapable of walking. It made Kate ashamed to be a Brit. The woman deserved the label 'lager lout', a term often used by other Europeans to describe the worst of her countrymen – or, in this case, women.

Before leaving the airport, Kate took the till receipts Vicky had given them from her bag, programming the address of the restaurant into her iPhone, intending to use the device as a satnav. Just as she was doing that, her phone rang in her hand. It was Lisa Carmichael and she sounded really excited.

'Vicky's sister still has that photo,' she said.

'Good job, Lisa.' Kate high-fived Hank. 'Send it to my phone.'

'It's on its way. Have a good trip.'

'Thanks. Call me if you get anything else.'

Hanging up, Kate started the engine. Turning left towards the E15/A70, she followed the signs for Murcia. Already complaining about the heat in the car, Hank opened the window, then closed it again, realizing the aircon – such as it was – would be rendered useless if he left it down. The vehicle was a Seat Mii, rented from Avis. A friendly Spanish agent had offered an additional driver for ten euros a day plus taxes. Despite the fact that the car was a glorified golf trolley, Hank urged Kate to accept.

She declined, telling him that they were on basic expenses. She couldn't justify the extra money. It wasn't the real reason. Neither was it that she didn't trust his driving. She simply preferred to be in control of the vehicle while driving on the wrong side of the road. He stopped whining only when she pointed out that he could sleep while she drove or drink within reason to give the appearance they were a couple of tourists looking for a place to buy in the sun – a legend they had hurriedly agreed upon as they waited for their flight at Newcastle International airport.

Before leaving the UK, Hank had questioned the rationale behind her decision to follow what could only be described as a long shot. And now he was having another go, asking what they were doing there. 'All we've got is a couple of credit card receipts and a photo of a holiday home, of which there will be thousands.'

Adjusting her sunglasses, Kate glanced at the speedo, reminding herself it was shown in kilometres per hour and not miles. 'Trust me, I have a theory,' she said.

'Which is?'

'Vicky told me that John took frequent golf trips to this area—'

'Right.'

'Wrong, Hank . . . he went nowhere near a golf course. Lisa contacted every club on the Costa Blanca and no one appears to know him. If he had been a regular, someone would have remembered him. I've got mates who visit every year. The welcome they get is amazing. Even the waiters recognize them. Some know them by name.'

'They're women,' Hank grunted. 'That's different.'

'No, whatever the gender, golfing is a closed community. Socializing in the bar afterwards is all part and parcel of the trip. People notice you.' Kate could tell he wasn't convinced. 'They do! Hoteliers and their staff are trained to retain that kind of information. It makes returning guests feel important. Feeds their egos. John Allen would soak it up. He'd expect it. In fact, he'd demand it. He liked the ladies too, remember? He'd hardly miss an opportunity to get his leg over while Vicky was at home in the UK, unlikely to find him out.'

'He was probably using an assumed name,' Hank suggested.

'Why would he if the trip was kosher? He travelled on his own passport and made trips twice or three times a year. Men only. No wives allowed. I think he was meeting his dad, not playing golf. That restaurant receipt may be all we have, but it's a kicking-off point and needs investigating.'

'Makes you think he didn't stop for a meal en route to somewhere else?'

'Two nights running?'

They exchanged a look.

Hank went quiet.

Within minutes he was hanging like a bat from his seat belt again. Kate drove on, wondering if narcolepsy was hereditary. Hank could sleep at a moment's notice, like soldiers are trained to do. Didn't matter what was going on around him, he could switch off. Another reason she preferred to drive. Not that he'd ever fallen asleep at the wheel – she wasn't taking any chances.

Kate liked Spain but there was little to recommend the area she was driving through. Baking under a relentless sun, it was too brown and scorched for her liking, a stark contrast to the beauty of the lush green Northumberland she was used to. It didn't surprise her that a few days ago, four hundred plus kilometres southwest of here, forest wildfires had damaged large areas around Marbella. In this country, a discarded cigarette had the potential to destroy great swathes of landscape. Fortunately, the recent fires were under control, unlike the signage overkill on both sides of the road.

The giant advertisements offended her eyes. *How could the authorities allow it?*

A blast of a horn from an impatient local woke her from her daydream. 'Yeah yeah,' she whispered under her breath. 'Gimme a break, I only just got here.'

'Are we nearly there yet?' Hank spoke through a yawn, stretching his arms above his head.

'Not far. If this idiot behind would just stop pushing me around.'

Another yawn. 'Show him a clean pair.'

'In this? Do me a favour, I could walk quicker.'

Kate took the AP7 motorway towards Cartagena and then the Torrevieja Notre C90. They were heading for Ciudad Quesada, inland from the coast, approximately fourteen clicks north of Torrevieja, ten minutes from the beautiful Orihuela coast. Not that they would be seeing much of that, unless Brian Allen had managed to bag himself a frontline apartment they weren't aware of, pretending to be like any other expat planning to spend his retirement in the sun. Mr Invisible.

Chapter Fifty-six

A STONE ARCHWAY led into the village. It was late afternoon when Kate drove through it, checking out the territory on either side of the road. It was a busy town, a small one, the main street consisting of souvenir shops, banks, cafés and restaurant bars.

Blink and you'd miss it.

Out the other end, the surrounding area was a collection of small urbanizations. Under a stunning blue sky, neither detective spoke as they drove up and down palm-fringed avenues of high-walled villas, getting a feel for the place. The properties were mostly white, cream or mustard, many with bars at the windows, tiled patios and roof terraces.

Brian could be watching them and they would never know it.

If he lived here, he could come and go with impunity.

In the Avenida de Malaga, Kate stopped the car.

To her left, a chain-link fence surrounded an area of rough, weedy ground, strewn with litter. It looked incongruous among the smart properties on either side of it. What was it? Another building plot? A bit of land earmarked for a park? Where the hell do the kids play, Kate wondered. In the centre of the field, a middle-aged man was having a smoke while exercising a mangy dog. Stepping from the car on to a pavement you could fry an egg on, she glanced at her watch – 5:10 p.m. – then sent Hank to speak to the dog-walker, telling him she'd meet him at the car in an hour. They separated.

IT WAS 6:20 p.m. by the time she reappeared. The streets she'd been combing all looked the same, the houses no different. She'd lost her bearings for a time and had to backtrack. Hank's face was bright red, a mixture of physical exertion and exposure to intense heat he wasn't used to – no hat, eye protection or suntan lotion. Beads of perspiration stood up on his forehead. Rivers of the stuff had run down the side of his face, wetting his shirt collar.

He was bushed.

Having lucked out, they got in the car with heavy hearts.

The water bottle was empty. 'Fancy a pint?' Kate asked.

Hank made a silly face. A big kid being told he was getting an ice cream.

She did a U-turn and drove the way she'd come. Parking at the southern tip of Quesada, they walked down the main street towards the town's archway entry, less than a ten-minute walk end to end. And still there was no let-up in the heat.

The sky was deep blue with the faintest wispy clouds Kate suspected held no rain. On a shady corner, she stood checking out the bars across the road. One in particular caught her eye, The Old Don Carlos, an Irish tavern mentioned by one of the people she'd spoken to that afternoon. According to her source, an English-speaking Norwegian, the bar was popular with visitors, a good place to start searching for Brian Allen.

Leading Hank by the arm, Kate crossed the street to an out-side table that afforded some shade. There must have been forty customers there, many of them sitting in full sun, their skin in danger of a silent killer.

Crazy.

She ordered an Americano, a big bottle of water, and a pint of local beer for Hank. When it came, he struck up a conversation with the barman, making up a story that he was searching for a father and son he'd lost touch with, showing him the photo of John and Brian obtained from Theresa. Clearly, she wasn't inter-ested in saving Brian's skin after the trauma he'd put her through. Either that or she thought he'd suffer the same fate as their sons, his arrest and detention better than a cruel death at the hands of Craig O'Kane.

'No señor! Lo sentimos.' The apology was all the barman could muster.

Hank tipped him and he walked away.

When they had finished their drinks, they took the ten-minute drive to Guardamar. Finding Brian was something that might take several days. Lisa had booked them into a hotel on the west-ern edge of the town, her reason being that a couple wanting to buy a property would probably head for accommodation with a sea view. Hoping the coastline would remind her of Northum-berland, Kate got horribly lost on the way there and had to double back for a second attempt.

Hank was getting frustrated. 'Do you even know what the hotel looks like?'

'No, I don't!' Kate snapped, turning round for the umpteenth time. 'I'll find it. And in case you're wondering, I'm not sharing beds. So if Lisa didn't book a twin room, you're on the floor.' She spotted a high-rise building at the end of the street. Although in a privileged spot, fringed by dunes and golden sand, the sight of the hotel made her shudder as she drove up. The three-star duck-egg blue building represented all she disliked about package holidays. It was a monstrosity similar to many hotels on the Costa Blanca, a frontline concrete structure with nothing to recommend it. Like the skyscrapers in crowded resorts such as Benidorm, it was her idea of hell.

'Oh God, Hank! Tell me that's not it.'

A sign proclaimed: *Parking Exclusivo Clientes.*

Kate drove to a spot under the trees, grabbed her bag from the back seat, slammed the door shut and led Hank inside. The interior of the building did nothing to allay her fears. Basic didn't quite cover the description. Thankfully they were given a twin room with two queen-sized beds and clean linen. She made a mental note to have words with Carmichael. The young detective needed educating in the finer things in life.

Thank God they weren't booked in for dinner.

At sundown, after a shower and a change of clothes, Kate decided to stake out the restaurant where John had eaten on his last trip abroad. It pleased Hank no end that they were going out for a meal. After a day of travel and trawling round in the baking heat, he was hungry and exhausted.

They arrived at Antica Italia ten minutes later.

The restaurant was situated on the first floor of a little terrace of bars off a main road, about half a mile away from Quesada. Parking the car near the entrance, they mounted the steps. It was pleasant inside with subtle lighting, decorative statues, a long bar on the right as they walked in.

A friendly member of staff offered them the pick of available tables.

Kate noticed a flight of stairs that led out the rear. The door she was looking at opened. A waiter entered carrying fresh supplies for the bar. As the door closed behind him, she caught sight of a stockroom. *A delivery entrance – and a bloody good escape route.* The nearest table to the stairs was where John and Brian Allen would've chosen to eat their meal. It had an excellent view of the front door and they wouldn't immediately be seen by anyone using the delivery entrance.

She chose that same table.

Italian food came a close second to Indian cuisine in the detectives' culinary choices. They ordered bruschetta to start. She decided on risotto with wild porcini mushrooms, Hank opting for the chef's special – *Bistecca di Manzo ai tre Pepi* – sirloin in light brandy cream and peppercorn sauce. By the time they reached the crêpe Suzctte, the arse on the next table was beginning to annoy them. Like Billy-no-mates he was sitting alone, trying too hard to be friendly, asking where they were from and why they were there.

That was all they needed.

Hank put his hand on Kate's, stroking it affectionately.

'Wedding anniversary . . .' He smiled at the guy. 'Fifteen years, I really don't know how she puts up with me.'

Hiding behind her napkin, Kate stifled a grin.

Without stopping to draw breath, the man offered his congratulations, telling them he'd been living in Quesada for over five years with his third wife, who was twenty years his junior. The lucky lady was indisposed this evening, whatever that meant. Probably bored stiff, Kate thought, wishing he'd drink up and sling his hook.

'Big fish, little sea,' Hank whispered, loud enough for the guy to hear.

His rudeness did the trick. The man never spoke again.

Ten minutes later, he paid the bill and left.

'So why didn't you question him, darling?' Hank asked.

'Why do you think?' Kate told him to drop the lovey-dovey routine. 'He's a loudmouth, the type to blab to his mates. If Brian Allen *is* here, we can't afford to tip him off.'

She called their waiter across.

He didn't recall John or Brian from the picture she showed him. All she got was a European shrug and a few words of apology. Taking the picture from her, the waiter consulted with other bar staff and came back none the wiser. He returned the photo to her, then walked away speaking in Spanish to another man who'd arrived on the scene, making Kate feel uncomfortable because she didn't know what they were saying.

Wishing she'd paid more attention to languages at school, she began to wonder if she'd bitten off more than she could chew. She studied Hank, her cheek propped up on her right fist. 'Someone must know them. They must. Vicky said John wasn't very adventurous. He was the type to keep going to the same place again and again if he liked it. He came here twice on consecutive days and it wasn't to impress a woman, I can tell you that.'

'Eh?' Hank looked around. 'What's wrong with it?'

'It's hardly flash.'

'It's hardly Maccy D's either. I like it!'

'I do too. What I'm saying is, it's not seafront, overlooking a marina or in a posh golf hotel. It's on a main road in the middle of a gigantic housing complex catering for retired expats and holidaymakers. The Italian flag we saw on the roof as we drove up is a catchall for passing traffic. You could see it for miles. Trust me, other than the occasional hungry motorist, the clientele will all live around here. It's nice enough. I can't see anyone going out of their way to get here, though, can you?'

Hank put down his beer, unsure of where she was heading. 'So what are you saying?'

'I'm just making an observation. John Allen either came here to do business or he was meeting his dad. I happen to think it was the latter and that they were staying nearby – two blokes who couldn't be arsed to cook. The till receipts suggest they filled up, had a few beers and left. They are timed at nine and ten p.m. respectively. Does that sound like a romantic interlude to you?'

'Unless they couldn't wait to get their kit off and hit the sack . . .' Gormley grabbed her hand. 'Like you and me. I can't wait to get you back to our room.'

She laughed. 'You crazy sod. Drink up, we're out of here.'

Chapter Fifty-seven

KATE ROSE EARLY and tiptoed across to the en suite bathroom. Once she was dressed, she woke Hank and waited on the balcony for him to shower and shave. The hotel might not have been up to much, but the view was stunning: deep blue sea and a long strip of fine golden sand stretching for miles either way.

The patio door opened and Hank walked outside wearing a flowery Hawaiian shirt and a pair of knee-length pink shorts. Her eyes travelled down his hairy white legs to a pair of tan Jesus sandals and black socks.

'What?' He stopped drying his hair, put on his best ever wounded expression. 'Hello? We're on holiday. *Señor y señora turistas*, remember? Give us a kiss.'

Kate creased up, her whole body aching with laughing so much.

She couldn't speak . . .

She couldn't stop . . .

It felt good.

Telling him to lose the socks, she suggested they go for breakfast in Guardamar before heading back to Quesada. The quiet coastal town boasted the best beach. It was eerily quiet for the time of year, with few bars and cafes open, the perfect place to keep a low profile for someone like Brian Allen.

Hank's face was tripping him as they walked down the beach, to their left a line of hotels and low-rise apartments, the sun on their backs, a light breeze in their faces. When Kate asked why he was so miserable, he told her that he'd always hated the feeling of sand between his toes, an admission that she couldn't get her head around. They had known each other for years and that was news to her.

In order to distract him, she talked about their case. The odds of finding Craig O'Kane were slim but she had to try. Bright was relying on her to bring him in and she was determined to do that. Her only hope of achieving that was to trace Brian Allen. She wondered how many criminals had allegedly died in Spain but were actually still walking around. That unsettling thought gave her an idea.

Before leaving the UK, she'd spoken to the head of SOCA's European operations. With the cooperation of Spanish police, they had launched *Operation Captura* on the Costa del Sol in 2006, an International effort that had led to the detention and prosecution of dozens of fugitives living abroad, organized British criminals who had either evaded arrest entirely or escaped from custody and fled the country. In the course of that conversation, Kate learned that any tip-offs SOCA received were fed through Madrid directly to Spanish police. Having added Brian Allen and Craig O'Kane to their most wanted list, Spanish police were already on the lookout for both men and primed to give her all the cooperation she required.

In the UK, Strathclyde force had offered to deploy officers to find Brian. But because Kate had initiated the enquiry in Newcastle to find Craig – a search that would involve tracing Brian too – Trewitt had agreed to wait until he heard from her. That made sense. Although technically they were after different men, even with Spanish law enforcement on board, there was a high probability that she might draw a complete blank. No point two forces wasting precious resources on what could turn out to be a wild-goose chase.

They were nearing a promenade of sorts. Kate could see tables and chairs, a collection of bars and restaurants, the sight of which put a smile back on Hank's face. Not for long. On the way off the beach, they had to run the gauntlet of street-sellers shoving knock-off copies of watches and bags, CDs and other crap in their faces to the chorus of, 'Good price for the lady.'

One scowl from Hank, despite his ridiculous attire, and they moved away.

That shirt was enough to frighten anyone off.

He was already leaking like a tea strainer and it wasn't yet nine-thirty. 'I wish they would shove off with their poxy stuff,' he moaned.

'Don't be so mean. They're trying to make a living. To be honest, I don't like it either, but it's the culture over here. No one minds.'

'Well, I do.'

'You can afford to.' Kate walked off, smiling to herself.

They were already sounding like a proper married couple.

A transaction John Allen had made in the duty-free shop at Newcastle airport was niggling her. According to his credit card receipts he'd bought no gifts to suggest he was carrying out a clandestine relationship, travelling to Spain to meet up with a girlfriend. He'd made only two purchases and this raised her suspicions.

She glanced at Hank as he lumbered along after her.

'What?' He was responding to the perplexed look spreading across her face.

'Carmichael said John Allen bought duty-free whisky and cigars at the airport.'

'Wish I had,' he grumbled. 'And your point is?'

'He didn't smoke, Hank. Vicky told me he hated cigarettes with a passion. His old man, on the other hand . . .' She let her sentence trail off. 'Where's that photograph she gave us?'

Reaching into his pocket, Hank scrolled through his phone and handed it over. She studied it for a moment. She had to admit the villa in the digital image was like so many they had seen the day before. There was nothing unique about it. It was probably one of hundreds of identical properties dotted around the estates, built by the same firm in the past twenty years before the recession hit.

A stagnant market meant that houses were two a penny – even two for one: Kate had seen an advertisement for buy-one-get-one-free in an estate agent's only yesterday. She'd also witnessed people scavenging in rubbish bins in broad daylight, and hookers – no older than fifteen – plying their wares from the main road in order to make money, just like Bethany. Outside a supermarket, a young man had held out a begging bowl, a homemade sandwich board hanging round his neck with the words *Dos niños – please help* – scribbled across it in thick red pen.

So sad.

With no time to dwell on the appalling situation the Spaniards were facing, a state of affairs repeated in many other countries, she tapped the photograph and handed him the phone. 'We need to find this place.'

Hank's expression was his answer: *Yeah, right.*

'We'll be here for ever,' he said.

'Stop whining, that's *why* we're here. I could easily have brought Lisa along.'

'Careful.' He grinned. 'You know what a jealous husband I am.'

Hank invited her to sit in the shade at one of the cafes along the promenade, offering to buy her a cup of coffee.'

'Make it an espresso and you're on,' she said.

She sat down as he headed off to the gents, telling her he'd order their drinks on the way in. As he disappeared into the cafe, Kate glanced around her. Customers were sunning themselves, taking in the view, some already on the beer. The vista was stunning. Jo would love it here: slow pace of life, wonderful weather, warm sea – what was not to like?

Everything . . .

It wasn't Bamburgh.

Kate couldn't wait to go home.

Hank came back carrying a beer for him, a double espresso for her, a small biscuit to go with it. He set it down on the table, parking himself in the sun. He took off his shades, wiped his brow and picked up his beer bottle.

'You think he'd make that kind of mistake?'

'Mistake?' Kate had no idea what he was on about. 'Who?'

'John . . . taking a photo of his father's villa – if indeed it is Brian's villa. It seems unlikely to me.'

Kate pointed at his San Miguel. 'After a few of those, he might. I reckon it was a spur-of-the-moment thing to keep Vicky sweet, maybe to prove his cover story of playing golf. She was highly suspicious of his trips abroad. She said as much the second time we met. I'm betting he snapped that photo and sent it without thinking through the consequences. I've done a similar thing myself, only to realize, after I'd pressed send, that it was a stupid thing to do. I'd shown my hand when I shouldn't have.'

'Doesn't sound like you.'

'Yeah well, we all let our guard down sometimes.' Kate smiled at the memory.

'What?' Hank was smiling too.

She hesitated.

'C'mon, spill. I tell *you* things.'

'When Jo and I first got together I was on a high-profile job and texted a photo to impress her. It could have . . .' She corrected herself. 'Would have, jeopardized the whole operation if she'd forwarded it on to anyone else.'

'She wouldn't though.'

'Vicky did. We should count ourselves lucky. If she hadn't, we'd be screwed. Taking that photo was a dumb thing for John to do. His old man would've gone ape-shit if he'd found out, but it just might work in our favour.' Kate took a sip of coffee. 'God knows we need the break.'

Even if her theory was proved right, that John had been visiting his father in Spain, Kate was well aware that Brian could have moved on since. It was a big country. They might never find him. That photograph could be leading them up a blind alley, wasting precious time. In order to rule the property out, first they needed to find it.

'Living the dream, my arse.' Hank shook his head.

'What?'

'These lot . . .'

Kate followed his gaze towards the other customers. Boredom registered on their faces. No one seemed to be having much fun. Mostly they were middle-aged couples, either staring out to sea or into the bottom of a beer glass. The rest were ignoring each other: eating English breakfast, drinking English tea, reading English newspapers. And suddenly she had an idea.

Chapter Fifty-eight

THEY SPENT THE best part of the morning driving around Quesada, searching for the villa in the photograph. By lunchtime, they were beginning to wonder if they would ever find it. Exhausted and downhearted, they lunched in a tapas bar in the town and then started again – reluctantly.

Despite having lost a shedload of weight – almost three stones – Hank was feeling the heat. Kate dropped him off at the edge of yet another housing development and went to check out something else on her own.

Back at the cafe, seeing all the ex-pats reading English newspapers had prompted her to canvass local newsagents to see if she could pin down a delivery to Brian Allen. She was thinking of sports magazines in particular. Like a lot of his countrymen, he loved his golf. Just as she was giving up hope, almost two hours after leaving Hank, a local man reacted when shown his photograph.

Kate wanted to hug him.

He was the owner of the paper shop in central Quesada. A nice guy, he understood English perfectly. Unfortunately, he spoke very little. He was short and stocky with dark curly hair, a goatee beard and sharp eyes. The gold crucifix round his neck matched a large filling in one of his eyeteeth. Kate envied his loose linen top. Having chosen a fitted shirt herself, one that wouldn't crease, she was beginning to regret it.

Behind him, a young girl, possibly his daughter, was sweeping the floor and earwigging the conversation at the same time, occasionally throwing a comment their way.

'*Inglès?*' the newsagent asked.

'*Sí*,' Kate said. 'You know him?'

He waggled his hand from side to side. He wasn't sure.

Despondent, Kate patted her own chest enthusiastically. '*Mi amigo.*'

The Spaniard raised an eyebrow, a smile playing round his lips, as if he suddenly understood that she'd been dumped by Brian and was trying to make it up to him. Glancing at the photograph again, he struggled to put his thoughts into words, eventually managing to get his point across in broken English. The man in the photo resembled a customer, but Brian Allen was not the name he was using.

'What name was he using?' Kate asked, fanning herself with a leaflet she'd picked up off the counter.

The man's brow creased. 'Smeeth?'

You don't say? His pronunciation made her smile.

Unable to understand what was so amusing, he turned his back on her, pressing a button on a desk fan. It whirred into action, making little difference to the temperature in the shop. A female dressed entirely in black pushed in at the till. Giving Kate a dirty look, she dumped some items down on the counter, gabbing away in her native tongue. Although the DCI understood none of what was being said, it was abundantly clear that the woman was making reference to her because the lass sweeping the floor was trying too hard to keep a straight face.

As the newsagent rang in the purchases, a dark look passed between him and his customer. When the woman left the shop, he returned the photograph, telling Kate he really wasn't sure if the Englishman 'Smeeth' was the man he thought he was.

Had the female customer warned him off?

Kate wasn't having that. '*Señor?*'

Another shrug.

Kate was about to push him on the matter when Hank entered the shop. He'd seen their hire car parked outside. In answer to her inquisitive expression, he shook his head. He'd lucked out. Giving him her keys, she told him to wait in their car. When he'd left the shop, she turned to face the newsagent, this time showing him a photograph of the villa she'd been trying to find all day, stressing the importance of tracing the Englishman.

'Is this where you deliver the magazines?' she asked.

The Spaniard screwed up his face, pointing at the photograph, specifically at the driveway. '*La entrada es incorrecta.*' He moved his forefinger to the other side of the villa. 'Here is possible.'

'Ah . . . the driveway is on the other side?'

'*Sì* . . . exact.' He beamed proudly.

'Is it far?'

Again he shook his head.

'*Por favor* . . .' Kate pointed through the open door at her excuse for a vehicle. 'Can you show me where? Please, *señor* . . . it won't take long and it's very important.' Holding up her hand, she spread her fingers. 'Five minutes and I'll bring you straight back.'

Rubbing his face, the Spaniard studied Hank slumped in the passenger seat of her car. Understandably nervous about taking a ride with two suspicious English strangers who were not what they were making out to be, he refused. Forced to lie to him, Kate explained that Hank was her husband, a great friend of the man in the picture. When that didn't satisfy him, she took out her wallet and offered him cash.

Money talked when times were tough.

Barking something to his young assistant, the newsagent left the counter and followed Kate outside, lighting a Marlboro cigarette as he got in the car.

They drove out of the old town along a wide tree-lined avenue. Considering the time of year, it surprised the DCI how many homes were up for sale or empty. Some were like Fort Knox – behind big gates and high walls – ripe for hiding fugitives from justice. On her travels that morning, someone had mentioned Russian mafia living close by.

Nothing would surprise her.

The Spaniard opened the window, letting the smoke out and the scaring heat in. Unsure of which was worse, Kate ignored the temptation to ask him to close it. Instead, she kept her eyes peeled for GB or Scottish registration plates in case John Allen had driven a car over from the UK and left it there as a runaround for his dad. Brian would need more than one getaway vehicle in case things went pear-shaped.

Tapping her on the shoulder, the newsagent told her to make a left-turn at the next junction a few hundred metres ahead. As she approached the turning, it wasn't possible to complete the manoeuvre. Two motorcycle cops had parked their bikes right across the road, blocking her entry. They were standing in the middle of the carriageway, feet slightly apart, hands on hips, not far from their guns. Designer shades on – *too cool for school.*

They were clearly waiting for someone.

Like characters from the cult TV series *CHiPs*, they kept a watchful eye on her as she passed by. Not wishing to attract unwanted attention, she didn't stop. Instead, she drove on with the intention of finding an alternative route, watching them get smaller in her rear-view mirror. With any luck, she'd require a police presence herself later. No point pissing them off by getting in the way of their current job.

One English expat she'd spoken to earlier had urged her to speak to the police if she was serious about finding her elusive 'friend', unaware that she was a detective herself. The woman had gone into elaborate detail on the difference between the Policia National, Policia Municipal and the Guardia Civil, telling Kate not to assume they ever talked to each other.

Kate smiled to herself.

There was a hierarchy the world over when it came to law enforcement. She'd communicate with Operation Captura when she had something to say.

Responding to more instructions from her passenger, she coasted round the block, turning left, left again, then sharp right, arriving in a wide avenue fringed with well-established palm trees. She was now in a much older part of town with some of the largest and most ostentatious properties she'd seen since arriving in Spain. About halfway down, the newsagent told her to pull over, pointing at a villa on the passenger side of the vehicle.

Bingo.

Tucked in between some much larger properties was the house in the photograph. There was no doubt about it. Pulling gently to a halt, Kate put on the handbrake and leaned across Hank to get a closer look. It was an unremarkable villa set back off the road. Nothing special – perhaps why Brian had chosen it – much easier to blend in with the locals than with a bigger place that might draw unwanted interest. The house was nevertheless well kept with a nice front garden laid to lawn, a selection of palms creating shade and privacy from neighbouring properties, a wonky For Sale sign in the front garden.

'You think he was wise to us?' Hank asked.

'Something's up,' Kate said vaguely.

'You got that right. We're wasting our time.'

Kate's eyes fell on steps that led up to a circular front porch that had arched windows and black decorative tiles. A shaded veranda ran around the whole of the ground floor. The railings enclosing it were repeated on the first floor. Each bedroom seemed to have patio doors and a private balcony. On the very top, a privacy wall enclosed a square roof terrace.

She swivelled around in her seat.

'Señor Smith?' she asked.

'*Sí.*' The Spaniard nodded.

'Let's go,' Hank said. 'Allen's long gone.'

'Out you get, Hank.' Kate took one last glance at the property. 'Keep your eyes peeled. I'll be back in ten minutes.' She handed him a bottle of water. As he climbed out, she put the car in gear. Pulling hard on the steering wheel, she did a U-turn, wincing as tyres squealed on hot tarmac as she drove away.

At the newsagent's, Kate got out of the car, meeting the Spaniard on the pavement directly outside his empty shop. Seeing him standing there, his assistant yelled from within. She came to the doorway, pulling her jacket on, tapping her foot impatiently on the ground, acting like she should have been away home several hours ago. The universal language of those on low pay and long shifts.

Kate shook hands with the man. '*Muchas gracias, señor.*'

She stuffed some euros in his hand, got in the car and did a reciprocal. The police motorcyclists had gone as she drove by. Two minutes later she was back at the villa.

Telling Hank to hang fire, she walked up to the front door and tried the bell. Not that she was expecting Brian to arrive at the door and answer it. Hell, for all she knew, it might not even be the right house. She looked around as she waited. The steps were dirty, littered with dead leaves and spotted with signs of a recent downpour. Her heart sank as she examined the hardened ground around the base of the For Sale sign.

It hadn't gone up recently.

She tried the bell again, heard it ring inside the house.

Nothing.

Signing to Hank, she walked round the side but couldn't get access to the garden. The gate to the rear of the property was secured with a large padlock. It didn't seem as if anyone was living there. But she couldn't be sure. Brian Allen was clever. Maybe this was the impression he was trying to portray.

A visit to houses on either side depressed her. According to the neighbours on the left, with very few exceptions, practically the whole street was a collection of holiday homes. The house next door had been empty for several months. Kate tried the other side. A man answered, wearing only his underwear and clutching a beer bottle. He glared at her, the cigarette hanging from his lips bobbing up and down as he spoke, his eyes squinting to keep out the smoke.

His speech was slurred as he confirmed that the house next door was empty, like most others in the street. Then he batted her away from the step, unhappy that she'd interrupted his lazy afternoon.

That's all Kate needed: a bloody ghost town.

Despondent, she returned to the car, her skin burning in the midday sun. The heat was so intense, the dusty street so deserted, she expected to see a couple of cowboys rounding the corner with Stetsons on, hands poised to whip out their pistols, only one of them getting on his horse and riding away.

Her own horsepower was covered in blossom, blown there in the wind. Getting in, she fired up the engine, turned the air conditioning up as high as it would go and then reached into the rear seat-well for a bottle of water. It was warm and tasted vile in her mouth. Opening the car door, she spat it out on the pavement, wiping a dribble away with the back of her hand as Hank climbed in beside her.

'Any joy?' he asked.

She shut the car door. 'No, we need to get in there.'

He made a face. 'What for? It's obvious he's scarpered, and you know what that means. No Brian Allen equals no Craig O'Kane. My maths aren't great, but even I can work that one out. We could hang around for months and never find either one of them.'

'You're probably right,' Kate conceded. 'If the neighbours are anything to go by, no one gives a damn about one more bloody Englishman taking up space in their country. They were so pissed when they came to the door, they didn't know what day it was. They were savvy too. I may as well have been wearing a uniform.'

'Exactomundo. Would anyone notice if Brian was here? Would anyone care?'

'*I* care. This case might be slipping away from us, but we're not done yet.' Kate put the car in gear. 'We need a double-U.'

Hank grimaced. With limited Spanish, he knew that securing a search warrant was going to take some time.

Chapter Fifty-nine

HAVING BEEN CONTACTED by SOCA, Spanish police were keen to cooperate with British law enforcement, even keener to dissuade the wrong sort of tourists taking refuge in their country. Organizing a warrant for the villa Kate wanted to search was no problem for them. It was secured within the hour. The officer-in-charge, Comisario Roberto Chavez, insisted on accompanying her to the villa, supplying a team of officers to do a thorough forensic job on the place on her behalf. Nothing, it seemed, was too much trouble. As they waited to gain access, he was at pains to point out that many of the fugitives living in Rojales had come from the United Kingdom.

Kate nodded a guilty apology.

What else could she do? She couldn't argue with him. It was a well-known fact that criminals had taken up residence in Spain for years, on the Costa del Sol in particular, many of them favouring the hills around Marbella.

She couldn't see the attraction herself.

Right this minute, she was too bloody hot and couldn't hear herself think. A family of screeching parakeets had taken refuge in a palm tree further down the street. They were making such a din, flying in and out of their nest, squabbling with one another over bits of food. In competition with the birds, Chavez began shouting instructions to his men. Kate left him to it, wandering off to take a photograph to share with Jo when she got home. They had seen birds like these at the Pets' Corner aviary in Jesmond Dene. Jo hated to see them caged. It was wonderful to observe them, free to enjoy life in the treetops, their habitat secure from prying eyes.

The noise they made was another thing entirely.

Kate wondered what the residents of the magnificent villa adjacent to the tree thought of them. How they stood the commotion day after day, though hopefully not at night. Presumably, even parakeets needed their sleep. As cute as they were, she'd be a bit cross if she'd bought an idyllic hideaway, ignorant of the noisy neighbours nesting in the tree outside.

As she snapped away, she thought of Jo's compassion for all living creatures; like the time she found a baby bird that had fallen from a nest and dug up worms for days in order to feed it. Daft really. The day it flew away was magical. Then it flew right back, landing on her hand as if it was thanking her for taking the trouble to save its life. When it flew off a second time she had tears in her eyes.

Kate smiled at the memory.

Life wouldn't be the same without Jo in it. That thought dragged her down, their broken relationship hanging over her like a shadow. She couldn't shake it off, no matter how hard she tried. It was all her fault. She had no one to blame but herself. Maybe a holiday together was just what they needed to sort themselves out.

Hank gave a yell: their Spanish counterparts were in.

Pocketing her phone, Kate joined them at the villa, heart sinking as she entered the house, stepping over a pile of leaflets and magazines on the hallway floor, further evidence that no one was living there. Crouching down, she used the end of a pen to move them around. There was nothing of interest. A film of dust covered the floor tiles; clearly the place hadn't been cleaned in a while. Magazine issue dates confirmed her worst fears. They had lain untouched for months rather than weeks.

'Why?' Kate whispered, getting to her feet.

'You talking to yourself again?' Hank asked as he approached. 'What's up?'

'That!' She pointed at the mail drop on the floor, fixing him with a hard stare. 'It doesn't make sense to me. If this is Brian's villa – and I think it is – then where is he? I can understand him being on the run now he's wanted for Finn's murder, but this lot suggests he's been gone for some time. If he'd been living here minding his own business since disappearing, what prompted him to move away so long ago? Apart from John, no one knew he was alive.'

'Maybe he found out John sent Vicky the photograph and decided to cut and run.'

'Perhaps.'

As they walked further into the house, she thought some more about Hank's suggestion. The dates on the stuff pushed through the letter box fit loosely with the timing of John's last visit to Spain. The only other explanation she could come up with was that John might somehow have got wind of the fact that the O'Kane boys were on his father's trail and had tipped him off a while ago. Either way, Brian had got the jump on them – *again*.

Hank stifled a yawn behind a sweaty hand. With no air conditioning it was sweltering in the house. 'Where do you propose we go?' he asked.

It was a good question: one Kate had to think about. She couldn't help wishing she were thirty thousand feet above ground in a tin tube on her way home. It would be a relief to get out of the stifling heat and feel a nip in the air. She longed to be surrounded by lush green grass. By the state of him, Hank did too.

He loosened his tie a touch.

While waiting on the warrant, she'd driven him to their hotel to change into something more appropriate. He was dying in his suit. She was about to tell him to take off his jacket when her phone rang.

Carmichael.

'What you got for me, Lisa?'

'I viewed the footage of Brian on CCTV. He travelled to Spain on a dodgy passport in the name of Ray Charlton. You won't believe this: airport security even frisked him.'

'You sure it was him?'

'Hundred per cent . . . hold on a minute, boss . . . yes?' Carmichael's voice was lost as someone spoke to her at the other end – *something about CCTV* – and then it all went quiet as she turned her head away from the speaker. Seconds later, she was back. 'Sorry about that . . . we have the images. I'll email them to you. Brian was travelling light. Hand luggage only – a small black bag. He bought fags and Irish whiskey on his way through duty-free. Paid with cash. He's a cool customer. I'm watching the footage now. He's strolling through the departure hall, not even breaking sweat.'

Kate wished she wasn't.

Thanking Carmichael, she hung up.

'You want me to check that lot in the hallway?' Hank asked.

'No need, they're just leaflets and magazines. Dead men obviously don't get much post.'

'Er, when in Spain.' He pointed through the window to a bank of mailboxes attached to the wall. 'It serves the whole block, complete with name-tags and keyholes.'

Kate grinned and asked Chavez if anyone had found a key to the postbox outside. He turned to yell at his men and within seconds an officer came running with it in his hand. Taking it from him, the DCI went outside to investigate, only to have her hopes dashed. Barring a small sheet of folded paper – some sort of bill for €157 – the box was empty.

Her head was down as she went back inside.

The only tangible lead to Brian Allen was proving next to useless. Without further intelligence, her search would end and the case would collapse. Wandering through the villa, she looked around, hoping to find something that might give away his whereabouts. There was nothing on the walls that spoke to her, no telltale prints that might point to a location he could be using as a hideaway. She had no doubt that he'd be lying low for a while.

In the bedroom, Chavez's men were dusting for fingerprints. One young officer was shaking a telephone directory in the hope that something would fall out. Nothing did. Cupboard doors stood open, drawers had been pulled out. The bed had been turned down and was being examined for trace evidence: hair, skin, dried body fluids. Proving that Brian had once lived there was the most she could hope for.

Kate wasn't quitting yet.

There was always an alternative if you looked hard enough, and she was not a detective who fell at the first hurdle. As she continued to search, Bright's voice popped into her head. 'You have one week to wrap up your search in Spain. Not a minute more,' he'd told her. 'We have finite resources, Kate. The budget for major incidents is already stretched to the limit. The Crime Commissioner's salary has to come from somewhere.'

Clearly, he was not a fan.

Kate sucked in some air.

She was wasting her time searching the villa. The place was empty. Cleaned out. No clothes or personal papers. Zilch. Despite her seven-day deadline, she'd advised Hank that if she hadn't found Brian within the week – and more importantly Craig O'Kane – she'd take annual leave until she had.

True to form, he said he'd do the same.

As she walked back down the hallway, there was a flurry of activity in the porch beyond the front door. Raised voices. It wasn't the Spanish being, well, Spanish. The tone of the conversation was far more urgent than that. Rounding the corner, Kate suddenly felt as if she was in her own incident room, surrounded by her own team. She knew elation when she saw it. Didn't need to understand the language to know that something exciting was going down. She could see it on the face of local officers.

Hell, she could feel it.

Hank arrived by her side, drawn by the thrill of a breakthrough. Whatever it was, he could feel it too.

'What's going on?' he asked.

Comisario Chavez grinned.

A suspicious stranger fitting Craig O'Kane's description had been spotted a short distance away at La Marquesa Golf Club. An alert member of staff had heard about two Englishmen local police were hunting. Putting two and two together she'd phoned the law. *Shrewd move.*

THE REVELATION HAD everyone scrambling into a convoy of police vehicles, racing towards the golf complex with blue lights flashing and sirens screaming. In their vehicle, Hank rode in the back, Kate up front. Normally comfortable at high speed, they endured a heart-stopping, white-knuckle ride, thanks to their driver continually crossing himself while overtaking and praying in his native tongue as he weaved in and out of traffic. At one point, Kate shut her eyes, bracing herself for a collision, before yelling at the idiot to slow the fuck down and keep both hands on the wheel. Advanced police driver he certainly was not. She wanted to live long enough to make an arrest, she told him. He took no notice and, despite the rapidity of his response to the perceived emergency, the stranger at the golf club was long gone by the time they arrived.

That was the bad news.

On the positive side, it was confirmation that Craig O'Kane was in the area, on the trail of the man who killed his brother. The receptionist, Neena Gil, had no hesitation in making the identification. Thankfully there was no need for an interpreter; she spoke perfect English, having taken a business studies degree at London Metropolitan University with a view to starting her own real estate agency on returning to Spain.

'No hope of that in this economic climate,' she told them. 'So I'm working here until things improve.'

'You're sure this is the man?' Kate held up O'Kane's photograph.

The young woman nodded.

'You said he was acting suspiciously?'

'And quite aggressive when I told him to be patient.' Neena glanced past Kate to the door. 'At first I thought he was waiting for someone to arrive. He kept looking over his shoulder at the entrance, trying to push to the front of the queue when I had other customers to attend to. He wasn't a tourist. No interest in playing golf or becoming a member. There was only one thing on his mind and that was finding Señor Allen. I made out that I knew him, even though I didn't. I kept the man waiting a moment while I checked the club's database, even offered him coffee or a drink on the house.' She thumbed over her shoulder to an office behind her. 'I went to call the police. When I returned, he'd disappeared.'

Kate wished that all witnesses were as good as this one. 'And Señor Allen?'

'We have no Señor Allen at La Marquesa.'

'Are you certain, Neena? It's imperative we trace him.' Kate showed her a photograph of Brian, just to be sure. 'He may be using the name Ray Charlton.'

'I'm sorry, I don't recognize him.'

That wasn't the answer Kate wanted to hear.

Chapter Sixty

THREE DAYS HAD passed since the last sighting of O'Kane and the trail had gone cold. To further complicate matters, the hire car he was using was found abandoned not far from the golf club. He was obviously aware he'd been clocked on CCTV. Taking the view that he wouldn't risk hiring another, Hank asked local police to keep a close eye on any vehicles reported stolen. Old ones. That was part of the offender's MO for no other reason than they were easier to break in to.

Together, Kate and Hank spent the weekend scouring the area, visiting every golf complex in a twenty-mile radius. A wasted few days, as it turned out. It looked as though their suspect had gone to ground. They were desperate for another sighting. When it didn't materialize, Kate had no option but to turn her attention once more to Brian Allen. After all, finding him had been the sole purpose of O'Kane's trip to the Mediterranean. Why else risk his neck travelling from his home in Scotland? He could so easily have been arrested at an airport terminal at either end.

Kate longed to detain both men and return to the UK with her reputation restored. If she went home empty-handed she'd be letting Bright down. Letting herself down.

Sadly, it looked as though she had no alternative. She was running out of ideas.

In the absence of fresh intelligence from Chavez and his men, she decided to up the ante and widen her search.

Dumping her belongings in the boot of the hire car, she waited for Hank to do the same and then slammed the lid shut. She was eager to be on the move and hadn't yet told him where they were going. Time to put that right. Walking round to the driver's side, she opened the door and climbed in.

'How d'you fancy the five-star treatment?' she asked. 'La Manga suit?'

'You're talking my language.' His face lit up. 'Why La Manga?'

'Why not? We're chasing a villain who thinks he's fucking James Bond. Anyway, I'm sick of waiting. We need to be more proactive. If we want O'Kane, we need to go back to plan A and find Brian. He's a man who likes the high life. O'Kane may be a Glasgow thug, but I'm betting he'll have worked that out. If so, he'll be hanging out in all the best places. Where better to start than at the most prestigious golfing venue in the area?' She turned the engine over and pulled away. 'Besides, that fleapit we've been staying in was getting on my tits. I need a bed I can actually sleep in. And since we're travelling light, a place with laundry service wouldn't go amiss.'

Laughing, Hank strapped himself in and made a meal of sniffing his armpits.

A signpost for Torrevieja and Cartagena saw them join the motorway southbound. For a while traffic was slow. It wasn't until they left the built-up area that they picked up speed. Kate took little notice of the countryside whizzing by. She was on autopilot, mind on the job, the frustrating near-miss getting the better of her. She'd come so close to catching O'Kane she could almost taste it, but he'd slipped from her grasp.

Time for a rethink.

'We should change our approach,' she said.

Hank pushed his sunglasses higher up the bridge of his nose. 'In what way?'

'We should stop and get you a hire car of your own.'

'Really?' He lifted a water bottle to his lips. 'I thought you said we were on a tight budget.'

Kate pictured herself arguing the toss with the guv'nor when they got home, possibly empty-handed. 'Yeah, you're right. Scratch that idea. It was pants.' Indicating, she pulled out to overtake, telling him they would stand a better chance if they worked independently. 'We'll book in together, as friends this time. It'll appear odd if we're a couple who spend no time with each other.'

'You kidding?' He almost choked on his drink. 'We're supposed to be married, remember? It'll look a damned sight odder if we're talking.'

'We just got a divorce.'

'On what grounds? My snoring keeping you awake?'

His wounded expression made her laugh out loud. 'It's not helping. I believe irretrievable breakdown is the correct term. My people will talk to your people. Mine will insist on a fifty-fifty split of all bank accounts and a large chunk of your pension when you retire. You can keep your car. I wouldn't be seen dead driving it. I never liked our poxy house, so you can have that too, along with the contents. I get the dog. Do we have a deal?'

They drove on, the banter between them lifting their mood. Only seventy kilometres to go – if they were lucky, they would make their destination by nightfall.

Chapter Sixty-one

KATE SLOWED WHERE tollbooths crossed the carriageway. Signs above each booth showed method of payment: cash, credit card or personal service. Fearing being left penniless in Spain, she drove towards one with a human behind the desk. There was no way she was using her personal debit card in case it was swallowed up. It had happened before, leaving her stranded.

A few minutes' driving and they came to another toll-booth – another three euros.

'Bloody rip-off,' Hank muttered under his breath. 'Bet half that goes in his pocket.'

'You're such a cynic!' Kate held up a receipt. 'Not everyone is on the take.'

Winding her window up, she drove on. Settling in his seat, Hank closed his eyes. She thought he'd fallen asleep, but the atmosphere grew heavy in the car. He was still awake with something on his mind.

'You going to spit it out?' she asked.

'What?' He opened his eyes.

'You reckon we're pissing in the wind, is that it?'

'A bit.' He looked out the side window, his tone flat. 'Much as I fancy a luxury hotel, Brian Allen has been in the country for days. He could be anywhere by now. I agree that O'Kane might make his way south, but you heard Neena Gil, he was nervous, keeping his eye on the exit. He'll be watching his six for sure. He's not going to be a simple collar, is he?'

'When was our job ever easy?' Kate glanced his way. Hank didn't answer. 'Anyway, O'Kane wasn't looking for us, was he? He was keeping obs on the door in case Brian walked in. He doesn't know we're on to him. How could he? Besides, he likes the premier treatment as much as the man he's hunting. He's arrogant enough to want the best, and that's where we're heading. Trust me, of all the places round here, La Manga is worth a try.'

'You ever been?'

'Years ago, it was wonderful. An oasis in the desert.'

'Who with – if you don't mind me asking.'

'Old boyfriend.'

He turned to face her, a wry smile on his face. 'How does that work then?'

Kate spoke through a yawn. 'What d'you mean?'

'I'd have thought that was obvious.'

'Ah, I get you. You don't know much about relationships, do you, Hank? Because I was with Jo doesn't mean I've had no men in my life. You *know* I have. They may not have lasted long, but they did exist. If you want to know the truth, I just happened to fall in love with her. It was as much a surprise to me as it was to anyone. It's hard to explain. It felt right, that's all, like we were the perfect fit.'

They fell silent again, the miles rolling by as the road cut its way through flat land, orange and lemon groves on either side, mountains in the foreground. A caravan of foreign bikers passed them, a road trip Kate longed to be part of, their panniers and backpacks full to bursting, bedrolls securely fastened.

Freedom machines.

She pictured her Yamaha Fazer gathering dust in her hallway at home. She hadn't ridden it in ages, something she promised herself she'd do as soon as this case was over. Maybe north up the A68, across the border to Scotland, an ideal route for bikers. The road took in the most dramatic countryside with plenty of view-points along the way. *If only . . .*

Instructing her to take the next junction, Hank broke her reverie.

Completing the manoeuvre, Kate glanced at her watch. 'How much further?'

He checked her phone. 'Twelve more clicks, if the satnav on here is accurate.'

A few minutes further on, the most spectacular sunset began to form on the horizon for the second night in a row. Pink and purple at first – then flame-red, orange and yellow – the whole sky on fire. It was a glorious sight. So much so, Kate asked him to take a picture to forward on to Jo. She'd appreciate that – *assuming they were still speaking.* Kate had lost track.

THE HOTEL PRINCIPE Felipe car park was an area of manicured lawns, pine trees and well-placed floodlights that came on as they entered the driveway. Reversing into the only space available, Kate felt the eyes of a concierge on the upholstered roller-skate she was driving. Most other vehicles in the lot were high-end hire cars with posh interiors and pristine paint jobs.

'Talk about the poor relation,' she said.

Hank grinned. He knew how much she loved cars and what a bummer it was for her to be driving the Seat Mii. Before she had time to moan, he was out of the car, his eyes scanning the car park for any vehicles or registration numbers that might suggest they were on to a winner. Returning seconds later, he helped her get their bags out of the boot, telling her there was nothing of obvious interest there.

Palatial was the word that sprang to mind as they entered the cool interior of the hotel. The lounge area facing them was an architectural masterpiece: a domed building with arched windows, marble pillars, a floor so clean you could eat off it. Chandeliers hung above sumptuous sofas, a place to chill out, read or write an email home – a thought that had Kate wondering whatever happened to postcards. Fiona Fielding, an artist she'd met on a previous enquiry, a woman with whom she'd had a brief fling, was the only one she knew who used them. She travelled all over the world sending cryptic messages to Kate, asking if she was hungry yet, an in-joke between the two of them. She was gorgeous too.

Kate was suddenly ravenous.

Hank went off to do a recce of the hotel bar while she checked in. As she handed their passports in at the desk, he arrived at her shoulder. Another shake of his head, almost imperceptible, was enough to let her know that there was no sign of their quarry. Picking up their bags, they walked to the lift that would take them up a floor. Kate handed him the plastic key to room 305.

It was too near the lift for her liking.

Shoving the key into the slot produced a green light. Hank pushed open the door to a luxurious room, made a joke about slumming it for a few days and stepped inside. Taking a quick peek, Kate fell in love. The contrast between this celebrated hotel and the one they had vacated at Guardamar had been evident the moment they entered reception. She had calls to make and asked Hank to meet her in the bar in an hour.

Room 308 was further along the corridor. It was perfect and smelled of fresh flowers. The bed was as wide as it was long, with crisp white linen and plump pillows that would send her off to sleep in seconds. There was a partner's writing desk, two chairs, a comfortable armchair and a bathroom dripping with wonderful bathing products.

Heaven.

It was deathly quiet too.

Exactly what she needed to think through her case.

Chapter Sixty-two

THEY ATE IN the hotel, their dinner conversation like a murder investigation briefing. No investigative theory would equip them with a nice neat plan of how best to proceed. For the most part, their campaign of attack was based on gut instinct rather than hard evidence. Intelligence had dried up and Kate was trying to second-guess what was going through the minds of the men she was chasing.

Murder, probably.

If she had a strategy at all it was for Hank to check out the clubhouse the next day. He'd fit in better than she would. Hearing this, Hank puffed out his chest, telling her he was on top doe. The three stones he'd lost following his reconciliation with Julie and his recent walking tour of Quesada were paying off. He felt energized, he told her, ready to take on anything. Glancing at his plate, she wondered if her eyes were deceiving her.

No, he'd actually ordered sea bass.

Even more impressive: he was still on his first pint. Not bad going. They had already been there half an hour. He'd made a real effort to put his unhealthy lifestyle behind him and had finally turned the corner. His face was tanned, his eyes bright, his skin clear. It was no exaggeration to say that it had taken years off him.

'I wish you wouldn't scrutinize me so intensely.' He studied her over the rim of his glass as he took a drink. 'People might think we're in love. I can see you're already regretting the divorce.'

Kate laughed.

She'd missed his sense of humour in recent months. It was nice to see him so obviously relaxed, so happy that his marriage was beginning to work out. On the way to La Manga he'd told her that his son Ryan had returned home. The boy hated the south coast and couldn't wait to get home to Newcastle and the mates he'd left behind. Curiously, Hank never once mentioned Julie. Maybe he didn't want to spoil the magic. Maybe he didn't want to tempt fate.

'Do we have a plan then?' he asked.

'Of sorts.' She picked up her knife and fork. 'First thing tomorrow, I'm going to have a wander round, check out local businesses and doctor's surgeries too.' She smiled at him, a knowing look. 'I know something you don't.'

'Oh yeah? What have I told you about keeping secrets?'

'Theresa Allen let it slip that Brian is diabetic.'

'What?' Hank nearly choked. 'When?'

'Lisa managed to drag it out of her this afternoon.'

He rolled his eyes. 'Theresa didn't think to tell us this before?'

'Apparently not. Anyway, it's a new lead, the only one we have. I intend to make the most of it. If Brian needs insulin to keep his hormones level, he'll run out sooner rather than later. Lisa did her magic on the Internet. Insulin has a relatively short shelf-life. After a month or so it begins to break down. It becomes less potent and therefore less effective.'

'Then he'll be forced to consult—'

'A doctor. Precisely!' Kate beamed at him. 'I'm glad you won't. How's the fish?'

'Delicious.' Lifting a forkful, he paused before putting it into his mouth. 'GPs have a Hippocratic oath here too, Kate. They'll quote doctor/patient confidentiality. I'm not sure they'll tell you anything. Sharing information on a patient could get them into a lot of trouble.'

'We'll see.' Kate raised a cheeky eyebrow. 'You know me, I'm a DCI, an SIO and one hell of an SOB, if pushed. I can lie for England if the job demands it. I'll make something up, say he's my big brother who's gone missing.' She feigned distress, putting on a feeble voice to make her point. 'I'm worried about him losing consciousness and going into a coma, Doctor. It's happened before. He nearly died.' She placed a hand on her chest. 'I can't, I just can't bear to lose him.' She winked at Hank, reverting to her normal voice. 'I might even cry – if I can remember how.'

'You're devious, you know that?'

'I'll do whatever it takes to find him. Brian Allen is the devious one. He's survived out here for years without detection. Chances are he has a whole new identity and a GP in his pocket who a) helped fake his death and b) could supply medication at the drop of a hat. He's a fugitive on the run now though. I'm thinking that it might not be so easy for him, especially if he's been forced out of his home. He needs that medication to survive.'

Pushing his plate away, Hank reminded her of Brian's assumed name: Ray Charlton.

'I doubt he's using it now,' she said. 'That would be plain stupid, the one thing he's not. Anyway, I have his picture. I'll think of something. We have to learn to out-think him, Hank – him *and*

O'Kane – it's the only chance we have of locking them up. Then it'll be down to the extradition process to work its magic so we can get them home and into a court of law.'

Kate stared at a fixed point in the distance as two pieces of a giant conundrum moved into place, something she hoped might take her enquiries in the right direction. Noting her concern, Hank gave her a moment of quiet before asking her what was happening on Planet Daniels.

'I was thinking about the doctor who certified Brian's death.'

'What about him?'

'Her. Her name is Maria Benitez.'

'Didn't you put an action out—'

'I did.' Kate sighed. 'I hate relying on anyone else to make my enquiries for me, particularly when I can't speak to them face to face. The officer I talked to over here said he'd investigated the matter thoroughly. Benitez has been practising for around ten years. She's well respected, by all accounts, a pillar of the community. As far as he was concerned, she was in the clear and wouldn't face charges. He took the view that she was a victim of theft, not someone under suspicion.'

'Theft?'

'Yeah, that's what I thought. Some months after Brian was supposed to have died, she reported a numbered death certificate stolen, claiming that she'd only noticed it missing after the event. I'm wondering now if she was telling the truth. She could've been covering herself. Quite clever too, if you think about it . . . or maybe not.' Kate held his gaze. 'You know the score as well as I do. When people are trying to conceal their guilt, they sometimes go that little bit too far to prove their innocence.'

A waitress arrived to take away their empty plates.

Hank waited until she was gone. 'Sounds like Benitez is unreliable.'

'I thought so too. It was a matter for the Spaniards to sort. No offence committed in the UK, so not my problem.' Kate lifted her glass. 'If a certificate was stolen and reported missing, you've got to ask yourself why no one picked up on it at the time. It looks like the Spanish registrar couldn't be arsed to check his records or raise so much as a concerned eyebrow.'

'Not worth the hassle?'

Kate sipped her wine. 'Yeah, especially as it involved a Brit.'

'So what do you intend to do about it? She's not going to talk to us, is she?'

'Not the official us, no. Finish your pint, I need to call Lisa and find out more about Benitez and where I might find her. Don't stay up too late, I want you to resume your search first thing.'

'*My* search? What you going to do?'

Kate locked eyes with him, a plan forming in her head. If her hunch was right, there was one way to find out what Maria Benitez was up to. It might involve a little undercover work.

Chapter Sixty-three

KATE SLEPT LIKE a dream and woke fully refreshed. Before getting up she tried calling Jo. The number rang out unanswered. Frustrated, she lay there dreaming of what she might be doing right now, seeing her face, her sparkly eyes, a cheeky smile on her lips. Raising her knees, Kate slid her right hand down between her legs, shutting her eyes, imagining Jo's hands, soft and warm, tracing the contours of her body, kissing her gently, as only she could. A single tear rolled down Kate's cheek as she brought herself to orgasm, an ache in her heart as her emotions flooded out.

In semi-darkness, she rolled over and tried Jo's number again with the same result, then got up and took a quick shower. Wrapping herself in a bathrobe, she opened her curtains to a lovely surprise that hadn't been available the night before. Beyond her patio doors was a stunning view across the golf course, the eighteenth hole, an ornamental lake and the Mar Menor. Stepping on to the balcony, she leaned on the railing, drinking in the view, the smell of freshly mown lawns carried on the breeze. The sight served only to increase her loneliness. She missed Jo so much.

Totally pathetic.

Raising her face to the sun, Kate would have liked nothing more than to sit on the balcony and relax with a good book. Instead, she dragged herself inside to dry her hair. Tying it up, she put on a bit more slap than she was used to, dressing in cool linen, a pair of navy trousers, a long-sleeved white shirt and a pair of strappy flat sandals she could walk in all day long. Satisfied that the detective in her was well hidden, she went down to eat, giving Hank a knock as she passed his room.

HE'D BEATEN HER down, was sitting in the breakfast room when she arrived. The food was like artwork, laid out beautifully: cereals and fresh fruit, several different breads, croissants and pots of local jam. To her right, a chef stood waiting to prepare cooked breakfast for those who wanted it.

Through the panoramic window, Kate could see that many had already eaten and were out on the golf course. At a table near the window, directly ahead of her and down a few steps, Hank gave her a wave. As she arrived at his side, he flicked his eyes left. Following his gaze, she found not Allen or O'Kane but Judi Murray, mother of Andy, the tennis ace. She was sitting alone, reading a newspaper, dressed to give a coaching session in the club's tennis centre. Feeling Kate's eyes on her, she looked up and smiled.

Returning the greeting, Kate pulled out a chair and sat down with Hank. He'd ordered coffee, lots of it, strong and black. She'd trained him well.

'Going somewhere nice?' he asked.

Kate shook out her napkin. 'Might be.'

'You look different.'

She blushed, shoving away the ridiculous notion that he could tell she'd been masturbating before joining him at the breakfast table.

'Sophisticated, I mean.'

'That suggests I normally look like a tart.'

'That's not what I—'

'Joking! Got my fishing gear on, haven't I?'

He was intrigued. 'Need me along?'

'No, Hank, I want you here tracking down murder suspects. I've got to go out for a few hours, check out the local medical centre and shops. I need to track Benitez down. If I can, I'll rendezvous back here at two. I'll give you a bell if not. Remember that little tapas bar not far from the hotel?' She took in his nod. 'Meet me there.'

DR MARIA BENITEZ's consulting rooms were in Quesada. Kate arrived as they were closing for lunch. An attempt to see the doctor was met with a resounding 'no'. Hardly surprising. Even with the funds to pay for it, Kate didn't expect to get in quite that easily. She'd have to come at the problem from a different angle. Beyond the reception desk was the means to do just that. Benitez's photo and that of other doctors were displayed on the wall.

Kate smiled.

'I'm sorry,' the receptionist said. 'You must leave now. We are closing.'

Thanking her, Kate went outside. A sign on the door said the surgery wouldn't reopen until four o'clock, so she waited. When Benitez left the building and got in her car, Kate seized on the one chance she might get. In a flash, she opened the passenger door and climbed in too. Visibly shocked, the doctor tried to get out again.

Kate leaned across her, grabbed hold of the door and held on tight.

'What do you want?' Benitez was clearly frightened.

'I'm not going to harm you,' Kate said.

They were about the same age, Benitez the better dressed. Better looking. Her eyes were so dark it was almost impossible to distinguish her pupils from her irises. She had perfect white teeth. This close, Kate could smell spearmint on her breath.

'What do you want?' she repeated. 'I have money.'

Letting go of the driver's door, Kate said: 'I don't want your money, Maria.'

The doctor scrutinized her, confused by the use of her name.

'I want to die in the UK,' Kate said. 'And live a long and healthy life in Spain.'

'I can't help you.' The woman avoided eye contact.

'But you do know what I'm talking about?'

'Please leave. You are mad, I don't do this thing.'

'What thing is that then?'

'I can't make you disappear.' Her English was perfect.

'Brian Allen says you can.'

Kate slapped a brown paper bag on the dash, thick and heavy. Benitez looked at it, a flicker of interest she couldn't hide. Although the car was parked in the shade, the heat coming in through the window was tremendous. But the doctor's high colour and the perspiration on her forehead had nothing to do with the temperature inside the vehicle.

She made no reply.

'Where is he?' Kate asked. 'I've not seen him in a while, I need to find him.'

THE MORNING FLEW by. Back in La Manga, Kate found Hank sitting outside La Barra tapas bar on a circular terrace with a lovely view of the mountains beyond. He gave the impression that he was like any other tourist on holiday; enjoying time off in the sun, shades on, a glass of something cool in front of him, nowt troubling him.

An English newspaper was on the table. The front-page headline: A Fitting Tribute Rises from the Ashes of Ground Zero. Images the world would never forget forced their way into Kate's head. Eleven years on from 9/11, a memorial to the victims who died in the World Trade Centre was finally visible.

Terrorists would never win.

A cool breeze blew between the building and the trees. Kate was glad of it. After spending an hour in the car, she needed to escape the searing heat. She sat down. The restaurant was very popular, not a table empty in sun or shade. A glance at the menu told her why. It served up wonderful Spanish cuisine but also catered for the English palate.

'Apple crumble . . . *really*?' She screwed up her face. 'How can anyone eat a heavy pudding in the heat of the day? What do people come abroad for, if not to experience something different?'

'It's like home from home.' Hank grinned. 'On Sundays they even have roast beef and Yorkshires. According to the owners, you can't get shifted at lunchtime. They have to bring in extra staff to cope with demand.'

'They're Brits?'

'Yeah, nice young couple, friendly enough to sit down and have a conversation about you know who. They don't know O'Kane. They're not too sure about Brian. The husband seemed to think he was familiar, but the wife didn't recognize him and she's the one who waits on tables, so don't get too excited. Let's face it, he looks much the same as other men of his age.'

'Did you show them the picture of John?'

Hank gave her a nod. 'Didn't register.'

They ordered a glass of wine and some local food: chorizo, chickpea and pepper salad; garlic and chilli prawns; cubes of potato in a spicy tomato sauce. As they ate, Hank advised her that his search of the golf club had come to nothing. There was no sign of either man at the clubhouse and therefore nothing of interest to feed to the incident room in the UK. He leaned forward, placed an elbow on the table, his earlier enthusiasm a little depleted.

'You fare any better?' he asked.

'Maybe.' Kate could see herself and the customers around them reflected in his sunglasses. She lowered her voice, making sure they weren't overheard. 'I lucked out totally at the medical centre. Nothing doing at the local shops either. Then I drove north in search of a certain doctor of dubious character. I got to see her, *eventually.*'

Hank leaned in. 'And?'

'Guilty as sin.'

'She admitted it?'

'Do I look like a woman you mess with?' She gave him a crazed face that made him laugh. 'Carmichael was spot on. Insulin won't last much longer than a month. Benitez last saw Brian on thirtieth August, when she gave him the drug. She said he was agitated, a clear sign he was in need of medication. It's the eleventh of September now. By my calculation, he's got a couple or three weeks' worth left before he has to find some more.'

'From Benitez?'

'Not any more.' Kate swatted a fly away from her meal. 'She's driven off with an envelope full of paper she thinks is money. I lied, told her I wasn't interested in her deception. She came clean in exchange for my silence, silly woman. Local police should be picking her up soon. She will of course deny our conversation ever took place. Ta-daa!' Kate held up her iPhone, a big smile on her face. 'I captured her admission on here. She'll be struck off for sure and will be going down if Chavez has anything to do with it. That'll stop the bastard crowing about British fugitives in his country.'

'Yeah, but if Brian gets desperate and can't raise her, he'll break into a chemist.'

'Which is precisely what I told Chavez. He'll feed us any burglaries as and when they occur. Didn't you get *any* whiff this morning?'

Hank waggled his hand from side to side. 'Not sure.'

'What did you get?'

'Well . . .' He stretched out in the sun, crossing his legs at the ankles, linking his hands behind his head. 'I did six rounds of the hotel corridors, one every half-hour. There's a sign on the door of room 210 that bothers me.'

'Sign?'

'*POR FAVOR – NO MOLESTAR!* I made discreet enquiries with the chambermaid. Whoever booked the room has been in there a couple of days. In all that time, the sign has been hanging on the door. He – and it is a *he* according to my new best friend; I tipped her well – never has turn-down service at night and she can't get in to clean the room in the daytime.'

'She's seen him?' Kate asked.

'No, so she can't make the identification, unfortunately.'

'So, how come she knows it's a bloke in there?'

'She knocked on his door. He barked at her to shove off.'

'Nationality?'

'English or American – English-speaking, certainly.'

'Dialect?'

Hank pulled an are-you-kidding face. 'She wouldn't know one accent from another.'

That was unfortunate, but the news set Kate's imagination off and running. Maybe Craig O'Kane was holed up here, watching and waiting for Brian to show himself. With no idea O'Kane was in the country, let alone in La Manga, chances were that if Brian was also at the resort, he was playing golf. Kate was in room 308, Hank in 305, both with views of the eighteenth hole. The DCI was sure that room 210 on the floor below would share that view. All O'Kane had to do was wait until his target came strolling up the fairway and pick him off. She could almost hear the shot ring out and pictured Brian dropping to his knees.

She studied Hank. 'You don't look too excited.'

'It feels too easy.'

Kate knew what he meant. Maybe she was clutching at straws. *Still . . .*

'The guy in 210 is probably hooked up with a married woman,' Hank said. 'Or maybe the lucky bugger has a sex slave in there. I could do with one of those myself. Wish I'd bought Julie along.'

Wasn't that the truth?

Kate felt hot, her eyes settling on anything but Hank. A thought occurred as she turned back to face him. 'Even sex slaves have to eat,' she said.

'How do *you* know?' Hank grinned.

Kate laughed. 'Just because the sign is on the door, it doesn't mean that he's actually in there. I stick mine on when I'm working, when I need a kip, but also when I leave the room because I can't be doing with people poking around in my stuff. Whoever's in there is either going in and out to eat or getting room service. So which is it?'

'Dunno. I'll ask the chambermaid to find out and check in with her later.'

'Fine. If he doesn't show himself soon, we'll get Spanish police to collar the hotel management. Provided we can get access to the room next door, we could be in business. As you say, it might be nothing . . .'

'Anything is worth a try.'

Hank raised his wine, hoping that finally they had reason to celebrate.

Chapter Sixty-four

BEFORE THE DAY was out, confirmation had come through from hotel staff that the man in room 210 hadn't moved, at least not during the day. His room-service bill was hefty. He'd eaten well and regularly, drinking only the finest wine. He'd made no calls from the hotel phone. Hadn't signed on for any broadband connection or ordered any newspapers. He'd accessed a number of adult movies on his TV, all between the hours of midday and eight o'clock in the evening, one of which Hank had also viewed.

'It was good too.' He made a smiley face. 'Any chance expenses will cover—'

'None,' Kate cut in. 'You want porn, spend your own money on it.'

'We could share!'

'Behave!'

His pet lip made her laugh.

They were sitting on a semi-circular settee in hotel reception savouring a cool drink. Apart from one guest who sat typing on a mobile tablet, they had the space to themselves. Everyone else was out enjoying the sunshine, keeping fit – something Kate wished she was doing too.

Hank nodded towards the reception desk where three very smart clerks stood waiting. 'How did you get on with them?'

'I spoke to the manager. Nice man. He's keen to cooperate. Even keener to avoid any embarrassment or, God forbid, threatening development that might upset or injure a hair on the head of one of his guests. Can't say I blame him. He has a reputation to uphold. His upmarket clientele won't take kindly to rubbing shoulders with a tooled-up Glaswegian thug.'

'Don't suppose they will. So what's the plan?'

Kate thought for a moment. 'The way I see it, O'Kane is slipping out at night in search of Brian, watching the course during the day hoping to spot him.'

'Good luck to him. We've not managed it.'

'Yeah, that's what bothers me. It's unlikely O'Kane will find him from the comfort of his room. Like us, he needs to move around. Ask questions. Flash the cash. I think he's out at night doing just that. Probably has a few hours' kip when he gets in, then amuses himself until he can go out again. I need to examine his room, but his curtains are drawn and I can't see in. That's where you come in.'

DRESSED AS A hotel maintenance man, Hank knocked at the door of room 210. There was a spyhole in the panel facing him. Wondering if anyone was on the other end of it checking him out, he knocked again. When there was no reply, he used his master key to access the room, calling out as he pushed open the door.

'Excuse me, sir?'

Cocking his head to one side, Hank listened. He scanned the room without making it obvious he was doing so. In his peripheral left vision was a cupboard big enough to hide in. Directly ahead, net curtains were drawn across patio doors obscuring his view of the balcony. O'Kane could be out there, waiting.

Improbable.

Kate would spot him.

Hank had timed his entry into the room knowing his boss would be outside.

'Hello,' he called out. 'Sir?'

As he waited for a response, his eyes homed in on a bag on the floor . . . a light tan Hidesign leather holdall, exactly like the one Lisa described O'Kane carrying when captured on CCTV at the easy-Jet check-in desk while his boarding pass was being processed at Glasgow airport. As quickly as his spirits rose, Hank's enthusiasm plummeted. On the table above the bag, an open laptop pointed in his direction, a red light blinking above the centre of the screen.

Surveillance camera.

The fact that the owner could pinpoint exactly where he was in the room from a remote device spooked Hank a little. He was glad of the Kevlar Kate insisted he wear underneath his overalls. Despite the weight of the protective vest, and the fact that it made him leak like a colander, it would give him half a chance of survival should O'Kane charge at him with a knife or pull a gun.

Although he'd rather not be there, Hank had no choice but to carry on pretending he was part of the hotel staff who'd come to fix a leak. Double doors led into the spacious bathroom. He rounded the bed, which was rumpled and unmade. Putting an ear to the bathroom door, he knocked gently. 'Excuse me, sir? I have to check your bathroom. There's been a complaint from the floor below. Hello? Sir, are you in there?' Sliding the doors open, Hank poked his head in, his heart hammering in his chest.

Silence.

A second sliding door led to the WC. The shower curtain over the bath was closed. Taking a lungful of breath, Hank checked the shower first, then slid the toilet door open. Nothing. He unbuttoned his overalls, pulled out his penis and had a pee to justify opening the door. Fortunately, due to the copious amounts of water he'd consumed throughout the day – something he never drank at home – he had a full bladder. The sound of urine splashing into the pan below left nothing to the imagination should O'Kane be listening in.

Kate certainly was.

With a wry smile on his face, Hank flushed the loo, washed his hands in the left of two sinks and dried them on his work overalls.

He relaxed.

If O'Kane had been hiding out in the room he'd have known about it by now. Getting down on his knees, Hank opened up his toolbox and proceeded to take the bath panel off. It came away easily. Whistling as he worked, he fiddled around for about ten minutes and then pretended to call a colleague on the bathroom phone, telling him he'd tightened up the dripping pipe, asking him to check that the leak was fixed in the room below.

Thanking the dialling tone, he hung up and packed his tools away.

When he was ready to leave, he took a few hairs from the shower tray, placed them in an evidence bag and put them in his pocket. He left the room, closing the door quietly behind him.

Giving his ear a scratch, he spoke into his sleeve. 'Where are you?'

Kate's voice came through his earpiece: 'Service room. Far end of the corridor.'

'Target not present,' he said.

Seconds later, he reached her.

Kate looked at him expectantly as he walked in. 'Are you sure it was his room?'

'Hundred per cent. Unless someone else has the exact same bag he carried through Glasgow airport *and* all he packed was one change of clothes and a toothbrush. He forgot his cologne. The room reeks of alcohol and stale sweat. I think we've been rumbled anyhow. He's got a webcam watching the door. Pound to a penny it'll be linked to his iPhone. It'll go beep. He'll clock me entering his room and do a runner. I carried on with the facade of fixing a leak, but I doubt he'll buy it. All we can do is wait.'

Kate rubbed her face. O'Kane was clever.

They both knew he was long gone.

Chapter Sixty-five

THEY SPENT A couple more days lying in wait, but in the end Hank's suspicions were confirmed. O'Kane had disappeared into the ether, leaving no trace. There had been no further activity in room 210, no room service, no movies ordered nor bill paid. That came as no surprise to Kate. Even dressed as a maintenance man, her DS looked like a policeman.

The only sensible option open to the DCI was to move in and seize what she could. When she did so, there was nothing of interest. The Hidesign bag contained a change of clothes and toiletries, nothing more. There was a pair of shorts and a crumpled T-shirt hung up on the bathroom door. Chavez's men took away a toothbrush and comb for DNA analysis. They didn't need it. No one was under any illusions as to whom the items belonged.

With no clue as to where O'Kane might be, local police made enquiries along the Mar Menor. With one hundred and fifty kilometres to cover, it was like looking for a needle in the proverbial haystack. Chavez didn't complain. As part of Operation Captura, he was as keen to apprehend Kate's target as she was. Besides, it was well worth a shout. Even in September, that stretch of coast-line was rarely busy. It was very Spanish there, not home from home for the English like the main resort areas.

While his men checked all the obvious places, Kate and Hank stayed close to La Manga. All morning, they had scoured Mar de Cristal, named after the crystal-clear waters on that part of the coast.

Looking out over shimmering waters, Kate turned her atten-tion to the La Manga strip on the horizon to her right, a beauti-ful sight, especially so accompanied by the sounds of a flamenco guitar drifting from the garden of a small cafe across the prom-enade behind her. The tranquillity of the lagoon and warmth of the sun on her bare arms did nothing to calm her frustration.

'We lost him,' she said, without turning her head. 'We bloody lost him!'

'Yeah, well . . .' Hank muttered something under his breath. He wanted to call a halt to the search. He didn't verbalize it. He didn't have to. Kate got his message loud and clear. What's more, she was beginning to think he had a point.

'I'm thirsty,' he said. 'Won't be long. You want anything?'

Shaking her head, Kate watched him go into the cafe, shoul-ders slumped in resignation. With all the walking they had done in the past few days, he'd lost even more weight. His long shorts were practically hanging off his arse. Despite the fact that Bright had given them more time abroad, increasing the budget expo-nentially, her DS was keen to get home to his family.

They both were – except in her case the family didn't exist.

Aware of someone standing beside her, Kate turned around and came face-to-face with an attractive woman of indeterminate age. She had a fit body, fair hair, a pale complexion and beautiful blue eyes under a wide-brimmed hat. The man by her side was a little older and a lot more suntanned. Two small dogs lay at his feet.

'First visit?' the woman asked.

Kate nodded, her eyes scanning the strip.

'It's gorgeous, isn't it?'

'Stunning,' Kate agreed.

'Did you know La Manga's literal translation is "sleeve"?'

'Really?' the DCI tried to sound interested. 'I didn't know that.'

She listened as the woman talked about the place she now called home. The 'strip', twenty-odd kilometres across, seven wide, separated the Mediterranean from the Mar Menor, the largest lagoon in Europe, a massive one hundred and thirty square kilometres in area.

'Have you been in yet?' the woman asked.

'Not yet.' Kate told her she had a fear of water and couldn't swim.

'Then it's perfect for you. The year-round bathing temperature is eighteen degrees. It's almost as buoyant as the Dead Sea. It's shallow too, only twenty-one feet at its deepest point. Do yourself a favour and try it.' Smiling, she held out her hand. 'I'm Shelley.' She pointed to her right. 'This is my partner, Tony.'

'Pleased to meet you both.' Kate shook hands with them. 'You come here a lot?'

'Yes, we live up the road.'

'Where you from?' Tony asked. He had a soft Irish accent. His whole persona screamed laid back. This was someone for whom relaxation was a way of life. He had no idea Kate was hunting a killer. Two even. Why should he? He was better off thinking he'd found his little bit of heaven on earth.

Perhaps he had.

He raised a quizzical eye. 'Durham?' he guessed.

'Next door, Northumberland,' Kate replied. 'My husband and I are thinking of buying a place around here. We wanted somewhere typically Spanish. A friend we lost touch with years ago recommended it.' She acted all melancholy, letting out an enormous sigh. 'He went through an acrimonious divorce, sadly. I'm still in touch with his ex. Such a shame their marriage should end that way; I always thought them to be a perfect match for one another. These things are never pleasant, are they?'

A flash of irritation crossed Shelley's face. Kate suspected she'd been in the same boat once herself. Tony saw it too and quickly changed the subject.

'This old friend?' he asked. 'He lives around here?'

'He certainly used to,' Kate said vaguely. Hank arrived by her side, drinking from a bottle of still water. She smiled at him with adoring eyes. 'Darling, this is Shelley and Tony. I was telling them about Brian, how we'd dearly love to find him before we go home.'

Hank proffered a hand, to Shelley first, then Tony. 'You know Brian?'

'Doubt it,' Tony said. 'Almost everyone we know around here is Spanish. What's his last name?'

'Allen,' Kate said. 'His ex-wife's name is Theresa. They have two sons, John and Terry.'

Least they used to.

Tony shook his head. The names meant nothing to him. The screeching of birds made Kate look up. She shifted her gaze to Hank, an urgent question in her eyes.

'What?' he said.

'The parakeets.'

'What about them?'

'They wouldn't nest here if these places were empty, would they?'

'They certainly pick their spots.' Shelley answered before Hank could. 'These birds aren't stupid. This is the only place that's open all year round, except Christmas Day, the only certainty of finding food for their young.' The woman turned, pointed towards the cafe he'd just come out of.

Tony agreed with her. Kate would have to get used to them or reconsider buying a home in Spain. Where there were palms and food, there were parakeets, impossible to avoid.

Kate had tuned him out.

She'd been transported to Quesada, was staring at a palm tree, taking photographs to send to Jo, the sound of Chavez yelling orders to his men reaching her from further down the street. She pictured the avenue, many of the houses empty, the magnificent villa adjacent to the tree. An idyllic hideaway, had been her first impression. Not far off the mark, she was thinking now. *Someone lived there permanently.* She hadn't found O'Kane but, if her hunch was right, she knew exactly where Brian was – and she couldn't wait to get there.

Chapter Sixty-six

'Wow!' HANK'S MOUTH literally dropped open. 'Mucho euros, I reckon. And a damned sight better than the pad a few doors down.' He looked at Kate. 'John Allen wasn't as daft as we first thought. He gave Vicky a bum steer as to where he was staying which led us up the wrong garden path quite literally. This is something else. Jesus! How much would a place like this cost?'

Kate didn't answer. She was too busy scanning the extravagant property from the pavement. It was so well protected she couldn't see in. A high stone-clad wall surrounded the house, topped with spiked wrought-iron railings to deter unwanted visitors. Behind the electronic gate, there was a large garage with purple bougainvillea scrambling up the wall on either side. A ceramic pot near the door held a white-flowered climber she couldn't identify.

It was very like clematis.

The residence itself was well hidden from prying eyes. All Brian would have to do was stand on the roof terrace and he'd be able to see for miles. He was counter-surveillance savvy. If he saw anyone hanging around, he'd be straight downstairs and into his car, fire the garage door open and away before anyone got wind of it. The place was like a fortress. Bin Laden hid in a house like this behind a privacy wall. US Special Forces had to breach it by using explosives. Unfortunately, Kate had left her dynamite at home. Once more, she would have to rely on Spanish officers to gain entry.

WITHIN THE HOUR, assisted by Chavez, they managed to get inside. Hank whistled as they entered through the front door, arriving in an atrium so big you could drive a double-decker bus through it. It had a high ceiling, a wrap-around balcony and ornate staircase leading up to the floor above. Upstairs and down, dark wooden doors led off in each direction.

The main living room was directly ahead, an airy space with lots of natural light flooding in through fold-back tinted-glass panels with a view over a formal lawn and swimming pool. It would be right at home in *House & Garden* magazine.

'This is more like it!' Kate said.

Inside, the temperature was cool, helped by white marble floors. The room she was standing in was filled with the most wonderful furniture and local artwork on the walls – a real feast for the eyes. Kate was mesmerized. She imagined sitting on the comfy sofa, doors open allowing the garden in, a glass of chilled wine, Joni playing softly on the iPod, Jo sitting on the floor at her feet.

And candles . . .

Lots and lots of candles . . .

Magic.

There was no TV, she noticed. That particular item was hidden away next door in a movie den, a gigantic flat-screen television almost covering one wall. The room was even more sumptuously furnished, with an open fire laid ready to put a match to. No expense spared. No windows to allow any light in here. Perfect for an evening's viewing cuddled up on the sofa.

Switching on the TV, Kate noted that it was tuned to a Sky Sports channel.

Turning it off again, she wandered into the lounge area where Hank was carefully searching some drawers, finding something of interest if the expression on his face was anything to go by.

She thumbed in the direction of the door behind her. 'Brian certainly has a penchant for the finer things in life. Check out the home cinema next door when you get a minute. To die for . . . and I *wasn't* being ironic.' She pointed through the window. 'John may not have liked golf, but his father certainly did. I could spend some time here, I can tell you. And they say crime doesn't pay.'

'They were wrong.' Hank pointed at the papers he'd found in the drawer, a wide grin forming on his lips. 'I do like Brian. He seems to have morphed into Richey Edwards, according to his utility bills.'

'Wasn't he the guitarist from the Manic Street Preachers?'

'Yup. They disappeared around the same time. If my memory is correct, Richey was presumed dead not that long ago – two, maybe three years? Brian obviously shares my wicked sense of humour. I think we'd get on.'

'Why would he *do* that?' Kate asked. 'I can understand him using the name if he rated the guy. I can even see how he'd find it amusing to take the name of someone else who had vanished, but he'd be mad to think people weren't searching for Richey. You'd think he'd want to deflect attention, not court it.'

'He's a risk-taker,' Hank said. 'It's what fires his jets. Besides, if Richey was alive he'd hardly be going by his real name, would he? I bet Brian only took his name after he was officially presumed dead. He'll have more than one alias. He's probably changed his identity several times.'

He was right. It was a demonstration of the cheek of the man they were dealing with. Nothing fazed the Glasgow gangster. Kate's eyes were drawn through the window. Beyond the turquoise pool was a putting green so closely cut she'd be terrified to walk across it for fear of spoiling the lay of the grass. It was a piece of art. Brian obviously had help in the garden, in the house too, Kate imagined. Perhaps his cleaner was the woman who'd gone into the paper shop in Quesada and spoken so hurriedly to the newsagent, warning him not to talk to her. Maybe she was another of his conquests.

Kate sighed. 'What is it with women who fall for shite?'

'Eh?' Hank chuckled.

'Never mind.'

She wandered off, arriving in the kitchen on the west side of the house a few seconds later. In the refrigerator she found food and fresh milk. Well, nearly fresh. It was out of date by days, not weeks. Something began to tap on the inside of her brain. She couldn't get a handle on it but it was connected to her present location, she was sure of that. It refused to surface. Hank joined her moments later and they toured the house together, eventually arriving in a carless garage.

There were no gardening tools, further evidence that hired help did all the donkey work. Kate noticed a BMW car kit bag, unzipped, a carton of polish sticking out the top. A man after her own heart: a petrol-head. She thought about John and Terry's pristine vehicles. They may not have lived with their father for years, but clearly they had his genes.

She examined the kit.

The products inside were hardly used.

'Looks like Brian may be driving a new BMW, probably under three years old.' She explained the theory behind that assumption. 'Anything strike you as peculiar in here?'

Hank didn't think so.

She urged him to look harder.

His eyes were still searching, trying to figure out what he'd missed. 'There are no tools here, if that's what you're getting at. Clearly he wasn't into DIY. Can't say I blame him. I'm useless myself. Bores me rigid.'

'That wasn't what I meant.'

'C'mon, it's too hot for guessing games.' Hank yawned. 'Give us a clue.'

'There are no golf clubs here, no trolley. If Brian plays golf, there ought to be. Check the house again. While you're at it, get Chavez's men to inspect the sunroom in the garden, any sheds, outbuildings – anywhere big enough to store large items.' Kate's eyes lit up as she remembered what had caught her attention on the way in to the house. 'If I'm right, O'Kane was working on more than a hunch when he took off for La Manga.'

'You've lost me,' Hank yawned again, covering his gaping mouth with his right hand. 'Sorry, my brain isn't functioning. No wonder Pedro takes a siesta every day. It would do my head in to work here permanently. Five minutes after I get up, I want to go back to bed. All the fresh air is killing me.'

Kate's eyes found the front door. 'I saw something on the way in – I think O'Kane saw it too.'

'Which was . . . ?'

Hooking her forefinger, she gestured for him to follow.

They went outside, both shading their eyes as they left the dark interior and met the glare of the sun. Kate put on her shades. This was the home of a golfer, for sure. She didn't play much herself, but what was lying on a slab of rock near the garage made her heart beat a little faster, reminding her of a charity game she'd felt obligated to play for the benefit of the force benevolent fund. 'A good cause,' was the way the Chief Constable put it, leaving her in no doubt that her attendance and financial support were mandatory. How could she refuse? At the end of the competition, players banged their shoes on the concrete plinth outside the clubhouse to get rid of grass that had stuck to the underneath. Circular tufts fell away from the studs – similar to those she was staring at.

Getting down on her honkers, she picked one up.

Even more exciting . . . little green shoots were poking out from the rings of turf. The rings were still soft and crumbly and therefore fairly recent. This side of the house was in full sun. If they had been there long, they would have baked solid in the searing heat. Kate stared at them, a smile forming on her lips.

'This is why O'Kane asked questions at the golf club, Kimosabe.'

Hank laughed out loud, impressed with her reasoning and cheerfulness.

She stood up. 'I think Brian's been putting it about here in Spain. As well as flashing the cash, he's probably screwing Benitez. He must be good at it too. Can't have been easy getting a GP to sign off on his death and feed him insulin all these years.'

'The guv'nor said he was charismatic, appealing to both sexes.'

'Yeah, and everything Theresa said supports that view. I bet he's charmed his way into the affections of several local women, including the one in the newsagent's I told you about. She was extremely agitated when she saw me asking questions. Some women like a bit of rough, even though, deep down, they know it's probably not going to end well. Including, I strongly suspect, a certain Neena Gil.'

'You think she lied to us?'

'Damn right I do. What better way for Brian to get rid of his nemesis than to have a girlfriend call the authorities and get him arrested? If it had worked out, it would have been a genius stroke. He must've been laughing his socks off, knowing the police were on their way. As it turned out, we didn't get there quick enough to lift him. But now we have an even bigger problem: Brian knows we're here in Spain. We walked into that one.'

Hank sniggered. 'You can understand why Bright rated him.'

Kate was unimpressed. 'He's a thug, Hank.'

'A smart one.'

'We're smarter.'

They raised their heads as a bird squawked above them.

'You think he fed them?' Hank asked.

She shrugged. Who knew? Maybe Brian had a heart after all.

Chapter Sixty-seven

STILL REGISTERED AT the La Manga hotel – and with the Spanish end of her enquiry very much alive – Kate sent Hank down there to pack up their stuff and settle the bill with a view to finding cheaper accommodation Bright couldn't quibble with. A Spanish officer kindly offered to drive him in an unmarked car, negating the need for him to travel by public transport, one less thing for him to complain about. It left her free and clear to revisit the Marquesa Golf Club and, if necessary, make further enquiries.

Chavez tagged along to avoid any problems of jurisdiction. He gave Kate the courtesy of conducting the interview with Neena Gil. They arrived around three o'clock and took her into the club secretary's office in order to question her again. Once the caution had been administered, the DCI wasted no time. She slid Brian's photograph across the desk, never taking her eye off the girl.

'I asked you once before if there was a member or visitor here by the name of Brian Allen, or anyone resembling him using another name. I'm asking you again. Tread carefully, Neena. Do you know this man?'

'No, I don't.'

'Think again.'

The girl's eyes found the floor.

Chavez yelled at her in Spanish, making her sit up and pay attention.

'You are a liar,' Kate said.

The girl looked up, a sullen expression on her face.

'In my country,' the DCI said, 'you'd be in serious trouble. It is an offence to waste police time, an even bigger one to harbour a dangerous criminal.'

Neena was resolute. 'I told you, there is no one here of that name.' The members' register was lying on the desk between them. She pushed it towards Kate, cocky as you like. 'Please check for yourself, if you don't believe me.'

Kate didn't bother.

The young woman shrugged, feigning indifference.

The DCI wasn't fooled by the show of bravado. There was something about people who were lying through their back teeth that she'd learned to recognize in her years as a police officer. The receptionist was good, but not that good. She wasn't used to being interrogated. Her eyes darted around the room, a sure sign that she was agitated.

Scared even.

Chavez interrupted, offering to take her away for more questioning, his way of putting the frighteners on. Kate declined, asked if she could have a few moments alone with the girl. Perhaps she could talk some sense into her and avoid further unpleasantness. Avoid locking her up. Hearing this, Neena appeared to relax physically. She thought she was home and dry.

She was wrong.

As the door closed behind Chavez, Kate leaned forward in her seat, clasping her hands together. For a moment, she stared at the girl. Saying nothing was often more effective than words. When the time was right, she asked, 'Is Neena Gil your real name?'

Caught off guard, Neena's brow creased. 'Of course.'

'So it's not Maria Benitez then?'

'Why should you think that?'

'Ah, I'm beginning to understand.' Kate paused for effect, chuckled to herself. 'Maria is Brian's real love, his soul mate. You're his bit of fun, someone he can use and discard at will, like the others. You did *know* there were others? Women who've helped him construct a false identity in this country, ones who've put themselves and their careers on the line for him.' Kate took in a breath and let it out in a long, loud, frustrated sigh. 'Men are bastards, aren't they?'

Neena avoided eye contact.

Kate could see she'd made an impact. The girl was mulling over her words. Hurting too. Time to put her under pressure. Time to ram home the truth. Time for Kate to show her that she wasn't talking bollocks.

'There's no disgrace, Neena. You're not the first woman to fall for a man like him. He made fools of all his women, one of whom is a respected doctor. She not only faked his death certificate, the silly bitch supplied him with the drugs to keep him alive. I think that makes her more valuable to him than you, no?'

There it was. A flash of recognition, so brief that Kate might've missed it. Neena knew about the doctor. Or if not, she knew of Brian's need for insulin. She was fast realizing she had nowhere to go. She was weeping.

Time to turn the screw.

'Neena, this doctor will not only be struck off, she'll go to prison. Are you going to follow her? Brian won't give a shit what happens to you, but I do. Believe me, I've met many men like him. Here, dry your eyes.' Kate handed her a tissue. 'That's better. If you know where he is, you need to tell me now. I'll be straight with you: if you don't help us, the Comisario plans to put you before a court of law. He's not going to be happy until your reputation is in shreds.'

'He's in La Manga,' she said, her voice hardly audible.

'I don't believe you. I just came from there.'

'He is! He stayed with me last night. He went this morning.'

Kate took a moment.

Neena might have lied to her before, but what she was now saying made sense when Kate put herself in Brian's shoes. He was clever. He thrived on risk. With a manhunt underway, there was no better place for him to hide than somewhere he didn't think the police would consider looking, somewhere they had already looked, the very hotel O'Kane daren't visit. She pictured him there, practising his putting and drinking Pimms in the sunshine. He'd get a fright when Hank walked in.

The door opened.

Chavez entered, his face ashen.

'There's been a shooting,' he said. 'I'm sorry. The news is very bad . . .'

Chapter Sixty-eight

KATE'S BREATHING WASN'T what it should be. It came in short, sharp bursts. She was hyperventilating, trying to push the unimaginable out of her mind as she rushed from the room. This was a nightmare. It had to be.

Details were sketchy. In the club's lobby, Chavez told her what little he knew, then just stood there gawping at her. It seemed to take him for ever to pull out his phone and call the hospital in Cartagena. As he asked to be put through to someone in authority, Kate watched his mouth move but heard no sound above that of her own heartbeat. Her stomach heaved. She feared she might pass out. Hank was everything to her. She thought of his family, Julie and Ryan, at home in the UK, unaware he'd been injured. How badly, Kate had yet to discover. She thought of the Murder Investigation Team: Naylor, Robson, Brown, Maxwell and especially Carmichael, Hank's protégé.

Lisa would be devastated . . .

As would Bright. What would Kate possibly say to him?

She knew she ought to contact Naylor right away but couldn't bring herself to do it. Best to wait until she had more information, she reasoned. Besides, her team would be packing up, heading home for the weekend, no doubt wishing they were with her in sunnier climes. Kate wished she were anywhere but Spain.

She searched Chavez's face.

It showed nothing.

She couldn't read him. Panic set in as it occurred to her that he might deliberately be masking his emotions because of the gravity of the situation. She wanted to grab the phone off him, scream at the person on the other end to give her something, a shred of hope to cling to. She couldn't accept anything less.

What was taking so long?

Chavez stopped talking and pocketed his phone. Sombre-faced, he told her that his men had responded to a call from a witness who had seen Hank lying on the ground with a man standing over him, aiming a gun at his head. Several shots had been fired. Officers and paramedics had rushed to the scene, but sadly it had taken them a while to get to him. As far as Chavez was aware, Hank had only taken one bullet. He was in surgery . . .

Only . . .

Blood rushed through Kate's ears, blotting out everything else. All her working life she'd dealt with death. She'd lost colleagues before, one or two in the line of duty, but this was different. This was Hank.

God! Please let him live.

Feeling her legs go, she put a hand out to steady herself, grabbing hold of Chavez with the other. He helped her into a chair and went to fetch his car.

A Traffic escort eased the way. The journey to the Santa Lucia Hospital in Cartagena seemed to take hours. Every kilometre they travelled was painful for Kate. Blue lights flashed and sirens screamed all around her, a reminder of the countless times she and Hank had rushed to a scene of carnage, swept along on the adrenalin rush of a new enquiry. This time there was no buzz of anticipation. She felt numb as the landscape flashed by.

A NUMBER OF policemen were waiting at the entrance to A & E, evidence of the seriousness of the situation. The car door was pulled open. Before Kate knew it, she was being assisted from the vehicle. Chavez said something to her. She couldn't move. She was stuck fast to the melting tarmac beneath her feet.

No one would look her in the eye.

'What?' she yelled. 'Tell me, you bastards!'

A female officer stepped forward. Taking Kate by the arm, she propelled her inside, showing ID to the triage receptionist. Under fluorescent lighting, they were escorted along a corridor. Images loomed up and faded away: doctors, nurses, patients and hospital orderlies pushing trolleys. Wheelchairs. Sick faces staring up at her as she walked by in a daze. Suddenly they turned into a side ward, and through an observation window to their left there was a view of the bottom half of a hospital bed.

Hank.

The female officer stepped aside, gesturing for Kate to go in alone. Kate nodded her thanks. Reaching for the door, her hand hovered above the handle. She turned it slowly and walked inside. Hank was pale and motionless in the bed, hooked up to a monitor, his shoulder and chest heavily bandaged, his arms resting on the sheet covering him.

No head wound.

Kate covered her mouth, suppressing a scream. Tears streamed down her face, tasting hot and salty as she licked them away.

She'd let Hank down, just as she'd let Towner down, Bright, Jo –
her father. Full of self-loathing, she sucked in a deep breath and
approached the bed, wiping her face dry with the back of her hand.

She pulled up a chair, reached for the hand resting on top of
the blanket. It was cool to the touch.

Hank opened his eyes, his lids heavy with sedation.

'I'm OK.' He squeezed her fingers gently.

Her bottom lip quivered.

Then she lost it.

Chapter Sixty-nine

LA MANGA'S MOST prestigious hotel was now a crime scene. From a police point of view it was as well handled as any Kate had ever seen. Determined to do things right, Chavez had locked it down, taped off the car park, allowing no vehicles in or out, safeguarding forensic evidence. With the full cooperation of hotel management, he'd commandeered the reception area and deployed officers to take witness statements from all the guests.

In the ensuing hours, mobile phones had been collected. Guests who didn't hand them over willingly were searched and had them confiscated. Images from those phones had been uploaded on to a computer hard drive so that detectives had access to all available data. Chavez had done a fabulous job. By studying those images, a major incident team had put together a comprehensive sequence of events that Kate herself would've been proud of.

By ten o'clock in the evening, her hotel room had been turned into a satellite of the incident room on the ground floor. Sitting at her computer, with only a desk lamp for company, she clicked on the file containing crime-scene images. She noticed there was also one video and she began with that.

What she saw chilled her to the bone.

The person holding the phone was shaking. His accent was American, his voice urgent and high-pitched: *Carole, stay back. Jesus! Someone shot a guy right here in front of me. Call the cops!* The image panned left towards the road. People were running from the scene, their heads held low. They ducked down to hide behind cars as best they could. The camera moved again, to the right this time, zooming in close. Hank was lying on the floor, motionless, blood seeping from a wound to his chest, his head lolled to one side. Kate could hear a woman's frantic voice in the background begging for someone to help him. It was like a movie scene. On the screen, O'Kane calmly walked into shot. *Fuck! He's going to shoot him again. No, I can't . . . believe . . . who is this guy?* O'Kane was standing over Hank. *Hey!* the Yank with the video screamed. *Leave him be, asshole!* Although O'Kane didn't look up, Kate detected a slight hesitation before he raised his gun calmly, aiming at Hank's head.

A shot rang out.

Kate felt her whole body shudder and shut her eyes. When she opened them again, the image had shifted. For a few seconds, the footage bounced wildly. Kate saw the ground, the trees and deep blue sky as the man grabbed his wife and ran for cover. The woman's distress was hard to listen to. A door slammed. *We're safe, Carole, we're going to be OK.*

The footage ended.

Kate's fury stuck in her throat. The incredulity and anxiousness told its own story. The images made perfect sense, fitting exactly with what Hank had already told her.

He'd thought he was a goner. He'd seen the whites of O'Kane's eyes and the wrong end of a gun barrel. Looking away, he'd braced himself. When the shot rang out, a gun fell to the ground a few feet away from him. He couldn't move in time to pick it up. Turning his head, he'd seen his attacker being dragged away by two men. He didn't know if O'Kane had been hit and dropped the gun, or if the gun had gone off as the men grabbed him. They'd bundled him into a waiting car, which was immediately driven away at speed. Hank had been unable to make out the registration through the plumes of dust thrown up by the tyres.

How they got past the security gate was anyone's guess.

Kate re-ran the tape, freezing on the harrowing image of her DS lying on the deck with a Glasgow gangster preparing to finish him off. If she lived to a ripe old age, she would never forget this moment. Sitting back, she shut her eyes and took a slug of pure malt. It burned her throat as it went down.

A tap on the door startled her.

Still traumatized by what she'd seen, she rose heavily from her seat. She opened the door expecting Chavez. Hank was standing in the corridor, sweaty and pale. He'd discharged himself from hospital. When he got inside, she went ballistic, telling him not to make himself comfortable. He wasn't staying.

'You . . .' she tried to inject a note of command into her shaking voice, 'are going straight back to hospital!'

'Don't fuss,' he said. 'I've had worse cuts shaving.'

His words made her laugh, then cry.

'You can't joke your way out of this,' she told him.

'Kate man, it's sweltering in there, bloody unbearable. I was sweating my bollocks off. What would you choose, hospital from hell or five-star La Manga treatment – an air-conditioned room and drinks on tap? I'll take my chances here, thanks very much. Besides, you need my detective brain.' He pointed at the bed. 'If you insist, I'll lie here and play Sherlock while you pretend you're Florence Nightingale.'

Kate wasn't laughing. The bullet designed to kill him had entered the left side of his chest, missing his heart by inches, and gone straight through. Fortunately, it hadn't hit any major arteries or bones – a miraculous escape. 'No chance.' She shook her head. 'Can't you take things seriously for once? Much as I'd like to play nursemaid, this is way beyond my first-aid skills. I won't accept the responsibility, Hank. It's not fair to ask me to. What if you suddenly take a turn for the worse?'

Hank didn't reply. Oblivious to the question, the focus of his attention had shifted to her computer screen. The image shocked him, she could tell. 'You put it all together?' he asked, changing the subject.

Kate killed the image. 'Pretty much.'

'I saw Chavez's handiwork on the way in. He did a good job.'

'He's got a hundred men searching for O'Kane.'

'They're wasting their time.'

'Yeah, I know. Chances are he's gone the same way as his brother.' Kate shrugged. 'Some you win, some you lose. I've run out of sympathy, Hank. Whatever Brian Allen is doing to him, I hope it hurts like fuck!' She held up her hand, pinched forefinger and thumb together. She was filling up. 'You came that close. You'll never be that lucky again.'

'Lucky? I've got Brian to thank for it,' he reminded her.

Kate had no answer, but she knew he was right.

Chapter Seventy

KATE WAS EXHAUSTED when she went to bed at midnight, more so when she woke suddenly a few hours later. She couldn't see anyone. She didn't need to. The strong smell of a cigar had disturbed her sleep and caused her to wake. The Scot was massive. He was standing in the shadows at the bottom of her bed, holding a handgun, a pensive expression on his handsome face.

She scrambled up the bed, drawing her knees to her chest. Naked and unarmed, she'd never felt more vulnerable. 'How the fuck did you get in here?'

Brian rebuked her by waggling his gun around from side to side. 'That's no way to greet a guest, is it? I have my methods.'

'So what happens now?'

Taking a couple of heavy-duty cable ties from his pocket, he proceeded to secure her tightly to the bed, his face almost touching hers. He wasn't rough with her. Neither did she struggle for fear that the gun in his right hand might go off accidentally.

'Your days of freedom are numbered,' she said.

'You're the one tied to the bed.' The irony made him chuckle. 'They told me you had balls. They weren't wrong. You must take after your guv'nor, Mr Bright. How is the old sod, anyhow? He and I go back a long way. Did he tell you that?'

'He told me.'

'I used to get a real kick out of taunting him. He didn't like me crossing the border, wreaking havoc in Newcastle. It was good sport until Dougie O'Kane tried to get in on the act.' He shook his head sorrowfully. 'I never wanted a turf war, Kate. That's why I made it my business to get acquainted with Bright. It pays to know who you're up against – I did the same job on you.'

'You know nothing about me!'

'You'd be surprised what I know.' He was enjoying himself. 'I know your mum is dead, you don't dig your old man, and you have a friend you'd rather not talk about. How's that for starters?'

Kate's stomach churned at the veiled threat to her family – to Jo.

'Relax . . . all I'm saying is, my snouts are better than yours. I pay them more than you do. Worth their weight in gold, informants – wouldn't you say?'

Was he talking about Towner? Was it possible that there was more to his death than a tragic accident? Had he seen something – someone – that made him bolt from the bench and run into the road? Towner hated the Allens, he'd always blamed John for getting Margie hooked on drugs; tipping off the O'Kanes that Brian was still alive would be one way of having his revenge.

No, this was just Allen mouthing off, Kate told herself. She was letting her imagination run away with her. It was running in other directions too: images of Brian's handiwork in a garage on the outskirts of Glasgow flooded her mind. Did he have something similar in mind for her? But then, why go to the trouble of tying her to the bed?

This is just a warning. He has nothing to gain by killing me.

'I haven't come here to hurt you.' It was as if Brian had read her mind. 'I just want you off my back. Neena gave you guys a starter for ten. Soon as O'Kane turned up at the club, she rang me. If I could've got there, I'd have killed the bastard, but I knew he wouldn't hang around long enough for that. So I told her to ring you. I'm a patient man, Kate. I was hoping you'd lift him and fuck off home, but you blew it. Not only did you let him slip through your fingers, you decided to come after me instead. So I put my boys on the job of tracking him down. Good thing I did, under the circumstances, wouldn't you say?'

Kate said nothing.

He laid his gun down on the bed, took a photo from his pocket and held it up in front of her face. It featured Kate and Hank and the expat couple, Shelley and Tony, on the promenade at Mar de Cristal. All four had their eyes turned skyward.

The parakeets.

'I knew then you had me.' Brian's eyes were smiley. 'A clever deduction. However, you made a fatal mistake. You were following me when all the time I was following you. Not once did you look over your shoulder. Even you must see the funny side of that.' He put away the photo, pocketed the gun. 'Right then, I'm out of here. You'll never find me, so don't bother trying.'

'Is O'Kane dead?'

'What do you think?' He kept his eyes fixed on hers. 'It's possible he could still be alive, but not likely. If he is, he won't look pretty and you won't hear him scream. He'll be meeting up with Finn right about now, I should imagine. Consider his death my gift to you.' He turned towards the door. 'Give my regards to Bright when you see him.'

'Brian!' Kate shouted at him, pulling at her restraints. 'I'm not going to stop!'

He turned, as if considering her words. In that moment a video image of Hank lying on the deck, a gun pointing at his head, flashed before her eyes. This thug was responsible for saving Hank's life. That must count for something.

'I need to find O'Kane,' she said. 'I don't give a fat rat's arse about you – that's Strathclyde's problem. In fact, I owe you – big style. My DS . . .' The words stuck in her throat. She had to swallow hard to keep her emotions in check. 'But I need to get a conviction. And to do that I need to find O'Kane, dead or alive, and prove he killed your boys.'

Brian nodded, suddenly less cocky. Behind the facade, Kate saw a beaten man, robbed of his sons, haunted by his past. 'Just so you know, my youngest had no idea I was alive. When those vicious bastards were torturing him, the poor sod couldn't have given me up if he'd wanted to. You saw my lads, Kate. Tell me it was wrong to take revenge.' He waited, melancholy eyes watching her. 'Nah, I didn't think so.'

She looked away, ashamed that she shared his point of view. She couldn't deny that, given the exact same circumstances, she too would want revenge. Wouldn't any parent? And if O'Kane had executed Hank in cold blood, as he'd clearly intended to do, she'd have blown him away in a heartbeat, no qualms whatsoever.

'Please,' she begged. 'Tell me where to find Craig's body. If you don't, I'll have no choice but to hunt you down.'

'There's some old mine workings around Portman. If you can be bothered to go fishing for the fucker, you might find him. Then again, you might not. Don't bother polishing up on your interview technique. He'll be dead by then.' He sighed. 'An eye for an eye has always been my way. If it'll make you piss off back to Newcastle, he's in the mine nearest to the coast.' He picked up her phone. 'I'll leave this under the wheel arch of your car.'

'You're all heart,' Kate said, but the door was already closing behind him.

Chapter Seventy-one

IT WOULD BE another four hours before the sun came over the mountains. Best part of the day, as far as Brian was concerned. As a lifelong golfer, he was often first on the course and finished before breakfast. Sadly, he'd not see it again, at least not from this location. Time to move on.

There was a flicker of a smile on his face as he wandered into the hotel car park, pulling Kate's mobile from his pocket. Scrolling through the address book, he found Hank's name and pressed the call key.

THE PHONE SOUNDED tinny and far away. Remaining flat on his back, the only position that was anywhere near comfortable, Hank swung his right arm out, his hand scrabbling around in the dark until he found the light switch. His mobile was lying on the bedside table. He checked the display. The name KATE was illuminated.

Who else, at this time of night?

He yawned.

Even to him, his voice sounded groggy: 'Either you've decided you're straight or there have been developments,' he said. 'What's up?'

BRIAN GRINNED. DS Hank Gormley was well worth saving. Less than twenty-four hours ago he'd faced his maker, yet here he was joking with his boss at three a.m. This was the sort of guy he could happily share a pint or two with, as he had done with Bright in the good old days. Brian hankered after the camaraderie, the 'them and us' mentality, the tit-for-tat between the prigs he ran with and the likes of Bright. He missed Theresa too. No one had ever floated his boat like her; not Neena, not even Maria, who'd kept his secret all these years. Family came first. Always had. Still did. He'd made a good life for himself in Spain and it didn't come easy, giving all that up, but no sacrifice was too great when it came to keeping Theresa safe. If only he could have kept the O'Kanes from going after his boys . . .

'KATE? YOU THERE?' Hank groaned as he tried to move himself up in the bed. 'Stop playing hard to get. We both know I'm irresistible.'

A male voice hit his ear. 'She's a bit tied up at the moment, Sarge.'

'Hello, Brian.' Hank's tone was flat calm. 'I'd like to speak to my boss.'

BRIAN WAS IMPRESSED. The detective was not someone who panicked easily. Another groan reached him from down the line. The guy was trying to get up, put some clothes on and ride to the rescue like a knight in shining armour. Who could blame him? His gutsy

DCI was quite something, in or out of clothes. Brian chuckled. If she wasn't 'on the other bus' he'd have fancied his chances.

'PUT HER ON,' Hank pleaded, trying to get one leg into his strides. 'Let me trade places. You know what women are like. I'll be less bother than her in my condition. I'm no threat, am I? I'm a one-armed fat man. She's a shouty, foul-mouthed dynamo. Don't put yourself through it, pal – you're on a hiding to nothing. Believe me, I know. She's been giving me earache for years.'

'You move from that room, she dies,' Brian said. 'Stay put and she lives to fight another day. Do we have a deal?'

HANK STOPPED DEAD in his tracks. He took a deep breath, wincing from the pain. Images of Finn O'Kane forced their way into his head. Weak as he felt, he couldn't let anything happen to Kate. Fighting off a wave of nausea he tried to think what she would do in the circumstances . . .

'Deal,' he said finally. 'How long d'you want?'

'GIMME FIVE.' BRIAN had always been a master of the double entendre. Mentally, he raised a hand to Hank in a gesture of goodwill. Placing the phone under the wheel arch of the Seat Mii, he got in his BMW and drove off into the night, flooring the accelerator, putting as much distance between himself and La Manga as possible. Hank Gormley was not someone who'd delay before taking action. Unless Brian was reading him wrong, he'd wait two minutes max before heading to the room of his DCI. Brian was counting on him doing that before calling the law.

IT WAS A monumental struggle for Hank to propel his aching body the short distance along the corridor to room 308. Injured or not, with one kick he had the door off its hinges, flattening it against the wall. When he saw Kate naked and tied to the bed, he covered his face, peeping out between his fingers.

'Did you not fancy the pitch and putt then?' he said.

Kate collapsed in a fit of laughter.

Chapter Seventy-two

'WHAT WE GOING to tell Bright?' Hank asked as they boarded a plane home to Newcastle. He was travelling back to the UK, tanned and relaxed, a good deal slimmer than he'd been when he arrived in Spain, looking forward to being reunited with his wife and son. Although his injury was healing nicely, his left arm was still in a sling and Kate had insisted on carrying his bag on to the aircraft.

Before packing up, they had taken the time to track down the gutsy American who had yelled out at Craig O'Kane as he prepared to pull the trigger. When she got home, Kate would make it her business to ensure that the tourist got a commendation for bravery. Although O'Kane hadn't looked up at the time, she was sure his hesitation in that split-second had made the difference between life and death for Hank.

The image of O'Kane standing over Hank's prone body was still vivid in her mind as she strapped him into his seat, but a glance at his smirking face told her he had a different image in mind. She narrowed her eyes. 'What happened in the hotel stays in the hotel,' she said.

'OK, no need to get arsy!' He grinned. 'What are we going to tell Strathclyde?'

''Bout what?'

'About Brian.'

Kate noted Hank's attitude to Brian Allen had altered significantly in the past few weeks. She too had started thinking of him on first-name terms; no longer the infamous criminal but the man who had saved Hank's life.

'We're going to tell them nowt,' she said. 'He disappeared. End of. Our offences are detected. He's not our problem. Time to let the Scots do their jobs.' She smiled at Hank. 'Besides, I like him.'

Hank settled back in his seat and shut his eyes.

He'd sleep easy now.

Not so Maria Benitez. She had been arrested, charged with serious offences too numerous to mention, and remanded in custody to await trial. It was highly likely she'd be struck off the medical register and sent to prison for an extended period. Comisario Roberto Chavez was determined to make an example of her and, in so doing, secure his position as one of the lead officers in SOCA's Operation Captura.

Despite a plea for leniency from Kate for information received, Neena Gil was charged with wasting police time and harbouring a fugitive. She too faced prison, although, after due consideration, Chavez had agreed to recommend that her sentence be suspended in exchange for further intelligence on Brian Allen.

Convinced that Brian wouldn't harm anyone unless provoked, Kate secretly hoped he'd continue to evade the long arm of the law. He'd shown during his time in Spain that he could lead a peaceful if not entirely law-abiding existence; it was only the brutal slaying of his sons that caused him to resort to violence. If Brian lost his liberty now, he'd spend the rest of his life in jail. In her mind, that would be a travesty of justice.

The Spanish authorities had already found Craig O'Kane's body. It was right where Brian said it would be, several hundred feet down a mineshaft in Portman. It took a specialist rescue team to extricate the corpse from the harsh landscape and bring it to the surface. With visual identification complete, Kate would write up the case and present it to her former guv'nor to be written off as detected.

Her phone vibrated in her pocket.

A text from journalist Gillian Garvey:

You can't stay angry with me for ever! C'mon, we both have jobs to do. How about calling a truce? Gimme the inside story and I'll shout you lunch. What do you say?

Kate held up her mobile, showing Hank the message before keying a reply:

Sorry, no can do. Switching to flight mode – it's a bit like silent mode only it also cuts out interference. Ask your pals in Strathclyde! ☺

She was about to switch the phone off when an email came in from Jo. She'd booked a cottage for a month in Crail, a tiny fishing village on the east coast of Scotland where the DCI could recuperate from the traumas of the past few weeks. 'Only problem is,' she wrote, 'it only has one bedroom! OK with you?' The email was signed with a kiss.

Kate elbowed Hank in the ribs as he read over her shoulder.

'Watch it!' he said. 'I'm recovering from a near-death experience.'

He was grinning and so was she. Kate was looking forward to spending some quality time with Jo. A call to Bright had sealed the deal for her to take an extended leave of absence. In fact, he'd insisted upon it. He was still pissed with her. A lump formed in her throat. He'd get over it – he always did. And so would she – eventually.

While on the phone she'd finally asked him why he'd wanted to see her that Sunday when he'd come into the incident room instead of playing golf. It seemed moons ago now, but the mystery had played on her mind during her time in Spain and she was dying to know what it was.

'Ellen and I are getting married,' he told her.

'Oh, guv, congratulations!'

Kate shed a tear at the news. She'd been close to his late wife Stella but, more than anything in the world, she wanted to see him happy. She glanced at Hank. Her two favourite men were doing well on the romance front. Maybe she was too.

Maybe.

Acknowledgements

WRITING IS OFTEN a lonely occupation. For long periods I switch off in order to listen to conversations going on inside my head. My characters become my friends, my family. Their real life counterparts understand this. They forgive and support, encourage and cajole; it is only right that I acknowledge the amazing contribution they make here.

Killing for Keeps is the fifth in the Kate Daniels series. Grateful thanks must go to the entire staff at Pan Macmillan: especially my editors, Wayne Brookes and Anne O'Brien, who have taught me so much. Thanks also to Louise Buckley – always at the end of a phone or email to offer helpful advice – and to my publicist, Philippa McEwan. Without her my writing life would be in chaos.

A special mention to everyone at A.M. Heath Literary Agency – in particular my brilliant agent, Oli Munson. This book is dedicated to him. His extraordinary passion and commitment is infectious. It motivates me to turn out the very best work I am capable of.

Appreciation must go to Joanna Cannon for providing insight into a busy hospital A & E department. To my brother and sister-in-law, Rob and Marit, for helping me negotiate Rojales – a part of Spain I was completely unfamiliar with at the early stages of writing this book.

I'm blessed with a wonderful family of cheerleaders, each one a constant source of inspiration: Paul and Kate, Chris and Caroline, Max and Frances – and Mo, without whom Kate Daniels would not exist.

About the Author

MARI HANNAH was born in London and moved north as a child. Her career as a probation officer was cut short when she was injured while on duty, and thereafter she spent several years as a film/television screenwriter. She now lives in Northumberland with her partner, an ex-murder detective. She was the winner of the 2010 Northern Writers' Award and 2013 Polari First Book Prize, and was recently shortlisted for the CWA 2014 Dagger in the Library Award.

www.marihannah.com
@mariwriter

Discover great authors, exclusive offers, and more at hc.com.